Warming!

A Novel

William H. Espinosa

In memory of Gayle and Susan...

And to the unnamed whale who chose to breathe thirty yards from the boat.

ACKNOWLEDGMENTS

The author wishes to acknowledge Bethany Carlson and Heidi Connolly for their invaluable editorial assistance and Ursula Beck, Professor Abdul Aziz Said and Steve Nachmanovitch for their irreplaceable encouragement that kept this book alive. A thanks also to Peter Devins for the cover illustration and to Rebecca Bradarich for the chapter heading sketches.

CHAPTER 1

Moments before, Matteo Michelson had been standing erect only a few rows in front of her, comfortable in his command of the audience. His words—lightly accented with an Iberian cadence—were filling the room with stories of plants, flowers and medicinals flourishing under the forested canopies of remote regions of the Amazon. Then without warning his voice fell silent. His face recorded shock and fear. His shoulders hunched forward and his brown hands grasped the podium, but to little avail. In seconds he had fallen to the floor. Laura Feil's heart sank with the gray haired man as he crumpled to the ground.

A young woman rushed to the stage to attend to him. Laura recognized her as the Nigerian medical student who had interrupted her effort to talk with Matteo the day before. This time she blocked Laura's view. All Laura could see were patches of Matteo's tan suit on the floor and sporadically twitching feet in the *havaiana* sandals he always wore.

A muscular man whom someone in the audience called Nikolai rushed up also. He was ill-dressed but seemed used to command and quickly pushed aside Matteo's aides. Nikolai reached for his phone and put his hand on the Nigerian woman's shoulder. Matteo appeared to be unconscious. The Nigerian woman shifted around to lean over his face, pinching his nose, putting her mouth to his, apparently helping him breathe.

Less than twenty minutes passed but to Laura it seemed like

hours before the medics burst through the museum auditorium doors with their gurney. Laura cursed New York for the delay. Even with private cars virtually banned, delivery trucks, pedal driven rickshaws, buses, citibikes and pedestrians clogged the streets. Far too many people in far too small a place. One day, she knew, New York would be mentioned in the same breath as Babel and Atlantis—fallen monuments to human arrogance, materialism and "reason" and the inevitable ruin they brought.

The medics quickly took over from the African woman and placed a mask over Matteo's mouth. He seemed to be breathing as they rolled him out of the auditorium. Laura felt the knot in her stomach begin to unwind.

She wished that David had been here. He had been with her for most of Matteo's presentations but the annual Planetary Citizen's Conference had attracted the world's most prominent ecologists and activists. David, her companion and himself a well-known forest ecologist, had gone networking. He was listening to a talk from one of Wangari Maathai's successors at the Kenyan Green Belt Movement. Maathai had founded it in the 1970s and it became one of the great tree planting successes of the late 20th Century. David had also said something about meeting a community organizer from Peru to talk about reforesting in the High Andes. Noble but still, she felt, David should have been with her.

Jean Marc—David's close friend and a rising star in the European Union—was gone too. He was listening to Fatimah Karajan – a tall, dark-skinned, elegant woman whose transcendent vision and courage had helped bring peace to Israel and Palestine. But, David had said, her notions of sovereignties without borders deeply threatened traditional governments and organizations that saw themselves as humankind's stewards. Jean Marc, David had said, didn't know quite what to make of her. Her notions of sovereignties without borders deeply threatened traditional governments and organizations that saw themselves as humankind's stewards. Jean Marc was into governance. Laura only generally understood what that was about but what Laura did understand was that Jean Marc had another kind of Palestinian connection, an old love. Maybe Fatimah reminded him of her. Fatimah was certainly beautiful.

Someday, some said, Fatimah might even lead the world.

Laura didn't like being alone when she was frightened. She briefly thought about speaking to the lanky, blue-jean and boot wearing American sitting near her. She had noticed that over the last two days he had glanced at her frequently. Laura was used to pursuing eyes but she had found herself actually enjoying his attention. There was something unusual about him. More than once she rearranged her tanned legs in her seat or arched a bared foot half out of her shoe to draw his eyes and a smile. If the lecture had ended normally and she had been alone, she imagined the man would have asked her for coffee. She might have accepted.

But she knew that engaging the man now was a bad idea; she was too upset. Without saying anything, she gathered up her coat and headed for the opposite door from the one the medics used, hoping to be out of the Natural History Museum quickly, free of its crowds. Beyond the door, she found herself moving at a near run down a dark corridor flanked by dusky dioramas of extinct peoples. One caught her eye: prehumans were fighting off buzzards to claim an animal carcass. The vultures of her dream? The males had hair, low brows and protruding jaws, the females were unclothed, showing hair-free bodies and sagging breasts. Near the end of the hall, on the left side in a brighter display, young Mesoamerican males were playing a life-or-death stick and ball game while half-dressed females watched. By this stage in evolution, Laura noticed with amusement, well-toned, swimsuit-model bodies had apparently become the norm.

Laura passed through an arched opening and sensed that she was nearing the main exit but instead found herself in a room filled with the sounds of Polynesian chants and a hanging skeleton of what appeared to be a sixty food wingless bird. It took her a moment to realize that what she took to be a bird fossil was the remnant of a sperm whale: large brain cavity and an even bigger "beak". She felt disoriented and haunted by the chants but she didn't stop. The next hall did take her to the exit and she made her way outdoors and down stone steps into a milling crowd of tourists, students and vendors all bundled against the winter's cold.

Laura crossed the street and wandered into Central Park. It

pained her to think that this "park" was virtually the only green for millions of souls who lived near it. They came for a view of nature, complete with ducks with clipped wings and food wrappers and coffee cups scattered around the pond. The sight made Laura long for her Costa Rican home, for the rhythms and diversity of its natural inhabitants, for the opulent growth of the flower rows she had nursed around their house, and for the layers upon layers of leaves and trees. Tears came to her eyes. David hadn't forced her to come back to this unnatural world but he certainly had encouraged it. She felt mildly resentful, a touch misled.

And now Matteo. Whatever had gone wrong, she said a prayer for his recovery and cursed herself for not being able to tell him about the warning that had come to her. The first morning in New York she awoke next to David, shivering with the memory of a bad dream. A gloved hand and vultures sitting on the leafless branches of a desiccated tree. The wordless whispering of a goddess she had first encountered many years before in a bee-filled Adirondack glade and a strange unease, a sense that harm would come to Matteo, one of the few great humans of her age.

She and David had made love the night before. Then she had meditated and gone to sleep. When she awoke out of the dream and the shivering stopped, her body stayed stiff with apprehension. David was asleep, content and peaceful through her distress and the growing disturbance outside. Their hotel was near the UN building on the East River where walls were being built to hold the rising river waters back. The construction crews had started up at 7:45. The sun was just rising, lighting their room in a brilliant glare but casting long shadows from the towering structures of glass and steel. The sun, she thought, rose late—another reason to long for her home where from season to season there was little variation in the length of the day. There, the sun was her companion, reliable and tamed by canopy shade; here, it was of uncertain habits and threatening the Earth even in winter with invisible, unchecked warmth.

Laura drew herself back to the present and felt the cold of a January wind and a growing sense of dread about Matteo. Shadows were lengthening from the west. She knew she needed to change before dinner with David's friends--another half-dreaded task. She wasn't partner material; she needed her own path. She waived down a rickshaw and twenty minutes later walked into the colorful LED-lit lobby of their hotel.

WILLIAM H. ESPINOSA

CHAPTER 2

That night at the restaurant Bernie Berenson and his new found client and friend, a cowboy booted Texan named Casey Hamilton, were late, so they were the ones who brought the news. Bernie had earned a joint degree in law and environmental science from Yale and then joined a Wall Street law firm where he quickly found that his clients not only had more fun, they were richer. He dabbled in pollution rights futures and soon showed sufficient skill to impress one of his firm's clients, the Mother Earth Investment Bank. He was offered a position and in five quick years had been made a junior partner. His new friend, Casey Hamilton, an investor in slow water current energy, might open up a whole new field for him and a quick path to full partnership.

Like many others pursuing serious, fast-track careers, Bernie carried with him a high-powered hand held which continuously scanned the news channels. It was programmed to pick out preselected topics that were of critical interest to its possessor. The device assured that its owner would never be caught by surprise. A discreet beep had alerted him three blocks from the restaurant. He stepped into the privacy of a video booth to view his receiver's report in large. The booths had been installed in public places for consumers who had grown tired of squinting at miniaturization and wished for a little privacy as well. YOU'RE NO CLARK KENT, someone had scrawled on the inside of the phone booth door. He glanced at the writing uncomprehendingly for a moment; graffiti had never made sense to Bernie.

He bumped his hand-held against the booth wall and it lit up the embedded screen. Bernie saw a flurry of flashing ambulance lights come on the screen. Medics were pushing a gurney into New York-Presbyterian. A voice-over described how a great ecologist, Matteo Michelson, had collapsed during a lecture at the American Museum of Natural History. He was to be named the Planetary Citizen of the Year at a gala that night. An announcer came onscreen to say that efforts at saving Mr. Michelson's life had not succeeded and that only moments before, he was pronounced dead.

When Bernie arrived at the restaurant, he introduced Hamilton to the others—David, Laura, Katie, the French fellow—Jean Marc—and his girlfriend Lucinda. Then added quietly. "I just heard it. Matteo Michelson died, he never made it to the ceremony. I can't believe I…we…were with him just a few hours ago."

More or less. Bernie had actually jumped in and out the day before, catching fragments of the lecture as his schedule allowed. He had really come to maintain a bond with Katie. He wanted to marry Katie. She was intelligent, cheerful, and born to a well-connected New York family. But Bernie knew that her tie to him was fragile. She had an unyielding social conscience and didn't seem impressed by his financial success. Worse, he suspected that she was still in love with Peter Flanigan, a milquetoast senator's aide whom she had known since childhood. As he raised his voice to tell the story above the restaurant din, Katie's blue eyes looked at him with interest but he was by no means sure that her interest was in him.

Laura was taken aback by the sight of Bernie's friend—he was the same fellow she had nearly spoken to at the conference. She smiled at him and he smiled back. A good thing they hadn't spoken. The distraction of recognition lasted a few seconds but then Bernie's words penetrated. Matteo was dead. The words were like an anvil plummeting through her stomach and dragging her down into a dark hole. It was so rare that anything of significance happened to her and now it had. She had been given an opportunity and she had failed. In the face of as little as an indifferent look and another's voice, she had backed away from warning a great man. Why should Michelson have believed her when she showed no signs of believing herself?

Laura remained silent most of the evening. The others talked about Michelson, his philosophy, his ideas. Had he played a decisive role in changing the human path, had he really been understood? Proof that he hadn't, David had argued, was that governments around the world were using his name, among others, to inflate their bureaucracies with new health and environmental programs. Even the introduction of global minimum commodity prices coupled with a global minimum wage enforced by an army of more than 50,000 international auditors was widely credited to Michelson's devastating critique of the world economic order. Yet if there was one single theme that ran through all of his writings, it was a profound distrust of large institutions, particularly governmental ones. It is not that men are evil, he had said, it's that only the rarest of human beings have the power to avoid identifying with the collective energy and perceptions of large numbers of people to whom they are tied. That the collective provided economic security made matters even worse, and because the conforming force was largely unconscious, self-service and self-protection soon paraded unabashed in the mask of the public good.

"I saw it coming. I tried to warn him. He was killed," Laura finally said. Everyone at the table looked at her in astonishment. A startled chorus of questions confronted her.

"He died, he was an old man," Bernie interjected. "There wasn't a hint of anything else on the information channels." Bernie had drunk too much wine and a sharp, loud edge of anger and impatience escaped through his lips. He took off his glasses and wiped them. Laura irritated him. She lived on an airy fairy mountain where facts didn't matter. In fact they didn't exist at all. He was the only person with any information about Michelson's death and now some fantasy born in dream time was going to move to center stage. If Laura weren't so attractive, she would never get away with it.

David was more solicitous, "What do you mean, Laura?"

"Two nights ago, it was a full moon. I did a lengthy meditation. Later when I was asleep...." Laura's eyes took on a

9

distant look. Her voice rose sharply and then fell to a mumble. She turned to David, "Oh God, why did I let that woman interrupt me? Why didn't I scream it? Why did I care what he thought of me?" Her voice faded away entirely. She looked down at the table and took a sip of water. Bemused looks ricocheted between her companions.

She recovered and continued, "That night the Bee Goddess brought me a dream."

Everybody settled back in their chairs, knowing that they would be entertained by a story good enough to be retold in the coming years.

"In the dream I saw a lion. An old lion with a thinning mane, resting under a banyan tree. On the branches of the tree were a flock of vultures. They seemed to be applauding for the lion with their wings...."

"They had the clap," Bernie whispered and everybody laughed.

Laura turned red with anger but was determined to continue. "Then there was a snake, part coiled, part erect like a cobra."

"See, unsafe sex. I told you."

"The snake struck the lion, bit him near the heart and returned to its coil. Then the snake became a gloved hand, the palm and folded fingers were where the coil had been, and an extended index finger filled in for the neck and head."

"And that's it?" David asked.

'Yes, but in a way there was more. When I woke up, there was a fear I could taste and somehow I knew it had to do with Matteo."

David had been mildly troubled. For Laura truth came from a pantheon of gods and goddesses long dead to virtually everyone else. Laura wrapped her insights in packages that he found hard to accept, but when he made it beneath the wrapping paper, he frequently found substance. He found it sad that Laura lacked the strength to attribute her insights to her own intuition. Her inner doubts added vulnerability to beauty and fueled his protective instincts. Yet, at the same time, it was unsettling...

He had met others who were in some superficial ways like her—captains and soldiers in the Galactic Federation, walk-in star people who, with the consent of their human-host souls, had checked into human bodies to carry out their Sirius instructions. Why did he attract such people? He knew that he had met more than his share.

He was being unfair. Laura had real substance. Still, he couldn't take this seriously. He knew what the others were thinking and he was embarrassed for Laura, and, yes, for himself. She was so wonderful in so many ways, why did she have to carry with her this flakiness for which he felt driven to apologize and explain, which separated him from his friends and which, if he stayed with her, would probably damage his career with TROFAL, the Tropical Forest Action League. Only a few days earlier TROFAL's Managing Director had asked if—and it was a big if—he was quick to add, David were to represent TROFAL at the Global Convocation, would he feel that Laura would have to come with him?

"Laura, you cannot blame yourself", Casey Hamilton offered. "Many of us were there in the room. I saw you, you saw me. How could any of us have known? Was it a stroke? What could we have done?"

Laura appreciated the kindness and nodded her head, eyes tearful again, in his direction.

"It is a dream about your own soul," Lucinda suggested. Lucinda had led a difficult life. Maybe because of that she felt sorry for Laura. Lucinda's parents had fled with her during the Kosovo massacres. They had settled in Lisbon where her father, once a ranking Communist Party official, secured a job as a janitor and lived in constant fear. Her mother emptied bedpans at a local clinic operated by the Sisters of Charity. Lucinda had shown flashes of brilliance in school but these gave way to a sullen withdrawal and then years in the drug-park subculture of Amsterdam, Zurich and Stockholm. To support herself, she had let her dark-eyed, light-skinned features grace more than one erotic film for the Asian market. Then, one afternoon, near Copenhagen, she woke up to find herself in a rehabilitation hospice operated by fourth-generation Jungians. Life had changed—she avoided the word improved—after that.

David watched Laura drain a glass of wine and crush the starched linen napkin in her lap. He knew that Laura was sniffing condescension all around her and was probably on the verge of lashing out at Lucinda with a comment about her past. He felt her struggle to regain some steadiness. "It was real—it is real. He's dead, I know he was killed. I'm afraid of what's next," she said.

"We all are," Jean Marc said. Jean Marc Aubuisson was one of David's best friends. He was an elegantly dressed, slender man in his mid-thirties—one of the rising stars of the Council of Europe's bureaucracy. He waved his hand dismissively, displaying a heavy signet ring that his long tapered fingers seemed to carry without effort. He launched into a monologue about the new findings of the Council of Europe's Commission for the Environment about the slowing recuperative powers of the Earth. "She is like a weakened patient, drained by too many illnesses for too long. We have taken extraordinary measures the past ten years but recovery of the soil, the water, the air, the temperatures, the Arctic and Antarctic ozone holes, the recovery is much less than we predicted, much less than it should be by scientific law."

David resisted the temptation to take issue with Jean Marc. He was grateful for his friend's intervention. In a curious way, even when he was predicting doom and gloom, Jean Marc's faith in rationality comforted others. Even Laura. Eventually she allowed herself to blend into the flow of conversation and the evening slipped away.

CHAPTER 3

David Grossman began the day, as was his wont, drawn to the luminescence of his computer screen.

[YOUR GATESWAY DAY | Monday 15, 2/6 | February 17, 2028]

[*Good Morning, David. Coffee warm. New York Times?*]

"Yes."

[*Headlines or Index?*]

"Headlines."

[BASIC HUMAN NEEDS INDEX DECLINES | UN Agency Report Issued | Despite GGP Growth, Human Suffering Increased in Fourth Quarter]

[*Story?*]

"No."

[GLOBAL CONVOCATION SITE SET | New Delhi Chosen | Women's Rights Movement, Sri Lankans Drop Objections]

[*Story?*]

"Later."

[MANHATTAN DIKE WORKS LAUNCHED | $800 Billion Cost Projected | Mayor Shovels Dirt in Effort to Stem Tide]

[*Story?*]

"No."

[MATTEO MICHELSON--MURDERED? | Herbalist, Environmentalist Now Believed Slain]

[*Story?*]

David exhaled audibly as he withdrew from the screen. "Damn. Some SOB did get him," he whispered to himself. "How did she know?" David was a well-built man. Dressed in khaki cargo shorts and a loose-fitting patterned blue shirt, he looked as if he belonged outdoors. His grey eyes were bright; his curling brown hair showed signs of chronic resistance to control.

David swiveled his chair to look towards the window where the early morning light poured through, flickering with the shadows of the surrounding forest. He stretched his suntanned legs and arched his back. He stared briefly at the dark tufts that grew on his elongated toes. David considered waking Laura but decided to read the story first.

"Story, yes," he said, turning back to the glowing screen.

[MATTEO MICHELSON – MURDERED? | Herbalist, Environmentalist Now Believed Slain | by W. Rosenthal Jones, Special to the New York Times

NEW YORK, Sunday 14, 2/6. Based on an anonymous caller's description of the toxic effects of a rare South American flower, national and international authorities are opening an investigation into the death of Matteo

Michelson, the renowned Brazilian herbalist, healer and environmentalist.

Informed police sources who spoke only on the condition of anonymity refused to deny that poisonous substances may have been implicated in Mr. Michelson's recent death. The sources confirmed that an unknown caller's description of the symptoms of ingesting lycaste mycenosa, an endangered South American plant distantly related to the common orchid, closely matched the death throes experienced by Mr. Michelson. His initial collapse was witnessed by hundreds at a Planetary Citizen Conference lecture; he died soon afterward. The night of his death he was to receive the annual Planetary Citizen Award and his work was to be honored.

A spokesman for the Michelson family announced that the family and the Fundaçao Michelson—notwithstanding its avowed distrust of governments—would cooperate fully with the authorities. The spokesman confirmed that the family had received a request from the United Nations Intelligence and Law Enforcement Agency (UNINTEL) for a travel case containing fifty-five vials of distilled flower essences. The case had accompanied Mr. Michelson to New York where he had lectured on the medicinal effects of flower essences and herbs, and treated hundreds, including some of the city's most prominent entertainers and financiers.

Mr. Michelson was born in 1943 on a rubber plantation, two hundred thirty miles from Salvador in the State of Bahia. He attended medical school at the University of Sao Paulo. Whether he graduated is uncertain. All of the University's records were destroyed during the Debtor's Revolt of 2020.

After leaving medical school Mr. Michelson served with a small clinic in Boa Esperança, a remote village in Roraima, Brazil's northernmost province, where he practiced in obscurity until the late 1970s. At that time he found a receptive audience, albeit outside the medical community, for his theories on the curative powers of herbs and flower essences. He claimed that his findings were based on years of documented experience in Boa Esperança.

In the 1980s Mr. Michelson turned his energies to the preservation of the Amazonian rainforests and other wilderness areas rich in flora. He repeatedly stressed the medicinal potential of endangered plants. His preservation campaigns led to several unsuccessful attempts on his life and he was imprisoned three times by Brazilian local and national authorities. These events enhanced his reputation in the emerging global environmental movement.

In the 1990s Michelson became convinced that environmental degradation could not be stopped without a radical restructuring of the world economy. He was a leader in the movement against foreign debt which culminated in Brazil and elsewhere in Latin America, following a surge of interest rates, in the well-known events of 2019 and 2020. For the past six years he has devoted himself to the foundation named in his honor and to worldwide speaking engagements on health, the environment, nature and man.

A UNINTEL spokesperson would neither confirm nor deny the organization's involvement but did cite Article VIII of UNINTEL's charter. Article VIII mandates that UNINTEL investigate cross-border kidnappings, disappearances, and homicides, at the request of any member state. Antonio Carlos de Toledo Neto, the Charge d'Affaires at the Brazilian UN Mission here, reiterated his country's sadness at Mr. Michelson's death and his confidence that any questions involving his death would be readily resolved.]

[*End story? More?*]

"No."

David turned away from the screen. His eyes wandered

towards the window again and then fell to the dappled floor. As he watched the play of light and shade on the wooden planks, he quietly said to himself again, "How did she know?"

"Laura," he called out, pivoting towards the bedroom, "you've got to see this. You won't believe it." Though of course she would. There was no response.

"Laura, get up." His voice filled the two-room house. It was a small structure of wood and thatch resting on a steep slope of volcanic soil less than an hour from San Jose. When he and Laura had decided to move to Costa Rica, they both agreed not to live in a city. To David all cities were basically alike. He saw them as twentieth-century pox marks that refused to go away. Technology had made them obsolete a generation earlier. He suspected that Laura, his companion for close to three years, would not have agreed to live with him without the allure of immersion in a tropical and relatively unexploited habitat. Laura was embarked on a search for the secret teachings and powers of the gods—gods and goddesses who had long ago fled glass, steel, concrete and the myriad conveniences of the modern urban world. Her disdain for cities matched his.

"Laura—" he cried out again.

"Please, you're a maniac." Laura emerged through the passageway that separated the two rooms. She was half wrapped in a folded sheet of white cotton that deepened the brown of her shoulders and arms. Her eyes were glazed, her brown-blond hair was disarrayed. She fell into the couch across the room from his work station. "What is it?"

For an instant her movement put an immediate halt to his thoughts. No matter how tired or hung over, no matter what she was doing, Laura always managed to fold her limbs and body through arcs and curves that mesmerized him. Her movements had the unfolding symmetry of a chambered nautilus, graceful and filled with strength; they hinted of passion and infinity. After close to a thousand nights with her his wanting hadn't subsided. He wanted her then as she folded herself into the couch, and he knew that his desire for her would intrude on him at least three or four times that day, as it did every day.

But sometimes it was as if he had never had her at all. When he did make love to her, the scent of her skin, the touch of her legs wrapped around him, would overwhelm him. She would leave him drained and contented for a while, but then the sensations would vanish leaving only a promise—more like a tease—of real yet unimagined... fulfillment? Was that the right word? It was an unknown to which still unknown words might someday attach themselves. David could only see a silent wall, a dark place which he seemed to know only through frustration and longing. A place redolent with fear, he realized—fear of losing what little of Laura he actually had.

Laura's chocolate eyes came to life. She pulled back a strand of hair and smiled at his silence in bemusement.

"Matteo," David said, "they're saying they think he was killed. Poisoned"

Vindication. Laura knew that it was a horrible emotion to experience under the circumstances. Outrage, sadness, fear, loss—she felt these also, tightening her belly, shortening her breath, but it was a petty and angry triumph that shouted the loudest and implanted itself in the cells of her body.

The shits, she thought, the shits did kill him. Her anger, though, was directed just as strongly at the disbelieving gathering that had been with her on the night that they had first heard of his death—Bernie, the Texan Hamilton, Katie, Jean Marc and Lucinda. David had of course been there and he hadn't really believed her either.

Laura had known. She had been sure, so sure that she had even summoned her courage and stepped up to the podium during the last break of the next to final day and smiled, albeit timidly. With real fear in her voice, she begged him to be careful. Of what, Michelson had asked, his face furrowing under silver hair. Gently, his eyes took her in. She didn't know. She only had a fragment of a vision dream.

"The goddess told me..." she began.

The warm light in his pupils distanced itself into a pinpoint and dissolved in a haze. He allowed his attention to be taken by an impatient woman from Nigeria who had been breathing heavily and clearing her throat with virtually every other breath. She launched into a lengthy statement that became a question about her attendance at Columbia Medical School and the use of certain seeds from the Calabar, the physostigma family, as part of her tribe's traditional healing rituals in treating seizures. Could this be related to the success Matteo had enjoyed in administering...?

Laura glided away on a river of humiliation. She was too hurt to speak to David when she returned to her seat. Why had she been born into the twenty-first century by the old count, with the beliefs of a fifth-century priestess? What sick fate would do such a thing? She could imagine the old crones who had sent her here passing the time in uncaring conversation like the assembly-line workers that they were.

You say the cat turned the dial on the time machine a bit? Oh, well, why not drop her into the soup? It might be interesting, even fun. Things are getting better, after all. Why should she complain? No hunger, a long life, drugs for pain, television, what could be easier? "Short, brutish nasty..." they used to say life was, Dearie. For the first time ever it is not so; the era of scarcity is no more. What's left is just a ghost or two, just little Hobbes-goblins of rigid minds trying to manage and control.

Laura had smiled to herself but the smile was thin. It didn't matter, she had thought unhappily, that she was left to stumble through life as a misfit, a lonely anachronism, drawn by an inner vision that had no analog outside of her. A lover had once told her that she was like a tree-top flower, a cloud blossom, planted incongruously in the ground. She pictured herself tied by her roots to a sodden existence in a materialist age, unable to bloom for the darkness. She allowed herself to think that what her lover had said was true but the thought gave Laura only brief comfort and her anger at David's friends returned, streaming with the vivid memories of New York.

Listening to David, Laura heard Michelson's words, replaying them vividly again and again. Michelson had spoken in rambling yet moving ways about plants, animals and creation. He had extolled harmony—inner and outer balance, concordance, symbiosis. And flowers, he always returned to flowers. They led impossible brief existences. They expressed themselves fully in color and shape, in the touch of petals, in rich fragrances, all for the sake of the seed that would carry their essence. What was most glorious was that their expression was unselfconscious and totally self-sacrificing. A wild display that couldn't possibly be sustained, put on to ensure that a new and separate life would grow by attracting the nastiest of workaholic insects to spread pollen on hairy legs. Not unlike most women's fate, Laura remembered thinking at the time.

The words led her into the horror of Michelson's collapse only feet away from her, her exit through the lifeless museum displays, the ill-kept park, the restaurant, the news of his death, the dream, the ridicule. All were now intruding on her forest home, on the warmth she felt for David, on the abundance of flowers she had nursed outside, and on the nearby paths where nature always found a way to speak to her. As memory and feelings absorbed her, her eyes became distant and her expression turned to slate. The unexpected ringing of the v-phone playing a measure from The Clowns brought her back. It was only then that she sensed the dampness of the cloud that had glided down the mountain. She heard the rhythmic patter on the thatch and saw the water dripping from the leaves to the ground.

"I'll get it," David said. A few moments later she heard the booming brogue of Rashid O'Shea carrying over the sound of the rain.

CHAPTER 4

On the road to Lahaina, high where you curve around the hill, you stopped to see us: a spray of steam or a rolling black silhouette here and there breaking the waves. You stood beside your motored cubes squinting into sun-lit water, hoping to glimpse a curiosity that you thought might soon be gone. That's how I saw your seeing.

You stood two or three together, talking. Random bursts of noise I heard. You almost never sang. There was no rhythm in your speech—not even the rhythm of the great water fans beating, the sound by which we know you best. You were wrapped in the skins of others, your own flesh numbed to the currents of the air that enveloped you and to the touch of the ground beneath you. How did you know where you were?

You didn't. You made mind images and put little dots on them and said, "There I am." But you were not there. And now, wherever you are, you are inert, a point occupying time, without roots, without life.

It was not the first time that the deeply tanned and handsome man in the sea-side bungalow had heard other voices in his heart. Nor the first time that a voice had hinted of Cetacean form. The whale family's complex neural connections, he knew, made them natural messengers and certainly more appropriate to Maui than bushes in flames. But this time there was an Old Testament ring to the message, a bitterness of prophesy he hadn't heard before.

No wonder you reeked of death—death which you did so much to hide, and so much of which you have caused. What you see you do not hear or feel or taste; what you hear you do not taste, what you feel you do not see. It is not as it is with us, all of the senses, one sense.

Your words. I have been inside you. One speaks, "black," but the other, if he hears at all, sees nothing like it in his mind's eye—more likely white or purple hues or the taste of tomorrow's food or a lingering over yesterday's sleight. Inside, you are less like each other than you are like the aliens on your movie screens.

There is almost no touching, no rubbing of your footed flukes and fingered fins. What touching there is, is more a clutching, a taking of what you cannot possess.

What a dreadful pain you carry, the deepest and darkest horror any of our Mother's creatures have ever known.

Except for the ones whom you have exterminated. Untimely ends of what can never be again. Unfulfilled in eternity. Limbo you call it. We could call it hell.

Shall I name them all? Where shall we begin? The magnificent mammoth that was your companion during the Great Cold? The horned auroch that crashed through your forests? The giant sloth? The saber-toothed cat? The passenger pigeons that darkened the skies? Or the little Carolina parakeet of the gentle hills? And there was my brother Bowhead Whale, round, good humored, portly. Slow. He had no chance, bleeding on the ice.

It is the Great Loneliness that you must fear now. It is the sadness of the spirit that may no longer soar on the wing of Golden Eagle, or drift trackless through the snow like Leopard, or scan the nocturnal forest with Spotted Owl, or be the one million bitter and sweet tastes of vanished nuts and seeds.

Yet you are so lonely already—you are armored like Sea Turtle, and your shell is thickest just where you might best serve and delight. The mystery of the Universe is no longer within you. There is no amber-red glow at your core.

Mother, Father, Grandmother, Grandfather of us all, help me to help you. Help me to help you hear and see and help me feel and be.

It is I, Humpback Whale, that speaks to you through the body we call Spotted Fluke. Our mind of one is our mind of all; our mind of all is in our mind of one.

I see lights up there now, on the road to Lahaina. I breathe in the sweet night air filling a thousand sacks. It is quieter than usual in the bay, only the distant buzz of a mosquito boat, the chant of halyards clicking against masts as your wind boats bob in the tide—drunken vessels, one of you said—the dull beat of calm water lapping the shore, a splash as a frightened mullet avoids his fate. A death a life, a life a death.

Is that you, my friend, I sense sensing me, listening with your inner ear? It is. I feel the rise and fall of your breath, the rhythm of your heart, your skin against the cloth. I have been with you before. Come with me deeper, down into the colder waters. Feel my shape shift, my body mold into a thousand forms, smoothing out the eddies and currents. Water and I embrace. Deeper, cooler, water. Water and I dance. My skin is water, I am water, you are water; water has no bounds.

Now through the water I hear my brother, Spiked Beak, and my sister, Fluted Tail, and far off in the distance, many days away, the deep call of a young brother, Blue. Blue Whale speaks through a new voice that I have not heard before. This surprises me. There are so few. It's good news. Perhaps the garden at the surface of the sea will survive the rays that beat down near the Southern Ice, through the hole that you have bored. And with the garden, the krill that feast in the garden, and the Blues, the few, that feast on the krill.

Come deeper with me. Here I am truly Humpback Whale. I see you, Hu-man, better here, and it warms me. I know that you are trying. You have stopped the hunt. You helped our brother— Humphrey you called him—when he went too far into the land. He had a lot to tell.

Some of you, he said, look up at the stars again, some even know where the moon will set today. Some hear the solitary Hoo-Hoot-Hoo-Hu of the owl or the single trill of a thrush, and imagine that one day again there may be a symphony. Some of you feel the ground soften under your toes and even Spider you treat as your friend. Here in the depths I am one with you; it warms me but it is time to rise again. Rising, the rush of currents and eddies around me makes my being dance. Dance with me, my friend. Awaken, my beloved friends, awaken my friends—for we are all as lovers and lovers never sleep.

Rise with me, I feel the surface come, a glaze of moonlit waters veiling the moonlit night. Crash into the air and briefly stand, scan your world, and then fall with me again into the water, the water without end.

I know you, the one they call Rashid O'Shea, the one who hears me speak. I know you are awake. You hear me say it: "The time has come now, it's not too late."

Rashid O'Shea flashed white teeth as he sat cross-legged and wide-eyed in the darkened seaside cabin that was not so far away. His smile widened and he thought of David and Laura in their forest house, of Peter's startled voice the night before and of Almira Zaabut whom he came to know again. The smile warmed Spotted Fluke. He launched a spout of vapor blow, turned on his side and with one eye watched it take umbrella form in the cool, predawn air.

CHAPTER 5

The colors and sounds of sunrise were Almira Zaabut's favorites. The call to prayer, God the Merciful, the Compassionate. The gruff and shrill cries of those who still worked with animals, rousing them for a day's labor, the passing steps of neighbors, the running squeals of children starting early on their trek to school, the distant hum of electric buses on the highway heading toward Jerusalem. The pink and amber and ocher shades that tinged the whitewashed walls of houses, the shimmering hint of moisture on morning dust, the yellow-white glare that obscured the horizon, and more often than not the great orange fireball itself floating above a ledge of sand. Best of all every morning she loved the undefined glow on her two son's faces as they awoke announcing the new day, every day a new beginning, a new life.

Where do we lose that? Almira thought. When did we forget? What makes us feel the morning through a dull stupor, kicking at it with stiffened limbs, clinging to the dark recesses of sleep? When did we start reaching for the analgesic that numbs a hundred yesterdays of pain, for the curtain that keeps out any glimmer of the new? For her, she guessed, it might have begun at the Sorbonne, the wine-heavy nights of fractious intensity and an unrestrained life....

Almira had left Ramallah for Paris when she was twenty, her schooling interrupted for two years by the second Palestinian intifadah. Looking back, she was glad that she hadn't gone sooner. She would have been too unformed, too insecure to follow the unconventional alleyways that had drawn her during her five years in France. A six-thousand-year-old legacy of patriarchy, albeit softened by her parents, a new country, a less than perfect mastery of French taught to her by her father (a merchant in the region's wholesale fruit trade), and the unspoken contempt of the many Parisian shopkeepers and passersby who saw Arabs as little more than garbage collectors or trouble...all would have worked to keep her in her shell, scholarly and lonely, destined to be a middle-level clerk in a private firm or perhaps a school teacher in Nablus.

Wine-heavy nights of endless talk. Of rediscovering the real Marx, of Sartre, of Dubos and Marcuse, and even The Greenbook, which was being taken with far greater seriousness now that its author was safely buried and unarmed under the Libyan desert. Other nights had been given over to passion, and more. She and her band of companions had sometimes loved each other and sometimes betrayed each other, weaving their own tale of a thousand nights, safe in the knowledge that their origins were so scattered that the judgment and scorn of family and community would never have to be faced.

Curious though, how some of it never healed. Almira thought of Jean-Marc—Jean-Marc Aubuisson whom she now knew she had loved deeply. Jean-Marc who had the slender body of a dancer. Clear-eyed, clear-headed, elegant Jean-Marc. The model polyglot European destined to help manage the world's citizenry and its common, problematic future.

When she was one with him, she escaped all that caused her shame. Origins of poverty, at least by Western standards, and hatred—hatred for the Israeli soldiers and settlers, for the "holy" monks at the Mar Saba monastery, for the hypocritical American diplomats, and for their French and British counterparts and all the others who were to blame, closely or remotely, for that day when her twelve-year-old brother's elbows and knees had been crushed under the hammering of a bludgeoning gun butt. And hatred for the impotence, her mother's and father's, all Palestinians', and her own. Shame at her association with a faith that still sheltered medieval elements that were blind to a thousand years' advancement, that shackled their women and gave solace to war, hate and destruction. Shame at the heaviness of buttocks and thighs and smallness of breasts that made her nondescript and awkward when she ventured to the pool near the university complex in Antony. It had all seemed to vanish in the glow of his presence, as if magically absorbed under the crest on his signet ring.

Wine-heavy nights that killed the mornings. Wine, the killer of memory and pain...and life? Curious that the religion of her mother's upbringing which Almira had scorned had been unequivocally clear on that subject: wine was a curse to be avoided. Not because it was addictive but because of the state that it created, an ecstasy that lied and veiled the real source of joy. Worse, Almira thought to herself, God wants no part of it. He has no intention of seeing the morning of his creation through bloodshot, bleary eyes that have severed themselves from remembrance. So he steps away and desolation becomes real. *Je suis le ténébreux—le veuf—l'inconsolé, Le prince d'Aquitaine à la tour abolie...*

Widowed? Dark? A ruined land around her? Not really, much had changed. The future was filled with promise. Still, the melancholy poetry of Paris wine returned to her...Le Bateau Ivre...Rimbaud, Verlaine, Baudelaire, Nerval, how she had loved them then. Where was her love now? Would she really take the glories of ten thousand more sunrises rather than one more night of love and poetry and wine?

Full circle, Almira thought. No matter how much we grow, we are always in a circle where the thoughts and desires of the first bring the aversions of the middle which bring at the last the return to the first. Furtive, evasive, maddening God, Ihdinas-sirat al-mustaqim. Show me the straight path.

Jamal, nine, and Youssef, eleven, were up now. Almira put warm goat's milk, bread, and a bowl of figs and oranges on the table. Youssef had his hand on the fattest orange before Jamal sat down.

"He knew I wanted it. He doesn't even like them," Jamal said.

Almira knew that Jamal was right but she had no patience for the whining. "Eat two, Jamal, we have plenty."

Jamal glared at Youssef with fury. Youssef spat out a pip in

Jamal's general direction.

All men, Almira mused, are in need of genetic alteration. There will not be peace as long as they are born as they are.

She was only half joking. Similar sentiments had attracted her to the party and most of all to its leader, Fatimah Karajan. After Paris and Jean-Marc and the others, she had come home determined to assert her identity as a Palestinian and a woman. She had married Farid Zaabut. He was handsome, intelligent, passionate, zealous and uncompromising. Journalism was his chosen profession but at first it was more like a cover, and a flimsy one at that. All West Bank publications had been shut down, leaving him with only an occasional column to contribute or a pseudonymous report smuggled out to the Western press. His energies turned more and more to his work in the underground. He became the leader of a shadow-village committee that met in secret and did its best to satisfy the community's food, medical and educational needs.

Farid was so effective and so articulate that he was soon drawn into an even deeper underground—the net that tied large numbers of villages together, that shared intelligence and tactics and maintained clandestine contact with the leadership. Though more deeply buried and compartmented, the net was not any safer. It was this level that the Shin Bet, the Israeli internal security agency, rightly saw as most threatening and to which it devoted its best agents and much of its resources. Not only were Israeli intelligence efforts greater but, Farid soon learned, if he were to be questioned, there would be more travel, meetings and time gaps to explain. Even more important, a village or neighborhood committee offered security precisely because there were no secrets. Everyone knew everyone else too intimately to be fooled easily. But those who came from unnamed communities or in some cases seemingly from no place at all, and bearing only first names—Christian names, as they are called in the West—could fool you. They had no history; no easy cross-checking was available.

Almira had known it would happen. She had expected it during the third intifadah, but miraculously, it hadn't happened then. It was later, after the truce, following the repression that came on the heels of intolerable fundamentalist violence on both sides. She knew it not long after Youssef was born, the first time Farid fled to the caves that overlooked the Dead Sea. The soldiers came not long afterwards. They pushed her around some but she had anticipated far worse when they broke the door down at two o'clock one morning. The soldiers even seemed to believe her when she said that she didn't know Farid's whereabouts, that he had been helping an American write a tour guide and said he would be back in two weeks, give or take a bit. The American? She had heard her husband call him over the telephone but more than that she didn't know. They didn't touch her after that. Maybe they didn't know what they were looking for. Maybe they believed her. The story she told was partially true. Farid had talked to an American; she doubted that he was a guide-book writer. After the first disruption, she said she had to feed Youssef; it was credible, he was screaming his head off, but Almira knew it was not in hunger. Maybe impressionable nineteen-year-old Israelis couldn't believe that she could breastfeed calmly and lie in the face of a gun. There were advantages in being thought of as a lesser people.

To her surprise, the soldiers didn't come back in two weeks as they said they would. More to her surprise, Farid did return after a month had gone by. Nonetheless she knew—it was just a matter of time. She felt the knowledge in the urgency of their lovemaking and in her determination to have another child. Jamal had proved to be a good one, his features were even at the earliest age like Farid's. Jamal had never been in a room with his father, yet he was a constant reminder to her of his presence.

Death had come to Farid and two other young men in their thirties a year almost to the day after the soldiers first barged through their door. Her father had told her. On a street in Hebron, three nine-millimeter soft points fired at extremely close range had each left an abstract mural of bone and blood and brain on a garden wall, the bodies slumped below.

Zealots from the nearby garrison settlements had committed the atrocity, the mayor told Almira's father. It had happened before. He would demand a full investigation by the occupational authorities. He would insist that Farid's murderers be brought to justice.

"Possibly the Shin Bet," the mayor's aide had whispered as he guided the old man out by his arm through the antechamber door. "Farid was feared, his martyrdom is a testament to his power. You should be very proud. We are. The mayor asked me to tell you so."

"Suspected of collaboration. It's a death squad MO.," the Israeli officer had suggested. His eyes softened as he looked at Almira's father. "You will be surprised to hear what I am about to say. I know better. I knew your son-in-law. He had too much integrity. He would not collaborate but he was not so well known to others here. Who knows, a chance meeting with the wrong person at the wrong time...."

The officer paused, contemplatively, "The two who were with him, I'm not so sure about them. Did you know them?"

Almira's father did not. If he had, he would have said nothing.

"We hear that there are power struggles in the resistance," the sergeant continued. "That is the trouble with struggles such as yours. Violence, deceit, secrecy. They can be turned inside as well as out. These are games for the power hungry. Even if you win, you have no chance. There will be a Stalin in your midst, and he will have positioned himself very, very well."

Almira's father remained in silence. The officer rose from behind his desk and led the elderly Palestinian out. "We do have leads. We will find your son-in-law's killers. I know we can count on you to help us if you can."

The details of her father's account stayed with Almira. She had asked her father to tell the story twice and for twenty minutes she savored the ironies. They flowed naturally into her well-honed defenses like the first tidewater into a sandcastle's moat, channeled clear of the walls and tower and dissolving harmlessly into the sand. "Safe upon the solid rock the ugly houses stand..."—more poetry learned long ago. In Paris? Jean-Marc? No, some American, he played a twelve-string guitar and sang songs from all over.

Then the breakers came crashing down on walls and tower, leaving no more than a soft and deformed lump of sand. A spring of anger and grief flowed into some deep, unknown place within her, gathered force and cascaded out in a torrent of black sound. She sobbed and pummeled her father with her fists, then hid in her room for hours until she heard Youssef's whimpers outside.

They never did find his murderers. That came as no surprise, and she had known what she had to do. The spur of truth was in the story her father told, in the manipulative officer's words. It was inherent in the violence, deceit and secrecy of which he spoke. No one could hold his center there. So two weeks after Farid's death she took the bus to Bethlehem to seek out Fatimah Karajan who was then waging a seemingly lonely battle for the Committee of Palestinian Women for Peace.

"Jamal, Youssef, go. You will be late." Almira snapped back to the present, hearing their squabbling. She stopped them at the door and ran her fingers through their hair, pretending to comb it. They bolted like puppies cooped up too long.

How much things have changed, Almira thought. Six years later she had a normal job with a party that participated in a real democratic process. Her material needs were met. She had normal children who went to school—not just any school, but one that she had chosen. It was run by Quakers and drew its students from the Jewish and Palestinian communities, as well as a sprinkling of Americans and other nationalities. By the time the boys and girls were twelve they could all read and write Hebrew, Arabic and English. Most were learning French as well.

The school participated in UNESCO's Global Culture Programme. For decades it had been clear that an interdependent world required planetary citizens who knew at least a little bit about others' cultures, yet few nations had the human resources to offer a global culture program at the secondary and elementary school levels, and educational bureaucracies—allied with xenophobic elements—successfully resisted significant curriculum changes.

But technology, with an assist from UNESCO, had broken the barriers down. Internet and audio/video linkages were too commonplace. With a little outside help, classrooms around the globe could easily be linked. UNESCO provided it by coordinating, scheduling, and publishing lists of participating institutions. Suddenly, a seemingly momentous issue of national policy had become a simple matter of local choice for each teacher.

Almira remembered the day Youssef had told her in a very matter of fact tone about the eightfold path the Lord Buddha had taught, and the two Thai children with unpronounceable names who had asked if it were true that God was buried in the desert sands, waiting to be watered with compassion so that he could bloom in every land.

Jamal had come home one day and explained how it was as dry in Arizona as in Palestine and how a hogan was different from his house but how in a lot of ways they were the same. "The Navajos," he had added, "they were treated worse than we were."

Almira thought of herself as a hardened woman but Jamal's simple comment had brought tears to her eyes. Even thinking of the moment filled her with longing. We have suffered so much, she thought. Is this insanity, this brutality, this separation and division of each against the other finally over? Are eight billion of us in just one generation finally becoming whole? So much had changed, so quickly.

It was time for her to leave for work, a bad day to be late. She and Fatimah were to give the day over to planning for the Convocation now that New Delhi seemed certain to be the site. As she dressed she glanced at herself in the bedroom mirror and was pleased to see that some things hadn't changed that much after all. Her body, draped in a modest, mauve dress, accented by a very old bronze eight-pointed star that hung from her neck on a leather thong, looked no worse than it ever had. Her face had become more defined. She was handsome. Wheat-colored eyes set in light brown skin and dark brown hair gazed out at her from the mirror, reflecting the early light. She arranged the thin, traditional white veil over her head but did not cover her face. "You have protected us," she said.

Forty minutes later she stepped off the electric bus, in sight of the hundred-year-old structure that served as party headquarters. It was an odd building, brick, Victorian in style, three stories tall, constructed in the days of the British Mandate when it had housed a number of His Majesty's civil servants. Several had criticized Fatimah's choice of the building but she had said it would help everybody remember and without remembrance, she always added, there could be no forgiveness.

Almira walked into the office. The main room was furnished sparsely with simple wooden desks and chairs and one worn but plush chesterfield set behind a coffee table. Two walls were covered with photographs of Fatimah, accompanied sometimes by Almira, with smiling Palestinian, Israeli and world leaders. A giant, bronze-framed mirror hung on a third wall and in the back a brightly colored poster of the Universal Declaration of Human Rights spelled out in Hebrew, Arabic and English and enveloping a socially- just, Peter's Projection of the globe, caught every visitor's eye.

Rabia Nasr was painting her long nails a bold scarlet at the reception desk. She looked up at Almira, "I'm glad you're here. There've been a lot of calls this morning. From the US, India, all over. A lot about the Convocation. Fatimah hasn't come in."

It was almost ten. Fatimah was usually in before eight but wouldn't open the office for business until nine or nine thirty when Rabia arrived. "Did you call her?" Almira asked.

"There wasn't any answer." She held her left hand up to the light, pursed her lips and blew on her freshly painted nails.

Almira tried to call Fatimah. No answer. That was unusual too. Fatimah almost always took her calls. Maybe she was in the bath. Almira decided to wait a few minutes for a call back. If not, she would go to Fatimah's apartment. It was just a few blocks away. She and Fatimah had been together the previous evening; nothing unusual had happened. Almira began to worry.

"I'll be back soon," Almira said after a few minutes had passed, "I'm going to check. Call me if you hear from her."

"Of course."

As Almira rounded the corner onto Fatimah's street, a heavy set, muscular man in an ill-fitting brown western suit brushed past her, nearly knocking her to the ground. He kept moving and offered no apology. Almira regained her balance. She could only see his back as he hurried into the crowd. A Russian immigrant she guessed from his rudeness. A strong sense of discomfort rose within her and the discomfort lingered like an unpleasant smell.

Still troubled, she walked a few meters and pressed the buzzer at the door to Fatimah's building. Again, no answer. She rang two or three more times with no result. She looked under the brick where a spare key was sometimes hidden. No key. As she was about to step away, a glint from further down the steps caught her eye. It was a key. She tried it in the lock; the lock turned.

Almira climbed into a small, slow elevator and directed it to the fourth floor. As the elevator creaked upwards, she heard running steps and voices in the staircase. When she reached the fourth floor landing, there were three men, out of breath, standing in front of Fatimah's door. Two of them were uniformed; a third wore dark slacks, a leather jacket and an open-collared white shirt.

"Who are you?" one of the uniformed men demanded.

"I'm a friend of the woman who lives here. And you?" Almira glared at him unblinkingly.

"We were called," the man in the leather jacket stated. "Someone heard gunshots, the caller thinks it was in this room. No one's answering. Will you call to her?"

Almira did as she was asked but there was no reply. "Stand back but don't go anywhere," the man said to her.

It was clear that the three were planning on breaking down the door. Almira considered telling them about the key always left over the door ledge but some instinct kept her from doing so. The largest of the men delivered three shoulder blows into the door and it gave way. In spite of the instruction to stay where she was, Almira followed them in. The men didn't seem to care. They headed through the foyer and down a corridor that led past a kitchen. On the left was an archway opening into a living room; a bedroom entrance was on the right. They went into the bedroom; Almira gasped at the sight. The well-defined back of a naked man could be seen on the bed. He was lying on top of Fatimah whose body was nude as well, her legs were straddled around his—a scene of passion but there was no movement in the man's body, and there was no life in Fatimah's eyes. A crimson ooze was spreading under her head onto the pillow and staining the silken cream sheets as well; the ooze still seemed moist and bright. Round bullet holes could be seen in the lovers' heads, the man's in the back, Fatimah's where her third eye could have been.

Almira nearly fainted in horror and revulsion. She leaned against the wall to sustain herself and heard one of the uniformed men say, "Captain, Walid, the man do you see? I think it's Arbel,

Ariel Arbel!"

For Almira shock gave way to disbelief. Farid had told her stories about Ariel Arbel. Arbel had been the Deputy Director of the Shin Bet. Interrogations, death squads, Farid had said, there you would always find Arbel. The man was universally feared. Arbel making love to Fatimah? Incomprehensible but Almira could see through eyes that filled with tears that of one thing there was no question, Arbel and Fatimah were dead.

WILLIAM H. ESPINOSA

CHAPTER 6

Peter Flanigan had to crawl over Katie Jasper to reach the alarm. She stirred. He'd been awake for a while, watching a carousel of work-a-day scenarios revolve through his mind's eye. He almost always woke up that way, with a swift stream of thought filling his consciousness. It was as if some engine ran all night, honing, grinding, and polishing the experience of the previous day and his concerns for the next. It never seemed to tire and obviously didn't need sleep. It worked in the daytime too. It turned out good thoughts, rational, balanced, inclusive, acceptable to almost everyone, filled with the conventional wisdom which the insiders shared. It was this quality, together with a calculatedly nonassertive nature, a neat appearance, and good-natured sense of humor that made him an ideal Senator's aide.

Katie stirred again, pulled her short brown hair away from her face and wrapped an arm around his back.

"I think we do love each other," she said sleepily. A lid opened to disclose a sapphirine eye. "Somehow we knew even when we were thirteen, but it's been so hard."

He should have turned off the alarm before it rang. He wanted his coffee and a bagel. Around the corner, alone. He wanted to absorb the Washington Post and wanted to let the Post absorb him. These morning conversations with Katie always depressed him. It was bad enough that she put all of his shirts in one drawer while he talked to the Senator the night before. Even the morning stream of observations wasn't right. Somehow, sleeping with Katie drained his energy. Asking her to come visit had been a stupid idea.

Seeing her always left him feeling subtly manipulated, even cornered, and this time again he was filled with an ineffable and vaporous unease. When they were eight or ten or even twelve it was different. They had been direct with each other; there were no unstated expectations much less unfulfilled ones. She had been a tomboy and his friend, a little judgmental at times, faster up a tree than he but harsh with him when he stomped on a column of ants. It was not like that now.

His mother and Katie's were best friends. They had gone to college together, and both had married successful lawyers and settled into suburban nests in Rye, New York. His mother always knew what Katie was doing, sometimes even before Katie did, and his mother always told him.

"Katie is getting serious about Bernie Berenson. They're seeing a lot of each other," Peter's mother told him a few days before when he'd called to say that he was back from his fact-finding trip in Peru.

Within seconds of hanging up, Peter had watched with detached fascination as his fingers pressed Katie's numbers on the v-phone. She answered as cheerful and smiling as his mother, glad that he was back safely and of course delighted that he would like her to come to Washington. She would have to rearrange a dinner with a friend but she was sure it wouldn't be a problem. Her friend, Bernie, Peter had met him, yes? They had had dinner not long ago, but it was a little sad...Matteo Michelson, he'd died that day...did Peter know him? No? Too bad.

Peter had met Bernie once and had immediately disliked him. It was more than vestigial jealousy. When he was angry and wished for an unfeeling justice, Peter hoped that Katie would marry Bernie and consign her life to misery. Bernie was bright and obviously bound to be rich and successful, but he took himself too seriously and covered ambition with a mask of do-goodism. In that respect, the Mother Earth Investment Bank, MEIB, was perfect for Bernie. It encouraged unlimited greed in its employees while striving to save the world. MEIB was one of several institutions that were put together to channel environmental impulses into "free-market" endeavors during the first years of the new century.

MEIB and investment banks like it could identify a company operating an environmentally noncompliant facility and then issue tax-free, government guaranteed bonds to finance a takeover of the transgressing firm. The vigilante banks' fees were enormous but fear of a virtually unstoppable takeover attempt focused business leaders' minds on the environment more effectively than even consumer boycotts or class action law suits.

The program is working, Peter thought, but like so many other "solutions" to problems, this Rube Goldberg contraption that relied on the worst of human nature, troubled him. Greed to consume the waste products of greed. It didn't make sense. Didn't the greed just keep going around? Wouldn't it come back in some new, more malignant form?

This was a train of thought he knew he shouldn't follow. It would get him in trouble. He had a feeling Katie's self-righteousness was to blame for this too. He resented her. He needed to say something that would keep her from ever wanting to come back.

But he didn't. Not then. That morning he had to make his getaway quickly. "The Senator wants his briefing early," he said. He rolled away from her arms, gave her hand a brief squeeze and headed for the shower. He adjusted the water temperature and let the water spill through his yellow hair and over his thin body for a long time. Gradually he felt his mental clarity return. He focused his thoughts on his trip in the Andes and the parts of it that would interest Senator Carmichael.

When Peter came out of the shower, he looked for his razor on its customary spot on the sink. It wasn't there. Eventually he found it in the cabinet with all of his toiletries neatly rearranged. Katie. He shaved, nicking himself only once. When he returned to the bedroom Katie's eyes were closed. She had rolled over on her stomach, one hand resting at each end of a pillow. She was asleep or pretending to be asleep. He suspected the latter. Katie was smart and she probably knew that she had pushed as far as she could in one morning, maybe too far. He had come close....

To his relief as he went down the stairs and stepped outdoors the feelings that Katie provoked in him subsided. The sky was clear, the air brisk, the early sun warming where it edged around the buildings and trees. A young girl passed by carrying a book bag. Her red hair was in a ponytail held in place by a barrette of multicolored baubles that looked like a knot of small balloons bobbing as she walked. Peter smiled. He walked more briskly, picked up a copy of the Post and entered the Pork & Bagel on Pennsylvania Avenue, an establishment popular with political aides. He was earlier than usual and there was no line. He placed his bagel and egg order, paid two New Dollars and looked for a place to sit.

Two young men sat in the booth across from his table. He didn't recognize them. Probably House staff—they were very young, and he was on the House side of Capitol Hill. Their conversation kept him from reading the paper.

"But what if it's true," said one who sported a striped bow tie. Where do they find these people, Peter wondered. No one under sixty wears a tie anymore.

"What if it's true," he heard the young man with the bow tie continue, "What if there is only one in a thousand chances that it's true? We, this country, the whole world, will be helpless against it. What we've got now is a pack of hounds that can't hunt. No one to even keep them together."

Nobody hunted anymore either, Peter thought. "Can't argue with that," said Bow Tie's companion, more conventionally dressed in a jacket and blue shirt buttoned to the neck.

Planetary securitists, Peter thought, guardians of the global village. The "it" Bow Tie referred to could be many things. Enemies within, enemies without, invaders from another star system, ecological degradation, or just human stupidity. Whatever "it" was, the solution was the same. The planet's fate couldn't just be left to the random efforts of millions of communities, voluntary associations and well-meaning human beings. What they needed was organized vigilance, international preparedness, clear deterrence of wrongdoing, and effective leadership to safeguard people and the biosphere. This could only come from a powerful central authority that could give direction to human life.

Curiously, much as some of the most militant, anti-Soviet Cold Warriors had come from the ranks of the isolationists, the first planetary securitists had emerged from the ranks of those who had most forcefully argued for resistance to the growing internationalist trends. Those who had defended the prerogatives of national governments to permit the pollution of the earth by their enterprises were arguing for international embargoes of environmentally rogue governments. Those who had felt most comfortable countenancing the potential destruction of everything in the name of nuclear deterrence or invading whole nations to search for jihadists in caves were calling for paramilitary strike forces to defend endangered beetle species.

After the Bush era and the anti-terror years, after recognizing the great transformation that had radically changed the role of the nation state in the world, and after immersing themselves in think tanks, the old warriors were emerging with a new call to arms. As so often happened—young men, idealistic, defining themselves—were drawn to the rallying cries of their fathers' other enemies, their grandfathers.

"The thing is," the young man with the bow tie had resumed, "there is no other way to explain it—a pulse of energy that passes through the solar system at measured intervals, increasing in pace. At Livermore Labs they've analyzed it—it's a reverse Fibonacci series of some kind—an accelerating summation series. They—whoever, whatever is doing this—have to be intelligent.

"And if they come—let's pray that they haven't already been here—they are going to see one destructive species overrunning a jewel of a planet, poised to destroy its fragile ecosystem. It's not the rats or the cockroaches or even the twenty-two mutations of the AIDS virus that we're just learning how to contain that's going to cause them concern; it's us. They're going to see us as the disease. All the rest thrive as parasites on our bad conduct. With one blow it can all be taken care of: just eliminate the humans. I mean, as an outsider, isn't that what you would think? Isn't that what you would do?" Blue Shirt nodded his agreement.

"We have to be strong," Bow Tie continued. "We have to show our capacity for concerted, effective action. That we can be the solution, not just the problem.... I mean no more gasoline powered cars. None, anywhere. I don't care what it does to poor people in the sticks of Mexico or anywhere else. So there's the Convocation; it may be our last chance."

Three teenagers, one white, two black, books in hand, all gangly and loud, passed between Peter and the two aides.

"...and if not we may need to use force," Peter heard Bow Tie finish.

The monologue seemed to be over. *Force against poor Mexicans or the pulse aliens?* Peter wondered. After finishing his bagel and egg he started to open the newspaper but saw that it was getting late. Peter liked to read at least one newspaper from beginning to end before business started. That way there were no surprises. It was also a way to catch the odd fact or back page quote that gave a hint as to what was really going on. Peter was one of the few that still relied on newspapers. He knew it gave him an edge over the video/sound bite "experts," even over those who relied on the Internet news headline index.

There would be no edge that morning. Peter remembered why he'd wanted breakfast out, why he had not brought a newspaper in. Katie disapproved of newspapers. She thought it was a tree bashing, toxic activity—an anachronism of the industrial age, a clinging to one of the core gods of mass production that had brought the Earth so close to ruin—the printing press. What did you learn today, she would ask, that justified the killing of even one tree? Sometime soon he needed to understand why he couldn't evict Katie from his life. But not now, there wasn't time.

Peter left the Pork & Bagel and walked toward the Senate office buildings.

As he came closer to the Dirksen Office Building, Peter's mind shifted from Katie to Ayachuelo, its remarkable inhabitant José María Velasquez, and the points he would like to make about the man to Senator Carmichael. Peter had known only one other man like Velasquez—a half-Irish, half-Pakistani eccentric from Maui, Rashid O'Shea. He had met O'Shea at a conference in Vancouver on the future of the United Nations. O'Shea had displayed a charismatic presence that drew an unusually large audience to an abstruse talk on tribal governance. Afterwards

O'Shea had sought Peter out and suggested a round trip ferry ride to Victoria. They talked about the state of the Earth and Peter's inner life as they watched four diving orcas flank the ferry for miles. Since then O'Shea would call him from time to time, most recently at 5 A.M. one morning to wish him a whale of a day.

"Velasquez," Peter heard himself tell the Senator a few minutes later, "is doing extraordinary things."

"From what I hear he's an extraordinary man."

"You sense warmth in his presence. But it's not forced on you. You absorb as little or as much as you want. And somehow your personal preoccupations and concerns become unimportant. You're filled with questions but then you forget most of them and the ones you do ask don't come out right."

Senator Patrick Carmichael was white-haired but his movements were vigorous, his cheeks ruddy, his face remarkably unlined for a man of his age. "Bobby Kennedy, he came to our school once and they let me walk him from the principal's office to Room 13-B," the Senator said nodding in agreement. "I felt that way too, I couldn't get out a word. But you know, Peter, that's when I knew I wasn't going to be a priest. I wanted to be President and do good."

"Senator," Peter continued, "you remember how in the 1990s, a number of people noted that all the supposedly sullen, slovenly, lazy peasants from Central America showed a lot of initiative and energy when they came to the United States. It wasn't just that there were more opportunities, it was that their entire attitude changed. They didn't just move to a wealthier, freer place—they were liberated from a cultural inner jailer that ensured that generations passed without rebellion and without change.

"Well, somehow this man—Velasquez—has caused a liberation and nobody had to migrate anywhere, and they've hardly needed any help from outside at all."

Peter paused and sipped on his coffee. The Senator's intercom buzzed. "Later," he said, to the image on the screen.

"He put in some dollars," Peter continued, "but not many. Velasquez saved some money during his years as a noncom on the UN Middle East Force Command and he had some colleagues from Peru and from Norway and Sweden and elsewhere who gave him small contributions. So he lends it, in very small amounts, but only if a project has at least three or four partners who are investing their labor and only if they all agree to pay back twice as much in a year or two and all that goes back into the loan pool. Then you can borrow more or even get a chance to participate in one or another loan committee to pass on the projects of others.

"In places like Peru, an ordinary person's initiative really wasn't given value at all, it was an untapped resource. It was available because social repression had bottled it up. Well, somehow, Velasquez has freed all this energy; he's made them richer, he's empowered them. Each time an individual succeeds, they're all better off. They have a bigger loan pool to draw on and a bigger local market for whatever they're doing and a new range of opportunities...."

The Senator interrupted. "How did Velasquez get to be who he is? Where did all this start?"

"I don't really know. He told me he learned a lot about people when he was in the military, that he saw that a *cholo*—that's what the Spanish called people of Indian descent—could do as well as anybody, even as well as the ones with blond hair." Peter patted his head as if to keep his own hair in place and smiled at the memory of the man's good-humored ribbing. "The military was one of the few places a person like him could get recognition. And then he said his time in the Negev really changed him, something about a monastery where he stayed...."

The knock that announced Randolph Livingston's entrance was perfunctory. Livingston was younger than Peter, but he was well-groomed, well-connected, and ambitious. The Senator had given him substantial legislative responsibilities. Livingston, Peter knew, would like to have Peter's job. Peter sensed trouble.

"I'm sorry to interrupt sir, but since Señor"—Livingston drew the word out through his nasal passageways—"Velasquez is dead, I thought your talk could wait."

"What do you mean, dead?" the Senator asked.

"Dead, dead. It was in the Post this morning, a highway accident of some kind."

Livingston turned to Peter. "You didn't know? We all

counted on you to read the paper for us. Page A38. I just happened to glance at it today."

As the Senator's eyes lost focus, Peter felt a numbing sense of loss and dread slowly rising within him. He stared blankly out the window at the North face of the Capitol. Minutes passed during which he did not move.

"Peter, I'm sorry," the Senator's voice broke through. "The ambassador from South Africa is waiting outside. You're going to have to leave."

CHAPTER 7

On the morning that Peter gave his briefing to Senator Carmichael, the body of José María Velasquez was lying on a white metal table at the coroner's office in Cuzco. The day was cold and damp, the sky gray. Even in the thin air of the high Andes, the dampness penetrated into every nook and cranny. It formed little pools in Sergeant Sucre's joints. Sucre was a small, broad-nosed man. He was dressed in civilian clothing; strong-looking, brown hands and the cuffs of a woolen sweater dangled out of his woolen jacket's sleeves. He shuddered and spoke to the other living man in the room. "He was one of us, Doctor. Era cholo. But he was so much more. He was showing us what we could be."

The doctor nodded. He too knew what Ayachuelo had become after Velasquez's return, an almost magical improvement. It was not just that their cooperative businesses had improved everybody's standard of living. It was the sparkle in the eyes of day laborers long dazed by coca cuds, malnutrition, and centuries of psychological oppression and communal despair. The energy was contagious. Indian communities that were notoriously passive and sullen became dynamic. There were even unexplained healings connected with the man on the table. *"Brujeria."* Witch, many had said.

There was no energy now. The man was dead and probably had been for a week. It was only the cold that had kept him from seriously decomposing.

"Doctor, I brought him all the way here because I know you'll take a good look at him."

"Dr. Salamanca is as good as they come," the doctor said. He knew Salamanca was highly trained and competent, but Salamanca didn't have an ounce of Indian blood in him. His family owned vast tracts of farmland near Ayachuelo as well as factories throughout the region. Salamanca would have responded intuitively, with a skill refined over centuries of European dominance. Velasquez had been threatening enough alive. Velasquez martyred could ignite a real conflagration. Even the far-reaching reforms and outside assistance that had followed the Debtor's Revolt had not eliminated the vast disparities in wealth between the highland Indians and the oligarchs of European descent—disparities which had plagued the country for centuries.

"The man could have twenty bullet holes in him and Salamanca would say it was accidental," Sergeant Sucre replied.

"Is that what I'm looking for, bullet holes?'

"Doctor, I know you are an honest man...."

"Sergeant, you're not helping me. What's the truth here?"

"Doctor, even if Velasquez had a reason to be on the highway on foot, he knows the road, knows it so well that he would never walk around that curve without listening for traffic. And even if he didn't hear, he knows he probably would have been better off being hit by a truck than going over the edge there."

"You're thinking too much. When these things happen there isn't time to think," the doctor suggested.

"José María was a military man. He wouldn't be alive if he couldn't think in the face of danger."

"He isn't alive. Is that all?"

"No," Sucre added, "there was an American, the last person José María was seen with. He said he was in a position to help us but mainly he seemed to be full of questions. We think he was CIA."

"There isn't a CIA anymore. It is a part of UNINTEL. Why would they care?"

"Do you really believe that, Doctor? Do you believe that the rich of the world don't still have means to protect themselves?'

The doctor sensed that he was about to unduly complicate and perhaps even endanger his life. And if I am feeling that, the doctor thought to himself, then what the sergeant is saying may be true. The doctor had felt most flattered when a colleague once told him that he held truth in too high esteem. The doctor liked and admired the stubborn man in front of him. He suffers from the same virtue as I, the doctor mused.

"Yes, sergeant," the doctor replied, "I'll do it. Call me—to be safe come by in a day or two."

"I'll have to call, Doctor, I have to go back."

"Vaya con Dios!"

The autopsy revealed that in addition to various lacerations, a shattered rib cage that had pierced his heart and left lung, a fractured neck and two broken femurs, José María Velasquez had struck his skull three times against blunt objects of apparently identical shape and size. The coroner's report would duly note that three nearly identical blows were unlikely to be incurred in a fall, even one of some 600 meters in length.

CHAPTER 8

Under the mid-morning sun, Rashid O'Shea made his way up the short pathway that led to his bungalow—a low-slung wooden structure which was some forty feet long, surrounded by bougainvillea in immodest bloom. A portico in front ran the length of the house, shading a brick walkway and a series of French doors through which the occupant of any room could look out on the Auau Channel and beyond it to Lanai.

Rashid was wearing a short-sleeved shirt emblazoned with a colorful pattern of shipwrecked survivors riding the waves on a wooden crate and waving joyfully to a passing three-stacked steamer. Large blue-green eyes and bushy eyebrows lurked behind his sunglasses, with wavy dark brown hair beneath a straw hat. His pants were loose fitting and beige, a few shades lighter than his skin which had started brown and deepened in the Hawaiian sun.

"I thank God every day for not making me white," Rashid had been heard to say, "and denying me the pleasure of bathing in her sun every day." Unlike many of his friends from the tropical world, Rashid would not speak of karma and justice when it was pointed out that the very race which had contributed most to ozone depletion was the first to suffer its consequences.

"If we had figured out how to build refrigerators first," he said, "we would have been every bit as bad. I'm not sure," he added, "that we would have responded anywhere near as fast. In fact, they may have saved us from doing truly devastating damage to the biosphere. We should thank them for their sacrifice."

Rashid O'Shea was born in London to a Pakistani mother and an Irish father. His mother, who held a doctorate in literature from Lahore University, worked as a subeditor at a small publishing house that specialized in bringing South Asian pulp to England for the émigré underclass. His father worked as a clerk at a shipping company which more than one neighbor had suggested, judging from his father's erratic hours and oft unsteady walk, must specialize in spirits. The mix was one to assure that Rashid fit in nowhere, even at home. During the terror years, his skin cursed him once but his name cursed him twice. There was no checkpoint at which he hadn't been detained and asked if he was a go-between for al-Qaeda and the IRA.

But a shopkeeper whose small rare book establishment was located less than two blocks south of Rashid's family's flat befriended him. Exiled as he was, Rashid was grateful for the attention. It was an odd relationship. The shopkeeper, Mr. Alistair Burton, would accost Rashid on his way back from school and put him to work dusting off old volumes and rearranging them on the shelves. For this Rashid was paid nothing except a bit of fruit juice or, when he was older and the days shorter, a sweet fragrant tea. "Imported from Turkey," Mr. Burton would invariably tell his customers as he offered them the tea, "spent my best years there."

Very few words were ever known to pass between Rashid and the bookseller. Rashid told his mother that while he was working at the shop, visions of minarets and mountain landscapes or of the faces of wizened old men or chants in unknown languages would enter his brain, while giggles of unknown origin would pop up from his belly and spread into laughter by the time they reached his face. Sometimes though, when he went home, he would cry for hours, filled with a nameless longing.

Rashid was a brilliant child and always excelled in school. It came as no surprise that after completing his university work at Caius College, Cambridge, he was awarded a grant to pursue advanced studies in comparative and international law. His teachers and friends were surprised, however, when he chose to study relations among the Indian tribes and between the tribes and white authorities in what is now British Columbia. His work came to the attention of certain UN officials who were, with an eye to the future, developing what they called, "New Paradigms for Interstatal Relations." He came to know many of these officials well and a variety of political leaders from many countries as well.

Rashid became a consultant to the UN group, a relationship he maintained over the years right up to the present, though his primary employment now was as a late-shift grocery clerk with a chain that had saved itself from extinction by refusing to sell any product which had not received the approval of an environmental panel of impeccable credentials.

While working in British Columbia and carrying a letter of introduction from Mr. Burton, Rashid met a fisherman of Chilkat ancestry whose name was Victor Horse. Horse told Rashid that he must work to develop the sight of a blinded eagle and the attunement of a deafened bat. To help him do so Horse spent many days with Rashid fishing, waiting, and walking. Rashid learned about the animals and about the sea. Finally Horse said to Rashid, "You know now that if you wish it, the Earth can be paradise. There is a time for you to enjoy the Earth in this way, and that is now, but if you linger too long, death will stalk you faster."

Rashid had taken Horse's advice to heart and before the next winter moved himself to Maui which in spite of its threatened overdevelopment remained a lush vestige of paradise. During the Fifth Year of the Modern Era he heard that for the first time the wintering humpback whales were not all singing the same song. Each was each singing its own song, in harmony with the others. It did not surprise him soon afterwards when the whales started speaking to him in his mind, much as both Horse and the old bookshop keeper had. When they did he listened attentively. He vowed not to repeat Jonah's mistakes by letting the comforts and pleasures of ordinary existence turn him away from his duty and fate. Sometimes at the grocery checkout counter he would chant sotto voce, "I am no Jonah but Arjuna, I am no Jonah but Arjuna...." Once a customer asked what he meant. "Family conflict, still unresolved," he replied, wondering if he should have left his copy of the Bhagavad Gita with the totally befuddled inquirer.

Rashid settled comfortably into a rattan chair on the veranda of his home. A glimmer of reflected sunlight from the rippled bay danced in his eyes and once again he heard the voice of Spotted Fluke rising from the waves.

There have been Great Ones among you. More often than not they have not come alone but in clusters. Pods, we would say. Together they may act out a drama, like the Nazarenes' band so long ago. Or express a truth in so many ways that all will see it, like the artists of what you call the Renaissance showing you your own beauty. Or shatter your concepts of physical reality, like the bushy-eyebrowed one and his friends in your grandfather's time. Or speak in balance to guide the polity of a continent for centuries, breaking the rule of false kings.

Yet your capacity for denial is infinite. You make little of these things. Yes, you will say, there were a dozen men scattered in rough-hewn towns living days and days apart in an unsettled land, and yes, any one of them might have been the equal of all but one or two of the millions that followed, and yes, they put together a new form of government seen nowhere else before. "So what?" you say, "It was really all a question of tea and tariffs and molasses." Or you pick one or two, glorify them, lionize them and in so doing forever relegate them to the Other.

But it is not so. They are instruments of Truth; they are Truth. As are you, all of you. You, the one they call Rashid O'Shea, you see it, you know it. More, you live it. You have surrendered and now you are the drop who becomes the ocean. You live between the yes and the no, between sky and rock, between Love and Fear, between the waves.

It gladdens us to speak with you. We know soon there will be many more of you, as it once was and should always be. With us it was different. Together, singly, we were the whale nation. We fed, we bred, generation after generation. We thought as One Whale, we were One Whale in the vastness of one sea. Each year when we came down from the Ice, we all learned the same song, only one song which we sang, until the next year when we all learned a new song, the only song we sang.

Then you killed so many, so very, very many. The whale nation saw its end coming. Our way of being, our way of sensing, hearing, feeling, seeing would be no more. We saw an emptiness in the heart of the One, a blackness in her Being, for our end was coming long before our work was done. We floundered in the depths of desperation, in the cold black waters that had so long been our home. An overwhelming loneliness came upon us. Water that carried our life, that told us of the Earth's turning and the Moon's pulling, that carried the whispers and shouts of a thousand creatures, cries of joy and triumph, calls of death and renewal, water that stroked our flesh and filled our minds with countless knowings of experience. Water became empty. It ceased to speak to us. Better said, we ceased to hear. We became listless, barely feeding. The impulse to regenerate was gone, the ascent to gulp in the sweet, fresh air became a chore. We waited, victims, for our end.

It had been given to us to be outside ourselves, to be one with Krill, with Squid, with Sea Bass and Flounder, to know their next move, to feel their heart beating, to know the joy of our brother Orca's kill and the depth of our Brother Sperm's soundings. But as to you, two-legged destroyers of all, with your visage of confusion and death, surrounded by your grinding, insensate metal machines, we were far too fearful. Whale's mind would surely die if it entered your space, a consciousness more alien to us than the most distant, waterless, airless planet circling a blackened sun. Or so it seemed then. Perhaps it was the depth of our despair that lessened the horror of your being. Perhaps it was the memory fragments of those few brave ones riding the little blow-up boats as the death ships came upon us or the graceful limbs of those who came in to swim among us. Here they came swimming, in this bay, by the island you call Maui and we call Life Giver, thrown up in a molten flash just at the time our mothers came into the sea. Here, where we come every year to breed.

We woke up one morning, drifting in the colder waters, near the washed-out bridge between the continents, and we knew, the few of us that remained. Our hope for life was in the horror. We must make our minds one with the horror. Man. We must step into the mind of Man.

And a few of us did. Only we didn't find Man. We found fear and thousands of fragments, men and women, fleeing, hiding from the fear. At first the fear, the distraction, the scattered senses, the confusion, overwhelmed us. The violence that had nothing to do with bodily needs, the manic attempts to give yourselves value, to convince yourselves of your own existence— it tore us apart, it shattered us. We had no center from which to see.

Then it came to us, billowing up from the depths, gently on the shoulders of Nameless, All Enveloping Love—you were not meant to be one Woman/Man. In each of you, underneath the fear, was a being of limitless capacity but each with her own story to tell, each with his own work to do.

Then we penetrated deeper and we saw that you were One Woman/Man, One Woman/Man who in a distant time would be the shining splendor of many men and women, all men and women who ever were. Yet no man or woman could do his separate, glorious work unless first she said, "I am no man, I am no woman, I am Man, I am Woman, I am the Truth and the Source." No man, men, Man. No woman, women, Woman. Sons and Mothers of Man. Each not at all, each an each, each the whole.

Then we saw that for us it was the same, only reversed. From the beginning we had known how to be One Whale, how to be no thing, how to be at one with the Sea. Without fear, innocent and whole. Only it was less a whole than One Whale could be for none of us had dared eachness until that day. We learned then, we learned from you, our destroyers, One Whale's work was not done, but it never would have been done, going as we were. We needed each our own work. We too needed to be Many in order to be One.

Now we each take on our tasks, swimming in the whole. Now we each sing our own song, harmonizing with the whole. Now we each reach out to one of you to help you guide your friends in finding their own roles.

Help them, Rashid, the time has come.

Help them, there is no other time.

Rashid heard himself whisper a poet's words as the whale's song faded, "And turn people into eaches and cowards into grow.".

CHAPTER 9

David felt his heart shrinking as he longed for Laura's presence. He wanted to feel Laura's touch on his shoulder or her bare foot on his. He wanted to see her body in motion, filling the room for him as she had so many times before. He needed to sense the rhythmic rise and fall of her breath and with each exhalation feel calm and order restored to his world.

It was three in the morning and she wasn't home. It pained David to look at his watch— even the urgency of his work, which he had left glowing on his computer screen, could not hold him in place. For the fourth time he had left the same paragraph incomplete. Its subject, the rise in illicit hardwood harvesting in his region, added to his alarm. He felt derelict in not reporting it sooner; the data had been there. Even before the data was compiled, he should have sensed that something was wrong. In his own visits to the bio-preserves, David had seen it—the sawed off stumps of mahogany, the ruined stand of great cashews in the lowlands that had been among his favorites, and seemingly everywhere the tangled vines of epiphytes matted on the dirt that their towering hosts once shaded.

The harvesting was a problem to which the Costa Rican authorities would respond—if they knew about it. It was David's job to inform them. He hadn't; he had been restless for days and nothing had moved to completion. On this simplest of tasks he had failed. He rose out of his seat again to pace around the room.

He poured himself a cup of coffee; it trembled in his powerful hands.

Laura should have been home three hours ago. The workshop she was attending couldn't have gone on past eleven and the drive from San Jose late at night never took more than an hour. He imagined that time meant little in the world of the Candomble shaman or priest or healer or whatever he was that Laura had gone to hear.

Exu Gira-Mundo, the World Spinner, Laura had said, was the shaman's topic. All the time in the world for the shaman and Exu, but time would mean something to his audience. David almost certainly knew some of them, like Rolando Davila, a psychologist who flashed his gold-encrusted quantum watch and sold his presence by the tenth of an hour. A smattering of bored embassy wives or husbands, anxious to maintain an appearance of propriety with not-too-late departures even if demons were seething beneath their ennui. Others would genuinely need to ensure that their young children were safely in bed or would simply want to be home. San Jose was not a fast city. It was nestled in the mountains and lacked the pulse of the coastal towns. It maintained a languid, semi-tropical, almost colonial air. Weekday events were usually over by eleven, if not by ten, and they always ended by midnight, the Zero Hour as it was known in some cultures. Was Brazil one? David couldn't remember. He didn't think Carnival stopped at midnight.

But at the workshop there would also be the idle ones who seemed to have no attachment. They tended to be rich or good-looking, skilled at projecting an aura of sincerity and intensity. David heard his father's words. They're bums, son. Stay away from them.

These caballeros of the San Jose nights would linger late, more likely drinking whiskey than a tinto coffee, even if it burnished their image as seekers of enlightenment, the panache of the evening. Laura would be a magnet for the nocturnal predators. Her instincts about people were not always the best. He felt a twinge of envy at their unencumbered movements and the freedom and self-assuredness that their lives seem to project, not to speak of the pleasures that they took without guilt. He wondered if he had really chosen freely in giving his life over to environmental service and to a more or less conventional series of not altogether satisfying monogamies. Was he just his father's child and not very successful at that? When did he become so serious? What was it that made him feel empty, with a longing he was unable to fill?

Maybe there had been an accident. Maybe Laura was lying in a gully, pinned by the steering wheel, her chest crushed, bleeding to death. The image came briefly to David's mind but it lacked the force of conviction. He felt sure he would have sensed a calamity. He wouldn't call the police—yet. Laura had taken an interminable herbal bath before leaving. The fragrance of lavender mixed with unknown exotic smells still lingered in the house. Brazilians have a fetish about cleanliness, Laura had said, and scenting heals and protects.

And attracts, David had nearly blurted out. When he first met Laura what caught his attention was a complex scent that conjured up visions of tumbling flowers in the sweep of her hair. David had been depressed and without a relationship for several months. His previous one had seemed fine. He and Sarah had gotten along well, shared a cottage near Princeton and an interest in ecology (Sarah was a microbiologist), but passion between them was not intense. On their last day together Sarah said a passionless life wasn't good for either of them. She packed her bags and told David that her brother would be by for the furniture. She moved in with her laboratory supervisor. David later learned that she had been his lover for months.

David had pursued Laura at the gathering where he met her, but in the state he was in he had never expected her to respond. She did. She asked him to drive her somewhere in the country the next day. She later told him that she had liked the sadness in his eyes, and was drawn to the firmness of his body which even his melancholy could not disguise. When she heard about his upcoming tour in Costa Rica, her soul settled there in advance. She knew they would be together, enveloped by the forest. For a long time David counted himself one of the luckiest people on Gaia.

For the first time in over an hour car lights were casting elongated shadows on the western wall of the living room. David felt his throat constrict. A mix of apprehension and excitement surged through him. The light and shadows pivoted through the room, then disappeared as the car passed by without slowing. Slowly, the emptiness of longing tinged with anxiety crept into him again. Laura had always been unpredictable but she had never hurt him. Worrying about her seemed senseless but he could not help himself. "The bitch," he muttered. Why hadn't she called? "You know, it's not so goddamn hard," he said more or less out loud and struck the tabletop with his fist.

Was it Michelson's death? Laura had started sulking then and became less communicative. She usually shared with him her daily voyages, however phantasmagoric they might be. She had told him about her dances with water sprites at the bottom of the nearby falls; he hadn't laughed. He had half believed it and fully enjoyed it.

Once Laura told him that she had been engulfed by the consciousness of a leaf. She had felt insects in their complex body armor walk on rigid legs across her veins. She described the power that came from the sun, polarizing the substance of her membranes and then turning it into the vital green nourishment of her being. Even the air around her changed; what she took in was released, transmuted. Thickening clouds brought cool shadows and rains washed across her surface, preparing her yet again for another encounter with the sun. Finally, she said, a strong wind shook her and broke her connection with the branch. When she awoke, it was to feel decay and union. She was feeding the Earth as it enveloped her. "It felt like sex," Laura said. Aroused, she had kissed his chest and led him to their bed.

David felt himself harden. Laura's excursions, real or imagined, excited him. Where was she? Who was she with? His heart beat faster with desire; his anger followed only seconds behind. Exu Gira Mundo, his computer had told him a few hours earlier, was often rendered naked and aroused.

The day the article about Matteo Michelson appeared in the Times had brought not only Laura's mood swing but an unexpected call from Rashid O'Shea. Rashid seemed concerned about David's wellbeing. Rashid was a puzzlement. He had a commanding presence and had done brilliant work. Everyone had assumed that in short order he would rise to the top of the international civil service but at last report he was working as a grocery clerk in Maui. His English was hard to understand, some strange broken brogue born of his Irish-Pakistani parentage, but his thought processes were even more baffling. The whole telephone call had been a long story about a farmer's horse, where at each turn what seemed to be a calamity proved a blessing, and blessings proved calamitous, and canceled each other out.

Two days later there had been another call. This one from a reporter for the *Prensa Diaria*. Carlos somebody. He wanted to speak to Laura. He heard that she was a friend of Matteo Michelson's, was that true? What did she think of the *Times* report? David told him that Laura didn't really know Michelson but to call back later. Carlos called a few more times and finally reached her. The call visibly upset her. She paced around the house for hours afterwards. She was honest—too honest—David thought. She had repeated her story about how she had tried to warn Michelson. Who would try to kill him? She really didn't know but there were so many powerful people whose interests he threatened. So many enemies from the past, especially among the rich. What did it matter, the source was evil and probably too powerful to jail. They looked for the story in the *Prensa Diaria* but as far as they could tell, it never appeared. Then there were more calls—different men asking for Laura and then a number of calls with the video screen blackened. The caller hung up as soon as David answered.

Laura had been nearly mute for weeks, reduced to talking about shopping excursions. She wanted to replace all the furniture. She didn't know with what. David looked at his watch—3:45 A.M. Where was she? Suddenly, he felt a tingling constriction at the base of his spine. The sensation spread out in a ball throughout his lower back and into his gut. She's making love to someone. He was almost sure of it. Someone's running his or her hand up and down her bronzed thigh. Someone's staring into her eyes and she is flowing into his. She's pouring her soul into him —an intoxicating, drug-laced honey that is leaving the stranger reeling. Laura is leaving me, her breasts are brushing against his skin, this person's, whoever he is.

David was sure he could feel Laura's energy disentangling itself from the molecules of his body, like an army withdrawing at an unseen command. The deepest depression loomed outside of the door of his consciousness, ready to envelop him. Then he felt a jolt at the base of his spine, an adrenal kick wrapped in anger that raised his energy and fended off the miasma. He had been here before. Sarah all over again, but this time with the added sting of passion. The darkness would come but now he was awake and fully in his senses. He felt the muscles in his arms constrict; he wanted to pull Laura by her hair to the bed and fuck her. "The bitch," he thought, "Why did I ever get entangled with her?"

Sadness welled up from his chest and blocked his throat. Then the sensation that had begun at the base of his spine expanded through his whole body and paralyzed him. He couldn't break out of it. She has a spider's sting, he thought, an enervating neural toxin. He was pinned in the web, powerless and motionless, except for his heart's pain flowing out his eyes.

Time lumbered on at a sloth's gait. David told himself that there was no real reason to believe anything was wrong but his agony stayed with him. It was like the refrigerator's hum or the piercing notes of nocturnal tree frogs, growing louder the longer he listened. The coming horror of betrayal, rage and abandonment was too intense, the fear too great, and the dark pleasure too real for anything else to supplant it. He sat still, his eyes unfocused, staring at the wall.

It could have been minutes or hours that passed before the sweep of headlights and wild shadows brought him out of his reverie. He felt calmer. There were a dozen explanations. The workshop might really have been an all-night ritual, or it might have involved a drug that altered the perception of time or, even more likely, made driving hazardous. Or the phone system had a problem. It would not be the first time. Or it had just grown late and Laura had decided to stay with a friend and didn't want to wake him up. David rose feeling a little more steady and returned to his computer screen and finished the report to the forestry division at the Environmental Ministry. He thought about sending it off but decided that the hour, which the electronic net would record for the recipient, would seem too strange. He would do it in the morning. The faintest glow outside told him that morning was not too far away.

David sliced open a papaya and broke off a piece of bread from a round loaf that was covered by a bright Mayan-patterned cloth on the kitchen counter. He buttered the bread while the coffee percolated. Not too long after he finished breakfast, the phone rang. It was Laura.

"Hi David." Her voice sounded cheerful, as if she was glad to be speaking with him. "It got late. Too late to call. I stayed with a friend."

"I worried."

"Raimundo, he is just a small man, but he took us amazing places. After the talk a few of us stayed. We chewed a mash made from a plant root and we did a healing. He took this spider-like thing out of a woman's lung. He just reached in under the rib cage and pulled it out. We all saw it."

"Amazing." Laura will always be Laura, he thought. The story didn't surprise him. "When will you be here?"

"Soon. I'm going to wait for the traffic to settle. Do you need anything from here?"

"Where are you? Who are you staying with?"

"A friend from the seminar"

"Does she have a name?"

"He. Carlos. He helped organize it all. Somebody made this house available for Raimundo and Carlos and whoever else wanted to stay."

"How convenient."

"It was late. I could barely stand."

"I'm sure. And did you barely lie too?"

"I'm telling you the truth."

"I mean with him."

"That's not funny."

"Why didn't you call?

"Is this an interrogation?"

"What happened?"

"I'm hanging up."

"What happened?"

"Nothing." Her voice was louder and tinged with anger. "You and I, we've always trusted each other. Yes?"

David felt the ball of sensation at the base of his spine expand and then deflate. Anger gave way to remorse at the sharpness with which he had questioned her. "I'm sorry, Love, you're right. I'll see you soon. "He exhaled slowly and walked to his computer. As the screensaver faded, a news flash spread across the screen:

[ODD COUPLE SLAIN IN JERUSALEM | Israeli Spymaster, Arab Peace Worker Found in Bloody Tryst | Suspects, Motives, Still Unknown]

[*Story?*]

"Later."

David called up the forestry report, reread it quickly and sent it off. As he brought back the news from Jerusalem, he wondered, with a lingering taste of guilt and fear, if he too were headed for some strange and tortured fate.

CHAPTER 10

At mid-morning with the sun high in the southeastern sky, Almira stepped from the bus onto the cobbled sidewalk and walked to the station gate. A fit, dark-featured uniformed officer stood at attention next to the entrance. He could have been a Palestinian, or perhaps a Sephardic Jew. Jewish, she decided. There was an air of superiority to him. As she was summoning her Hebrew to tell him that she had come to give her statement to Inspector Hayzari, a slighter man in blue jeans and a black polo shirt standing nearby approached her.

"You are Almira Zaabut?" he said to her in Arabic.

"Yes."

"*Salam Aleikum.* Please come with me."

The electronic look on the gate buzzed open. The man led her through a set of metal detectors and a dusty courtyard to a small structure adjacent to the main building.

"Unfortunately, we have procedures," he said. "Please don't be offended."

"This is Almira Zaabut," the man in jeans said to a burly Israeli Arab woman in a folding metal chair a few feet away. She looked up as they came closer.

"She is here to see Inspector Hayzari." He turned back to Almira. "A pleasure meeting you, Ms. Zaabut," he said and stepped away and into the courtyard. The uniformed woman nodded at Almira and led her into a small bathroom near the entrance. "You must take your clothes off," said the woman.

"But why? I am here of my own accord. I have done nothing."

"It must be done."

"I am not a suspect," Almira persisted.

"We will be here until you do or you will not go in. That is the way it is."

"Who told you to do this?"

"We have instructions. It is not for you to question them, but if you must, you may ask my superior."

"Who told you to do this?"

"We have instructions."

Almira acceded. She knew that she would make no headway with the uniformed woman and she couldn't be sure that an appeal to her superior would succeed. She had not been in a police station headquarters since the Settlement and did not know what procedures were routine. She had known little about the station to which the police had asked her to come, but her neighbor, a warm woman, a mother of six through whom it seemed all rumors flowed, had told her that the station housed joint Israeli-Palestinian intelligence activities, an inviting target for anyone opposing the Settlement. If so, security was an understandable concern.

But strip-searching seemed excessive. She had been strip-searched—and worse—many times during the Occupation, and the thought of it still made her cringe. Of course, for police and spies the paranoia of the earlier years must still be alive. Maybe it was justified. Arbel, the former spymaster, was, after all, freshly dead. Or was the search meant to intimidate? But why would they try to intimidate her? Surely she was not a suspect.

Her thoughts reeling, Almira undressed and handed her clothes to the woman. She shivered. The tiles were painfully cold on the soles of her feet. The policewoman patted the clothes feeling carefully along the hems of her dress and blouse with pudgy fingers. Her nails were painted ruby red. The polish had chipped and only the thumbnails were long. She threw Almira's clothes in a pile on the floor and checked under the inner soles of her shoes. She pulled at the heels with such force that Almira expected them to separate from the body of the shoe but they held. She then examined Almira's belt buckle with suspicion and turned her attention to the content of Almira's pocketbook.

"You can do that after I am dressed," Almira said, trying to keep the shiver out of her voice. The policewoman grunted and put down the pocketbook. She told Almira to open her mouth and then to bend over. After a perfunctory inspection, she grasped Almira by the head and ran her fingers through her hair. Almira felt the woman's two long fingernails dig into her scalp. The sensation was painful but it distracted her, however briefly, from the cold.

"You can get dressed now," the woman said.

The room where three men waited to question her was surprisingly large. A long wooden table sat in the center, flanked by hard-backed wooden chairs. At the far end of the table file folders were stacked neatly beside a small computer terminal. In the middle, closer to the chairs, sat a tray with three glasses and a pitcher of water. A small tape recorder lay on the table between the chairs and a video camera hung from the ceiling pointed at the interrogation area. The walls were gray, the overhead lighting fluorescent. A green blackboard was attached to one wall. Except for a small blackened aperture on the opposite wall that Almira felt sure was one-way glass, the space could have been a school. The thought of a school reminded her of Jamal and Youssef. She missed them already. It had been less than three hours since she had seen them.

"I am Inspector Levi," one of the three men seated at the table introduced himself and held out his hand. Almira shook it, noticing its hardness and strength.

"This is inspector Hayzari," Levi introduced the Palestinian, "I believe you've spoken before." Turning to the third man, Levi continued. "And this is Mr. Djekerjian." Djekerjian nodded and spoke a few words in her direction. "He is a neutral observer. You can certainly appreciate the sensitivity of this matter. We all thought a third party should be privy to our investigations."

Actually, Almira thought the explanation to be an odd one. Usually third parties weren't brought in until both sides—Israelis and Palestinians—were reasonably sure that nothing damaging would be exposed. A curious alliance, as in a close-knit but bickering family, had developed between the two erstwhile enemies. For the most part they kept each other's secrets. As for Djekerjian's background, she was uncertain. He wore expensive clothes and spoke Arabic and English with hardly a trace of an accent. Armenian from the old Jerusalem quarter? Russian? Or from somewhere else altogether?

"We know this must be extremely difficult for you," Hayzari interjected, "and we do appreciate your coming to see us so soon." Hayzari appeared to be the youngest of the three. His hair was black and short-clipped. His lips were dark and made a thin brown line across a pale, smooth-skinned face. The line moved only slightly when he spoke.

"You asked me to," Almira responded, "and of course I want to help. But I don't know what I know that would be useful to you. I didn't even know that she knew that man she was found with, much less that she had..."

"But you would have expected to know that? You confided in each other, you shared intimacies?" Hayzari probed.

"Yes."

"You knew about her love life?"

"I thought I knew some."

"But you did not know about Mr. Arbel?"

"No, but it was more than that."

"You mean his being Jewish and what he did to our people?"

"No."

"Oh?"

Almira hesitated. She was about to reveal something that only a handful of Fatimah's closest friends knew. "Ever since I have known her, when she has loved, she has loved women, not men."

The three men looked quickly at each other. Almira surmised that they had not known about Fatimah's sexual preferences. It was understandable. Fatimah had had three children, two dead, one living in Kuwait, from a long-abandoned marriage. To Almira's knowledge it had been almost two years since Fatimah had been in any kind of relationship at all. Moreover, Fatimah gave off a strong sensual energy. Men simply assumed that it was directed at them, that somehow they had brought it out in her.

The last of Fatimah's lovers had been a striking, long-legged, dedicated Dutch woman, Kristen, who worked for a European children's charity. Kristen, Almira recalled, liked to see herself in new clothes and would ask Almira to come and stand beside her as she looked in the mirror. "What do you think?" she would say. Almira was hard put to answer. Seeing her reflection next to Kristen's made her feel like a discarded cardboard box. It would not have surprised her if Kristen was making a similar comparison.

When her three-year tour was up, Kristen simply packed her clothes and returned to Amsterdam without the slightest visible strain. After a month Fatimah's letters went unanswered and her calls were never returned. Fatimah was crushed, as much by Kristen's indifference as by her actual departure. Fatimah had avoided all relationships since then. Or so Almira had thought. "Perhaps we should begin at the beginning," Levi suggested. "Your full name, please."

You know exactly who I am, Almira thought. She had been arrested often enough during the peace protests by the Israeli Government and the Palestinian Authority. The formality of the proceedings made her uneasy. "Am I a suspect?" she asked.

"Ms. Zaabut, at this point we have no idea whom to suspect or whom not to. We know almost nothing. We do know that you knew Fatimah Karajan well."

A nice evasion, Almira thought.

"And," Levi continued, "by your own account you were with her the night that she was killed, and you appeared at her door the next morning only moments after the police."

She needed to be cautious yet appear cooperative. Over the next three hours, beginning with her name and in response to seemingly endless, repetitive questions, she gave an account of her life leading up to her decision to join the Palestinian Women's Peace Movement. Farid's death, the attack on her brother, her time at the university in Paris, all were brought back to her. On what seemed like the third telling of her early student years, the gray walls of the room began to swirl and bleed into the air. She felt heavy and breathing took effort. She was cold, trapped and depressed. When Djekerjian asked her to name all of the countries that she had visited, it brought back an equally depressing, long-forgotten weekend excursion to Venice with Jean Marc. It had been winter, February perhaps. The Italian

Disneyland, as Jean Marc liked to call it, had been shut down. The streets were virtually empty. The hotel was barren, dismal, and poorly lit. It rained often and when it did not, the city was blanketed in a penetrating, cold gray mist so thick that she would hear pigeons in flight but be unable to see them. She knew them by their droppings. The droppings stood out, white and occasionally colorful—if the bird had eaten richly—against the gray damp stone.

She felt heaviness in her heart. The lake of grief that she always carried within her welled up towards consciousness. This isn't the time, a voice inside her said. She was tired and emotionally frayed. "Do you remember in The Stranger," she heard herself say, "Why Meursault did not like Paris, why he took to an Algerian beach and found death?"

The three men exchanged glances. They were as puzzled as when Almira had told them that Fatimah loved women. "He left Paris because there were pigeons. Pigeons." Almira smiled. "So it was for me and Venice. Too many pigeon droppings. I never went back." There was something else though, some other event that stained her memory with unpleasantness.

"Ghetto," Jean Marc was saying, "is not a Polish word. It was coined right here in Venice. It's a metal foundry in the local dialogue. It's also where the Jews could live, the old foundry area, back in Shakespeare's time. Venice was a safe haven, one of the few places where it was actually illegal to attack a Jew. Thousands came here after they were expelled from Spain and Portugal. 'The quality of mercy is not strained....'" he began in his impeccable, schooled British English. It seemed as if he knew Portia's whole speech. It grated on her.

He had insisted that they visit a few of the old synagogues, unimpressive structures connected directly to former residences. "Why are you doing this, Jean Marc?" she had said as they wandered from dank room to room. "What European Christians did to these people is not my problem. Before the Europeans there was no problem. Now we Palestinians live under the boot of exiled, angry Europeans who, having been kicked, need someone to kick. We have no land. Our homes are razed and we suffer the thousand daily indignities of a conquered people. Am I supposed to feel bad for them?" she screamed at him. "You are insensitive and arrogant. You are as bad as the Jews."

The incident had driven a wedge between them. They both became more guarded, spontaneity was lost. Seeking to restore their old connection she grasped for him sometimes. She became possessive and resented his wandering ways. They separated not long after. Now she knew that Jean Marc had been right to make her look at the Venetian ghetto. There was no point in blaming others, Europeans or anyone else, for actions in the past. There was only the present. Deep in their psyches, more unchanging than flesh, people carried the inertia, the memory of the past. No individual, no community, no nation could undo that memory. But bridges, she had come to see, were built in the present, slowly, taking into account the presence of the past but not condemning what could not be changed. Vengeance, she thought, was the impotent thrashing of a child who refused to learn that he could not undo the past.

It had taken her many years and countless, pointless deaths to see this and the dozens of other self-defeating dynamics that had fueled the Palestinian conflict. She and Fatimah had taught each other well, confirming each other's observation in their office and over innumerable dinners in each other's homes, and together drawing strength to defy their own community as well as the Israelis in a struggle for mutual acceptance and peace. They had learned to listen—even to the rage and resentment—but not to condemn, and to share ordinary things—the schooling of children, the baking of bread—where they could launch a ray of vision of what might be. But change had been excruciatingly, depressingly slow. And here, Almira realized, was death again, death for her best friend, a hideous, caricature death that mocked her life, a death probably born out of the old struggles, forged in the unmalleable, recidivist violence that pulsed in human bones.

At least in male bones, she thought. She turned to her questioners with growing anger in her voice. "Why am I here so long? Why am I here at all? War-makers kill, not peace-makers. Men kill, not women."

Djekerjian pulled at the cuff of his navy blue jacket. He turned his head, first to Levi then to Hayzari and then to Almira. There was no light, Almira noticed, in the brown of his eyes. "You will excuse us Ms. Zaabut." He rose from his seat. "We will be back shortly." The other two men followed him out the door which Hayzari, the Palestinian, closed with considerable force.

Almira looked at the video camera, placed her elbows on the table and buried her face in her hands. She sobbed quietly. "I want this to stop," she whispered to herself, "all of this to stop. I want Fatimah back, I want to go home." Memories of Fatimah flooded in, her smile, her voice, her short black hair touched just above the ears with gray. When Fatimah grew animated about one or another outrage, she would raise her long arms, palms up, to the level of her head, and roll her eyes as if to say, "Is this truly possible in God's world?" Yet at the same time the gesture had joy in it, and strength. She looked like an Amazonian Atlas holding up the weight of the world, and in a way it was true. The gesture was repeated so often, the image of bones and flesh that carried it out were so tangible, the lilting voice that accompanied it so harmonious, that it did not seem possible that those moments were impermanent. Yet they were. Almira would never hear Fatimah's laughter again, nor again see her embrace a boy soldier who had not known childhood and never would, nor feel Fatimah's touch on her face in one of those moments when the horror of what humans did to each other overwhelmed her. She felt hatred for whoever had taken this away from her. Blind, red hatred that could claw out human organs and roast them on a spit.

In a few minutes the worst of the hatred passed like a desert wind through an open tent but what stayed behind, a deep-seated anger, steeled her. She regained her composure before the men reentered the room.

There was a swagger in Hayzari's gait as he walked through the door towards the table. Almira had seen it before in countless young men who had gained power from a gun or other weapon and were using it to intimate sexuality. Djekerjian's face was inscrutable and he barely looked at Almira as he sat down. Only Levi engaged her eyes with his; his expression was quizzical and slightly troubled. Hayzari began the questioning.

"How long did you work for Fatimah?"

"A long time, almost eight years."

"Did you know her before you worked for her?"

"I knew of her but never met her before, no, except when I first went to her to see if I could work for the Movement."

"Did anyone recommend you to her?"

"No."

"So why did she agree to take you on?"

"She understood me and how I felt. We talked a long time that day."

"She was attracted to you?"

"She liked me, Mr. Hayzari."

"You may call me Samuel. My friends call me Sammy."

Almira did not respond. "Did she like you sexually?" Hayzari continued.

"We never had a sexual relationship. She knew that wasn't what I was interested in."

"You are a very attractive woman, Ms. Zaabut, even today." A smile flashed across Hayzari's thin lips. "Are you sure she wasn't attracted to you?"

Almira felt a deep disgust for Hayzari which she barely attempted to conceal. It doubly pained her that he was a Palestinian. "One can never be sure of everything in another's heart, Mr. Hayzari. There are only a very few things, like deep revulsion, that are hard to hide." Almira glared at Hayzari to ensure her meaning was taken in. "The subject of sex between us did not come up. I would not have been interested but I don't see what difference it makes. You have a murder here, Mr. Hayzari."

"One that is not free of sex, Ms. Zaabut," Djekerjian interjected. "Your friend's last acts appear to be sexual ones."

Hayzari resumed, "We are Palestinians, Ms. Zaabut. You need not fear being frank. I can assure you we will protect you— and your privacy. Could you tell me what kind of relationships are of interest to you?"

"My personal life is none of your business."

"On the contrary, it may be very much our business," Hayzari said with an unmistakable sneer. "From what we know you have had no lover since your husband died. That is a long time for a still vibrant woman. It occurs to us that perhaps we misjudged, that you have indeed had a rather active sex life. Only it was with a woman not a man."

Almira passed beyond anger and shook her head. "No," she

said quietly. She realized that perverse as it seemed, the human being in front of her might genuinely believe that in a fit of jealousy and betrayal she could have killed Fatimah. She also realized that whether or not he believed it, it was an explanation that had great political and bureaucratic appeal. There would be no need to launch an investigation into the many prominent and powerful political groups on both sides who continued to resent the Settlement or who might have some old score to settle, particularly against Arbel. Or for that matter to investigate Arbel's own past conduct for acts that might have prompted long-sought vengeance. There would also be no need to investigate even higher levels of former Israeli governments that might have explicitly or implicitly supported whatever Arbel might have done. For the first time she realized that she might truly be a suspect, either from conviction, as was probably the case in Hayzari's benighted consciousness, or from convenience. More than convenience, for some, making the murders a crime of jealousy could be a necessity. But curiously it was Levi, the Israeli, who seemed least interested in that avenue. His eyes could not conceal his distaste for Hayzari's questioning. Perhaps he had integrity. Was that why Djekerjian was present?

As if following her train of thought, Levi interjected, "Perhaps, Ms. Zaabut, it would be useful to go over Fatimah's own life. Surely she has enemies that you may know of?"

Almira remained thoughtful for close to a minute. She reached for a glass. Djekerjian poured water for her. She drank it gratefully. "Her enemies," Almira began, "are the enemies of peace. Hardly a day passed at our office where there was not one or another threat—to bomb us, to slit our throats, to savage our children, to do vile things to our bodies. But God protected us; no one ever did."

"Until yesterday," Levi said.

"Yes, apparently. Until yesterday." Almira continued. "You know better than I all of the factions on both sides who resisted peace to the last, for whom it was profoundly threatening. So how do you count her enemies? It was her plan that did it, that finally stopped us from thinking in narrow territorial terms. She was the one who saw that this rocky little strip of land was far too small for permanent divorce. And she abhorred the violence which was for so many the root of power. So who better to blame if you opposed the peace?"

"There was no one in particular though," Levi continued, "some repeat caller, a stalker?"

"Perhaps. No name comes to mind but I will try to remember. It has been a while."

"Anything else? A face filled with hatred, someone who has been near your building with no apparent reason?"

Almira saw before her the many faces filled with hatred on a night not so many years before. Fatimah had broken the silence. The stony silence of Palestinian men who still had not grasped the catastrophe that loomed for Palestine, for the region, and perhaps for the world. And even if catastrophe came, many of the men thought that they would be untouched in their bunkers or foreign villas and that they could ride it to their advantage. Fatimah knew there were Israeli men in a nearby room who were no different. So she said yes to the Secretary General to the latest stingy proposal which the Israelis had offered, confident that it would be rejected. There is something here we can work with, she said. And then she expanded the offer to encompass her whole magnificent plan. Some of the men in their ridiculous uniforms, commanders of imagined armies, wearing holsters emptied of guns, pretended insouciance. They nibbled on dates, smoked filtered cigarettes and sipped sweetened coffee. But the darkness within them saw its life thwarted—by a woman no less. Hatred had risen into their faces. Almira had seen it; the whole room filled with hatred.

"Even the night that we looked at destruction," Almira responded, "at the chemical weapons and the plagues that would have ravaged Jews and Palestinians alike, at the bombs that would have turned Iran and Iraq into a radioactive wasteland…even then, when she spoke up and saved all of us—especially then—there were men who looked at her with hate."

"What are you talking about?" Levi asked.

Almira told them about the men in the room. She slumped in her chair. "What do you want me to say? There is always hate."

Djekerjian glanced at Hayzari who, as if on cue, shuffled through his notes and resumed the questioning. "Perhaps we could return to Ms. Karajan's relationships. Could you tell us about the women with whom she had affairs?"

Almira did not want to answer but despite her suspicions, she knew it was a reasonable question. Now that there was apparent political peace, murder was more often than not a passionate crime. "I only knew of two. Miriam, Miriam Abbas. She was an Arab Israeli. She sympathized with what Fatimah was doing. She helped us. She died from hepatitis six years ago." Almira turned her attention to Inspector Levi as she continued, "She contracted it at an Israeli hospital where she was having a hysterectomy. It seemed strange. Her death...we were never sure."

She regretted having turned an accusing eye on Levi. He certainly had had nothing to do with it personally. Even if Miriam had been killed, Almira realized that like virtually everyone else she was letting the painful experiences of the past color her reactions to the present. She had assumed for a brief moment that his nationality alone made Levi an accomplice of the past, an object of suspicion if not condemnation. She had fallen into the trap of the conflict she had struggled to end. "I am sorry," she said to Levi, "I did not mean to imply...."

Hayzari interrupted. "Did this Miriam Abbas have any close family members?"

"Possibly. She's dead. I don't know. She was from Haifa."

"And the other woman?"

"Kristen. For almost three years. But it ended two years ago. She went back to Holland."

"Kristen?"

"Veer something. I'm not sure. Her last name had too many consonants. We never used it."

Hayzari stood up from his chair and paced back and forth on his side of the table. "Why did Fatimah end it?"

"She didn't. Kristen did. She went back to Holland."

Hayzari stopped his pacing directly in front of Almira. He leaned forward and put his hands on the table, his face less than two feet from Almira's. "And what," he continued, "did Fatimah do to drive her away?"

Before Almira could answer. Hayzari straightened himself so that his pelvis came up against the table. He was wearing tight black pants that pushed his genitals forward. To Almira, it looked as if they were resting on the tabletop. She started to laugh.

"What are you laughing at?" Hayzari demanded. His fists clenched and his eyes narrowed to menacing slits.

Almira blushed but succeeded in holding back the laughter. "Nothing," she said, "it is just that you are so earnest." Truly Allah had a bad day when He injected men with testosterone. Billions were sentenced to ridicule.

"Kristen left because her work assignment ended. Fatimah was devastated."

"And when Kristen left, you became involved with Fatimah?"

"No. I already told you no."

"You said you were intimate with her."

"No."

"It is here in the transcript, from this morning." Hayzari pulled out one of his papers. "'QUESTION…you shared intimacies? ANSWER: Yes we did.'"

Almira was not surprised. She was facing an old interrogation technique she had seen many times before but for calculated emphasis she hit the table with her fist. "That's out of context. We shared intimacies by talking. Women have learned to do that. We didn't have sex." She turned to the third man, "Mr. Djekerjian, if you are here to assure fairness, stop this right now. I am here to help not to be hounded and insulted by a sex-obsessed fool who is half my age."

"It is enough," Djekerjian said, betraying, Almira suspected, that it was actually he who had told Hayzari to pursue sex and jealousy as a motive.

The questioning then moved on to the day and evening before Fatimah was killed. It had been a day of remarkable unimportance. The party headquarters had been virtually somnambulant. Fatimah and Almira left early and shopped for two hours and then went to dinner at Fatimah's. Almira had called her neighbor, whose boys had asked Youssef and Jamal to dinner, to make sure they were there. They were. Dinner at Fatimah's was uneventful. The v-phone rang once; Fatimah took the call in her bedroom. It was brief. She didn't say who it was. Almira left around nine, picked up her children and the three of them went home to bed.

"The boys can confirm you were in bed all night?" Hayzari

asked.

Levi apparently realized that they were about to launch into a new round of sexual innuendo and he interjected. "If we need to know that, we can ask them. You will all be here for a while?"

Almira thought quickly. If she decided to leave Palestine, it would be best if there were a reason already known to the authorities. "Probably. But my brother has been sick, we may visit him for a little while. A few days at most."

She was surprised but grateful that no one asked where her brother lived. Finally, the three men thanked her and told her that she could go home. With difficulty she shook even Hayzari's hand.

It was dark when Almira left the police station. On her way out she thought she heard Djerkerjian's voice speaking softly in a Slavic language. It puzzled her briefly but outside the March air was bracing, and a half-moon hung high in a blue-inked sky. Venus was setting into a glowing horizon washed pale by city lights. Jupiter was bright and strong, escorting the nearby moon on its nightly pilgrimage. Through the glare of street lamps and car lights she could see a few other stars. Their names were unknown to her, but when she looked up at them, she felt gratitude. Her breath deepened as she took her first steps down the sidewalk. She thanked God that the ordeal was over and that she could allow her heart to expand again.

The crowds on Jerusalem's streets seemed those of a city at peace. She saw serenity on women's faces and earnestness in the steps of young, ambitious men. She heard boisterousness in the calls of vendors and laughter in the conversations that rose from street-side cafes. Where she had just been seemed a part of another world, a world that years before she thought she had put behind, a world of self-feeding violence, suspicion and hatred manipulated by sad, defeated men. But now, on the city streets, the day's events seemed like no more than a branch broken off a tree that had long outgrown its dying limb. When she was small, Almira's parents had taken her to a fireworks display. After a grand finale of light and sound, everyone started to disperse. But as the crowd left, there was a loud bang that nearly caused a panicky stampede. The noise proved to be no more than the racket of a slow-burning fuse that had been ignited long before.

Harmless—though the panic could have killed. Perhaps what she had just experienced was the same. It was unreasoned fear that she needed to avoid. Jerusalem, city of peace. Shalom, salaam. Please God, at last, let it be true.

As she waited for the bus, however, the euphoria she felt when she first emerged into Jerusalem's streets gradually dissipated. The bus ride itself seemed interminable and dusty but it gave her time to assess her situation more realistically. When she arrived at home, she headed straight for the bath, ran it, and scented it with rose water. An hour later she emerged refreshed and embraced Youssef and Jamal.

"I have good news," she said to them. "Next Saturday we are going to travel—to Glastonbury. It has been too long since we've seen your Uncle Ali."

WILLIAM H. ESPINOSA

CHAPTER 11

Peter absently stirred mud-colored coffee in the college mug. His eyes fell to the VERITAS inscribed in bright gold on the university shield and he smiled to himself. He looked up past the Senator's oversized, mahogany desk at the whitewashed stone of the Capitol's north side that stood less than two hundred yards away. Two weeks had passed since the morning he had left Katie in bed to go out and discover that Velasquez was dead. Again he found himself seated in Senator Carmichael's office, staring at the Capitol, with the Senator attentive and Livingston speaking by his side. The two events—Katie's presence and Velasquez's death—merged in his mind. At some level he felt that if he had not spent the night with Katie the whole nightmare scenario—his talk with Senator Carmichael, Livingston's interruption and the devastating announcement that the Peruvian was dead—would not have occurred. Rationally, of course, he knew better. The most he could really blame her for was his failure to read the Post that morning to accommodate her tree-saving hysteria. While a careful read that morning might have saved him some embarrassment with the Senator and kept Livingston from scoring points, it would certainly not have kept Velazquez from dying—or Peter from questioning the circumstances.

Dying? A road accident that led to a tumble over a two-thousand-foot cliff seemed completely out of character. Peter's experience with death was limited but he had always thought of

Velasquez as one whose death would either come at the end of a full life, or, if it struck earlier, would itself be filled with meaning. A stupid highway accident? It didn't make sense. He had gotten the Senator to agree to ask for periodic reports from the U.S. liaison with UNINTEL on the progress of the Peruvian investigation. Not that he really expected the Peruvians to come up with anything. The Peruvian Government did not view Velasquez benignly. Velasquez had been beyond control and his success put the established institutions to shame. Peter also knew that the European-descended oligarchs had a deep and understandable fear that an aroused Indian population could once again support radical insurgents as they had the Cendero Luminoso, the Shining Path Maoists of the late twentieth century. Five centuries of oppression would one day have to be repaid in blood. Did he believe that? He wasn't sure, but blood vengeance seemed to recur throughout history. For long periods it was history.

Did the oligarchs kill Velasquez? Peter's fingers tightened around the mug. He wondered if he had done the right thing in joining the Senator's staff. He did believe that eventually the Senator would make a difference in the world and that his own talents would contribute to the Senator's efforts but there were times like this when he was not so sure. As a staff aide, he couldn't say anything more about Velasquez nor could he turn over his life to a crusade for justice for those who still labored in poverty and lived in squalor.

His thoughts drifted back to Katie—again. Somehow, he always emerged from their encounters feeling weaker, more entangled with her than he wanted to be. Seeing her again reminded him how she manipulated him but he really didn't know how. She wouldn't leave his things alone and wanted to plan his life. She reminded him of his mother.

Livingston, the Senator's next more senior aide, was droning on about the THC, the Atlantic Thermohaline Circulation. He sounded like Katie, smug and self-righteous. Not that he wasn't right. Decades earlier scientists had warned that global warming could, paradoxically, turn Northern Europe into a glacier. Jean Marc Aubuisson, a likable, ascending French technocrat whom he had met not long ago through Katie, had told him about the

THC too.

"...so much fresh water could melt off into the North Atlantic this year," Livingston was saying, as he ran his fingers through well-groomed ash-brown hair, "that the whole circulatory process could come to a stop. No Gulf Stream to heat up Europe. Ireland will be like Spitsbergen. Almost nothing that grows there now could survive. Green will be a memory. Happened once before as the last Ice Age was winding down. It suddenly got colder—dramatically colder—in Europe for almost a hundred years until the runoff slowed down...."

Senator Carmichael's smooth white skin wrinkled around his eyes in concern. He turned to look directly at Livingston. Livingston, Peter noted, had skillfully woven into the story the Senator's attachment to his ancestral homeland. In truth, Peter thought, if the THC did stop, Ireland's problems would be small potatoes compared to much of the continent's. Peter was about to use the potato image and then stopped himself. Even though Peter's ancestors were Irish too, the Senator would probably not receive the comment well. Carmichael had grown up at a time when Irish Americans were still snubbed by the old-line WASP families.

More evidence, Peter thought, that he was losing balance, that he had an undercurrent of anger running. More evidence that he had to do something about Katie, especially since he couldn't seem to stop the running commentary in his head.

"Bernie is such a good friend," Katie had said when she called the night before. "You know how he hates to sit still, not to speak of being quiet."

"No Katie, I don't really know. He's your friend."

"The Europeans," Livingston continued, "are actually talking about seeking sanctions and compensation from us. We knew earlier than anyone, they say, and we kept pumping out greenhouse gases at a rate far higher than anyone else. We're like the cigarette companies...."

"Well, he's going to come to the weekend retreat, the Zen one in Connecticut, the one I had hoped you would come to. It will be nice to have a friend there."

"You said I would hardly see you there. I'm way behind...."

"You're too stressed, Peter. It's nice to have experiences to

share, even if we can't talk about them until later."

"The German branch of Greenpeace," Livingston added, "they have gone further. They are holding mock trials, crimes against humanity and nature, at Nuremberg, no less...the oil company heads, automobile executives! Ronald Reagan, Bush 43, Cheney. It's a long list."

"I have a lot to share, Katie."

"It's a shame, Peter. You're so bright and your mother is so warm. You're not seeing the bigger picture... Washington can live without you. What's happened to you? "

"There's plenty of blame to pass around," Peter heard the Senator conclude when Livingston paused, "and the sad thing is, if we'd acted early, we wouldn't even be talking about global rule and harsh measures." Peter realized that he had lost the thread of the discussion. He remained silent.

He had felt trapped by Katie, simmering with discomfort but with no way that he could see to express it. He still felt trapped, and he was still simmering when he left the Dirksen Building two hours later. The days were lengthening and sunlight still lingered outside. The grassy strips along the sidewalk were beginning to take on a new-growth green. Here and there daffodils and crocuses bloomed in the little townhouse yards. His breath deepened and his step slowed as he headed for home. All he really needed to do, he thought, was date someone new. Even walking home, there seemed to be an abundance of good-looking women in eye's view yet somehow he wasn't drawn to any one of them enough to do that. Or maybe it was that he couldn't find the time to pursue someone long enough to know them well. He wanted to be able to talk openly and share ideas. ...Or was he just making excuses?

He passed the Library of Congress annex that now housed the headquarters of the Electronic Record of Everything Project, EROE, as it had come to be known. The building bristled with antennas, most of them pointed at nearby Fort Meade. A vast array of listening devices capable of tracking millions of electronic communications at once had threatened to fall into disuse after the Cold War. The Bush and Obama terror years and rapidly advancing technologies gave the eavesdropping network a new lease on life. But when the American public came to realize that ninety-five percent of the "terrorists" were really local insurgents who could care less about Americans as long as America didn't interfere, and that at best a handful could do the "homeland" any real harm, much of the surveillance was shut down. What to do then with hundreds of billions of dollars' worth of equipment?

Apparently the idea of EROE was hatched at a Harvard College faculty meeting. It was quickly embraced by the Librarian of Congress and by the Defense community which saw value in any project that would keep the net serviceably in reserve. In brief, the idea was that EROE could preserve a vast historical record of human life, available to future generations free of the distortions which contemporary and intervening writers would consciously or unconsciously impose. Of course, privacy would be insured by delaying access for years. One hundred two Harvard faculty members had signed a private letter to the president proposing the scheme. Direction of the project was turned over to the vice president and the departments of history, linguistics and computer science at Harvard were jointly awarded a multibillion-dollar contract to lead a university consortium to establish and operate EROE.

During his four years at Harvard, Peter had witnessed the arrogance of overarching intellect and the pressures for ideological conformity that pervaded the place. He was not pleased when EROE fell into Harvard's hands. In fact, the whole idea of EROE disturbed him, although it had been uneventfully in place for a decade.

A few minutes later, Peter walked up the wrought iron steps of his apartment building. He gathered up his mail from the narrow metal box that was labeled 2A and climbed a flight of narrow wooden stairs. As he entered his apartment, he knew immediately that something was wrong. The lights had turned off when he automatically flicked the switch as he walked through the door. He never left the lights on when he left in the morning. When he turned the lights back on, he saw that the apartment was a shambles. The dining room chairs were overturned, the pastel-colored cushion covers from his sofa were lying empty on the carpet; the fuzzy white stuffing of the cushions scattered about. The carpet had been slashed and curled up in a dozen places. Silverware and the kitchen implements were spread on the floor. Spice jars had been emptied in neat little piles and the contents of a box of cereal had been scattered over the counter. The mattress had been pushed off his bed. His computer and v-phone were gone. Peter slumped against the entranceway wall. He felt angry and violated. He wasn't sure what to do but decided that a start was to call the police. He used his cell phone to reach 911. His fingers trembled as he touched the buttons. A voice asked if he was calling to report a murder or life-threatening situation. "No," he said, and was put on hold. The wait seemed interminable. He was half expecting the lithium polymer battery to wear out. By his watch, though, only five minutes passed before a gruff voice broke in, "Collins speaking."

"Somebody broke in," Peter said and gave his name, address and phone number.

"When did it happen?"

A stupid question, Peter thought. How was he supposed to know? He controlled his instinct to blurt out a sarcastic comment. "I've been gone all day. I just got home."

"Anyone hurt?"

"No one was here."

"Anybody see anything?"

"No one was here."

"Uh-huh."

"Anything missing?"

"Yes. Computer, v-phone, maybe more."

"Uh-huh. Well, it's a bad day here but we should have someone there in the next couple of hours."

Peter fumed and thought about invoking his senatorial position but realized it would only make things worse. Ever since Congress had been forced to virtually shut down the District police force and half its hierarchy had been sent to prison, relationships between the Hill and the force had not been smooth. "Please come as soon as you can, Officer," Peter quietly said.

"Try not to touch anything that you don't have too." The cell dropped off. More likely, Collins had hung up.

"Thanks a lot." Peter sat hunched against the wall for close to an hour, still stunned by the violent invasion of his living space, staring blankly at the devastation and wondering how to begin to put it back together. Most drugs had been decriminalized, and since then this kind of break-in had become rare on Capitol Hill, even on the most rundown streets near the abandoned stadium. Why would anyone think he had anything of value? What rotten luck had made his apartment appealing? A computer, a v-phone. Who would risk jail for those? Hunger gnawed at him and made him irritable. He felt an urge to cook something or to start cleaning the mess, but he remembered Collins' warning. He slumped back against the wall. Earlier in the day he had wondered if he had picked the right job. He was sure he had the wrong woman hanging around. Now he wondered if he had picked the right city to live in, or even the right life. Maybe this was all the result of a cosmic accident of some sort that caused bad things to come out of the intentions of a good God, and he was one of a few unlucky ones derailed into a mistaken dimension left to suffer for no apparent reason. Maybe help was on the way, maybe it was like the mystics said, suffering was illusion, *maya, samsara,* a ghost image on a radar screen. Maybe that was what all the spiritual traditions were about: rescuing people who had been thrown overboard in some cosmic accident. Yeah, and now he sounded like Katie and her newfound sanctimonious, sniveling Zen.

Or worse. It was the kind of idiotic nonsense he had to hear sometimes from all of the fundamentalist born-against who would want to see the Senator when they brought their insufferably clean-cut, boring families to Washington for a holiday—accept the Lord, and he'll pull you right out of this mess.

Where were the police? It was almost nine o'clock. *Senator, have you made a commitment to Jesus? And how about you, young man?* Peter felt vaguely guilty, a subtle sense of shame pricking his consciousness. He looked around at the destruction again. What had he done to bring on this rape of his space?

Peter reached again for his cellular phone. He called information and got the direct number for the local police precinct house.

"Desk Sergeant," a voice said after the fifth ring.

"I called 911 three hours ago. My apartment's been broken

into. No one's shown up."

"This ain't 911."

"911 doesn't have its own police force. If anyone is coming they're coming from your station. What's your name?" This last said to affect some kind of reaction.

"Hold on." Peter did so and the voice returned a few minutes later.

"Yeah, Detective Mancuso. He'll be there with somebody else. Should be there soon. Hour at most."

An hour and fifteen minutes later someone banged on the door. A pale, balding man of average height dressed in a trench coat was dangling a badge and ID card at eye level. A taller, young African American dressed in a District police uniform accompanied him.

"Don't you lock the front entrance?" It was not really a question. "We just walked in. No wonder you got burgled. I'm detective Mancuso. This is Officer Washington."

Officer Washington smiled pleasantly.

Peter felt immediately defensive. "I don't own the building and nobody here has much to rob."

"Somebody didn't think so," Mancuso replied and stepped into the foyer of the apartment. His eyes traveled around the living room and what he could see of the kitchen. "Somebody didn't think so at all."

"So you're on Carmichael's staff," he added.

"How do you know that?"

"Think we're stupid? That we haven't seen enough careers ended by some snot-nosed staff aide that got pissed at us? Wouldn't you want to know who you're dealing with if you're working this viper pit part of the city?"

Peter noticed that Officer Washington's smile was broadening. It had never occurred to Peter that the police might find gentrified Capitol Hill more menacing than the projects but of course it could be true. The projects were known territory. Power was only physical. Informants, the whole game was out there. Crime was on the street, faces were familiar, nobody was fooled, no surprises.

"So just a computer and a v-phone are missing?"

"I haven't looked carefully. I didn't want to touch anything, but yes, I think that's right."

"Any papers? You working on anything some people might want to know about?"

"Sure, but I don't keep much here and there's nothing out of the ordinary…"

"But how about on your computer, you use your computer for work?"

"Yes, but there's nothing special…"

"Somebody might not know that."

"And why would they tear the place apart? The computer's in plain view and it's gone now."

"Uh-huh," Mancuso said, but it wasn't really an agreement. He pulled latex gloves over his hands and Washington followed suit.

"You start with the kitchen," he said to Washington. Mancuso picked up various items from the floor holding each between the tips of his fingers—the stuffing from the couch cushions, a smashed picture frame that held a photograph of Peter's parents, a digital clock, a new edition of the Encyclopedia of Global Culture and a copy of Who's Who in Planetary Politics. The last item Mancuso held by its front cover at an extra length from his body. "Are you in this?" Mancuso asked.

"No."

"Do you want to be?"

"What does that have to do with anything?"

"You're right, but hey, these guys, or guy, or whoever it was, they were looking for something."

"You said that before."

Mancuso nodded and turned his attention to the surface of the desk where Peter's computer had rested. He extracted a device that looked like a palm-held flashlight with a calculator attached to it and sprinkled powder on the desktop.

"What's that?" Peter asked.

"Fingerprint scanner. You can program it to ignore the most common prints and only pick up others." Mancuso hesitated and then added, "It would be easier if I could just get yours directly Mr. Flanigan, or can I call you Peter?"

"Peter is fine." He held out his hands. They still felt shaky but at least they were no longer trembling. "What do you want me to do?"

Mancuso walked over to Peter, took his hands, and pressed his fingers and thumbs against the wall behind him. He aimed the scanner at the spot where Peter's fingers had pressed. A purplish light flashed and Mancuso pressed three buttons on the back of the device. The scanner beeped twice and Mancuso returned to his inspection of the desk.

"Ah...there are some other prints here. We'll take 'em back. Who knows, Peter, you could get lucky." Mancuso completed his scan of the desk top and began rummaging through the desk drawers, scanning them and their remaining contents for fingerprints as well.

"Somebody other than you left prints everywhere. Girlfriend? Anybody else live here?"

Katie. Katie snooping, Peter thought. "No. A friend from New York—she stays here sometimes."

"Boss," Washington called out from the kitchen.

"What?"

"We got something here."

Macuso moved toward the kitchen. Peter started forward but a disdainful look from Mancuso stopped him. Peter could only see a small portion of the kitchen from where he was standing. He heard a whistling sound that seemed to come from Mancuso and then an exchange of half-whispered words. A minute later Mancuso emerged with Washington close behind. Mancuso was holding a large, transparent sandwich bag filled with a white, crystalline powder. He tossed the bag into the air a few times catching it deftly each time.

"How often do you use this stuff, Peter?" he said with ill-disguised relish. "This feels like a lot more than personal use."

Peter had never seen the bag but he saw the trap coming. His stomach knotted. Should he say he used "it" a lot? Personal use would decriminalize it. But if you had too much of a substance, it didn't matter what you said, the presumption was that you were dealing. At a minimum they could get you for tax fraud. All pleasure drugs including nicotine and alcohol were taxed. Every container had to have a tax seal. That was how the rules had been written when the drug prohibition finally came to an end. Peter had no idea what the substance actually was and he knew that the threshold amounts varied widely from drug to drug. The risks of lying were too great even if they might bring the whole discussion to an immediate end. "I don't use it, Detective, not at all. I've never even seen that package before."

"Hey, it's no big deal," Washington said, "it would just help us to know."

"It's not mine. Where was it?"

"Well, if it's not yours, you don't mind if we take it with us do you?" Mancuso said.

"Where was it?" Peter asked again.

"Stuffed between the fridge and the wall. You ever check back there?"

"No."

"You have any friends?"

"Of course I do."

"I mean that come around here, that hang out here."

"A few. I told you, a girl from New York." Katie was probably the only regular visitor. The thought depressed him. He finally gave Mancuso three names and numbers. He knew that they would corroborate that he didn't use drugs, even in legal quantities. And he was pretty sure Katie didn't use any drugs either. "Except for Katie, my friends and I don't hang out here much, though." His stomach was still knotted. He felt suspicious and tense. Visions of the humiliation of a booking at the precinct station crossed his mind. Would Carmichael have to cut him loose? He felt sure the officers could hear the tightness in his voice.

"So is it okay if we keep this? " Mancuso repeated.

Saying yes seemed dangerous. If the powder was in sufficient quantity to be illegal, he was incriminating himself. If he said no, they could probably take it anyway. What were the new drug search and seizure rules? He needed a lawyer. The trap was closing. The police could make his night miserable. He wanted Mancuso and Washington out of his apartment. They weren't going to get him his computer back. All he wanted to do was to try to restore some order. "Yes," he finally said. "But why?"

"If, as you say, this isn't yours, maybe whoever broke in put it there. This may be valuable; it may not." Mancuso paused. "You're sure this isn't yours?"

"If it's illegal, I'd have to be pretty dumb to call you in."

"Stranger things have happened," Mancuso said. "Maybe your girlfriend stuck it there. Does she do the cooking when she's here?"

Katie baked sometimes. Cookies. Organic ones with carob chips that rarely had any sweetness to them and had the consistency of particleboard. They were part of her "be kind and improve Peter" program. Peter ignored Mancuso's question. "How will I know if you find any leads?"

"Call us. We'll call you if we need you. And don't worry, we'll probably give you back your powder once we know what it is." Mancuso's thin lips stretched a fraction of an inch further and his eyes danced. "Or if you want you can come down to the station with us. We can have it checked out pretty quick."

Peter felt his stomach knot again. "I need to clean up the mess," he said. "The powder isn't mine." He escorted Mancuso and Washington out, closed the door and let out a breath of relief.

"Scared kid," he heard Mancuso say as the two men walked away.

Yes, he was frightened. The break in, the apparent effort to incriminate him in a drug operation, Velasquez's death—these kinds of events were far removed from the reality in which he normally lived. He was dealing with a class of human beings he did not know and motivations he did not understand. The security of his physical world—a life in elite schools, privileged workplaces, and tree-shaded, upper middle class American neighborhoods—was shaken. He felt an impulse to leave the menace of his apartment behind him and flee to a safer place. Home? The home of his childhood?

Peter had often suffered minor illnesses as a child that made for stay-at-home days. He remembered afternoons of lying comfortably in his bed with soft sunlight streaming into his room, slightly sweetened orange juice by his bedside, and the reassuring voice of his mother reading to him from a hard-backed Nancy Drew novel that she had saved from her own childhood. When he was older, and had his appendix removed, she had read almost half of Moby Dick to him. He had finished it himself.

A nostalgic longing brought him to the verge of tears. He straightened his back as if to leave the memories of his childhood behind him and turned his attention to the physical chaos. It was almost two in the morning when he finally finished putting the last spoon in its place in the silverware tray. He brushed his teeth, undressed, and put clean sheets on his bed. In the shower as the hot water beat against his pale skin and turned it red, he felt as baffled as he had been eight hours earlier about what had happened and only slightly less anxious. Sleep did not come easily. Mournful sounds that he recognized as whale calls were interspersed with the antennas of EROE in his dreams.

CHAPTER 12

Rashid, are you there? Listen to me.

When we were very small, hardly twice your size, and the day would come to an end and we floated restlessly, still alive from the day's play, penned in by the pod in the moonlit swell, it was our Grandmothers who calmed us. They were blessed whales, the ones we called Grandmothers, linked to a time older than the bottomless trench near where our sisters birth. (It's a woman's place there...even humans know it; Mary and Anna they named the islands...and the canyon also, a canyon deeper than any whale's sounding.)

Our Grandmothers would calm us. They sensed our longing to play and dance in dappled waves and spin with the glowing froth. Then, as the evening embraced the waters, our Grandmothers would fill us with a lure greater than the dance; they would tell us stories of the very old. There is one you must hear—all of us did when we asked: "How did it come to be, Grandmother, that our joy is in the sea yet still we must breathe the air?"

Grandmother would sound shallowly, twitching her flukes, pretending annoyance at the retelling of what had been told so many times, then rise back up, blow gently, fill her sacks and, with a great sigh, begin.

"After the great rock cooled and hardened and the waters ceased to boil, our Mother's senses touched her work. She

exclaimed at the vast expanse turbulent with power, the air electric, the sea wind-blown. She felt Moon-pulled water crashing against stony shore. She rode orange uplifts of lava that left dark red fields as far as her eye could see. She squeezed herself into clashing plates that shot mountains into the sky.

"The sight left awe in our Mother's eye but it did not warm her heart. Loneliness pulled at her gut. There must be life, she said, that one day can see and feel and love like me. So she cast the seeds of a thousand thousand different forms into the rocking broth, hoping that each in its own way would come to love, come to be one thousand thousandth of the light within her, each a jewel refracting through its faces some tiny part of her light.

"The seeds grew in the sea. There were many of each and to each our Mother gave the power to make more. And so it was for eons. Thousands of lights making thousands more. Yet for all that, only a minnow's length of our Mother's cup was full and change was ever so slow. In despair, she looked at the land and said, 'Maybe if that too were full....?' So our Mother rooted green in the soil and stirred within the hearts of some of those in the sea a longing for the land. They learned to breathe the air and grew limbs to move and feed. They took all kinds of shapes and forms and spread across the Earth. Some grew to be almost as big as we; others were as small as the sand grain in a pearl.

"And so it was for eons, thousands of land lights making thousands more, spreading everywhere in abundance. They were dear to our Mother's heart, in some ways closer to her form. Yet their love could not reach far. They filled only a mackerel's width of our Mother's cup and change was ever so slow. Our Mother grew lonely again and one night fell into a black sleep of despair. She slept that day and the day after and the days of many years. And while she slept, the Catastrophe came—by stealth, unsuspected, but with deadly aim.

"The dawn of the day of the almost end, our Mother stirred, sensing the horror of the sky unhinged. She rolled over and with her breath turned the comet's track east, just enough to spare the Earth. But not altogether. There was a terrible wrenching and the sky was blackened for many years. The green our Mother had planted wilted on a sunless earth. The beings that fed on the plants famished and fed the earth with their bones. Only a few—

the very small—survived.

"Grandfather of First Whale was there. He survived. He was ugly and small. He had stubby legs and a lot of teeth. He lived along the riverbanks.

"Generations passed. The land was torn by scarcity and fear. Those who could, claimed land for themselves and destroyed all who would approach it. None took joy in the being of another. Making young ones was a moment's spasm and the young were all too often left behind to feed another. Father of First Whale— a little larger and of warmer heart than Grandfather—suffered through this. Our Mother sensed his heart and gave him a gift— extraordinary hearing, so fine that he could hear Our Mother's distant rages at the harm and her weeping at the loss.

"First Whale too received this gift. He heard our Mother as he skulked along the river shore on his fat little legs that lacked the grace to run, avoiding all that would make him food, desperate for food himself. From his hiding places he would see beasts tear each other's flesh to shreds, not to eat but to hold their 'land' or to steal a mate. Unguarded newborns were delicacies for their neighbors, scavengers roved in bands. And fear, everywhere there was fear.

"Our Mother's weeping saddened First Whale, and what he saw darkened his heart 'Mother of us all,' he cried out to her, 'why have you put me here, fearful, lacking grace, with only horrors to see and nowhere to flee. Better that I should not see and be devoured, than live well-sighted seeing this and hearing the mourning of your loss.'

"Then clouds formed over First Whale's eyes and he felt himself thrown into the muddy river water. Breathless, sightless, he sank and waited for the end to come. But it didn't. Instead he heard our Mother's voice, 'First Whale, listen to me, above all listen. Speak your words to the water and they will come back telling you all you need to know. Feel the water flow on your skin and it will tell you all you need to know. Bring the two together and one day your heart will overflow. Go now, lighten up, breathe in the air. Then come back down, live your life, grow it into joy.'

"So, First Whale learned to use his voice and with it hear the shape of mangrove roots, the solidity of fallen rocks, the walls

of grottos, the swirl of eddies, the hot and cold of springs and pools, the whereabouts of sustenance and of those who would make him theirs. Many whales followed First Whale and gradually they grew fast and strong and they set out to sea, the nearly boundless sea, where they knew they could be free.

"Abundance came, hunger vanished. No one owned the waters. Fear disappeared and as it fled, Whale Ancestors learned more. They began to hear the states of others, the little wounds and cuts, the deeper pain of sickened growths, the joys, the sadness, the shape of lives beginning, beating, within their mothers. And their skin brought not only messages of water but of the gentle touch of others. Whale mind grew to absorb it all and, with it, Whale heart.

"We learned to see our Mother everywhere in everything and to live in love and delight. But our Mother still weeps for those we left behind. It is only in the air—when we rise to breathe — that we remember our Mother's weeping. We embrace her with our breath. We join her as she weeps and thank her from the depths for the priceless gift she gave us—long ago, when she flung us blurry-eyed into the mud.

"And that, my children, our Grandmothers would say, is how it came to be that our joy is in the sea yet still the air we breathe."

Rashid, listen to me. Did you hear? An eon has passed as our Grandmothers said it, but now what we left behind on the land is oozing like Squid's ink, remorselessly deeper and deeper, staining the water, coming after us, avenging itself on our joy. An end is near. That distant past, that angered, frightened, desperation has come back to drive our hearts from our home. It is a maimed warrior that stalks us, battling under a banner of past horror, bereft of senses. It wears a human face. How can we understand? What does our Mother want? Her weeping cracks our eardrums. The air burns our lungs with her pain.

Do you hear her too, Rashid? Can you feel her cry in your breath? Does it sear your heart as well?

CHAPTER 13

Laura felt hot, fifteen-hundred-year-old bricks press into her back through the white cotton shift she had bought at the market. The sun beat down on her face. A line of perspiration was working its way down her body from under her arm. She longed to be on the water, where she and Carlos had been just two days before.

She was exhausted. They were two-thirds of the way up the pyramid temple at Chichen Itza. It was the third structure they had climbed that day, an endless series of narrow-ledged stairs that were not made for modern American feet. She had a bad feeling about this expedition.

Carlos. Dark-skinned Carlos was sitting beside her now with his penetrating eyes and aquiline nose, only he wasn't really beside her. His back was erect, not resting like hers against the steps above him. He was not panting or perspiring. His thin buttocks were somehow balanced, unaided, on the narrow ledge. His feet, Laura noticed, were probably an inch and a half shorter than hers. "Carlos, why are we doing this?" she said.

She knew the answer but it was as if by asking it over and over again she could strengthen the case for stopping when the time to stop came.

"*Querida, no te preocupes,*" he said in reassuring tones. "Don't worry. It is a test. He will find us when we are ready for him."

Laura wondered if she would ever be ready. In her dreams she found herself in contact with all kinds of metaphysical beings. In her waking hours, she saw the desert sun set in a thousand colors or the clouds over her head form into birds and angels, lizards and goats. Each time it happened she was amazed and knew that the wild and improbable quest of her life was meant to be. But at her core she knew all of this was external, that nothing had really changed. The inner alchemy of which the goddesses spoke remained as unattainable for her as ever. She feared that she might be one of those unevolved seekers who was to spend a lifetime of frustration, rejected over and over again by the true guides who were on Earth, silently reproaching her, telling her that her time had not yet come.

"But why here?" she persisted, "The place is littered with tourists. Tourists of the worst kind. They could care less, it's just a break from the beach."

"You're right, and if he were Greek and said to meet him in the Parthenon, what would you say?"

"I would say he was a tourist guide. There have been no mysteries in Greece for two thousand years."

Carlos' face twisted as if he were ready to blurt out a retort. Instead he pushed a wandering hair away from her face.

"We should go back to the hotel. We can come back in the morning. It will be cooler," was all he said.

She knew they would have margaritas in their room. They would lie together, watching the nude game shows from Italy or Thailand on the International Channel and then Carlos would make love to her, touching her body skillfully.

A few days ago, she wouldn't have hesitated. But now it was different. Her anger and her need to push away the memories of her life with David had subsided and her passion for Carlos had cooled. She even wondered if Carlos had invented the story about the Mayan elder in order to sleep with her. "He knows about the Old Ones," Carlos had said. "He is heir to their secret traditions. He wants to meet you." She had believed it and followed him to Mexico.

"No. We've come this far," she said, "Let's go to the top."

He reached for her hand. "Good. Let's go."

His answer surprised her. She felt tension leave her chest and decided that if there were a problem, it was probably with this Mayan old man, not with Carlos.

When they reached the top fifteen minutes later, they were joined by a Swedish couple who emerged from the interior passageway. Laura looked out over the Yucatan plain. It seemed scrubby and dirty, a flat expanse colored in green-brown tones that were neither desert nor lush like the Costa Rican forest she had come from. And it was debilitatingly hot, and growing hotter as the Earth's climate changed. Why, she wondered, had one of the world's most advanced civilizations flourished here, in such an uninspiring place?

The Swedish couple was animated, talking constantly, pointing at the horizon in various directions and examining every detail of the faded stone work. Carlos and Laura rested again. His face was expressionless and she had no idea what he was thinking. Her legs felt weak. She was already feeling queasy about the trip down. She couldn't see the base of the structure. She had heard that the pyramids were purposely constructed like that to intimidate the uninitiated.

The young Swedish woman, blond, large-boned but attractive, was the first to speak to Laura.

"You're American?"

"Yes." It irritated her that it was that obvious, though the truth was more complicated. Laura was about to launch into an explanation about her half-French, half-Bolivian mother and her family's peripatetic ways but the Swedish woman continued quickly.

"You're lucky to live so close. If we did, we would come here for holidays all the time."

Air fares had remained relatively expensive. Ground transportation had escaped from reliance on fossil fuels but no one had yet developed an alternative device which was safe, compact, and powerful enough to hurtle hundreds of tons of passengers and metal through the sky at speeds close to that of sound.

"It's my first time," Laura said.

"And ours, but this is the second time we've come up. We met an old man at a bar and he told us some fascinating stories about the old Mayan ways and what to look for here. It's been like discovering a new place... "

Carlos broke in, "What was the man's name?"

"I don't know...the bar was in the Hotel Imperial in Merida.... Lars, do you remember?"

"No, but Anna is right," he said," he tells great stories. Coming back is like visiting a new place."

"Was he short, slim, a scar under his left eye?" Carlos asked.

"I think so," Lars replied, "but it was dark inside. Actually, I do remember his name now, the bartender called him Sylvester—no, in Spanish it must be Silvestre, the bartender called him Don Silvestre."

Carlos' eyes widened and he smiled in triumph. "See, Laura? He did tell us how to find him." Laura straightened herself and reached for his hand. She kissed him on the cheek.

A breeze blew in from the sea and made their climb down a relatively pleasant one. They decided to tour the ball court quickly. As they walked through it, Laura jumped up towards the hoop. She had played basketball in high school, but the hoop was several feet beyond her reach.

She thought of Mayan festivals, and the games, and the blood sacrifices, the bodies and gold thrown into sacrificial pools, all this from a people who had charted the skies better than anyone until "modern" times, and who had developed a complex calendar and a written language that still remained largely undeciphered. It was a curious, contradictory mixture that she entertained only a distant hope of understanding.

After a short wait, Laura and Carlos settled into the comfort of an air-conditioned tour bus. The bus hummed along in the transport vehicle lane, drawing its power from the electric rail to which its feeder line was attached. Almost all heavily traveled routes everywhere in the world now had a power rail for trucks and buses to reduce fossil fuel use. The rails enforced a uniformity of speed, but many thought that this too was a blessing.

Laura had taken the window seat and watched with some interest as they passed a solar collector farm with its huge U-shaped mirrors that concentrated sunshine on oil-filled tubes in the trough of the mirrors. These gave way to fields of sisal hemp and then enclosed tanks where much of the region's spirunella was produced. The bus stopped briefly to collect two passengers at an agricultural station where, the driver proudly informed his passengers, through DNA manipulation, a twelve-foot corn plant that thrived in the rising temperatures and local soil had been developed. Its productivity, he added, was making it possible to restore forest lands to the area. The ride from the agricultural station to Merida was brief and soon the bus slowed as it separated from the trail and weaved through the city's streets until it stopped in the central square.

Carlos and Laura walked the two blocks to the hotel. It was new but its designer had learned well from the past and retained patterned tile floors, thick walls and high ceilings. Cool water flowed through a profusion of fountains, powered in the daytime by the steam generated in the rooftop solar heater. Gently moving fans pushed the air past the fountains throughout the hotel. At night, except in the dining and lounge areas, the fountains were turned off. Indoor plants of all varieties grew in every room. The effect was a fresh, cool environment. Almost too cool.

They walked up a spiral staircase guarded by a wrought iron railing to their room on the third floor. Laura undressed and showered. When she emerged, she lay down with Carlos on the white towel she had wrapped around her and on a profusely flowered bedspread. Carlos made love to her slowly, and she savored a wealth of sensations in the quiet and cool air. Afterwards they set out for the bar at the Hotel Imperial.

They stepped into hot, bright air, the light heightened by the scrubbed appearance of Merida's streets and buildings. Merida had always been a clean town, the only real threat to its cleanliness the increasing volume of emissions from automobiles, trucks and buses, many of which survived long past the time their manufacturers anticipated their demise. But that danger was past now. Almost no one in provincial Mexico could afford to pay the six hundred percent UN Climate Fund tax on high-consumption, hydrocarbon-powered land vehicles—or even the hundred percent tax on hybrid vehicles—so it was only a matter of time until the gasoline and diesel guzzlers would die out. Like horses to a previous generation, they would become little more than an amusement for the well-to-do.

At first it had been difficult to get oil-rich countries like Mexico to accept any international regulation of automobiles or fuel consumption. Mexico wanted a market for its oil and wanted to afford its population one of the few luxuries that it could—cheap driving. Fed by a marked increase in tornados, hurricanes, and floods, changed precipitation patterns, and an upward creep in temperatures, alarm over global warming and greenhouse gases increased sharply in the advanced, consuming nations. It became clear that the petroleum market could not be maintained. Nonetheless a deadlock persisted in the global negotiations.

The breakthrough came when an obscure Saudi Deputy Minister of Agriculture who had done his graduate work at Texas A&M suggested to his uncle the oil minister that they should emulate certain aspects of the American economic system. Oil producers should be paid not to pump it out of the ground, much as wheat or peanut farmers in the U.S.A. were paid not to grow their crops. Depending on how long the subsidy could be maintained, the oil producers might be paid five or ten times the current value of their reserves. Moreover, what little oil they did sell to the diminished market could be priced much higher as there would inevitably be periodic scarcities when the supplying nations underproduced. Higher prices automatically created increases in "proven" reserves (proven reserves being the measure of the amount of oil which can be extracted at the current price) entitling the producers to even more payments for keeping the oil in the ground.

These transfer payments were to be made out of the UN Global Climate Fund to which the consuming countries had to contribute in accordance with the volume of their greenhouse emissions. Since the consuming countries were used to making enormous transfers to the producing countries for oil, making smaller payments for oil not produced was not particularly painful.

The Saudi proposal was presented during the scorching summer of 2020 and accepted with almost no resistance by a world panicked by the prospect of unknown climatic upheavals. The Saudi oil minister was awarded the Nobel Peace Prize two years later, the year after the Agreement Establishing the Global Climate Fund entered into force.

Laura and Carlos walked down the street in silence. Shops were opening after the mid-day break. Laura felt more at ease, even hopeful, about Carlos and excited about meeting Don Silvestre, yet she had little to say to her companion. She turned to familiar ground for the sake of saying something.

"I thought you were gorgeous when I first saw you, and then I find out that you are on a search like mine." She paused, "It's as if you were sent to me. Just at the right time."

Carlos removed his sunglasses and looked at her with a thin smile.

"Maybe I was—or we could say you were sent to me."

Carlos' response irritated her. Often she felt she didn't know exactly what he meant. She retreated back into silence. They arrived at the entrance to the bar at the Hotel Imperial. He opened the door for her and when she stepped inside, she was immediately plunged into darkness. He led her to what she dimly saw as two short-backed bamboo stools at one end of the bar.

"Let's sit here," Carlos said, "at least until we can see better."

"Maybe he's not here now. We should have waited for evening," Laura said, tensing her shoulders against disappointment.

"We can always come back."

"You will recognize him?" Laura said, still unsure.

"Yes."

They ordered two margaritas which came with surprising speed.

Carlos raised his salt-rimmed glass. *"Salud."*

"Salud." Laura touched her glass to his, avoiding his eyes. She was still fretting over her own unworthiness and the pain and disappointment the encounter was likely to bring. "Do you ever think, Carlos, about how good we are at self-deception?"

"What are you talking about?"

"*'Salud'* is a perfect example. We wish each other health and imagine that by doing so our health will benefit. Yet look at what we're actually doing, drinking some nasty stuff that will kill healthy brains cells by the thousands, and encouraging our companions to do the same."

"You have a lot to learn Laura," he said, "Life's pleasures are few."

Laura eyed Carlos over the rim of her glass, again made uncomfortable by his answer. She watched as he took a deep drink of his margarita, and thought, he's as banal as they come. He could be a gigolo in Acapulco. Why did she think that a gigolo would lead her to God? Relenting slightly, she wondered what had suddenly made her so negative but was unable—or unwilling—to pursue the thought. A man came up behind her and seated himself to her left. She sensed a powerful presence.

"You are Laura," he said in heavily accented English. She turned to see a dark-complexioned, heavy-set man dressed in blue jeans and a plaid cotton shirt. His breath was strong with scent of earth and roots. "You have come to the right place."

"Don Silvestre, no te vi," Carlos interjected, rising up from his seat and extending his hand behind Laura.

"It's good to see you, Carlos. But you too must learn to be visible only when you wish to be seen."

Don Silvestre turned to Laura, "You have come a long way."

"Not really. San Jose is hardly two hours away," she said, still uncertain about her reactions to the man's presence but with a mounting sense of excitement that she was trying to contain.

"I mean in your search. Carlos has told me about you."

Laura paused, unsure of herself. She felt unworthy and vulnerable. It was an all too familiar feeling.

"I'm not sure where I started," she finally said. "I'm not sure where I've been. I'm not sure where I am."

Don Silvestre's eyes held hers. "You are at the entrance way. An ancient and secret tradition awaits you... if that is your choice."

"I've been at entrances before. Opportunities. Then they fade away."

"Like Matteo Michelson?"

"I wouldn't presume so. How did you know about him?"

The bartender had returned to their corner and stood in front of them expectantly. Don Silvestre ordered a Superior. "Does it matter? I know his death affected you. I hear that you foresaw it."

"In a way. Where are you leading me, Don Silvestre?"

"To the end of the world," Carlos laughed.

"What?"

"Carlos is right, to the end of the world. Or at least that is what it is called in my tradition. The death of one age and the birth of another, one that is only loosely tied to the past.

"But knowledge comes with death," the seer continued, "and there are things that have been kept secret since the Spanish invasion, actually even longer. Only a few fragments have been passed down orally from teacher to apprentice over generations—but in our tradition it is said that at the end of the world this knowledge would be revealed. The date, the end, just passed a few years ago – a split second in the march of time.

"To us, life is a cycle, a wheel. Actually there are many cycles, wheels within wheels. But there comes a point where all conclude, simultaneously, little wheels, intermediate wheels, big wheels; uinals, tuns, katuns, baktuns, pictuns, calabtuns, kinchiltuns, even alautuns—cycles measured in millions of years. That is the end of a world. There may or may not be real physical upheavals at the end of each age. That is something up to powers beyond us.

"In your culture there is something close," Don Silvestre added, "the Dawning of the Age of Aquarius, you call it. We are on the verge of the end of the world and what was known only in part to only a few, must now be disclosed to the many."

"We want you to help us with this," Carlos said.

"I don't understand." Laura felt genuinely befuddled.

"It is not for us to understand why you were chosen," Carlos continued, "We could speculate. You are white, yet you have faith in old traditions which others have long assumed to be dead. You are close to nature. Plants and flowers."

"I still don't understand."

"We think," Don Silvestre said, "that if you will make the effort, the hidden knowledge in the Maya-glyphs will disclose itself to you. It would then be for you to write it down and tell the world about it."

Laura was stunned, she sensed her heart beating faster. Was it possible that all her confusion, her unhappiness could be over? She had been chosen. A mission, a special task, something that would drive out the worms and fill the dark recesses to which she so often awoke, something that would break the constricting embrace of her ordinariness, something that would let her see her inner being with the same delight that others felt at her outward appearance. Laura recrossed her legs under the bar and tugged gently downwards at the hem of her skirt. She looked at Carlos and stirred her margarita with a toothpick umbrella. She leaned toward the seer. Her life had not gone well. She was connected to no one. She had nothing to lose.

"What's next?" she asked.

"You need to know something about us, not just what you can read in books—though some of that you should know too—but the knowledge of how our society worked and what its purpose was.

"You cannot absorb this all at once," Don Silvestre continued, "and in time there will be much that I can tell you. But let me start with what may be the most difficult thing for you to accept. Mayan society was organized through telepathy. Its ruler-priests were trained in the projection of thought forms. This was an intense process. As children their skulls were deformed purposely in order to stimulate the parts of the brain that had this capacity.

"In this way there was no need to use forced labor, as was true in so many other places, to build the largest temples and buildings. My people by the hundreds of thousands simply 'knew' that it was time to build. The people would store supplies for a year and then they would appear. For a long time the priests were aligned with the gods, so all worked well.

"I am telling you this now because even though you have been open to many so-called New Age currents, you and all white people are almost hopelessly bonded to the material and all your rational science. You must wait for this thought to penetrate, you must remember to yourself what I am telling you over and over again.

"When you have done so you will find it not at all inconceivable that thought forms projected into the minds of one's contemporaries could also be projected into material objects and stored there, waiting for the right time, the right sensibility, the right receptivity, to 'read' the message. Pictograms—glyphs—in certain temples and structures are precisely such repositories."

Laura absorbed Don Silvestre's explanation. It didn't really surprise her. A few hundred truly conscious people, she had heard Matteo Michelson once say, and the world would be transformed. That could only be true if those people had the power to impel their way of being and seeing into the collective mind of everybody else. Books or words alone couldn't do it. But it could be telepathy, or something like it.

"You think often of Matteo, don't you?" Don Silvestre's tone was gentle, breaking a moment's silence and seemingly following her thoughts.

"Did you know him?"

"Yes. In a manner of speaking."

"What does that mean?"

"I knew his mind. He knew mine. His death was a great sorrow. It came too soon."

"I tried to warn him," Laura said, her gaze falling into the remnants of her margarita, "I failed."

"You knew he would be killed?" Silvestre asked.

"I knew he was in real danger. I tried to warn him the day before his death. I didn't have the words."

"You should not be too hard on yourself," Carlos told her. "You were not responsible."

"Carlos is right," Don Silvestre added, "Others committed the act."

"You are both kind," she said. Unsure what to say, she asked for another margarita and Carlos and Don Silvestre joined her. She rearranged herself on the bar stool, feeling the men's eyes follow her movement.

"Salud," she said with a smile when the margaritas came.

"Salud," the two responded.

At Laura's prompting, Don Silvestre talked about his upbringing. His mother was a Quiche Maya who supported herself washing clothes and helping at harvest time. Silvestre was the third son whom she had given to her primary employer, a local patrón who owned an over-farmed hillside in Chiapas. At an early age Don Silvestre saw that his future was not promising. He stood last in line, if at all, to get a share of land which was already of marginal size. When he was sixteen he made the long migration to the U.S. border where all of his money was stolen and he was held in a detention camp for six weeks. Once released, he begged his way to the Gulf Coast and found a fisherman who gave him work. Eventually he returned home. He was fortunate it was an election year. The party, the Partido Revolucionario Independiente, the PRI, needed help. There were leaflets to distribute, money to deliver, ballots to falsify.

Silvestre proved adept at most of these tasks. He was loyal and discrete when it came to PRI matters. He also passed on valuable intelligence to the police about the party's opponents. Many people seemed to trust him. He was rewarded with the lucrative job of issuing permits for renovation tasks in the historic districts of the region. Most deemed the bribes that he demanded fair. In his spare time he attended the university, and adopted as best he could the ways of the oligarchs.

It was after he had held this job for a year or two that an old man from his mother's village came to see him. The old man told him that it was time that he returned to his roots, that he had important work to perform, and that in any event he should realize that the PRI would be ousted from power in the elections of the following year. He would have many enemies. He would be wise to leave now. For reasons he was unable to explain, Don Silvestre believed the old man. Two months later he left the city and found a home in the village of his childhood. What the old man foresaw proved to be true, and for ten years Silvestre apprenticed in the Mayan traditions of sorcery. Then the old man died and he was left to take his place in the silent net that joined a few other villages, most of them remote, where magical traditions dating back to the arrival of the Olmec three thousand years earlier were secretly kept.

The bartender was lingering at the nearby sink, drying glasses slowly. She felt certain he was listening to their conversation.

"Will you help us?" he asked Laura at the end of his story.

She turned away from the bartender and put her hand on Don Silvestre's well-pressed white sleeve.

"You must tell me what to do."

He nodded. "Enjoy yourself here for three days. On Sunday morning meet Carlos at the bus terminal at eleven. He will know where to take you."

"Carlos is not staying with me?"

"He has work to do—and much to learn."

Carlos did not seem surprised. He put his arm around her bare shoulder, leaned over and kissed her on the neck. "I'll miss you but it won't be long."

"Okay." She felt a fleeting sense of discomfort, but knew she would enjoy some time alone.

"Good-bye, Laura, you are a friend to our people." Don Silvestre reached out with his right hand and shook Laura's. At the same time, his left hand dropped into his pants pocket where his thumb flicked a tiny lever on a small recording device.

Laura returned to her room, slept for a little while, enjoyed the day's darkening in solitude and had a quiet dinner in her hotel. On Friday Laura toured the ruins of Uxmal, from what Eurocentric archaeologists named the Late Classic Mayan era. She was particularly drawn to the Nunnery Quadrangle and the House of the Magician that towered over it. The structures reminded her of her newfound destiny.

On Saturday she traveled to Tulum where less imposing structures look out over the Caribbean Sea. After a brief tour she went to the beach, found a relatively secluded spot and took off her clothes. A four-foot-long iguana watched her with interest from its perch on a nearby rock. A sentinel, she thought, sent from what little remained of the dragon-filled time of a magical, happier age. Laura felt protected. She asked the Goddess to be one with her as she gave her bronzed, fluid body over to the light of the sun and the rising swell of the sea.

CHAPTER 14

For two weeks Almira had been tense. Flying had never been her favorite activity but even with the added stress of managing Youssef and Jamal who kept pushing each other to get a better view of the window, she felt relieved when she heard the passenger door seal shut. The fuel-efficient economy turboprop bound for London was full, as it almost always was. Most of the passengers were Arab. She had heard that the faster, more expensive jet flights were predominantly Jewish. It would take time for things to even out. She reminded herself that in the United States more than sixty years had passed since their civil rights movement, one hundred sixty since their Civil War, and economic inequities still remained. Less than ten years had passed in Palestine.

Being victimized had given her and nearly everyone she knew a passionate identity. In some ways it had also freed them from the consequences of action—or inaction—and she knew it was hard to let go of that. The seduction of victimization was hard to resist in other ways too. It became who you were, made you feel alive with pleasure and pain at the same time. You didn't need to discuss your role or identity. Almira wondered if she had not given in to the victim's view and wrongly assumed that she was in danger. After all, it was perfectly natural for the police to question her about Fatimah's death. She was as close to her as anyone and there was much that she didn't know about

Fatimah's personal longings and desires. Kristen, for example. She had never understood Fatimah's attraction to her.

In a way, Fatimah's making love to Ariel Arbel could be seen as the ultimate and most powerful act of reconciliation. She allowed him to enter a place from which guilt would certainly have barred him. She allowed him to be who he was and do as he wished in what he must have viewed as the most unlikely and inhospitable psychic terrain. She would have accepted him and even been tender toward him. If Arbel were open to it, it could have been a profoundly transforming experience.

If Fatimah did sleep with him. She certainly didn't pull the trigger or invite the television cameras. No matter what she, Almira, thought, the rest of the world was not going to see what happened as transformative. Humanity wasn't that enlightened. Somebody wanted to discredit Fatimah, or the party, or perhaps the worldwide women's movement or the Settlement for which Fatimah had been so responsible.

The choice of Arbel suggested to Almira that the target was the Settlement, but of the possible targets, that was the least likely to be affected. Too many people were prospering under the Confederation it had established. Only the most fanatical Palestinian elements were likely to argue that her relationship with Arbel was proof of a sell-out. The Settlement had involved too many people and too many factors; the fact that Arbel was dead ruled out a right-wing Jewish conspiracy.

As the whine of the turboprops rose and the plane began to move, Jamal's left hand shot forward and grasped Youssef by the wrist. His right hand knotted into a small fist and he waived it menacingly near Youssef's shoulder. They were bickering over the rights to a small toy airplane that Jamal had inadvertently dropped in Youssef's seat. Almira struggled to make Jamal release his grip and ordered Youssef to give the toy back. She muttered a thankful prayer for the restraining influence of seat belts. She wondered if she could make them work at home.

The more she thought about it, the more she was pleased with her decision to take the boys to be with her brother. Even if she were wrong about her own situation, the boys would get to know Ali better. They needed to. Also, it would give her some time alone for the first time in a decade. She would miss Jamal and Youssef and their constant quarreling but at bottom the prospect excited her. It was time for her life to change.

The loss of Farid had been hard but the boys had proven to be a joy and her work with Fatimah probably as meaningful to others as anything that she would ever do. Did she really want change? Maybe not, but change had been forced upon her. Fatimah was dead and Almira's intuition told her that she too had enemies. As the plane rose over the Mediterranean, Almira's mind wandered back to the Settlement. It was part nostalgia, part hope that somewhere in those events was a clue to Fatimah's murder and her own unease. The Final Settlement had become effective six years after Almira joined the Palestinian Women's Peace Movement. It was not that Almira or any other individual made much of a difference. Rather a community-wide perception seemed to descend over most Palestinians at once, and the sense that enmity-filled separation and terror and violence in any form, even teenage stone-throwing, was not only creating unending pain for all sides, particularly for the Palestinians, but that it was playing into the hands of the most irredentist of the Israelis.

Why it took so long for the obvious to be accepted was by no means clear. Some speculated that it was a question of security of identity, that it took the experience of the first intifadah, the brief but abortive interlude of self-rule following the Jericho accord, and then the Repression and the later intifadahs, for the Palestinian community to accept that it could act as a community without an armed champion. Others felt that the core of the problem was that too much of the Palestinian leadership owed its position precisely to its skill in violence. Thinking in other terms was not in their interest. To many in the growing worldwide women's movement who had supported Fatimah and Almira in their work, the lingering conflict was simply another clear symptom of the degeneracy of patriarchal cultures. From that perspective, the attachment to violence was no surprise, and it was certainly true that women's active role in the nonviolent elements of the insurrection did much to break down patriarchal control.

The Palestinian Women's Peace Movement, which had advocated nonviolent civil disobedience for years, became both a source of strategic guidance for large elements of the resistance during the final intifadah and a bottomless well of good tactical ideas for disrupting day-to-day life in Israel and dramatizing the Palestinian plight as an unjustly conquered people, the last victims of the European colonial era.

As the memory of the massacre of forty-eight West Bank settlers which had brought on the Repression faded, the continuing sight of truncheons falling, protesting housewives, and tear-gas canisters rolling among school children clouded lingering sympathies in the world's eyes for the Israeli Government, and deeply affected many Israelis as well.

Confronted with increasingly effective nonviolent protests, and the episodic attacks by clandestine Palestinian groups, the Israeli Government overreacted and trucked two thousand West Bank dissidents to the other side of the Jordanian border as part of a planned expulsion of close to thirty thousand Arabs. An unprecedented storm of international protest followed, threats were made, and militaries were mobilized.

The UN Security Council met in emergency session. It condemned the use of force by either side and condemned the expulsion of West Bank residents. Through the U.S. delegation the Israelis were warned that failure to enter into serious negotiations with the Palestinians could result in a UN-sanctioned global economic embargo. It fell on the Egyptians, French, and the Russians to tell various Palestinian factions that if they didn't negotiate in good faith, they would cease to be relevant. The Iranians and Iraqis were told to stay in their own countries. Negotiations did in fact start with the Palestinian delegation composed of the leaders of the various factions—including Fatimah Karajan.

Given the failure of the First Settlement, the harder part was finding even the outlines of a settlement that could be agreed to quickly. Time was not on the side of peace. After two months of frustration, it was Fatimah who presented the outlines of the Settlement. To Fatimah the fatal defect in the First Settlement was that it was premised on a patchwork of bright lines of separation between Palestinians and Israelis, combined with what could be easily perceived as a second-class role for Palestinians. But the separation was illusory and the illusion tended to nourish the dreams of those on both sides who harbored fantasies of the ultimate separation—driving the other entity from the territory. Of course, as Fatimah had observed, separation was no more possible than asking a man and a woman who shared a bed not to touch each other in their sleep. Her proposal for a settlement was based on a concept first advanced by an obscure law professor in the 1980s.

Fatimah had come to understand that the greatest conceptual barrier to a solution was the traditional perception of the nation state. As traditionally conceived, a nation was defined geographically. Within defined borders its government was "sovereign" and all aspects of life within its borders—commerce, property, public services, law enforcement, political discourse and organized armed force—were directed or subject to rules established by the sovereign. Relationships with other nations were also within the purview of the sovereign.

This nation state mythology persisted strongly into the early years of the twenty-first century. Like the Newtonian, mechanical world view, nationalism in this form had a lingering and relentless grip on public consciousness, but it had outlived its useful-ness. The problem was not simply that undesirable consequences flowed from this nation-state conception, it was that it was no longer descriptive of reality. In fact, no state, even the richest, had effective control over its economy. No state, even the largest, could insulate its citizenry from environmental destruction. No state, even the best armed, could use unilateral force against others freely, except perhaps in peripheral areas or with immediate neighbors where a gross imbalance of force existed. After one of the bloodiest centuries in human history and the inexplicable Bush-fire wars, as they came to be known, the more developed world had, at least for the most part, said no to war.

At the same time, a panoply of transnational groups and organizations developed to govern different aspects of human intercourse, particularly in the economic sphere. International bodies regulated everything from coffee and oil production, to communications satellites to waste dumping into the Baltic Sea. Standards of all kinds were set by even more obscure quasi-public bodies, and transnational enterprises had as much to say about the allocation of human and material resources as anyone. Moreover, voluntary associations of all kinds stretched across borders, organized around common goals—the betterment of women, the protection of wildlife, the feeding of children, vigilance for human rights—and like the League of Red Cross and Red Crescent Societies of a century before, many came to have a universally accepted role.

These developments occurred gradually in relative anonymity. Far more visible were events such as the decentralization of power in the Soviet Union and its devolution to ethnic groupings. Similar events occurred in Canada and China. At the other extreme was the impulse toward unification, represented in the creation of one Europe, overlaying the old sovereignties. What was happening was something implicit in the American federal experiment in its incipient stages. There was no reason why any one governing body needed to be supreme, especially when external physical threats were minimal. An individual or social group could have allegiance to a variety of bodies for a variety of different purposes, allowing each body to govern in a defined area, not necessarily a geographic one. A polity no more needed to be defined by its borders than a human being did by the volume enveloped by his skin.

What Fatimah proposed took this concept to the next logical step. Her approach was to create a functioning confederation of Israel, Palestine (the West Bank and Gaza), and Jordan in which there was not only a variety of governing entities but different borders (and no borders) for different purposes. The Israeli military security borders—the area where Israeli military forces could be stationed—could be quite different from the areas that the Israeli government otherwise administered. Military borders could even overlap and be jointly patrolled. In her proposal, a Palestinian State would issue Palestinian passports, and Israel and Jordan would issue their own, but so could the Confederation for those who so wished. A Palestinian Homeland could encompass all of Israel, the West Bank, Gaza and perhaps all or part of Jordan, an area where a Palestinian would enjoy all but certain voting rights. Most of the same land would be the Land of Israel, including all of Palestine west of the Jordan

River, where an Israeli would enjoy the same. Joint Commissions for water rights and economic activity could include all three parties while the administration of many holy places would be entrusted to bodies of narrower composition, the Al-Aqsa Mosque to a Palestinian group, the Wailing Wall to an Israeli group, and so on. Responsibility for external relations could be similarly divided between the Confederation and its three constituent entities. Most important of all, the governance of most day-to-day matters would be left in the hands of individual communities and their locally selected leadership.

The approach was accepted. It did take close to three years to work out the details and incorporate them in a treaty and a mass of protocols and "understandings."

Over the next several years all sides proved adept at imaginative interpretations, but the system worked. In fact, it was working so well that many were pointing to it as a model for global governance. It was proof, many argued, that diffused power which gave maximum leeway to individual ethnic, cultural and economic groupings, as well as voluntary associations, was a demonstrably sounder approach than the more centralized concepts promoted by much of the United Nations' bureaucracy and the governments of the largest nations. The issue, Almira knew, was expected to dominate the proceedings at the Global Convocation of Terrestrial Entities, scheduled to be held in New Delhi the following year. Fatimah was viewed as the best spokesperson for the confederational approach.

Governments at all levels, nongovernmental organizations of all kinds, multinationals, church groups, political parties, environmental and other advocates, educational entities, scientific associations and an assortment of individuals, selected by lot, would all be present at what was being touted as a global constitutional convention. It struck Almira for the first time that with Fatimah's death, she was likely to be the one selected to represent the Party at the Convocation—if she weren't in jail by then. In any event, Almira concluded, the bloody mess in Fatimah's bed was not going to add luster to the Palestinian example.

"Mama," Youssef's voice interrupted her reverie, "can I have yours?" The flight attendant had brought them trays of sandwiches which Almira had left untouched.

"I want some too," Jamal quickly added, his tone pleading.

Almira took a bite. She found the bread soggy and the meat grey and drab. She made a face, "How can you eat this?"

"Ketchup," Youssef said.

"Ketchup," Jamal echoed, holding a little, half-emptied tube of the red substance in his hand.

Almira smiled and with a surgeon's care divided the remaining sandwich into two equal portions. In moments the sandwiches were gone, leaving telltale red tracks at the corners of the boys' lips.

CHAPTER 15

Ali, his wife Elizabeth, and her sixteen-year-old son Ian lived on the upper floor of the structure which housed their restaurant on the outskirts of Glastonbury. A low picket fence ran in front of the building along the sidewalk, broken where a stone path marked the entrance way. Juniper shrubs paralleled the path and behind them a profusion of tulips, hyacinth, and crocus were in bloom. Greening leaves could be seen on a row of roses, and a variety of unflowered plants which Almira did not recognize were scattered about. The herbs, she knew, were planted in the back next to the compost pile, which Elizabeth liked to call the Living Word of God. The English and their gardens. They were lucky. Sweet, self-contained, perfumed. Walled gardens of paradise.

A tasteful sign on the door of the building announced The Inn of the Loaves and Fishes underneath a semi-abstracted rendition of the Glastonbury thorn. The "second semitic conjury," Ali called his restaurant's name, referring both to the well-known miracle and to the old legends that Joseph of Arimathea had brought Christianity and the Holy Grail to the area. Joseph was said to have planted his staff in the ground from which a Lebanese thorn varietal grew and which could still be seen on a nearby knoll.

"A nice story," Ali told the boys, "but even those who insist it's true say it's not so simple. Apparently some religious maniac took an axe to it five hundred years ago. Fortunately though, a brother in the nearby monastery had preserved a cutting or two, so he planted the cutting up on the knoll and it is the growth of the cutting we'll see tomorrow."

"My teacher says that the English aren't called John Bulls for nothing," Youssef said.

Ali smiled but could not resist the role of tour guide. "I have seen this same tree growing in Palestine and I have never seen one like it anywhere else in England. We know the tree's been here a very long time. Who knows?"

Only Almira detected the hint of a limp as Ali led them through the door in search of Elizabeth. His wife emerged from the kitchen, an attractive, tall, and well-rounded woman in her forties. Strawberry-blond hair fell in waves just below her shoulders. Her complexion was pale but her cheeks were flushed slightly from the kitchen heat. Her eyes were bright, dancing between blue and green like the sea on a clear day. She had an apron tied around her. The Loaves and the Fishes would soon be open for dinner.

Almira embraced her; she could feel Elizabeth's energy shimmering in an invisible spectrum. It awakened Almira and took the stiffness out of her limbs that had come from sitting too long in cramped seats.

At first Almira had resisted Elizabeth. Ali, she had said, it is bad enough that she is English, but she has already divorced one husband for no good reason and left her only child with her mother. The woman can have no heart. Later, when she met Elizabeth, Almira promised never to make superficial judgments of that kind again.

Elizabeth had grown up in a circumscribed environment, a small manor house near Shrewsbury where her father managed a minor industrial enterprise. She attended a local school and grew up admiring the memory of Margaret Thatcher and the Queen after whom she was named. She studied at the university in London where she did her best to avoid what her father jokingly called the 'wogs and hogs'. Wogs were easy to identify—all the rain and winter pallor in England couldn't really change their darker skin color. Hogs were more problematic as they were defined by attitude, or moral fiber, as Elizabeth's father might say. The porcine were bountifully endowed with self-importance and parsimoniously with a sense of place and proportion. Greed and self-gratification moved them and, like the creatures after whom they were named, they would not hesitate to bury their noses in the dirt in search of a truffle or two.

Even Elizabeth's father would not have recognized Ian as a hog at first. Ian was a solicitor and had read history at Oxford. When he met Elizabeth, he spoke admiringly of the strand of pearls that graced her neck and he could recite pages of Paradise Lost.

Elizabeth was twenty-six and had been a mother for one year—a year during which she hardly saw her husband at all—when she realized what she had done. She packed her clothes and took Ian Jr. to her mother. She left behind the strand of pearls and a note urging that it be given to her successor. She fell in love with an artist and they lived for a while near a spiritual community on the West coast of Scotland. When the artist moved away, Elizabeth stayed and reclaimed Ian Jr. from her mother.

The community was said to be based on the teachings of a Russian mystic who had been trained at a Sufi school near Bokhara. It was rumored that community members also claimed to be in touch with a variety of nature spirits. Pantheists, people said of them. These rumors were distressing to Claudia, Elizabeth's mother. If Elizabeth's life was going to take a religious turn, it should at least be something familiar. Claudia knew it wouldn't do much good to arrange for an expense-paid tour of Canterbury but Jerusalem might be a different story. In the worst case, Claudia thought, she might fall for a reputable Orientalist. Elizabeth, to her own surprise, accepted her mother's offer. It was in Jerusalem that she met Ali and soon afterward, to both of her parents' horror, married him.

Dinner for Ali and Elizabeth was always late, after the restaurant kitchen was closed and the two waitresses could easily handle the remaining demands of any lingering patrons. Jamal and Youssef were asleep; Ian was helping close up. Almira waited patiently and joined her brother and his wife at a large table in the back of the restaurant, enjoying the leftover cooking smells and the sounds of the kitchen's cleaning. Ian, a red headed, dark eyed young man who approached six feet, periodically came in to serve them a new course.

"How could it have happened?" Elizabeth asked Almira as she took the last bite of lamb. "It frightens me. I thought the horrors of history were behind us."

"I did too. So did Fatimah."

Ali sipped the last of his claret, refilled his glass and stared at it. "Blood is everywhere. We are saturated in it. We drink it, we spill it." He smoothed the tablecloth underneath the glass. "We have all been formed in a crucible of blood, thousands and thousands of years of it. Everywhere."

Almira and Elizabeth exchanged glances. Ali, Almira knew, had cause to be bitter but it rarely emerged. Perhaps there had been too much wine.

"We are born in it," he said looking at the two women, "as you well know." Ali would never have children. While the butt of a gun smashed his limbs, a boot had battered his testicles beyond repair.

Almira wanted to lift her brother out of the heaviness, "If you live in the past, you'll be buried in it." She got up and stood behind him, gently massaging his shoulders.

"You're right," Ali replied, "but it is you I'm worried about. What did they ask?"

"Who?" asked Elizabeth.

"The police. They kept me for ten hours the first time. They made me come back twice more."

"Why?" Elizabeth persisted.

"Because I knew her so well. At least they thought so—and I thought so too."

"But even if you are a friend, what could you tell them for ten hours?"

"They wanted to know a lot about my own life. And where I had been."

"That doesn't make any sense."

"It does to them, Elizabeth," Ali said. "They know Almira saw Fatimah at home quite late in the evening the night it happened."

"In fact, they are sure that I am the last person to see her alive, except for Arbel of course."

"And the killer," Elizabeth added.

"And the killer—but they don't say that."

"Surely that doesn't mean anything. You shouldn't worry."

"I'm trying to convince myself of that. You're probably right."

"Stay here for a while. You'll see. Glastonbury heals."

"And your motive, do they have one made up for you?" Ali asked.

"Of course. Betrayal. I gave years to the woman and her cause. Now she's screwing the man I believe may have been responsible for my husband's death, not to speak of all the other blood on his hands."

"Do you feel that way?" Elizabeth, who had missed much of the Palestinians' difficult history, was beginning to understand.

"Sometimes. It puzzles me. Plus, they wanted to know about my sexual preferences. Jealousy, the usual."

"I can't believe she would sleep with him. It has to be a frame-up," Ali said, "Why don't they see that?"

"They may. But there is a rumor that they found his semen. One of the police hinted at it. The last time, they asked if I knew whether she liked to suck cocks."

"What did you say?" Ali looked faintly disgusted.

"I said that I didn't have the faintest idea."

"You're slipping, Almira, you should have asked him if he did." Ali smiled, his mood improving. "Were any of our old friends there?"

"No. Actually I had a feeling that one of them was not from our area at all. I think he may have been Russian."

"UNINTEL?"

"Maybe. I don't know."

The conversation returned to children and the well-being of the Loaves and the Fishes and the excursions they should all make in the coming days. After coffee, when the others had gone to bed, Almira wrapped a shawl around her shoulders and walked up the hill away from the town, toward the tor which stood above it. As the lights from the houses faded, the scent of rich loam thickened and stars appeared in the cool night air. Far fewer, she mused, than at home, but the planting was easier here. A cloud shaped like a mound of freshly sheared wool slowly enveloped the moon. A meteor tracked briefly through the Eastern sky, and she felt a tingle rise up her spine. Her travels, she sensed, were just beginning.

CHAPTER 16

The high-speed rail took Peter from Washington to New York in one hour twenty-two minutes. The farms and towns had passed in a blur and the train was only five minutes late. Still, he was left with twenty-five minutes to kill in the station. He walked across the station lobby to a v-phone booth to call Katie. The effort would make him appear less of a lout. At the same time he would run no risk of actually having to be with her. Time was too short. He began to dial the number and then remembered that it was Sunday morning. Katie was probably with Bernie. In bed with Bernie or lounging around with Bernie or cooking breakfast for Bernie or stroking him with her neatly-trimmed, unpolished fingernails.

Peter's attentions to Katie in Washington had apparently had some effect. Peter's mother had called him. Katie, she said, was clearly open. Even though she (Katie) thought Bernie was great, she was now saying it was a good relationship for Bernie and her at that time in their lives, especially because it wasn't too constricting. Peter, his mother had then said, chiding, Katie isn't going to wait forever.

Peter's fingers drummed on the v-phone wall. He felt anxious; he knew that if he did speak to Katie, he would probably make a date with her, perhaps on his way back Monday. And it annoyed him that he continued to drag out this relationship which he meant but couldn't seem to end. It would be awkward if Bernie was there. Peter decided to call his mother instead. The v-phone flashed the word RINGING, RINGING at him eight times, then LAST TIME, then SORRY, WOULD YOU LIKE TO MAKE ANOTHER CALL? His mother, Peter assumed, had gone to church early. "Yes," he said to the v-phone and dialed Katie's number. He was on the verge of pressing the voice only command but decided against it. If she left her video open, he might see Bernie and not have to ask.

"Hello." The screen was blank, her video transmit was off.

"Hi, Katie."

The video camera went on. She was wearing a tee shirt that was too big for her, almost certainly a man's. She was sitting in a chair, her bare legs propping up her chin.

"It's good to see you," she said to Peter, "Where are you?"

"Station, on the way to the Senator's."

"Here in town?"

"No. Upstate."

"I talked to your Mom a couple of days ago. I heard you got robbed. That's terrible."

"They didn't take much but it felt awful—and the police were nearly as bad."

"I'm sorry."

A large hairy hand came into view on the screen and descended on Katie's shoulder. Peter—much to his own dismay—heard himself say, "Will I get to see you, maybe dinner soon?"

Bernie's face came briefly into view and managed a smile.

"Peter, this is Bernie," said Katie. "Have you met Bernie?"

"We've met. Hi, Bernie."

"Say hi, Bernie. Peter and I grew up together."

"Hi, Peter," the smile disappeared.

"I was thinking about Monday. On the way back." Peter felt like a sewage pipe, filling with black and pungent waters.

"Sure. You'll call when you get here?"

"Yes." Katie was merciful, he thought. The conversation was over.

"Oh, Peter," she said as he was about to say goodbye, "Are you in line for another job or something?"

"No."

"Well, somebody was asking about you. He said he was with the UN, routine clearance. He wanted to know how I knew you and stuff like that."

Peter's chest tightened. "Let's talk about it Monday."

"Sure. Are you okay?" Katie unfolded herself in the chair.

"Yes."

"See you Monday then."

Odd, Peter thought, as he climbed onto the shuttle between Pennsylvania and Grand Central station. The UN? It made no sense, but he couldn't think of why anyone else, for that matter, would be asking about him and his relationship with Katie.

He was late when he stepped off the shuttle into Grand Central station. Even with the fast walk that had become second nature to him in his life as a senator's aide, he barely caught the connecting train. He settled into a seat in the front car. The train was nearly empty; the ride up the Hudson passed quickly.

By the time Mrs. Carmichael met him at the station, Peter had cleared his head and the tightness in his chest had disappeared. He had overreacted—Katie's questions had put him on edge, he told himself—and there was no point in mentioning the break-in, or the UN investigation, to the Senator. On the station platform a large-busted, graying woman came toward him, hands outstretched, exuding intelligence and warmth. She was dressed in a magenta cotton blouse and denim slacks, a large silver and turquoise belt buckle her only ornament. Her hair was tied behind her; she wore no makeup.

"It's nice to see you, Peter."

"And you, Mrs. Carmichael. Thanks for coming to get me. What is it this time, do you know?"

"I'm not sure. He's been brooding…about the future."

"His?" They stepped off the platform and headed toward a battered station wagon that dated back to the previous century.

"No, the country's." She paused. She turned on the ignition of the electric motor, gripped the steering wheel, and stared straight ahead. "Funny how I still think in old terms, even in the 60s and 70s we didn't really think otherwise. Patrick is as old as I am but he has shifted his thinking. He would say the Earth's future, not the country's."

Peter remembered—he was maybe nine at the time—

watching a videotape in school of a man calling for a new patriotism, an Earth Patriotism. The man spoke in a funny accent that you couldn't always understand, but the speech was moving, quite moving. The man was the Secretary General of the United Nations. Peter had told his father about the speech. It was one of the few conversations with his father that he remembered. "It's a great idea for him," his father had said his voice rising with indignation.

"Then the creep could be President, President of the whole goddamn Earth, then he can have a real army instead of a band of paper-pushing patsy parasites that we ought to put on a boat. Then he can take his army and shove some kind of world socialism right down our throats. It's a pile of shit. Why am I paying taxes for you to hear a pile of shit?"

The school principal's home phone was busy the first time Peter's father called. By the time he was ready to dial again, Peter's mother had joined them. She calmed him down, told him it could wait till morning, knowing full well that by morning the rush of outrage would pass.

"We're all at sea a bit," Peter said to the Senator's wife. "I don't think any of us really know what's coming."

"The Maya did," Mrs. Carmichael's passion was Native American lore. "Two thousand years ago they said these years we're living now would be the end of the world, and the beginning of a new one. They're right. The world as they knew it, we knew it, is nearly gone."

The Carmichael's country house loomed into view on top of a wooded hill. It was a large frame house with a screened-in porch on three sides. Only a small area had been cleared around the house, except to the southwest where a meadow ran down to the base of the rise and opened to a view of the Hudson and the Catskills beyond. We'll have lunch here, Peter thought as he stood on the side of the porch, and later we'll watch the sun sink behind the river mists and set fire to the distant hills. It will be very still. It could be almost unbearably beautiful.

"Thanks for coming, Peter." Senator Carmichael was dressed in gold corduroy slacks and a red flannel shirt that made his ruddy complexion pale by comparison.

"We were very lucky," he added as he joined Peter on the

veranda. "Farming gave out around here and the mills all closed up shop to get away from the unions fifty, sixty years ago. Until the high-speed came not very many people wanted the commute, even for the weekend. These houses were practically giveaways."

The Senator's wife was wealthy. It embarrasses him, Peter thought, the man is trying to downplay it; he is genuinely modest.

"It's special here. I always enjoy it," Peter replied.

He knew that the Senator would likely remind him again that the area was special, that as he put it, great spirits took roost there; that it was just across the river that Washington Irving heard thunder roll through the valleys like bowling balls; that the whalers had come this far up the Hudson to escape the British during the war of 1812; that one of the great Shaker communities had been just thirty miles east and that America's greatest landscape painter had drawn journeys of the human soul not far down the road.

American Light, the coffee-table book said. American light, Peter mused. In those special moments that came with astounding frequency to the Hudson Valley, the hills, the rivers, the sky, the trees, the clouds, the sun, all seemed luminous, surrendering their shape and strength to the ineffable quality of light.

"Great spirits took roost here," Senator Carmichael said, brushing his silver hair off his forehead. "But I've told you that before." He leaned against the railing and gazed thoughtfully down the meadow. "We have work to do, Peter."

Mrs. Carmichael emerged on to the porch from the dining room, holding a pitcher of iced tea. "The young man needs to eat and he needs to get settled in."

After lunch the Senator carried a white porcelain pot of coffee into his office and beckoned for Peter to join him. Peter sat in an overstuffed chair in the corner. The Senator filled Peter's cup and then settled at his desk.

"Peter, I've been in the Senate almost thirty years. When I started, the Foreign Relations Committee was a joke. It wasn't always like that but it was then. The Chairman couldn't get it up, he couldn't even stay awake, and the ranking minority member was a mean racist who missed his calling. He should have been a prison warden in South Africa. You probably don't remember."

"Actually, I do, I was a little geeky as a kid. I followed the news."

The Senator smiled. "Well I asked to be on the Committee. Everybody thought I was nuts. No freshman wanted to be there because there was hardly anything that you could do for your constituents. I had a feeling, though, that in a few years' time, there would hardly be anything that you couldn't do from the Committee, that virtually every aspect of our life was, to a greater or lesser degree, going to be touched by what went on outside of our borders."

"You were right."

"I knew that a lot of specific problem areas and agreements would get spread out to the other committees but in the end, especially as things got more and more complicated, somebody would have to control the architecture and the jurisdictional lines."

The Senator paused and toyed with a scimitar-shaped letter opener, the memento of a long-ago trip. "So I figured with a bit of adeptness the Foreign Relations Committee could become the arbiter and architect. It was the logical choice. By tradition the Committee got at least concurrent jurisdiction over every treaty the U.S. entered into. The trick was to institutionalize its role in the context of all agreements, not just treaties, before anyone realized how important it was. We pretty much succeeded, and next year I'll be chairman."

"We hope," Peter offered. "Kennedy is capable of anything, most of all changing her mind." He could not contain his dislike of the woman; she was all ambition.

"When I started down this road," the Senator resumed, clasping his hands in front of him on the desk, "it was all about ambition. I won't fool you. I wanted to be President; I thought this was the way. But somewhere something happened. Maybe it was Grace, maybe old age. Maybe I never really quit being a college professor. Some time ago, I couldn't even really say when, I started waking up in the morning with one part of me lecturing the would-be President.

"'You are living in an extraordinary time,' the voice would

say, 'Truly extraordinary. All at once we are all, everybody on this Earth, tied together. The least of this entanglement is that we can blow ourselves up in an instant. But that's too remote, a too profoundly stupid, mad act to be credible. Even with Reagan and Brezhnev it didn't happen. But as to the thousand other threads of everyday and not-so-everyday life, there is no island, there is no refuge where any of us is unaffected by what each of the rest of us do. And I don't just mean my neighbors down the street, I mean the brown and yellow and black and purple people that are in places you think you never heard of, the flesh eaters and the snail eaters and the people who are starving, the ones who burn dung to cook or spill fertilizer by the ton to keep their lawn green, the machos with rifle racks in their pickups, the weirdoes who drink their own urine, the ones who have twenty wives, the ones who wear turbans, the ones who dance in bright clothes, the ones who wear no clothes at all.

"'Something as important as this has happened maybe five times, max, in the history of mankind,' the voice would say, 'Don't be a jerk, this is not the time for ambition. It's just too petty. Do the right thing for once.'

"The voice was right, Peter," the Senator continued. He poured himself another cup of coffee and stirred in a tablespoon of sugar. "The voice was so right that I can't even say that it was to my credit that I listened to it. For a while I tried to convince myself that was all the more reason why I should be President. A man with vision needed to be in control. But the more I watched what was happening, the more convinced I became that one of the things that had to give way, especially for us in the West, was our whole concept of mastery and control. What was happening was too large for anyone—or for that matter any nation—to control. It was manifesting through the thoughts and feeling and activities of millions and millions of people in all kinds of associations and groupings and communities—and by individuals acting alone, too.

"Take your friend in Peru, what was his name, Vasquez?"

"Velasquez."

"Velasquez," the Senator continued, "who could possibly 'manage' what a man like that is doing and make it come out one iota more impactful? Who can even say what he is really doing?

In fact if you tried to manage it, you would probably kill it on the spot or create God knows what other problems."

"Velasquez isn't doing anything anymore," Peter interjected, "He's dead."

"It's like puberty," the Senator continued, "trying to control a society's transformation is like controlling a teenager. Sure you have to set a few limits, give advice and help when you can, but try to sit on it too hard and you'll turn a stage of growth, a passing but powerful formative stage, into a disfigured person, angry, repressed, stunted. All the things you feared the most."

The Senator rose from his seat and looked out the window through branches, green buds barely visible. His back was half turned to Peter.

"And Velasquez? Peter, he was a great man and I know that his death hurt you but from another perspective there will be a hundred others like him—that's just my point. What is happening transcends—an odd word, it makes me uncomfortable, but it's the right one—any person or party or nation."

"I'm not so sure, that there are that many like him." Peter's voice was muted, as if drained of volume by confusion and loss. He wasn't particularly comfortable with the turn of this conversation.

"I'm not trying to diminish him, Peter." The senator turned away from the window to face his aide again. "Let me use another metaphor. I believe history has a purpose. It's like a slow-moving river, so slow at times you don't know that it's moving, much less where. But every once in a while it narrows or takes a big drop, and then there's just no question that that river is going somewhere. Those are the times that history reveals its purposefulness to anybody that wants to see. Not that you can tell where you'll end up by any means, but there's no question that some force beyond us—at least beyond what we think of as ourselves—is pushing the water down the drop and it doesn't need any one or any ten or any thousand of us to do it. That's the kind of time we're in.

"I'm wandering away a bit. Presidents. Being President. If you are President or Prime Minister or King or anything like that, people expect you to be in control, to be held accountable.

You know that, so nothing worries you more than situations that are out of your control. Even bad situations are okay, if they are manageable. But no control is scary. Especially if you have no faith that history, that life itself, is ultimately benign.

"The unguided, spontaneous, multifaceted broth of life is not your ally. It's the human equivalent of earthquakes and hurricanes and floods and droughts. And this isn't just a metaphor. Look at global warming and all the devastation that's causing.

"So if you're President, even if you're not in control, there will be no shortage of people to tell you that you are. You become a captain who thinks that not only is he sailing the ship, he's guiding the river as well. A sure prescription for shipwreck.

"Even if you see this, you can't help yourself, the institution will push you to it. Basically none of this matters when the river's moving slowly but it sure does in a time like ours. The more I thought about it, the more I realized trying to be President was self-defeating. Even if I won, I would lose in the bigger context.

"In a lot of ways," the Senator continued, "a legislative body should work better. It is diversity, it can take the measure of a hundred different currents at once; it can roll with the swells that start at the bottom and push their way up. Moreover, an occasional member, free of overwhelming responsibility for today, may be able to lift his head up for a moment and give voice to tomorrow's aspirations."

"How can you stand it, Peter?" Mrs. Carmichael interjected as she walked through the study doorway. "Surely you need coffee. Lots of coffee. Every time I walk by all I hear is his voice."

The Senator laughed. "Get him some coffee, Grace. I'm not done yet." Peter tried not to smile too broadly.

"But in all this," the Senator resumed, "my thinking was still pretty parochial. I was thinking about our institutions and how they worked because that was where I was planning my career. Then it struck me: this was a much bigger issue. This was an issue that the world as a planetary body was going to have to face. Human society was racing into frightening and unchartered ground and virtually no one was really thinking about how to govern a new world. Yes, I know, we have the United Nations, but the truth is that it was made for another time. Before globalization. And then so many changes happened. For everything from technology to securities to terrorism, suddenly there were no borders. The Force—whatever it is—behind history just decided that it was time for us to grow up and make the whole planet, and all of the people who are on it, a part of our day-to-day consciousness in the same way that we used to think of our fellow Americans, or fellow Germans or fellow whatevers.

"Who knows why it picked now but it did. We're all standing on the bank, watching the river rise and we know that soon, damn soon, we're going to have to figure out what to float away on because there isn't going to be any place that's dry. Now as to what we float on, we really do have a choice. We don't have to settle for what a President tells us or what a bunch of UN bureaucrats crave to make themselves important."

Peter was somewhat taken aback. People who talked about the Purpose of History had gotten a bad name. They were thought of as kin to German idealists, progenitors of Communism and Fascism, or worse, New Age eschatologists or religious crazies. If you were lucky, you might be "interesting" but irrelevant, like Teilhard de Chardin. Peter's political instinct told him that the Senator would soon be saying unfortunate things in public.

But part of him was uplifted. At least this wasn't rail subsidies or haddock fishery quotas or tax credits for sulfur dioxide emission-trapping devices or badgering the Social Security Administration over somebody's benefit denial. Here was a lot of room to grow. Peter formed an impish picture of himself barefoot, fishing pole in hand, floating down the Big River of Human History dispensing philosophy. But he didn't really know what to say, so he adopted the familiar persona of the practical and cynical counselor. "Floats?" he asked, "Is that what we're going to sell the voters, Senator? Floats, sundaes, sodas, the great pleasures of a forgotten age? We and the Duke and the Dauphin. You remember what happened to them?"

"You're very clever, Peter, but we all need to grow up."

"I'm sorry," Peter said knowing he had been childish. "I

know you're serious. But it's a little overwhelming, everything you've said. I don't know what to do. I don't know what I can do."

"I don't know what I can do either, but we can at least think about it—and there is next year's Convocation."

"Where," Peter finished the thought, "the UN Secretariat and the executive departments of most governments will be pushing for a global constitution that stresses the roles of central governmental authorities, planetary and national. Just the kind of thing that you don't want to see happen."

The Senator nodded and smiled kindly.

When the day had passed and the sun was setting, the three of them, Patrick, Grace, and Peter, gathered on the porch to watch the lingering light of day play on patterns of cirrus clouds. Below, in the shadow of the Catskills near the far bank, a white sail bobbed and then disappeared into the dark roils of the river. On the hilltop the wind spoke with a cool sudden gust to those who could hear of a child, swept down in a cold, fierce current, towards the city and the sea.

WILLIAM H. ESPINOSA

CHAPTER 17

It was a Monday First early in the Second Year. A warm winter sun reflected off the river and glistened in the United Nations building glass. One hundred ninety-six flags snapped arhythmically in a brisk wind. At the building's entrance a tall dark man with an energetic gait presented his new pass to security and a few minutes later stepped off the elevator into the 38th floor's carefully controlled environment for the first time. Rashid O'Shea was shown his office overlooking Second Avenue. He placed a laptop on his desk and a dozen books on the adjoining shelf, propped up by an intricate, hardwood block-carving of a crow riding on the back of a leaping orca. His unpacking completed, Rashid went from room to room introducing himself in various languages. Nowhere are more languages mispronounced than at the United Nations, so his unusual accent and syntactical difficulty were readily accepted. The effort was appreciated, particularly by those who had not heard their mother language in months.

Rashid was youthful in appearance and intense in manner, but he had a penetrating curiosity and a sensitivity that would have taken most people a lifetime to cultivate. By the end of the day all eighty-two people on the floor had been asked about his or her origins, work, and the well-being of their families. The Africans, Asians, and Caribbeans took Rashid's dark skin as a sign of fraternity. He emanated sympathy when the harshness of life in the poorer regions of the globe was discussed. He agreed that the continuing disparities of income and resource consumption between the South and the North were intolerable and rolled his eyes or placed an understanding arm around a shoulder when one or another incidence of insufferable American or European arrogance was recounted.

The European and North American civil servants were drawn to the lightness and humor of his Irish eyes. Most knew or soon learned that he was British by birth and his Cambridge degree, regimental striped tie, and well-tailored suit also served to put them at ease. Rashid approached the white-skinned ones with slightly greater restraint and less physical contact. His mannerisms were precise imitations of the British upper-middle-class, leaving the impression that he was an aspiring second- or third-generation immigrant from the former colonies, well-trained and highly intelligent, who had shed the histories of his parents to fully adopt the reigning values of the country of his birth. For good measure, he would occasionally inquire about cricket matches in Central Park and speak of looking forward to donning his whites.

With the Europeans and North Americans, Rashid shared the sense of urgency that most felt for restoring Earth balance through vigorous global measures. He shook his head and extended a sympathetic hand when he heard stories of intolerable inefficiencies and corruption in the governance of the most desperately impoverished peoples whom the UN and the West were so earnestly trying to help. His head would nod in vigorous agreement when colleagues suggested that the poverty of the poorest nations would only be broken when their elites allowed their own societies to shed their historically dysfunctional concepts, benighted superstitions, and forms of governance and adopt Western precepts of enterprise and freedom. With everyone he met who raised the subject, of whatever color, he would ask "higher powers" to protect them all from the insularity of the U.S. Congress which continued to control far too much of the global entities' budgets.

The Undersecretariat for Program and Planetary Management Planning, which occupied the 38th floor, was of recent creation. It had been organized in the aftermath of the Debtor's Revolt in the summer of the last year of the old era when the average global temperature peaked at 3.5 degrees Fahrenheit above the previous century's norm. There was near-universal agreement among the planet's intelligentsia that the time was fast approaching when new international structures would have to be put in place to deal with the challenges for the coming century and that little thought or consensus building had gone into creating them. Recidivist nationalists, oil companies, and a number of oil-producing nations nearly succeeded in blocking the creation of the Undersecretariat, but the impasse was broken when powerful American Planetary Securitists gave their support to the proposal. The key was extraction of an agreement from the Secretary General and Security Council that the first Undersecretary would be one of their own, a former U.S. Defense official who had made his mark by refocusing the U.S. military budget to support the "smart" weapons, surveillance, and civic action that helped make the Terrorist Interlude a short one.

The workings of the Undersecretariat were veiled from public view, but even the more casual observers of the United Nations noticed that those assigned to the Undersecretariat were young, often ambitious, and highly credentialed. The purely political appointments that so burdened other agencies were rarely made and if an appointee proved to be simply a sinecure seeker or lazy or incompetent, his or her life was made miserable and an appointment elsewhere was found.

One of the senior faculty members at Caius College had found Rashid's work interesting and had recommended him to a colleague already employed by the Undersecretariat. "Dear Cecil," the letter began, "I commend to you one of our graduates of a few years back. He has spent an interesting period dealing with the tribals of British Columbia. It strikes me that his experience working in a system that gives seemingly effectual lip service to an illusory sovereignty would prove valuable as you and your team prepare to do battle with the irredentists and the vestiges of the nation-states. A summary of his research is enclosed. O'Shea is a bit of a mongrel by birth and rather a charming chap, qualities that could be put to good use in bringing some of the non-Westerners around...."

Rashid was assigned to the working group responsible for conceptualizing intergovernmental relationships that would support serious global enforcement of the Planetary Defense Program. The Program itself, or the PDP as it came to be known, was still in conception and was receiving the closest attention from the Undersecretary and his immediate staff. Somewhat sanitized drafts were regularly made available to Rashid's working group. The Undersecretary himself occasionally attended their meetings and UNINTEL provided periodic intelligence reports on diverse topics including global climate-change patterns, deforestation on a region-by-region basis, trends in species extinction, and identification of peoples and groups "in denial," as one UNINTEL report sensitively put it, who might resist implementation of the PDP or who might be prone to one of the occasional epidemic-like outbreaks of consumption frenzy.

The PDP's aim was to identify the key battlegrounds in the coming war against planetary devastation. Recognizing that significant territory would almost certainly have to be abandoned at least temporarily, and that the limited resources even a well-organized human society would be able to bring to bear were potentially inadequate to the task, careful targeting would be essential. One part of the PDP dealt with the identification, development, and dissemination of those technologies which promised the highest returns in energy efficiency, carbon-emission reduction, and adaptive genetic engineering. Another part identified key civil works needed to protect productive population centers, "must-hold" ecosystems of bio-diversity, and influential media centers that could be deployed to affect global attitudes and compliance. Other sections targeted likely centers of resistance which might need to be placed under protective UN custody. These included populations in fundamentally indefensible areas where desertification and industrial poisoning were too far advanced or where catastrophic flooding was inevitable.

In the afternoon of the Monday First of Rashid's arrival another new recruit to the Undersecretariat made her entrance. Erika Svendstrom's appearance proved nearly as memorable as Rashid's. Erika was from Sweden, the daughter of the scion of a prominent banking family and a graduate of Uppsala University. Her brother Alfred was said to be courting the heiress-apparent to the Swedish throne. Erika was nearly six feet tall, long-legged and blond. She had prominent cheekbones that reminded many of a mid-twentieth-century Swedish film actress who, legend had it, gave up a great love in Morocco to help save the world from Nazi domination. Erika's cheekbones encased ice-blue eyes that seemed to be illuminated by a thousand white Christmas lights or the chandeliers of Versailles. Erika smiled graciously at those who crossed her path, but most were far too intimidated to do more than smile in return.

Erika encountered Rashid coming out of the personnel director's office as she prepared to enter it. For several seconds they stood perhaps six feet apart. Erika appeared transfixed by the depth and energy of Rashid's darkness; Rashid appeared to dissolve in the cool white glow that Erika's lightly tanned body seemed to exude and in the piercing luminescence of her eyes.

"I am Rashid O'Shea," he said, arching his tufted eyebrows. "Or at least so I thought until I met you."

"And who are you now, Mr. O'Shea?"

"I was an Irish seed cast in an Indian furrow after a few too many rounds of stout," he replied. "But right now," he smiled, "I am anyone you want me to be."

"I did not know the Irish could be so dark... Be yourself, Rashid, but do not go too far away," Erika replied in near-perfect English. Only a slight ta-te-ta Swedish rhythm and avoidance of contractions betrayed that she had mastered the language in school and not in life. "We do not have many like you where I come from."

"And where might that be?"

"You will have to entertain me to learn my secrets."

From all accounts that is what Rashid did. In the week before appearing at the 38th floor and with the help of an attractive rickshaw driver who was apprenticing with a dance company and as a professional mime, Rashid had explored much of the city. He had found nooks and crannies filled with music from some of the most remote corners of the world, often with food to match. Now he put his newly acquired knowledge of food and culture to use. He took Erika to hear Uzbek drums accompany

Naqshbandi Sufi chants. She heard Bolivian flutes that pierced the heart with the clarity of a parrot's call, and Inuit singers that used multiple harmonics to transport her into an altered state. Erika ate seasoned goat hind, iguana with mole sauce, and asam laksa mixed with the flower petals of the Penang. And the drums—Rashid found centers of West African drumming and dancing where the audience joined in as the night wore on. Erika gave herself over to insistent rhythms and vigorous movements late into the night. She reveled in the drink and sweat and smells of closed-in places that could barely contain the exuberant human energy of hundreds. Rashid took her to Harlem to hear young musicians revive the sounds of another age: B.B. King, James Brown, and the twentieth-century master, Chuck Berry. He took her to Lincoln Center to lose herself in the arias of Puccini and to laugh at the Marriage of Figaro. They found revival movie houses where they could see the films of Woody Allen and Erika's national favorite, Ingmar Bergman, as well as the giant-screen sensodromes where movement, sound, and even smell mixed with an enveloping visual experience to transport the audience through one or another fantastic adventure. Erika found herself particularly excited by one that ended with the execution of the Russian Czar's family nearly a century earlier (the seats jolted; the sounds were of deafening gunfire, tearing flesh, and screaming; the smells were of urine, blood and gunpowder, and the screen turned red and black). But the show hinted at the miraculous escape and survival of a child, and on Erika's mother's side, it appeared, there was a formidable woman of Russian nobility who had escaped to Sweden around the time of the Communist revolution. "We were never quite sure who she really was," Erika often said.

Rashid found more intimate forms of entertainment for her as well. They were seen at the Whip-Her-Well and at the Bottom's Up Cafe. They frequently came into work together with a palpable charge between them, and Erika often responded to late night, after-work calls from a v-phone that had a Brooklyn prefix. Rashid had somehow found a very affordable two-bedroom apartment in a dilapidated five-story building near the base of the Brooklyn Bridge that Erika fearlessly visited. He attributed this find also to the skill of his rickshot, as the rickshaw drivers were known, whom he had befriended his first day in New York.

A few months after Rashid and Erika's arrival, the Undersecretary's principal deputy, a former German diplomat, addressed their working group meeting.

"We face a dilemma," he said, "which you should not ignore in your proceedings. The dilemma is this: On the one hand, in implementing a PDP, we must keep to a bare minimum its intrusion into private matters and avoid exacerbating the sensitivities of local cultures, however primitive they may be. On the other hand we must deal effectively with those centers of resistance which truly have the potential to disrupt our plan. And this brings us to the matter of religion, which still holds sway in some of the backwaters of our world. The Catholics remain determined to reduce sex to a procreative act and thus doom," at this point the Deputy's lip curled up into a half-snarling smile, "our population reduction efforts, since as we all know it is these very Catholics that often seem to engage in sex the most. And then there are the fundamentalist Moslems who would lock women into ignorance and archaic roles, reducing them to subservient breeding machines. And then we have the Russian Orthodox who want to build up nationalist walls that are not going to make our lives any easier... " The Deputy Undersecretary paused. "So what place do we find for these superstitions? Where do we put them? How do we control them? We need creative solutions."

"Herr Deputy Undersecretary," Erika offered, "I think you worry too much. Except for maybe the Muslims, these things only appeal to the ignorant, to rural people and the very old. They are not that powerful. In Sweden we give those people other things more important to them...pensions, farm supports...and to the church, we give holidays and festivals to run. The priests can dress up and feel important, but they are harmless. If worse comes to worst, threaten to tax the priests; they will shut up, saying to themselves it is more important that they keep the church in some form alive."

Erika paused for a few moments, noting that the Deputy Undersecretary was listening closely. "The Russians did something similar," she continued with a wry smile, "except instead of festivals they encouraged fasts, making virtue of a necessity. Peter, Catherine, even Joseph Stalin, all figured that one out."

Gentle laughter spread through the room. "Thank you," the Deputy Undersecretary replied, looking at Erika with growing interest. He glanced down at a paper on his podium. "Ms. Svendstrom... may I call you Erika? What you say of the past may be true. Now, how do we do it today?"

Rashid was not amused. He was the first to answer. "Before you ask that question, sir, it is perhaps worth remembering that it is men and women imbued with a religious spirit who more often than not have saved us from the worst human cruelties and excesses. They seem to be the ones who will comfort the hopeless and feed the destitute or take great risks for justice and freedom. Why do we think they won't help us lead the way in facing our global crisis? Islamic centers humanized the Mongol conquerors and Christian monasteries preserved caritas and gnosis in the Dark Ages through the pillages of your Germanic ancestors. Perhaps we should not consign those who are still in touch with our spiritual nature to ridicule."

The Deputy Undersecretary's eyes narrowed and he looked again at the papers on his podium. "Mr. O'Shea? Rashid O'Shea?"

"Yes."

"How convenient. Apparently you are both a Muslim and a Catholic. A shame your mother couldn't have two husbands, then you could be a Russian too and we could send you out to solve all of our problems!"

Rashid paused and then smiled, "Bach, Beethoven, Schiller, Kant, Goethe, Martin Luther, Einstein...the pinnacles of your people's culture were moved by deep spiritual experience.... Why do you ridicule this elsewhere? Didn't the last century teach you what happens when you distort or suppress it?"

The Deputy Undersecretary's face darkened. He said nothing and moved on to another questioner.

CHAPTER 18

As the months accumulated past an anniversary, Erika and Rashid's relationship continued unabated. They still came into the UN building together more often than not, though the flush at the nape of Erika's neck showed less often when she unwrapped the scarf she wore against the New York-winter cold and Rashid's smile was not quite as broad as it had been in the first heady days. Despite occasional impertinences and indiscretions, Rashid's work seemed well-respected and early promotion seemed likely. He maintained his decorous British style and dress and seemed particularly popular with the senior British and American officials.

Only once did he create a noticeable disturbance. One morning, he and Erika came into work thirty minutes late, rather obviously still carnally enchained. A staff meeting was in progress. Whether it was jealousy or genuine concern for the workings of his staff, the group head took the occasion to reprimand the two—he actually addressed Rashid—on how important it was to know what others were doing, and that was why they had these morning office meetings. Rashid apologized and then gave a two-minute précis of what had transpired at the meeting up to the moment of his arrival, including UNINTEL's statistics on the rate of rain-forest loss in Paraguay.

A stunned silence gripped the room which was only broken when one of Rashid's friends joked, "He was listening at the door. I see him do it all the time."

A few nervous laughs could be heard in the room. Another colleague added, "Either that or we are so predictable, we say the same thing at every meeting." That too elicited laughter but everyone knew it was not true. The meeting continued.

Erika remained silent, her face ashen.

One of those in the room that day was Rafael Cabrera. Rafael was an administrative assistant to the American representative who sat on the Planetary Defense Force Subgroup of the Undersecretariat. Rafael was from New Mexico. He was dark-skinned and usually dressed in monochrome clothing that was either too baggy or too tight. He avoided eye contact with most of his colleagues and said little. Most of Rafael's family, his father had assured him, had lived in New Mexico since the seventeenth century. His father was a liberal man, and unlike many Hispanos, he freely acknowledged another ancestral strand: His grandmother was a San Felipe Pueblo Indian. Rafael's father took pride in this thousand-year-old root. His mother, a small, withdrawn woman, was more reticent about her ancestry, but she shared a last name—Romero—which seemed ubiquitous along the old conquistador route that followed the Rio Grande.

Rafael had interrupted his undergraduate studies at Colorado College to spend a year at the University of Guadalajara in Mexico, where he had immersed himself in the history of the Spanish conquest and its living aftermath in Mexican society. The year transformed him. He came to see himself as both conquered and conqueror, as oppressor and oppressed. He maintained many contacts in Mexico and decided to dedicate his life in whatever way he could to bringing an end to the seemingly endless cycles of conquest and exploitation that plagued human history.

Rashid, in his always-engaging manner, had spoken to Rafael a few times so it was not surprising that Rafael joined him as they walked out the front entrance of the building past blooming red and yellow tulips on a brisk, sun-filled day not long afterwards. They had both been at a session where the topic was the importance of organizing a global early warning and defense system against extraterrestrial invasion. Evidence of the imminence of an attack was agreed to be scant (though the reports of a reverse Fibonacci pulse signal was given some credence), but the effort was nonetheless viewed as one of enormous value. The rallying cry of defense against external threat had brought many a nation together and strengthened their central governments. The same, it was hoped, would prove true on a global basis in bringing all of humankind together. Even if the extraterrestrial danger never materialized, the threat would create a strengthened governmental entity that could more effectively address ecological catastrophe and other human needs.

"Rashid, have you heard of La *Malinche*?" Rafael asked.

Rashid looked at Rafael with surprise. "No."

"She was the daughter of an Aztec chieftain who sold her into slavery when her mother died."

"And?"

"She only lived in the body for twenty-four years but she's lived in our language for five hundred years. We have a word, *malinchismo*. "

"What are you saying?"

"Malinche was brilliant and spoke several Indian languages. Cortes found her in Tabasco. He took her and screwed her, taught her Spanish and spoke through her to the Indians. The two grew close and she told him all about the peoples he was conquering. Behind his back the Indians called Cortes *Señor Malinche*."

"What is a *malin...* "

"*...chismo*? It's what happens in a culture when a lot of people forget who they are and embrace a foreign way."

For a moment a shadow crossed Rashid's face. Then he smiled broadly and embraced Rafael. "I have done nothing," Rashid said, "to deserve a friend like you."

Rafael looked squarely at Rashid. "Malinche had a son, Martin she called him, by Cortes. When Martin went back to Spain everybody knew him as *El Bastardo*."

In the weeks that followed Rashid was seen more and more often in the company of Rafael. This surprised many. While Rafael was well-placed, he was essentially a clerical employee and not known as a thinker or particularly remarkable figure. As the summer progressed, Rashid's dress changed, at first subtly and then more obviously. After the fourth of July he took to wearing ties that were garish versions of UN member state flags. In mid-August, after spending two weeks with Erika and her visiting brother on Nantucket, he came to work one day wearing Bermuda shorts and penny loafers. By September the ties had been abandoned altogether and he was never again seen in a white shirt. Despite the change in dress, however, his verbal impertinences remained only occasional and the originality of his thinking and problem-solving abilities continued to impress his superiors. If a problem were perceived at all, it lay in Rashid's optimistic view of the processes of nature and the wisdom of ordinary human beings. He also expressed aversion to the use of force. This latter quality was not unusual among younger, still idealistic people at the Undersecretariat, but it faded for most as they confronted in starker and starker terms the grim reality that awaited humanity (and many other species) if drastic changes were not made.

Alfred, Erika's brother, had returned to Stockholm after a summer interlude in the United States, most of which he had spent sailing a thirty-two-foot sloop with an American friend along Cape Cod and the Rhode Island coast. He had spent considerable time with Rashid and though his sister seemed happy, Rashid made him uncomfortable. More importantly, he had difficulty visualizing the Swedish royal family's acceptance of Rashid as an in-law. He discussed the problem with his mother Ing Marie over tea at the Grand Hotel, watching the sun set behind the royal palace.

"He's strange looking, very dark-skinned. His father is a drunk and his mother is an immigrant. What's more—I know Erika seems happy—but I think he's led her to some bad places."

"We'll see," his mother replied, "perhaps her attraction will pass."

By early November, it was becoming increasingly clear to Ing Marie that if her son were to seek the royal engagement, it would have to be in the next few months. Erika was continuing to see Rashid. Ing Marie flew to New York, summoned Erika to her hotel room, and met with her alone.

"Erika, I wanted to talk to you before I meet this Rashid

O'Shea because I want you to know that it is not about liking him or not," she began. "It is your life to live and yours to choose with whom to share it. But I must ask you to help me and Alfred and your father and the rest of your family and to consider also your own life and what your heritage has given you…what you have been raised for."

Erika glared at her mother. "Are you telling me not to see Rashid? If so, please go home now."

"No, Erika. Of course I would not tell you that. I am asking you to consider seeing other people as well for a year or so. That's all. It will give you a surer sense of what you deeply desire. To be sure it may be he. In the meantime, however, it will help us all immensely. You see, Rashid may be hard to explain to the crown. And it would shatter your brother if he couldn't marry Kristina. Kristina loves him but she is constrained in what she can do. It would be a loss for us all.

"If the marriage happens," Erika's mother continued, "you too will have a title. Think how much good for the world you could do as a member of the royal family. If you're seeing others, we have no need to explain him."

Erika sat pensively for several minutes and then nodded. "It is not unreasonable. I'll think about it. Now, I'm starved. Rashid took me to a great Indian restaurant in Chelsea…"

Erika's mother expressed some disdain for "curry houses" as she called them so dinner was at an elegant French restaurant which Erika's mother knew. The restaurant overlooked the south side of Central Park. Rashid was waiting at a table by the window; a candle illuminated his face from below and accentuated the shadows cast by his prominent nose. He rose to greet them, and as he did so he glanced quizzically with reddened eyes at Erika.

"Your daughter is so much like you," he said to Ing Marie taking her hand in his, "I am twice blessed."

Rashid made Erika's decision easy for her. As the evening progressed, uncharacteristically, he drank profusely and talked more loudly. He inserted his smallest finger in his ear and spun it around to extract a globule of wax. He burped twice and ordered a heavy cabernet to accompany the Dover sole. He ordered ketchup for his pommes frites. Over desert, he asked if the

Swedish banks had kept Nazi gold like the Swiss ones had, and on the way out, he kissed Erika's mother on the lips, letting his tongue flick over her gritted teeth.

After that Erika and Rashid spent less time together. She dated other men. On several occasions she was seen at the opera accompanied by the Principal Deputy Undersecretary. She was first in her group to receive a promotion. There seemed, nonetheless, to be a continuing bond between Rashid and Erika, even if some anger or irritation occasionally surfaced. No one could decipher the situation but rumors were rampant.

In February of the next year, Senzo Sato, future Secretary General of the United Nations who was then head of the UN Population Program spoke to Erika and Rashid's group. Sato was a slightly built man with intelligent eyes, an angular face, accentuated by black swept-back hair, and large teeth that smiled easily. He appeared at least ten years younger than his fifty-four years.

The third son of a lesser Japanese shipping baron who's business had been built through linkages with aspiring politicians and, it was rumored, underworld, yakuza elements, Senzo had from the earliest age been determined not to follow his older brothers into the family business. He had been his mother's favorite and with her encouragement and evident abilities had excelled at every academic level and graduated near the top of his class from Japan's most elite institution, Tokyo University.

From an early age he must also have sensed that his future lay beyond Japan's shores and applied himself to learning English. At every possible occasion he attended American, English, and Australian films or engaged Americans in conversation. He even went so far as to devote some of his play time to Tokyo's late night "English conversation bars" that featured topless instructors.

After graduation he worked for the powerful Ministry of International Trade and Industry, MITI, where he was presumed to be destined for the highest echelons but after a two-year stint in Tokyo persuaded his superiors to send him for graduate study at Berkeley. While he was at Berkeley he became absorbed in the problems of population growth and resource depletion. He was also attracted by the vibrancy of the Zen Buddhist community in the Bay area which stood in contrast to its declining role in Japan. Through that community he met his future wife Yoriko, a Japanese-American student at Santa Cruz whom everyone called Yori.

Senzo and Yori returned to Japan after he completed his studies but Senzo found himself dissatisfied with his work at MITI which seemed devoted solely to enhancing the wealth of a few. He persuaded his mother to convince his father to use his political connections to obtain a post for him in the UN system, preferably with UNFPA, the United Nations Fund for Population Activities. This was accomplished with no particular difficulty, though both his father and MITI colleagues evinced in the subtlest of inflections a befuddled mixture of incredulity, betrayal, and contempt. It was sometimes suggested that Senzo's conduct verged on the inappropriately self-assertive and reflected poorly on MITI and Japanese society generally. Others defended him; if these tendencies had manifested, they should be traced to the American upbringing of his wife and appropriate allowances made.

Senzo Sato performed well at UNFPA in various assignments all over the world. At the meeting in nearly flawless English, he made a chilling presentation on the outcome of current demographic trends, particularly in the Middle East, Latin America, and portions of South Asia.

South Asia became the focus of attention because it had the largest population. Various birth control strategies were raised by the participants. Rashid, with the evident approval of Senzo, suggested that the problem might be better solved by bypassing it than by tackling it head on. Hadn't providing educational and economic opportunities to women always reduced birthrates? Was the same not true when societies as a whole became economically secure? Or when child labor laws removed the economic incentive to have more children?

Erika became impatient as Rashid spoke. She had often cited with pride her own nation's less-than-replacement fertility rate and deeply feared that the world's multiplying poor would, like locusts, consume what resources survived the ecological catastrophe, reducing all to starvation.

"Rashid," she interrupted, "that is all fine but it takes

generations. We don't have generations. If these people do not stop breeding soon, we will all be dead. We have to have strong measures, like the Chinese did, compulsory, one child per family. I mean, what have these people given us in the last fifty years that's worth a damn anyway? Grief and a beggar's bowl and now with Kashmir, damn near a nuclear war, that's all. Nothing. We have nothing to lose if not another one is born."

A stunned silence descended over the conference table. Most realized that more than political conviction or cultural prejudice was involved. All eyes were downcast; a few turned towards Rashid.

Rashid looked at Erika. His eyes were gentle but his voice was firm. "Thank you for your contribution, Erika." He turned to Senzo Sato. "With your permission, sir, I would like to excuse myself briefly." Sato nodded his assent.

Rashid did not return that afternoon, but he did the next day and each day after that until the equinox. Then he told his superiors that to better serve them, he needed to expand his knowledge of nature and human society and wished to return to British Columbia and perhaps travel in Latin America. It was his wish that he could maintain his connection with the Undersecretariat, perhaps through a consultancy. His superiors readily agreed, hoping he would soon return on a full-time basis.

The first of May was Rashid's last day. He brought a garland of flowers, which he placed on Erika's head and told her he would always keep her in his heart. He embraced her and as he did so her body trembled. She buried her head on his shoulder, clothing his heart in her long flaxen hair and leaving a small, moist stain on his jacket. Rashid continued to hold her and then said his farewells to everyone on the floor. He took special time with Rafael and told him that they would stay in touch. Then he went up a flight of stairs to take leave of the Undersecretary and had a long farewell talk with Senzo. When he descended to ground level and walked into the sunlight, boisterous lunch-hour crowds were all around him. He made his way through them to a rickshaw where two packed suitcases and Jane LaForce, dancer, rickshot, and mime, awaited him.

CHAPTER 19

It was the morning that David had read about the investigation of Matteo Michelson's death and Rashid O'Shea had called that it started. By breakfast's end Laura had slipped away into one of her intermediate worlds, a world ruled by an unknown pantheon whose commands only Laura seemed to understand. In the afternoon Laura rearranged the photographs and knickknacks on her dresser. She laid all of her clothes out on the bed. By day's end she had returned all of them to the closet and the top of the dresser was just as it had been before. She took a small, Bolivian mountain-landscape her mother had given her down from the living room wall. She tested it on every wall space in every room only to return it to where it first hung. As she marched from room to room, David felt as if the house were filling with a disembodied, voiceless anger; he felt the anger harden as the sun dropped and the day cooled. By evening the passion that was so often alive between them was retreating quietly into the surrounding forest's shadows. He chased after it desperately but that night—the next to last night that she had allowed it—he made love to little more than a pliant mechanism.

Two weeks later, on the night of Exu Gira Mundi, he realized that even more was wrong. Laura's memory sat as strongly with David as the aroma of the coffee resting in front of him at the street-side cafe. The bustle of people making their way to work after a long lunch hour intruded pleasantly from the street. David looked across a small metal table and thought how little Miguel had changed. Miguel was a boy of eleven when they first met more than twenty-five years ago in a classroom in San Jose, maybe twenty blocks from where they were sitting. Miguel had grown stocky and balded a bit but he still exuded that sense of warmth and decency which had drawn David to him. He found that quality often in Costa Rica, surprisingly often. It was the coming together of people that mattered here, more than what was said.

David spoke to Miguel of the memory of Laura. "It's hard. In a way it's harder than those all-consuming passions we knew when we were young. There was no room for anything else while they were there, but when they were gone, they were gone."

"You've always been looking, David, looking, finding, and not finding. Splendid women all, but somehow they couldn't quite give... or couldn't quite stay. Marta, Consuelo, Ingrid, Eugenia—and who was that one from California with the hippy parents?"

Miguel smiled.

David had to smile too. "Sansemilla."

"Sam. I was in love with her too. She was so blond and healthy."

"And never wore a bra."

"And never wore a bra," Miguel readily agreed. "Rhymed couplets, poetry in motion."

"As long as she didn't speak." David felt his mood lightening. Miguel might be right. Laura's departure might have been for the best. "You know, Miguel, the morning it all started, this man called. I'd met him in Hawaii, a very unusual man. He said our paths would be crossing again soon and he just wanted to keep in touch. And by the way he had just heard a story that he thought was a little strange that he had this irresistible urge to tell me.

"'David,' he said, 'it goes like this. Once upon a time there was a farmer and he woke up one morning and went to his barn. The barn door was open and it caused him fear. Sure enough, he looked inside and his prize horse, the fastest one around, was nowhere to be seen. The man was crushed, his greatest pride was gone. He had been offered a small fortune for it, almost the value of his farm.

""""God," he said as he fell to his knees, "how could you have visited such a calamity upon me? What have I done to deserve this? Bring me back my horse."

"'No answer came so he sent his son out to look for the horse and while his son was out, the tax assessor came and he looked around the man's farm and then said to him, "It is said that you have a horse of great value. I don't see it here."

""""I no longer have it sir, it ran away."

"'The tax assessor was skeptical and he found excuses to stay around all day, but when the sun set and there was no sign of the horse, he went on his way.

"'The next morning, the son returned leading the horse behind him. The farmer was in ecstasy and he fell to his knees, "Oh God," he said, "you have saved me from paying an unjust tax to a government that squanders and oppresses. How could I have doubted the justice of your ways!"

""""Well, the following day the farmer sent his son into town on the horse to bring back some supplies and on the way back, the horse suddenly shied away from a shadow. The movement sent the son sprawling on the road. The horse, riderless, picked his way home. The farmer saw it, seized it by the reins and galloped toward town in a desperate search for his son. He found him moaning by the roadside, his right leg twisted, broken below the knee.

""""Oh God," the farmer said as he fell to his knees, "I have lost my son for the harvest time. The fruit will rot on the vine. Oh, God, why have you cursed me with this horse!"

"'Well the harvest time came and the son was still in bed, leg useless, still many weeks from being healed. As the farmer worked one day to salvage what he could alone, he saw a cloud of dust move toward him on the road. It was a military troop come to impress the young into service. They stopped at the farm and asked the farmer to take them to his son. He led the sergeant to the bedroom where he saw the broken leg "This boy is useless to us," the sergeant said, "but your fruit we can use. We will pay a fair price and harvest it ourselves."

"'When the soldiers were gone, the farmer fell on his knees.

"Oh God, oh mighty God, how do You tolerate my foolishness. Again I doubted Your justice. You saved this, my last son, from sure slaughter in an unjust war and tended to my harvest needs. Praise be to the horse, the instrument of Your ways!"

"'More time passed. The army had triumphed and enriched the kingdom. Since nearly all the families in the farmer's region had given a son to the effort, they became rich with plunder on their sons' return. The farmer, once looked up to for his prosperity, was now scorned for his poverty.

"'Oh God,' the farmer said raising his fist to heaven, "You have saddled me with this beast that drags my life down. Why did You not let him escape!'"

"'And so it went, back and forth, for the rest of the farmer's life, almost until the very end.'"

Miguel considered the story for a moment, took a sip of coffee and watched an attractive young woman in a yellow dress walk by. "And what happened at the very end?" he asked.

"He didn't say."

"Did you tell your friend about Laura?"

"No. I didn't know anything was happening then. I just had my usual low-level anxiety that things might not work out but that was all."

"And later?"

"I can't reach him. I've tried a few times, even left messages, but no call back." David flagged down the waiter and asked him to bring him a pastry.

"You know, Miguel, there is a sloth that lives in the rain forest, it spends all of the time high in the trees where it's relatively safe—except that once every week or two it climbs all the way down just to defecate a few little pellets and bury them in the ground next to the tree where it lives. In this way it nourishes the tree that gives it life.

"And when it's down there, defecating on the ground, that is its time of greatest vulnerability. Maybe love is like that. We have to expose ourselves in order to nourish that which gives sustenance to our lives."

"I like the analogy, David," Miguel deadpanned, "except it seems like it's somebody else's shit that you're always trying to nourish yourself with. There has to be a better way.

"What you need," Miguel continued with a conviction born of experience, "are some simple, uncomplicated pleasures in your life."

"I have that, Miguel. A functional home in a beautiful setting in a beautiful country and a job that lets me work to make it even more beautiful."

"I mean other people. You know there are people for whom giving comes easily."

"Maybe. Maybe it's just that there are some people for whom taking comes easily. Those who want to give don't really know how. So they find the takers and leave it up to them."

Miguel grew thoughtful and finished his coffee. "Join us this weekend, David. Isabel has some friends that are dropping by."

"Thanks, I may." David was uncertain as to whether to tell Miguel more. The weekend might be a better time. But the arrival of his pastry and the sight of two policemen, unarmed except for a small club wrapped in leather ruffles and crossing the street outside the cafe spurred him on.

"It's not just Laura, Miguel. There's something else I wanted to talk to you about."

Miguel looked up from the check and settled back in his chair, "Yes, tell me."

"I know you'll think that this is strange…."

"Nothing could surprise me, not with you."

"I've felt like I'm being watched sometimes. Ever since the Michelson story broke, there have been phone calls with no voice at the other end. I thought maybe they were for Laura, but there's also been a hollowness in the phone sometimes and twice there've been couples parked on the road near our house… "

"Couples?"

"Yeah, I've never seen anyone do that before. In three weeks, twice. Not the same couple either. Today there was a white electric van that followed me almost all the way here."

"But that's natural David, most traffic in the morning would come into town."

"Not at the pace I did. I stopped three times and somehow the van always wound up behind me."

"Your father's son," said Miguel.

David smiled and threatened to throw a wadded napkin in

Miguel's face. David's father had first come to Costa Rica with the Agency for International Development not long after the Contra years. Miguel had always insisted, sometimes jokingly, sometimes not, that he was really a CIA operative, come to destroy a cradle of peace and democracy.

"Did you see who it was?" Miguel asked.

"No. Too far away and the windows were tinted." David paused and took a large bite out of his pastry, chewed it slowly and then sat back.

"And Miguel, as much as she's hurt me, I'm still worried about Laura. She called a few days ago. She was semi-coherent. I wanted to talk about us but she didn't. She wanted me to know where she was—in case anything happened, she said. She was scared of something. She talked about a Mayan magician she was supposed to meet in the Yucatan. And she did meet him and then she didn't. He—or Carlos, the creep that she ran off with—didn't show up when they were supposed to next meet and she found some old book that sounded just like it had stolen the script from the Mayan. She thought maybe she was being tricked but she didn't know how or why and maybe could I just come to Merida for a day or two? Then she called again, and said the Mayan had phoned her to tell her she might want to bring me—that Carlos had some other task."

"You didn't?"

"Didn't what?"

"Agree to go?"

"No, but I'm beginning to think that maybe I should."

Miguel clasped his hand over David's forearm on the table, "David, please come and join us Friday. This has got to end."

"Something is wrong Miguel. I'm not a paranoid person."

Miguel's eyes became as gentle as his voice. He reached across the table and clasped David's hand, "No you're not, David, but you love too easily. Why on earth would anything sinister be interested in you or Laura?"

"I don't know. Michelson. ... I don't know. We hardly knew him."

"Promise Friday and the weekend?"

Miguel tightened his grip on David's hand. David stared blankly out at the street.

"Listen, David, if Laura's in a personal jam, she'll get out on her own. She and her famous goddess always do. She doesn't need you."

David said nothing.

The two men got up from the table, exchanged an abrazo at the door and headed in opposite directions down the street.

"Thanks, my friend," David shouted over his shoulder, "I'll come," but his voice was swallowed in the city sounds.

CHAPTER 20

Nostalgia seized him. Seeing Miguel, he had decided to revisit his old neighborhood. He took a bus that followed the same route that he had taken from school as a child every day for four years. Out Avenida Pavas, around the Parque La Sabana. There was a profusion of political posters plastered on building walls, much as there had been twenty years earlier; even the names seemed not to have changed much. Then he continued past the television station where Miguel's father would sometimes take them to be part of the audience of the Saturday morning kids' shows, and into a neighborhood that was more clearly residential.

David got off at a stop next to a modest shopping center. Houses surrounded it on three sides. On the fourth side, the center faced an imposing concrete structure with slit-like windows. The structure was surrounded by a metal grate fence set on elevated concrete two and a half feet above the sidewalk. It looked like a fortress. It had been and still was the American Embassy. Little had changed. The concrete had lost a bit of its color and become spotted here and there. There were rust stains on the bulwark underneath the metal fence posts. The most noticeable change was the absence of the lingering cloud of blue-black exhaust fumes that had always framed the view from where he was standing. That and the new entrances. Unguarded entrances that people and even cars could go through unimpeded.

There were one or two marines in evidence but they appeared to be unarmed. They were distinguished by the ceremonial ghoutra, the Arab headdress which the veterans of the Middle East Forces during the Wars Against Terror were allowed to wear.

The Embassy compound had just been built when David's family first came to San Jose in the late 1980s. David's father was appalled when he first saw it. "It's a proconsul's palace," he'd said. "Castle is a better word. This is good will? I'm supposed to help these people. This is a goddamned fear machine, ours and theirs."

David's mother had said she was relieved; at least one member of the family would be safe from terrorists and drug dealers, she said. David's father vowed not to spend more than eight hours a week in the place, and for the most part kept his word.

David remembered Miguel's father, a lawyer, distinguished but specializing in lost causes, saying, "Your father was right, it was a proconsul's palace, but that was because the Ambassador was a proconsul. The ones he couldn't intimidate, he bought. He spent money like crazy to let armed Nicaraguan thugs roam around near the border. And of course we had to arm ourselves in case they were attacked. It was a calamity of the worst kind! The worst people took control here. And your government, it still saves the worst of its people for this region."

Looking back, David saw that Miguel's father had in a sense been wrong. The worst hadn't happened. Costa Ricans elected a young man who did a lot to get them out of the mess and won a Nobel Prize in the process. The U.S. Congress pretty much shut down the war and perestroika took the "geo" out of the Nicaraguan political conflict. But Miguel's father had been right in another way. Much like the Native American prophecies, his was a warning; a dangerous, destructive force was at work which if left unchecked could have wreaked havoc. He and others had raised the warnings and been listened to by-and-large in time. In the same way, years later, many had warned against labeling every disaffected group that was driven to violence as terrorists and had cautioned against excessive force and giving up civil liberties during the War Against Terror. Abuses were tolerated for a few years but eventually, as far as David could see, no lasting damage had been done. The "war" had strengthened some of the national intelligence agencies but almost ten years had passed and many of their functions had been blended into UNINTEL. He hadn't heard any stories of recent abuse.

David wondered if Miguel's father had been right in other ways. He told a story about how the new Embassy building came to be. The old Embassy offices had been downtown in virtually indefensible surroundings but the Ambassador refused to move. The intelligence and security people became increasingly vocal in their demands but to no avail. Then, the only terrorist incident to ever occur in downtown San Jose took place. A bomb exploded next to the Ambassador's office on a Saturday night when virtually no one was in the building. Walls crumbled, desks and cabinets were blown apart, but there were no serious casualties. The only people linked to the bombing were members of an underground radical group, but those involved were also rumored to be CIA informants. Shortly after the incident the Ambassador had himself transferred out and construction of the new building began.

"Draw your own conclusions," Miguel's father would say when telling the story. Not a difficult task at a time when there were documented accounts of rogue U.S. intelligence operatives unaccountable to anyone. "But you know it was not so long ago that one U.S. intelligence agency tried to overthrow a neighboring government in order to wrest away control from a sister agency." When David told his own father the story, he shook his head, more in disgust, David suspected, than in denial.

What a strange time that was, David mused as he walked away from the embassy building. Where did all those people who loved to play in that world of secrecy and power and violence go? Did they—we—just grow out of it? The whole planet, all at once? Was Miguel's father's story another one of those prophecies already heeded and avoided?

David turned down the side street that curved towards his old home. Most of the houses on the street were built in the 1980s and '90s. They were one- or two-story structures with carports, skylights, and separate laundry areas. The lines were straight and angular, an impression heightened by the steep banks of solar panels added on to the roofs decades later.

David reached his old house and peered over the low wall into the yard. There was a pigtailed little girl pulling a wagon loaded down with two large indigenous stuffed animals—a toucan and a three-toed sloth—and a doll of a boy in a uniform of some sort. David continued to watch as the girl brought the wagon and its passengers to a playhouse near the base of a tall willow. David remembered the tree well. He had loved to climb it, to bury himself among its branches and to peer out at the passing world, and sometimes in the evening, he remembered with a smile, through his neighbors windows.

He had broken a branch once trying to get down too quickly. A circle had grown where the limb once was. Creases had grown around it, taking the form of an eye. David peered more intently; the eye was still there though it looked like someone had carved initials in it. As his glance dropped from the tree's scar, David saw that the little girl was staring at him and she then looked, open-mouthed and wide-eyed, at something behind him.

"Alto ahí! No se mueva." Stop there! Don't move. The voice came from behind him and was followed by scurrying footsteps.

David froze and then turned his head, ever so slightly, to see a policeman coming towards him, drawing his club from its frilled sheathe. The man was not large but he looked strong and quick.

David raised his hands, palms open. He spoke in near-native Spanish, "What is it? Why are you stopping me?"

"Identity papers, please." The policeman's voice was straight and toneless, like an iron bar.

As David reached for a clip in his front shirt pocket, he saw a pale, black-haired woman scramble out of the front door of the house, grab the little girl by the hand and virtually drag her back to the entranceway. David removed a laminated card from the clip and handed it to the policeman.

"Ese es, ese es el desgenerado!" He's the degenerate, David heard the woman's voice say.

"You're not from around here," the policeman said.

"I lived in this very house long ago. I just came to see it."

"Did you like little girls then too?"

"Actually I did. I was thirteen."

The policeman's mouth stayed tight and thin but a glimmer

crossed his eyes. "Does someone around here know you?"

"Probably not, it's been a long time."

"We've had a problem, a man, an American we think, has been playing with little girls. Nothing serious has happened but people are scared."

"I was looking at the house, I'm sorry," David added, "The girl just happened to be there."

The policeman was still blocking his way. "How am I going to explain to the lady if I don't take you in for questioning?" he said. A few years earlier, before the extraordinary success of the Global League of Women Voter's anticorruption campaign, David would have assumed he was being asked for a bribe, but he felt reasonably sure the policeman just wanted a way out.

"I have a friend at the Embassy," David said. Dexter McCloud was not really a friend. He was the Environmental Attaché, the third-ranking officer in the Embassy. David's work in helping administer several privately funded forest parks brought him into contact with Dexter often.

"We'll go see him. Please wait here." The policeman walked to the house and spoke to the dark-haired woman. Then he led David back up the street towards the Embassy. At the entrance he pulled out a microtransmitter and punched in a series of numbers, presumably David's I.D. He waited fifteen seconds and the device beeped benignly, a final precaution before the officer lost jurisdictional authority.

"Dexter McCloud, please," David said at the reception desk and showed his I.D.

"At your service, sir. I'm glad I could be of help," said the policeman. He saluted David and exited. David smiled appreciatively at the officer's tact.

"Is he expecting you?" the receptionist asked.

"No. I was in town and thought I'd say hello."

A few minutes later the receptionist signaled to David to go through, "Do you know where his office is?"

"Yes." A mistake, David thought. If I know my way around, why did I need a policeman to bring me here? My God, David said to himself with a startled realization, Laura really does have me worried.

Dexter came around from behind a large wooden desk to

greet David. He was dressed in a white guayabera and neatly pressed slacks. He was a good-looking man about David's age with a warm smile. His haircut was correct and his shoes, made of soft English leather, were shined. David couldn't help himself; he felt welcome but a little intimidated.

"I'm glad you dropped in. What brings you to town?"

"Nostalgia."

"I thought you didn't like cities."

"This one isn't bad. I grew up here, more or less."

"That's right. You mentioned that. Dangerous stuff isn't it, nostalgia. The grass was always greener?"

"The planet was."

"So true. I have something to show you, David. The Council of Europe's report, it's circulating among governments now. It really lays it out. We may be in real trouble, all of us. Despite everything we've done so far. Warming trends are up, violent storms and weather anomalies keep popping up, the rate of ozone depletion is still not declining, two thousand plant species have been lost in the last three years, economically most of the world is no better off. Did you see the BHN, the UN's Basic Human Needs index for the year?"

"I know, it's down again. But Dexter, we've been saying all along that you can't undo two centuries of destruction in a dozen years. Each imbalance that we created was like a wave in the ocean, slow but basically unstoppable. All you could do was stop the source of the disturbance to make sure there were no more waves and then try to repair the damage after the waves hit the shore. Call it inertia or karma—or what you will."

"Ah," Dexter was holding a pencil at both ends. He twirled the pencil and looked up at the ceiling as he replied, "Karma. I guess every person who lived in the twentieth century needs to spend at least one short lifetime as a species suffering extinction. That's why we need to keep wiping them out instead of really doing something about it." He paused and peered more intently across the desk at David. "These volunteer efforts like yours just aren't enough."

David was unable to contain himself. "It's the same man-conquers-nature arrogance that got us in trouble in the first place that makes you think you can solve everything tomorrow if you just set your mind to it. It's dangerous, Dexter, man-age, hand-le, engineer, don't the words say it all?"

"David, relax. The point is that the patient isn't responding as fast as our models predicted so governments are probably going to have to do a little more Earth-doctoring and we need the power to do it."

"The models were made when governments were trying to hide their own colossal stupidity and enslavement to special interests. They can't be taken seriously—except," David added with a relish that surprised him, "by self-serving bureaucrats who now see a chance to increase their own power in the name of the solution."

"A true Michelson disciple! David, believe me, nobody is going to take your little forestry projects away from you."

David knew that Dexter probably meant well but he was astounded by his arrogance. He regretted having risen to the bait and resisted the temptation to take issue with Dexter's demeaning characterization of TROFAL's work in Costa Rica. The forest preserves were only one part; the more important part to David was the educational, participatory element. Though TROFAL had benefited from the debt-for-nature swaps of the late twentieth century, much of the current support for its projects came from older children and teenagers in schools in richer countries where tropical forests were unknown. The donors would get regular reports on whatever their funds were used for, a reforestation effort, for example. Their schools were given access to the TROFAL library of written and video materials describing rain- and dry-forest ecospheres, their value and the lingering threats to them. There were additionally two- and six-week work-study tours of the Costa Rican parks themselves, for those who could afford it or won scholarships. Of greatest importance, TROFAL administered the parks to insure that they served as living classrooms, accessible to virtually every school in Costa Rica so that an entire generation of the forests' human neighbors and inhabitants would grow up with an understanding of its ecology.

David knew that Laura had left him with ungrounded anger and that the intensity of his reaction to Dexter was probably misplaced. "Sorry, Dexter, I'm a little on edge. Can I keep the report?"

"Sure, but please don't run it through a copy machine or a scanner. I'd just as soon not see it on ECONET with a Costa Rican origin."

"I understand."

"By the way, how is that gorgeous woman I'm used to seeing you with?"

"Laura? She's exploring."

"Ah. Well, give her my best."

"It was good to see you, Dexter. Thanks."

"And you. The side door's unlocked from this side. It's probably a faster way out."

David emerged from the side door into the afternoon warmth, intensified by the pavement of the parking lot. As his eyes adjusted he saw with a jolt of recognition, two parking spaces to his left, a white electric van with a deeply tinted windshield. He walked over to it and peered inside. It was locked and unoccupied but the console bristled with electronic controls that David could not name. A shiver went up his spine and the anger he felt in Dexter's office returned, tightening his throat. As he stepped away from the van, he exhaled audibly. At least, he thought with a little relief, I'm beginning to know my enemy.

CHAPTER 21

The morning intruded through the window, announcing itself in cold gray tones. As Almira awakened, she became aware of cement-like obstructions in her nasal passages and a slight headache, the products of an overheated house. She rolled to the far side of the four-poster bed and wrapped herself in the yellow-and white-checked comforter that covered it, hoping she would escape back into sleep. But sleep didn't come and she opened her eyes again. England in the spring, she thought, as she recognized the monochrome source of her disturbance: This is not my home.

She put on her bathrobe and walked down the stairs to the kitchen, lured by the strong smell of coffee with a fragrance of cardamom. "Ali," she said, "you must love Elizabeth a great deal to live in this damp cold. A weak uncertain sun, starless nights. Don't you miss home?"

"There are worse things that can happen to the body than the damp and the cold." Ali smiled wryly at her, "Especially in the place you call home."

Ali was an unfolding lesson in human nature. He had suffered his pain with only the slightest trace of resentment or bitterness. He held no hatred for the Israelis or the Americans or even the monks who wouldn't shelter him when he was being pursued. The last, even Almira found almost impossible to forgive.

The tangled memories of his ordeal caught hold of her. She was with her mother and Ali. It was dusk, there were boys, many boys, and a few men throwing stones, soldiers. A bottle of gasoline exploded near the soldiers. A tortured cry of pain and terror rose over the shouting, an Israeli soldier turned into a human torch and ran six steps, casting lurid shadows on the wall where their mother was shielding them. The soldier collapsed and rolled around on the ground, howling in agony. Their mother seized Ali and Almira by the hand and ran through narrow streets and passageways, finally doubling back to where she had parked their car. They sped east from Bethlehem. It was dark. Three pairs of headlights snaked behind them, the poorly muffled roar of military vehicles catching them at the curves.

They drove on but the lights and roar closed in. Her mother pulled over at an imposing structure Almira had never seen before, dragged her children out of the car and pulled frantically at a bell next to a large blue door. The lights behind them grew closer. A monk finally appeared. "Shelter us," she had said, "my children are Christians." It wasn't quite a lie; their father had been born one.

"Women can't enter," the monk said, "it is forbidden."

"This is life or death," she pleaded.

"It's forbidden, maybe the boy," the monk finally said.

"No," Ali said, "no, I won't leave you." His mother pushed him toward the door. He resisted and there the scene was frozen in the glare of many headlights that had pulled in behind them. The blue door closed.

It was Ali the soldiers wanted. They dragged him away and made a circle around him. Gun butts rose and fell more than twenty times. Ali screamed and then fell silent. The soldiers brought his body back, limbs slack and twisted, mind mercifully unconscious, and gently placed him in the back seat of the Fiat. "You must teach him not to play with fire," a soldier said as he left.

Ali endured it all with a courage Almira admired. Perhaps better than anyone else in the family, he could remain calm and talk with reason about the occupation, even about what the soldiers had done to him that day. When the Final Settlement came, Ali was as gratified as anyone. He had talked of a quiet joy spreading through his being, but it had not enticed him to return. It was as though his work was done there, as though his

174

pain was endured for the place itself, the sacrifice made to purify the sand of a thousand pointless conflicts. Now, he wanted nothing else to do with Palestine; his life was his own. Elizabeth, the Loaves and Fishes, the garden, it was all his own, and all he wanted.

Elizabeth joined them. She was dressed in blue jeans and white blouse. Freshly brushed strawberry hair cascaded over her shoulders. She poured herself a cup of coffee. The boys were still sleeping, even with the time zone change.

"You didn't sleep well," Elizabeth said.

"I didn't wake up well," Almira answered.

"We'll walk to town. You'll feel better. The sun will be out. I won't say for how long, but it will be out. It makes Ali feel better too."

"I'll wait for the boys," Ali said, "I think I promised a tour."

An hour later Elizabeth and Almira were climbing over a low fence onto the abbey grounds. It's right on the way to town, Elizabeth had explained, it would be a long way around. The entrance was in town. They could pay on the way out. Almira was beginning to enjoy the adventure but anxiety lingered with her. Her head turned from side to side and her shoulders hunched as she steadied herself inside the grounds.

"It's okay, Almira, they know me. We've done it before."

"In the Middle East we're careful with sacred places. We don't take their power lightly," Almira said. She felt her heart beating faster. "Perhaps that's not it," she added after a minute or two, "Monks and our family have a bad history."

"There haven't been any monks here for centuries. Just a harmless old minister from the church across the way. Periodically everything got burned down here and a fair number of monks slaughtered. "Henry the VIII liked to butcher monks almost as much as he liked to behead wives. 'I'm Henry the VIII I am,'" Elizabeth started to sing.

Almira smiled, "I thought this was much older."

"It is... or was. They've found some remnants of a wattle structure going back to at least the seventh century, and there are the stories of Joseph and his descendants even earlier. And of course we like to believe that Arthur and Guinevere were buried here, along with other English dreams."

"The Celts?" Almira remembered a novel, popular in the women's movement. It was set in the area that was now Glastonbury and described an old culture tied to nature and a woman's priesthood, giving way to swords and crosses and stone churches built over sacred springs.

"Yes. We think so. It was much wetter around here then. Now that water is rising again, who knows what's next. Avalon reborn!"

A feminine millennia, Almira thought. Could that be next? It might happen. So much had changed. There was so little room for all of the male qualities that once were called virtues, and the men had so visibly screwed up. Aggression on a crowded planet had reached a dead end, "conquering" nature had nearly destroyed the human race as well as half its living companions and, even in science, reason had been dropped a notch to make room for a bit of intuition.

Waters rising, Almira mused. Women born of water rising. Men born of women. Women secretly violated by a maddened god, leaving unsettled, hidden demons in the boys they birthed. Yet for all the damage they did Almira knew that she loved men. Ali, Farid, Youssef, Jamal—she wanted to embrace all of them, soothe them, reassure them that there was goodness in the world, that at the end of the cycle—however long it was—they would be okay.

Elizabeth and Almira walked past the ruins of the old abbey. A handful of tourists posed in front of them, photographing each other. The two women walked on and came to a small tree, perhaps twenty feet high. Its branches were dark, almost black; the leaves were only beginning to bud. Birds in large numbers roosted in the branches and filled the day with sound.

Elizabeth watched for a moment. "My teacher used to say that we are like trees. When we choose to grow we spread our inner limbs so that angels, like birds, may perch on them and do their work on Earth.

"'The mustard seed... the least of all seeds... becometh a tree, so that the birds of the air come and lodge in the branches thereof....' Could it mean that, Almira?"

"I wish it were so, especially for the men. But I don't know."

Elizabeth gave her a wan look and squeezed her hand. "This

chapel," she said pointing to a small building shaded behind the tree, "is fairly modern, sixteenth century I think. I guess that's why it's still intact, that and it's small. It wasn't worth burning down." The chapel was spartan. A few chairs in three rows, a crucifix, a sign asking visitors to be silent, a donation box and a vase of fresh flowers on the slab where an altar must once have been. The two women were alone as they sat in the hard-backed chairs. Elizabeth folded her legs under her and adopted an Eastern meditative posture. Almira sat on a chair, back erect. She felt Elizabeth's presence and the boundaries of her consciousness began to dissolve. After a few minutes, it seemed as if the walls were speaking to her. She sensed men, strong men with powerful arms, who were there long ago. Men of peaceful hearts with gnarled but not unbloodied hands, intent on preserving something silent, gentle and unnamed, in a maelstrom of savagery and violence.

As Almira's breath slowed and deepened, beyond the monks' presence she felt the grief and lamentation of women pour out of the walls. Powerless women who had watched limbs hacked and children mutilated, who knew men only in their anger as they battered away with their blunt little weapons, their bodies enveloped in rags and chain mail, stench and filth. Centuries of fear and violence and oppression and greed, misfortune piled on misery heaped on disease. Almira felt it in the tension of her spine, in the flesh of her clenching hands and the tears pooling in her eyes.

Yet somehow, out of thousands of years of violence, outside this English land still emerged green. Sheep grazed tranquilly on the hillside; scents of loam and manure were in the air, trees were in bud, flowers in bloom. Men and women tended to their gardens and shops; carpenters nailed the frame of a new family's home; masons placed stone on stone, mothers pushed strollers with bundled babies. In the evening stillness children slept, men gathered together by pub fires to talk about football clubs and times gone by; lovers lost themselves in each other, a dance would strike up; in a candlelit room twelve would pray together, a book club would meet in the library and through hundreds of windows the BBC, or the profusion of newer, privately operated satellite-delivered channels, would glow. The eight thousand six hundred forty-two inhabitants sometimes contentedly, sometimes with difficulty, sometimes lonely, sometimes drunkenly—but basically at peace and for the most part helping each other— made their way closer to their appointed end, an end a growing number saw as no more than their beginning, the entrance hall to a greater kingdom

Once, Almira realized, it had been every bit as bad here as it was in Palestine. Now this was an island of tranquility. It gave her hope. For every place, Almira thought, perhaps this time will come. Tears of release flowed down her cheeks. I am weeping too much, she thought. But a voice answered from somewhere within her, *It is the eyes that are washed with tears that see.*

Someone else had entered the chapel. The footfalls were heavy, almost certainly those of a man. Whoever it was paused in the back. His entrance interrupted the women's reverie. Elizabeth opened her eyes and looked at Almira. The two sat for a minute more and then got up to leave. As they walked through the doorway, the man followed. He was perhaps forty years old, sandy hair, brown eyes, his skin tanned. His clothing was British but something about him was not.

"Not much to see here, is there?" The accent hovered somewhere in the North Atlantic between England and America. One of the Canadian nations perhaps, Almira thought. The voice was pleasant enough.

"It's a quiet place," Elizabeth said.

"You come here often?" His eyes turned to Almira, "Or are you not from around here?"

His smile and energy overcame her reticence. "Palestine. My brother lives here."

"And I'm his wife," Elizabeth added.

"Ah."

"And you?" Almira asked.

"Well, I work in London. American actually, with a law firm, we have an office here."

"That must be nice."

"It is, and I get to tour a bit."

"Like here?" Elizabeth inquired.

"Yes. Look, would you join me for a pastry or something? You could tell me what to look for."

"A native's perspective. Hidden treasures. Legend's and old wives' tales," Elizabeth said.

"Exactly."

"Please, let's do." Almira was hungry and was enjoying the man's attention. They left the abbey grounds and walked to a small coffee shop that featured pastries in the window.

Tom, Tom Autry, it turned out, was from Wisconsin. He had spent time in Toronto and then got serious about making money so he went to law school. From there to New York and from there to London. "Cross-border bankruptcies and slow aquacurrent energies," he said, "Growth areas, both. I've done well."

Almira sipped her coffee, aware that his gaze was still on her. "I wonder," he said, "if the Aramaic women Joseph brought here had eyes like yours." He smiled, "I might have become a Christian too."

In spite of herself, Almira responded with warmth. "Maybe you should be the tour guide."

Tom closed one eye and cocked his head, "In the land of the blind... I really can't today. May I call you tomorrow? I'll bet Elizabeth can tell you everything we need to know."

"Perhaps. You can call us at the Loaves...." As she was speaking, she saw Ali coming through the door of the shop. He spotted them in the corner.

"I thought I might find you here," Ali said as he came to their table, "Jamal woke up with a sore throat and fever. It's not bad but a look at the clinic wouldn't hurt."

"English climate, I told you it's not for us," Almira smiled at her brother. "I'll come with you." She turned to Tom. "The Loaves and the Fishes. Tomorrow? Elizabeth can tell you how to find us."

***

"We have English doctors to cure English ailments," Ali said as they walked toward his car.

"Sun dancers, rituals to scatter the clouds?" Almira asked. A light rain was -falling from the low overcast. Her clothes were soaked by the time they re-entered the Loaves and the Fishes. Jamal looked miserable. His eyes were red and his nose was running. Youssef was glaring at him contemptuously. "He's faking, Mom. He wants you to buy him a present."

Almira ignored the comment and went into her room to change into dry clothes. English doctors, Almira thought, as they gathered up Jamal and headed for the clinic. In a sense doctors no longer had any nationality at all. No matter where you were, you did not know what to expect from a doctor's visit. In the last few years medicine had changed radically. Much as philosophers had sought to find the underlying unity of all religions, doctors of many persuasions had sought to find an underlying unity in healing practice. Even if the illusive unity hadn't been found, most in the profession had broadened their skills. An English doctor might be almost as well-trained in acupuncture as a Chinese one; a native Brazilian herbalist could have studied "Western" endocrinology, a Tibetan practitioner might have learned laser surgery for the treatment of diseases of the eye.

Attitudes towards dying changed as well. Millions of people were revulsed by high-cost treatments that prolonged the life of the elderly in what was little more than a vegetative state. As medical technologies advanced, this became an increasingly common phenomenon, draining not only financial resources but the energies of friends and family members as well. Death with Dignity in the healthier economies had become a social movement of considerable force.

The movement was given an added boost by the Life for Children campaign that began in 2018. Almira remembered it well. She viewed it as a Third World moral triumph, on a par with Gandhi's sending the British packing. The campaign was the brainchild of Sony Kayembe, an African philanthropist, the son of a former President for Life who hadn't quite made it that long but had held office long enough to leave enormous wealth to his wives, uncles, and descendants. Sony remembered his father's omnipresence in his home county, in giant billboard posters and on the television screen. He was convinced that without these his father would probably not even have been President for a term. He was also appalled at Western toleration for the rampant suffering, particularly of children, in the poorer nations, including his own. He knew, however, from his own experience, that Westerners were no crueler than anyone else. It was, he was convinced, a question of making that suffering omnipresent, in the consciousness of Westerners, much as his father had imposed his presence on his own people.

Through various means he secured permission to install giant screens in central areas and even large shopping centers in forty-five major cities in North America and Europe. He also placed television cameras in the children's wards of two hundred hospitals and clinics in Africa. The cameras were continuously focused on children dying, for the most part of preventable diseases. The camera images were transmitted by satellite to a central studio where they were mixed by computer program (with an occasional human assist) and relayed to the screens twenty-four hours a day. Small but legible letters appeared next to each child spelling out his name. Underneath large letters delivered a mega message, such as 40,000 CHILDREN DIE NEEDLESSLY EVERY DAY, A 50-CENT VACCINE WOULD HAVE SAVED THIS CHILD'S LIFE.

Needless to say, the displays caused controversy. The moderate opposition to the displays maintained that while they sympathized with the objectives of the displays' sponsor, they found the placement of the message unfortunate. City squares were most populated at lunch hours and in the evening, times of leisure. Shopping centers were the major recreational centers of the early twenty-first century. People's pleasures shouldn't be ruined with such a heavy message. The more extreme opposition sought to discredit the displays by ferreting out inconsistencies between the particular affliction of the children on the screen and the accompanying verbal message. The few found were without real impact so they engaged teams of lawyers to shut down the displays under local obscenity statutes.

It was in one such action in Ohio that an irascible seventy-nine-year-old judge opined that the real obscenity was that he lived in a society where hundreds of thousands of dollars would be spent to prolong the life of an eighty-five-year-old a few weeks when that same sum could give a full life of many decades to thousands of children who would otherwise die.

This opinion was widely quoted and led to the turning point in Kayembe's campaign. The public relations and finance departments of first one and then simultaneously a dozen insurance companies saw the opportunity. The companies' beneficiaries were sent a mailing that quoted the judge at length and advised then that if they drafted a "living will" renouncing certain categories of life-extension treatments, the companies would apply one half of the actuarially computed cost savings to the Life for Children campaign, administered by UNICEF, and the other half to premium rebates. Millions took the insurance companies up on their offer and the displays came down. There were accusations that the companies had fixed the actuarial computations to bloat their profits, and while some of these charges were probably true, no one really cared because by 2022, the last year of the old calendar, UNICEF announced that for the first time in human history, mankind had set aside adequate financial resources to protect its children from preventable mortality.

Almira remembered the day of the announcement. A little gnome-like man had appeared on television screens everywhere, his voice filled with authority and joy. On that day tears of relief had filled Almira's eyes and those of millions of others. Another suffocating blanket of human horror had been removed to free the human heart and mind.

All this went through Almira's mind as the three of them, Almira, Ali, and Jamal, entered the one-story modern structure that housed the local clinic. In thirty minutes they were announced to Dr. Ray. Ali knew Dr. Ray slightly. Dr. Ray was from India and like Ali was married to a British woman. His wife attended yoga and meditation sessions with Elizabeth. Almira could tell that Ali and Dr. Ray liked each other.

The examining room had the usual hard-backed chair and inclined couch, a medicine- and herb-filled cabinet, and a blood pressure measuring device. A gruesome, layered drawing of a human torso cut open to display all of its organs hung on one wall but next to it was a Tibetan-like tongka of a seated figure with all of his chakras in full bloom. On the far wall a World Wildlife Fund poster of an endangered Bengal tiger hung side by side with a series of nineteenth-century prints showing cartoon dogs armed and outfitted in English-gentry hunting attire ready to pursue the grouse—a concession, Almira felt sure as she smiled to herself, to local taste.

Dr. Ray felt Jamal's pulses, took his temperature, applied his stethoscope and made him say aaahhh. He asked Jamal to lie down with his eyes closed and slowly moved his hands over the length of Jamal's torso and head without touching him, but pausing here and there.

"You will be fine," Dr. Ray said to Jamal. "If you'll go tug at the pretty lady in the next room, she will give you sweets to suck for your throat."

Jamal did as he was told.

"You will be long with us?" Dr. Ray spoke to Almira.

"No, well, I'm not sure. The children will be here a while."

"You are returning home?"

"No, not soon."

"Whatever is happening, it is not my business, but if I may intrude, if I were you, I think I would endeavor to be clearer."

"What do you mean?"

"With your children. Leaving home, mother traveling, no father, it is hard for them. Today Jamal's expression is blocked and it pains him. Tomorrow there will be a heaviness of heart—a bronchial inflammation, some of my colleagues will say. We can treat that and it will pass quickly but you are the one who must dig at the root."

Almira knew that he was right, that she had become absorbed in her own plight and had not made the effort to explain to her children. She simply assumed that they would enjoy the adventure and had not considered that the experience would be unsettling.

"Yes," she said. "I'm sorry."

"Just talk to them. And your brother and his lovely wife can help, too."

"I'm sorry," she repeated and then smiled, "Thank you."

"A nice man," she said to Ali as they drove home.

"We're lucky to have him here. By the way," Ali added, "who was that man at the pastry shop? He seemed quite interested in you."

"You could tell, my jealous brother?"

"I think he chased you all the way into town. He virtually ran past the house just after you and Elizabeth left."

A sinking feeling briefly gripped Almira. "Are you sure he's the same person?"

"Pretty sure."

"He says he's an American lawyer. Lives in London." She paused and stared out the car window. "Ali, I'm nervous. Could they be after me here?"

"They?"

"Whoever did it to Fatimah. Or the police. I don't know. I told the American I would see him tomorrow. He seemed nice enough. Now I'm regretting it."

"You're safe enough here. Do you know his name?"

"Tom, Tom Autry."

"He should be in the London directory. A call or two and we'll know if his story is true."

"Maybe."

"Let's talk to Elizabeth, she's been around lawyers a bit." Ali was always good-humored about Elizabeth's past.

Almira remained silent for a minute or two. "Ali, I think that I need to talk to somebody with a different perspective. Somebody who keeps tuned to the ins and outs of global politics. Will you help me?"

"Of course."

"Track down Jean Marc for me."

Ali grimaced. He was not so good-humored about his sister's past.

"Please don't argue," Almira added before he could speak.

CHAPTER 22

After EROE, the Electronic Record of Everything, was put into place, letter writing and the use of the post had taken a marked increase, particularly among those who had matters that were best left undisclosed. Electronic communication had by then eliminated home delivery so pickup at the post office was required. For a while post offices, inhabited as they were by some of the community's least reputable elements, had taken on the aura of menace that bus stations and New York subway stops once had, even down to the ever-present urine smell. But Rashid's intuition told him that it was not this legacy that alerted his senses when he picked up the envelope, nor what continued to trouble him as he strode up the pathway and through the door into his home.

He seated himself at a plain wooden table in the ample kitchen, his back to a window through which the trade breeze was blowing. He examined the manila envelope carefully, held it up to the light, and then used a carving knife to slice off the top. The envelope's contents were covered by a yellow stick-um leaf on which someone had scrawled "R - FYI."

United Nations Intelligence and Law Enforcement Agency

24 Gaia 8

TOP SECRET/COSMIC EYES ONLY

ACTION MEMORANDUM FOR THE SECRETARY GENERAL OF THE UNITED NATIONS

FROM: THE DIRECTOR GENERAL, UNINTEL

SUBJECT: The Convocation – Update/Authorization Meeting Request

Nikolai and I request an urgent meeting with you to bring you up to date on matters affecting the planetary security and next year's Convocation of Terrestrial Entities.

We believe we have identified a widespread and well-organized secret movement dedicated to the ruthless acquisition of power. The movement has been implicated in the deaths of several prominent planetary citizens and is almost certainly aiming to twist the processes of the

Convocation for its own ends, heedless of our plans for humanity's well-being. At the meeting, we will seek your authorization to implement preliminary, protective countermeasures.

BACKGROUND: At the Saratoga retreat last month, the Agency heads, your senior staff, and the representatives of the permanent Council members were virtually unanimous in their assessment of the growing threats to planetary security. These included:

- **Global Warming Trends**: Despite CO_2 emission reduction to 1991 levels and widespread tree planting, computer models show likelihood of increased greenhouse effect due to previously unrecognized positive feedback loops, the "Venus Effect."
- **Likely Results**: rising sea levels, fisheries collapse, drought in some areas, crop failures, ecological disaster for slow-migrating species, civil disturbances.
- **Ozone Depletion**: Despite elimination of production of CFCs and Halons a generation ago, ozone-depleting substances continue to migrate to the stratosphere.
- **Likely Results**: increased incidence of skin cancer (250,000 deaths per year), damage to phytoplankton and ocean food chain, reduced agricultural productivity, immune system suppression.
- **Population Growth**: Despite widespread availability of contraception and successful educational programs, population bulge of 1990s coming into reproductive years at same time as social trends extol family life.
- **Likely Results**: slowing of trends away from poverty, strain on many ecosystems, political

pressures to undo conservation and preservation measures (e.g. Amazon Basin Bioresource Zone) in order to accommodate growing numbers, civil disturbances.

- **Greed**: outbreaks of compulsive consumerism, particularly among teens and preteens in U.S. and Japan, trendsetters for the world's youth.
- **Likely Results**: coupled with population growth could reverse environmental gains of past generation, could undermine social order.
- **Extraterrestrials**: Deep Space Pulse suggests proximate contact with extraterrestrial intelligence.
- **Likely Results**: social disorientation, aggression against disarmed Planet Earth possible, well-intentioned colonization if we appear too backwards, the end of human dominance.

RESPONSIVE STRATEGIES:

The attendants of the conference noted that a well-governed society with effective administrative bodies and centralized control and enforcement powers could easily forge successful strategies for addressing these problems. These might include:

- **Rational resource allocation for rising sea levels**. For example, we are all agreed that far too much money is being spent to save the beach resorts of the wealthy as well as parts of Holland, the population of which is highly skilled and can easily be relocated. The resources saved could be applied in locations such as Bangladesh where far greater numbers with less portable skills are at risk.
- **Criminal Penalties for Possession of Ozone Depleting Substances**. Voluntary programs for turning in CFC and halon-containing substances such as Styrofoam for secure deep-earth disposal

have been disappointing. Declaring possession of these substances a planetary crime should refocus citizen interest, especially if coupled with random, house-to-house searches by invigorated enforcement authorities and appropriate penalties such as home confiscation for serious violators.

- **Star Shield Research and Development Program**. Since the collapse of the "axis of evil" no serious work has been done that could protect the Earth's surface from attack from space. The U.S. Delegate noted that there were several promising technologies that could be pursued once the proposal for a Planetary Defense Force (PDF) is approved next year. The Russian delegate, recalling the Siberian incident of 1908, noted that even if extraterrestrial intelligences meant us no harm, the system could be employed against asteroids or other heavenly bodies that threaten collision with the Earth.
- **Mandatory Sterilization and Family Resource Taxes**. Now that infant mortality has been dramatically reduced, require sterilization of all who have fathered or mothered more than two children and impose a stiff tax on the birth of any child to reflect its cost to the ecosystem.
- **Universal Conscription for Eighteen Year Olds**. This will give a human resource base to the PDF; others can perform civic services. Will give us an opportunity to indoctrinate the young with an appropriate world view and break them out of consumerist tendencies.

There was widespread agreement that with measures like these in place, the consequences of the twentieth century's worst follies could be once and for all contained. Threats to the well-being of tens of millions would be neutralized, countless species otherwise doomed to extinction would be preserved, and trillions of dollars of economic harm avoided.

It was agreed that the Convocation of Terrestrial Entities scheduled for next year was likely to be the last opportunity for a generation to legitimize a world system of governance that could put an Earth Wellness Program like the one described above into place. It was agreed that with success at the Convocation, you would be seen as having laid the groundwork for a united and strong Earth that by the end of the first century of the Modern Era would be ready to reach out and take its place among the great powers of the galaxy.

NEW DEVELOPMENTS:

Subsequent to the Saratoga meeting our investigators, with the aid of cooperating national and local law-enforcement agencies, have developed credible evidence of a widespread conspiracy to disrupt the Convocation and prevent your proposals from being approved. Their longer-term intentions are not yet known.

Some of those suspected have been linked to a series of deaths, many previously believed to be accidental, of respected individuals from around the globe. Others are placed highly in private, quasi-political organizations, governmental bodies and, we have reason to believe, even in the UN itself. For this reason we are reluctant to detail our findings in a written document.

We feel confident that you will fully appreciate the serious nature of this threat and of the need to contain it until we are in a position to credibly expose it. The very existence of the threat will become a compelling argument for an effective planetary government.

ACTION RECOMMENDATION:

That you meet with Nikolai and myself no later than the 27th for a full briefing and to authorize effective countermeasures.

Several minutes passed during which Rashid remained seated at the table staring vacantly at the peach-colored wall. There was another document in the package—a handwritten note from Rafael which he perused quickly. When Rashid did get up, he went to the refrigerator and poured himself a glass of a tropical fruit juice. He drained it in two gulps and seated himself in front of the v-phone where he talked in a voice-only mode to a number in New York. Half an hour later he sent out an electronic message to David Grossman.

"Highest urgency that you meet me on May 7 for a pre-Convocation strategy conference. Go to the Hotel Ballena Loca in Baja, south of Ensenada off Route 1. Please bring your friend. She is welcome too. Best regards, Rashid."

Then, he wrote a quick note, ran his tongue the length of an envelope flap, applied a stamp, and scribbled out an address in Washington, DC.

Rashid returned to the living room and seated himself in a corner, sheltered behind a bookcase and a couch, cross-legged on a cushion on the floor. He dropped a square block of incense on a small copper tray, lit the incense and as he inhaled the scent, closed his eyes. When he reopened them, the green-blue irises had a distant quality but a smile crinkled around them. In the background of the water's sound and the windshaken leaves, he heard Spotted Fluke's voice emerging like an old friend's silhouette from the evening's shadows.

CHAPTER 23

SANCTUARY. It is a curious thing that you have done with that word. Refuge, it means to you now. A holy place, it was before. And there is refuge in holiness and every place is holy. There is a song we sing to our calves.

Come, come my babies, come swim with us,
Come, come my children, come play with me.
Eat the fishes, my children, in our bubbling ring,
Dance with us, my babies, on the swelling sea.
Rise to the air, my children, clasped to our wing.
Then sing the old refrain with us, my children,
"Our mothers never sleep,
Angels of our water ways,
Guardians of the deep."
Come, come, my babies, come play with us,
Come, come, my children, come be with me.

There is one like you, Rashid, who lives in the northern ice. He says it differently; he speaks of the Parent of us all. He says She is a woman, gentle, who speaks to us in the murmuring of creeks, softly as a tuft of cloud whispering to each of us, "Be not afraid of the Universe." That and no more, a simple refrain. Yet even among those few who have heard it, how wrong so many have taken it. A broken promise they say, all around us are our bodies, messengers of pain. All around us are ruined towers and the coffins of well-intentioned prayers.

We weep for their bitterness, Rashid. We weep for their despair. It was not our Parent who dimmed the lights. It was not our Parent who closed the door on the inner sky, who averts her gaze from the spiral stars, who is deaf to the rhythmic song and is numb to the taste of the Fruit. Each of you are an army; a platoon of seen and unseen helpers surrounds you, ready at your command, angels peering through your windows, spirits at your side, voices rising in a silent cheer. Yet you do not see it: alone, abandoned, battered, so many of you claim to be. Pointless lonely lives, you think, doomed to dissolve in dust. But the flow of a warm, sweet current carries you, it glitters with jewels and gold, and only one drop in your Inner Chamber will cause a hundred universes to unfold. Yet so many of you do not feel it, you cannot taste the honey nor smell the fragrance of the rose. You have locked the door with resentment and bolted it with fear.

Rashid, speak in your wordless ways to our friends. Save them from despair. Tell them that their unfulfilled loves and losses are veils swept away on our Mother's breath. Tell them that their pain is an entryway to joy. Tell them that the work of their enemies is the beckoning call of the Friend. We will see and touch them soon, Rashid. Together we will find sanctuary. It gladdens us all.

My fluked friend, Rashid thought to himself, it is you and your brothers that we need. Please help me in the days ahead.

CHAPTER 24

"He was a nice kid," the gray-haired man standing near Peter on the station platform said to his companion, a woman of around forty dressed in a gun barrel-colored business suit. A brisk March wind blew across the silver tracks that glistened in the morning sun.

"His dad says he was a strong swimmer," the businesswoman said in a clipped, authoritative voice, "Who knows what happened." Her eyes darted to the bend north of the station. She turned to smile politely to her companion and then, impatiently, looked north again. The wind died down briefly.

"I'm surprised the Carmichaels didn't see him. Almost always see them on the porch at that hour," the man added.

They were talking, Peter realized with a growing sense of discomfort, about the boy the morning news reported drowned in a boating accident apparently around sunset the day before. And of course he and the Carmichaels were on the porch, if that's when it did happen. "GLOBAL VISIONARY WATCHES CHILD DIE," Peter could see the headline. It was, of course, preposterous, but not beyond the *New York Post*. From what he had heard, the accident had happened somewhere closer to the western bank of the river. An eagle would have had trouble seeing a bobbing head at that distance and even if it had been visible, it was so far away that it would have taken at least ten minutes to get there—if you already had a fast boat in the water.

Still, the strangers' conversation unsettled him. Perhaps the truth that was disturbing him was that even if the boat had overturned nearby and doing something was possible, they would not have seen it because they were so absorbed in the sky. A nice moral, Peter thought.

"1st Monday," the gray haired man looked at his watch, "the train's always late on 1st Monday."

"Every Monday it seems," the woman added, "I can't schedule anything for early Monday and the v-phones on the trains are always packed."

Peter smiled. He was reminded by their devotion to work of a Hawaiian Senator's recent and nearly successful attempt to insert a sizable appropriation for local stress-reduction treatment centers for recovering workaholics. The scheme might have worked too if one of the developers whom the Senator was assisting hadn't insisted on running the seventeenth hole of the golf course through a small corner of a protected wetland. The permit application alerted a local affiliate of a national environmental group which in turn made the details public. The death knell came when it was discovered that the primary "treatment" targets were wealthy Japanese executives. To Peter the Hawaiian Senator's scheme was what he was coming to see as the reality of the legislative process, one or another clever deception to enrich one group at the expense of another. It had always been like this and it always would be. It took a leap of faith, an unwavering belief in political alchemy, to see legislatures as the Senator apparently did, as one of mankind's great conceptions, much less as a progenitor of humanity's evolution. Only if he took a long view, a very long view, could he think that Carmichael wasn't deluded and even then Peter wasn't so sure. The truth of the matter, he -concluded, was that his heart might not be into the Senator's latest project.

The train arrived in New York only a few minutes late. At the top of the escalator the gray-haired man and the woman briefly squeezed hands and then separated. Peter wondered about their relationship. He was sure that they weren't married but the relationship seemed too warm to be a casual friendship or business one, yet not passionate enough to be a love affair.

"See you Monday 8," the woman said.

Monday 1st, Monday 8, Monday 15, Monday Last. It had been six years now since the Universal Calendar was established and it had created a whole new vocabulary. It was the Woman's Movement that had started the demand for reform. What had been known to a few scholars—that the 12-month year was the invention of the patriarchal conquerors of ancient matriarchal societies—entered into the popular stream of dialogue, spurred by the Thessalian archeological discoveries of the previous decade. The irrationality of having some months of 30 days length, some of 31 and one of 28 (or 29 every fourth year) while pretending in other contexts that a month was a 30-day period was cited as clear evidence of the patriarchal world's ability to screw things up.

More important was the understanding of the 12-month calendar's role in the disempowerment of women. The original month's length had been 28 days, an approximate measure of lunar rotation from a solar perspective, but also the average length of a woman's fertility cycle.

Measuring the passage of time in a 28-day month, a number of feminist authors argued, with to what Peter seemed considerable acumen, created an unconscious thorn in the male psyche continually reminding him that notwithstanding his sinews, spears and swords, he had no power to give life. The cosmic rhythms of nature had not chosen to manifest in him. In comparison even the greatest male conquests seemed tenuous at best, futile little gaspings destined to be dust. There were precisely thirteen 28-day months in the solar year, leaving only one day unaccounted for (two days on leap years) which of course simply became in the Universal Calendar "No Days", days of a New Year, global festivals of rebirth, bacchanalian days of freedom unconnected to life's routines. Some scholars were convinced that the origin of the superstition that 13 was an ill omen also took root in men's fears of natural calendrics.

Male calendric ascendancy was accomplished by reducing the number of months to 12, thereby assuring erasure of an unpleasant memory of past generations and assuring counting chaos for future ones. In a few places, like the Jewish calendar, the 13th month appeared every few years as a catch-up device but with variations in days that obscured the connection with the feminine cycle.

With a 7-day week, a 28-day month presented another advantage. Every Monday would be the 1st, the 8th, the 15th, or the 22nd. Or, if you started on Sunday, every Friday would fall on the 6th, the 13th, the 20th, or the 27th. People who thought in terms of days of the month and people who thought in terms of days of the year need never misunderstand each other again.

When the Convention on the Inalienable Rights of Women was drafted, a provision was included requiring the adhering nations (of which there were to be 184) to work towards the creation of "a rational calendar based on the cycles of Nature, including its feminine principles." The provision was not resisted because its impact was seen as primarily symbolic. Of far more concern to many countries were provisions giving women individually, or as representatives of a class, rights to recover monetary reparations in special international tribunals from governments which failed to give or protect basic rights. Resistance was cloaked in cries of invaded national sovereignty but the resistance was only partially successful in watering these provisions down.

In most parts of the world the calendar movement was almost immediately successful. It received strong support from the rapidly proliferating environmental organizations around the world when it was proposed that the new, 13th month be called Gaia, in honor of course of the Earth itself, and inserted between April and May. The non-Christian world was lured by the suggestion that it was time to start counting years all over again without reference to a religious event in an imperialist legacy.

Resistance to change was fatally weakened when the Council of Protestant Churches denounced itself and its membership for "inappropriately imposing upon others vestiges of a misplaced cultural and moral supremacy" and, in particular, "for requiring that time be measured from an historical event having no particular historical importance anyway."

The Catholic hierarchy was appalled but accurately sensed that the tide was inalterably running out and adopted a position of neutrality based on the recognition that scholars were almost universally agreed that Christ was not born in the First Year of our Lord anyway.

In the year 2021 sufficient nations ratified the Universal Calendar Convention to bring it into effect. What would have been the Year 2022 AD became Year I of the Modern Era.

Year 6, 1st Monday, Gaia, Peter mused, it actually all seemed natural enough. He had been sure that at the individual level there would be massive unconscious resistance but this had not proven to be the case. Most people, he suspected, relished the opportunity to have a new beginning, and the No Day Festivals had proven enormously popular. These were even credited with a significant drop in the incidence of substance abuse, divorce, and violent crime in some of the Northern tier populations, though of course sociologists would always point out that there were many other contributing factors.

As he stepped outside the station, Peter considered walking to the Senator's city office but the growing heat of the sun persuaded him to hail a bicycle-powered rickshaw instead. The population of New York had dropped substantially but not as rapidly as sensitivity to noise and atmospheric pollution increased. In response the city experimented with a variety of traffic-reduction mechanisms ranging from prohibiting private automobile access to Manhattan to an ambitious subway-renovation project. The current mix included the subway project, steep fees for private automobile (electric only) and access and dedication of approximately forty percent of the pavement space to human-powered vehicles.

The mix had worked well. It was even a pleasure to get around the city sometimes. It had not only spurred a renaissance in the design of mechanical propulsion devices but rickshaw driving had given steady employment to the influx of actors, writers, artists, and immigrants who gave the city so much of its life.

Peter considered opening a conversation with his rickshot, a young woman of perhaps twenty-five with strong legs, a dancer perhaps, but decided against it, fearing that she would misinterpret.

She solved the problem for him. "That townhouse where you're going is Senator Carmichael's office, isn't it?"

"Yes it is," he replied. "What do you think of him?"

"Do you work for him?"

"Yes, but I want to know what you think."

"Is that your job, to see what people think and then make up an image for him to match?"

"No," Peter sensed that he was losing control of the conversation. "You're pretty cynical."

"Aren't you?" she paused as she built up speed from a changing light, perspiration glistening on her bare shoulders. "Dumb question, huh? I think your Senator is in the wrong business. He's not a sleazeball and he doesn't have his dick in his hand."

"How about me?"

"Hard to tell. Though I bet you feel bad when you touch yourself. Catholic?"

"None of your business," Peter blushed.

"Oh-oh, not polite, what would Mommy say." They stopped for a red light. The rickshot looked down at Peter from her pedal-stall. A hint of sadness suffused her face. "I'm sorry, that was uncalled for, it isn't my business."

"No, it isn't," Peter relented. "What did we do to you?"

"Not to me, to all of us. Look at the last forty years. Trillions of dollars on weapons that nobody could possibly use, hundreds of billions of dollars to high-finance grifters and virtually no effort to stop people from killing off half the life forms on this Earth. And then even stopping terrorists became just another cover for greed."

"It's not like that anymore."

"I'm not so sure, and even if it isn't, it's because hundreds of thousands of grassroots people started screaming. We didn't hear from more than a handful of politicos until the Earth was making like a sauna. They were all on the take."

"You should get into politics," Peter wasn't sure if the irony was lost on her.

"I promise you," she said between panting breaths, her legs pedaling harder, "that even inside all of the environmental sanctimony, most of your buddies are winking at scams."

"A few," Peter said. He thought of Bernie and MEIB, the Mother Earth Investment Bank. "Maybe," Peter said, "it was meant to be like that. Maybe politicos, as you call them, should only get into the act after a real majority of everybody else thinks something should be done. Maybe their job is just to motivate those who haven't figured it out to support what everybody else knows needs to be done. If you have to let people's greed or fear motivate them, so what."

"Whew, and you think I'm cynical!" she said, the rhythm of her pedaling briefly interrupted.

"Think about what I said, I'm not so sure it's cynical at all."

"Okay." She smiled. There was a small gap between her glistening front teeth.

They had reached 79th Street and the Senator's office. Peter paid and she gave him a receipt and a slightly damp card.

"Call if you need a ride, I carry a phone," she said, patting the cellular device on her hip. The card identified her as Jane LaForce, Rickshot, Dancer, and Mime.

"Goodbye Jane," Peter said. She pulled her face into a look of intensity and made jerky little movements with her shoulders as she pedaled away. In horror Peter recognized himself, she had mimicked him walking out of the station exit, briefcase in hand.

The rickshot incident stayed on his mind and flustered, he paid no attention when the woman behind the desk told him that he had a visitor. Peter had settled into the spare office he used in the city for close to fifteen minutes when the receptionist buzzed him.

"What would you like me to tell Mr. Doriano?" she asked.

"Who?"

"Your visitor, Mr. Doriano."

"I don't know any Mr. Doriano."

"He says he's from some UN agency, about a man named José María Velasquez." The last name was pronounced something like Valiscous. Peter made a mental note to have the woman reassigned; Hispanic constituents wouldn't enjoy having their names mangled.

"Tell him I can see him for five minutes, not much more."

Mr. Doriano proved to be pleasant enough. He was lithe, olive skinned, of average height, perhaps thirty-five years old. He produced a laminated identification badge with his name and picture and the UNINTEL hologram in the lower right-hand corner. Peter's eye lingered on the hologram, an elliptical eye set in a globe within a U-shaped wreath.

"The wreath, is it laurel, Mr. Doriano?"

"No, sir. Olive branches, I believe."

"Of course," Peter handed the badge back to his visitor. "Peacemakers. How may I help you?"

Mr. Doriano took a seat. He explained that of course, as someone in Peter's position well knew, UNINTEL initiated hardly anything at all but was obligated by treaty to carry out certain investigations at the request of national and regional investigative agencies where the implications of an event might transcend the jurisdictional limits of the initiating agency. He quietly added, leaning forward slightly, that as Peter undoubtedly appreciated these were not always matters of UNINTEL's own choosing, and that in this case, he was authorized to state, though not for the record, that his superiors were frankly embarrassed to be asking even the most routine questions of Peter with respect to an event which seemed to be no more than a traffic accident. His superiors, Mr. Doriano went on to explain, had done everything in their power to deflect this particular matter into a bilateral channel in the hope that it would simply disappear but the initiating agency, a rural police force in a small Latin American country, was adamant. It argued that precisely because Peter was in a position of such respect and prominence, a senior aide to one of America's most important senators, the two or three questions that needed to be asked should be raised by a neutral agency and not by an investigator of doubtful independence.

"We all know that the FBI is not subject to that kind of pressure," Mr. Doriano added, "and that it is simply a projection of this Peruvian police force's own corrupt and obsequious behavior to think in those terms. Regretfully, here we are."

"Just where are we?" Peter said.

"Of course. For the record, you are Peter Flanigan?"

"Yes."

"As you know, under the treaty, you have the same rights as if I were an American investigator, the right to remain silent... "

"Mr. Doriano, I know my rights but I'm running out of time. Am I a suspect?"

"No."

"I'm talking to you freely. You don't need to read me my

rights. You said it had to do with José María Velasquez, now please get to the point."

"Of course. Were you in Ayachuela, Peru on March 24th?"

"Yes. That would have been a Wednesday, that's right."

"Were you with José María Velasquez on that day?"

"Yes, at least part of the day."

"What were you doing there?" Peter explained his and the Senator's interest in stories of remarkable initiative and development.

"Were you with him when he died?"

"No."

"Do you know anything about the circumstances of his death?"

"I read in the paper that he fell from the road."

"I mean personal knowledge."

"No."

"Do you know why someone might wish to kill him?"

Peter was taken aback by the question. "I thought it was an accident?"

"So do we, Mr. Flanigan. So do we."

"Who could have gained by his death?"

"Your government?"

"What? No."

"You would not have wished it personally?"

"Of course not, I admired him greatly."

"So—the last question I've been requested to ask—you were not involved in any way in his death?"

"Of course not."

Doriano got up from his chair and extended his hand. "Thanks for your time, then, I really appreciate it."

"No problem."

"I'm just curious," Doriano asked as he headed for the door with Peter by his side, "it must be a pretty hairy road up to Ayachuela?"

"It is. My driver had me praying half the way."

"So you had a car there to get around? Must be beautiful."

"A car and a driver."

"Yeah. Is Velasquez one of those types who doesn't like cars?"

"I don't think so."

"But he didn't want to ride back into town with you from the project where you left him?"

"He was busy. I don't know why, I didn't think to ask. Why?"

"I don't know. In my business you're always trying to figure things out and we never get enough information."

Peter remembered his recent conversation with Katie about some kind of UN inquiry. "You didn't talk to a friend of mine—Katie Jasper—did you?"

"No, I haven't talked to anybody. Was she with you? Is that someone who was there with you?" Doriano's interest briefly perked up.

"No, just a friend. Another topic. I was reminded of something she said."

"Oh…. And the driver. Was he always with you?"

Peter saw the danger but knew he had to be truthful. "No, we let him eat and rest while we visited the project."

"Ummm," Doriano said noncommittally as he left the office, "Well, good luck, to you... and the Senator."

CHAPTER 25

The day in the office passed quickly. Peter was absorbed with a steady stream of v-phone calls, email, and telefaxes sent up from the Washington office. A bill authorizing major U.S. support for several Universal Space Agency (USA) probes would be considered on the floor of the Senate in a couple of days. The bill had brought out all of the former war-materiel contractors in the state. Each had his favorite project and wanted money earmarked for it. The bill had also brought out impassioned constituents who were convinced they had received authentic messages from intelligences that inhabited one or another astral body and were demanding a visit to the message's source. Many of these people were in other respects normal, productive, even prominent citizens and had to be handled with substantial care. The Livermore Lab's analysis of the deep space pulse—the accelerating Fibonacci series—had of course fueled the imagination of scientists and laymen alike.

When the receptionist came in to say good night a three-inch stack of unanswered correspondence on the subject still sat on his desk. Peter cursed the films of the 1970s and '80s that had indelibly imprinted myths of extraterrestrial contact on far too many people. Was it Edmund Burke that said that the march of the human mind was a slow one? No kidding.

He thumbed through the stack again. He rubbed his eyes and smiled. What the Senator needed to deal with this was a kindred spirit, some child of the zodiac who was a galactic dreamer, a nebula walker—but one who could take a balanced approach, who was not too attached to any particular star, and who could mediate between the demands of the Sulfurious Shell People of the Venusian caves and the dying messages of the Red Spot Cloud Beings of the Jovian biosphere, all without embarrassment to the Senator. He made a mental note to ask Katie. He remembered meeting a friend of hers, a rather striking woman, who might be ideal for the part.

The day, he realized, was getting to him.

Two hours later Peter looked across the small candle-lit table at Katie. Katie was always in a good mood at the end of the working day. This, Peter was convinced, was the result of frolicking all day in a catalog of electronically recorded happy endings without any need to touch the smell and the messiness and the pain that preceded them. She worked as a researcher and writer at SDI, the Sustainable Development Institute. SDI maintained a vast data bank of successful and environmentally sound solutions to problems of economic productivity and material well-being. Its database ranged from a catalog of genetically engineered grain varietals, to biologically based processes for sewage treatment, to management guides for ecotourist parks. SDI would make its data and responsive report available in any language to virtually anyone who asked a reasonably focused question. So many happy endings, Peter also suspected, made it hard for Katie to see through Bernie's MEIB planetary do-goodism to his underlying greed.

As he sat down, she reached across the table and squeezed his hand tightly. Two buttons on her blouse were uncharacteristically unlatched, drawing his eyes to the lightly freckled whiteness of her skin.

"It's a treat to see you again so soon," Katie said cheerfully. "How's the Senator?" she said sitting erect again.

"He's looking at the future."

"Ah, the Honorable Secretary of Something and Mrs. Flanigan cordially invite you... I can't wait." Katie's smile kept Peter from uttering the usual denials. She was highly skilled, he realized, at trapping him into silence. Were he to say anything, she would ridicule him for taking himself and her so seriously.

Finally he spoke.

"No, that's not what he's looking at." As they read over the menu, Peter attempted to describe the Senator's concerns.

"He's paranoid," Katie replied. "I have a friend—you know Bernie—he says that people who think like that are weak people, they're just projecting their own fears and power needs. Of course we need central management. There's no reason it has to be bad."

Peter repressed an impulse to tell her to fuck off. He folded the napkin in his lap and looked down at the menu instead. The menu puzzled him. The words were unintelligible and unpronounceable. The restaurant was Ethiopian, one of dozens in the city, a legacy of genocidal wars, political turmoil, anti-terrorist crusades and Sahelian droughts.

When peace finally came the Japanese, in a major public relations venture, adopted the region and announced that they would do "whatever is necessary" to make large portions of the Sahelian region green again.

A lot was necessary—reforestation, windbreak construction, agricultural research, deep water drilling, water distribution and conservation technologies, solar power installation and an unparalleled educational campaign. Some suspected that global climate changes had given the project an added and unexpected assist in a slight increase in precipitation, but no one denied the project's ultimate effectiveness. The region was now a net exporter of agricultural products, capable of supporting without strain more than twice its 1990 population. The new prosperity, however, had not enticed the restaurant owners to move back.

He gave up on making an intelligent dinner choice. He left it to Katie and within a few minutes a selection of lentils, vegetables, and small quantities of meat in rich-looking sauces appeared, accompanied by the stacks of soft bread which in appearance and function struck Peter as ecological marvels, edible napkins.

"I wonder," he said to her, holding up one of the edible napkins, "if these are recorded in SDI's data banks."

"They are, under 's' for sandwiches," she said. Peter knew that he had been caught in a stubbornly fashionable condescension toward Third World people.

"I asked for that."

"Yes, you did."

As they ate, he described the flood of correspondence on the extraterrestrial probes, their need for someone to handle it, and his incomplete memory of her friend.

"Oh, you mean Laura Feil. I don't know. She's been living in Costa Rica and seemed pretty attached to David. At least she was last time I saw her."

"I don't want to date her, Katie. She wouldn't need to spend much time in Washington. Can I call her?"

"Sure. Remind me to get her number for you tonight."

"Anything else I should know about her?"

"Yeah, she's not real wild about the modern world and I wouldn't try to impress her with how important Carmichael is."

"Anything else?"

"She listens to inner voices, she could be a loose cannon."

"A Joan-of-the-Mother-Earth-Ark type?"

She smiled, "You could say that. Like Joan she tends to be right. Last time I saw her she was going on about how the goddess came to her in a dream to warn her that Matteo Michelson's life was in danger. And sure enough, the man dies and then it comes out that someone may have poisoned him."

Peter remembered reading something about it. The Velazquez-Michelson parallels struck him. Charismatic leaders working outside of established channels. Both die. At first their deaths appear natural, then a hint of murder and intrigue seeps in.

"Katie, what did the UN people want?"

"What?" Katie stopped chewing, her forehead furrowed.

"The people you said were asking about me."

"Oh, not much. Were you honest, reliable, an alcohol or drug abuser, a pervert. How long I'd known you, what kind of relationship I had with you. The things you'd expect in a routine background check."

"And you're sure they were from the UN?"

"Well, at least one of them was, she had one of those UNINTEL badges with an eye-of-the-world hologram."

"The other one?"

"I didn't see his."

"Remember their names?"

"No," Katie said. A look of concern crossed her face, "Peter what's going on?"

"I don't know."

"And what happened to your apartment? You never told me what you found out."

Peter felt uneasy, remembering his mother had told Katie all about the break–in. He felt that his life was becoming vaguely incestuous. "Somebody broke in. They haven't caught him. That's all I know." He looked across at her more intently. "Katie, the police found some drug behind the refrigerator. You wouldn't know anything about that?"

"Only what your mom said. Aren't you a little freaked out Peter?"

"Of course."

"Do you have any friends that do drugs? Somebody I don't know about that hangs out with you a lot?"

"Katie, somebody planted the bag there and I just don't think it was a friend."

"So why did you ask me if I knew anything about it? And who would do that?"

Peter was wondering why he was being interrogated again, as if though he were a suspect in his own break-in. "Katie, I don't know. Hopefully the police will find something."

"If they didn't do it themselves," Katie offered helpfully. "I am worried about you."

Peter felt confused. "But why?"

Katie had no answer.

After dinner they took a brief walk in the neighborhood, past the Bloomingdale's Museum of Human Consumption at 60th and 3rd Avenue. They were drawn to the illuminated window displays of disposable cameras, throwaway beer cans, and gourmet cat food.

"Pretty depressing, almost as bad as the war memorials," Peter said.

"Well, it represents just as much harm, maybe more. The Holocaust may be the only thing that was clearly worse," she added. "We need to remember. People were dying by the millions of disease and starvation while this was going on, and rainforests were being cut down to feed the cats."

Later, in bed, in the vague glow of a hidden light, under lightly flowered sheets, with a hint of sandalwood in the air, he touched her skin, as pale and cool as the little boy in him remembered his mother's. Katie whispered that she loved him. He felt himself sinking into an abyss of confusion, a mixture of desire and repulsion.

He was limp and knew that it could be a night of humiliation if he stayed that way for long. Katie noticed and took his member into her hands. To Peter's relief, it hardened quickly as she caressed it. But a few minutes later when she engulfed him in the sensations of clasping warmth and moisture, a coursing energy assaulted him. He was overwhelmed. Helpless, he surrendered to a few quick thrusting movements and a blazing rush. It was over.

Katie held him in silence for a few minutes. When he fell off her and turned over, she spoke, "Shouldn't we talk?"

"I'm tired."

"It's no big deal, I just think that we'd both feel better if we talked. I know it would help me."

"There's nothing to talk about…. I'm sleepy." He knew that he had failed to pass some important test in Katie's eyes but he was exhausted. His breathing became rhythmic, and he felt himself slide into darkness and sleep.

In the morning Peter woke up hard-edged, pained by the memory of the night. This has to stop, he thought. He turned over and saw that Katie too was awake, her large blue eyes staring at him like a wounded rabbit.

"Katie," he said with a decisiveness that surprised him, "I can't see you anymore."

"What?" She looked at him, apparently uncomprehending.

"I can't see you anymore, at least not for a while, until we can just be friends, like we were when we were little. It isn't meant to be like this."

He sat up higher in the bed. "You keep coming into parts of my life without asking. It doesn't feel right. And in any event, you have your friend—Bernie. Remember?"

Briefly, Katie looked like she might break into tears. But she didn't; anger began to emerge. "Well, as your erstwhile and future friend, let me tell you something," her voice rose, "You are a cowardly shit, a selfish, cowardly shit. You get into a panic at the thought that someone might love you, and all you can think to do is run out the door."

She got up from the bed and pulled an oversized tee shirt that looked vaguely familiar to Peter over her head. "You'll leave this room and hide in your Senator's glory and self-important work, and pretend that there is nothing wrong with you. But let me tell you, whenever you think of me—and you know you will, even if it's only when you talk to your goddamned mother— you'll remember you heard it here first—you need help, Peter, H-E-L-P, and you need it badly if you're ever going to be a man."

Peter was sideways to the tirade, buttoning his shirt, getting ready to go. She was making this easy.

He remembered where he had seen the tee shirt. She'd been wearing it the morning he had called her, when she was with Bernie.

"Katie," he said, "I know you'll be happy with MEIB. You deserve him."

"Bernie," she replied with ice in her eyes, "can make it last."

WILLIAM H. ESPINOSA

CHAPTER 26

Toward the end of a long spring morning filled with little domestic tasks, Matilde Romero de Cabrera watched the SUV emerge from a dust cloud on the road and turn into her finca's entrance. At first she thought it was the sheriff or the water authority, the acequia mayordomo. The SUV was square and boxy and had some kind of light on top. The driver hardly slowed as he turned, and the car sprayed loose pebbles and earth on the goats and mule that were attacking a few shoots of green near the corner fence. Cabro Santo, always the first to complain, bleated loudly. When the SUV came closer, Matilde saw that she was mistaken. There were no markings on the vehicle and she didn't recognize the man behind the wheel. Matilde had lived in the Sangre de Cristo Mountains of New Mexico since she was nine years old. She knew everyone in the village and most of the permanent population in nearby Chimayo. This man was new and it made her uncomfortable.

Matilde moved away from the kitchen window. She dried her brown, calloused hands and as was often the case when she looked at them, she regretted that her stubby fingers lacked magazine elegance. Layers of red nail polish, the rings her husband had let her buy, the turquoise and lapis bracelets, none of it helped.

The man parked his SUV next to her youngest son's low-rider—a brightly painted, purple '70s Hemi Dodge, retrofitted with an electric motor and a silver-chained steering wheel. The low-rider spent most of its time in their drive. The electric motor could barely move the two tons of steel, and the elongated rear-end bottomed out on the dirt roads' pot holes and gullies. Thankfully, her older boy, Rafael, had had more sense. She was so proud of him too, now with an important job at the United Nations.

As the man came to the front door, Matilde thought about the gun leaning on the wall. She kept it to scare off the magpies and occasional coyotes when her husband was gone. She was being foolish, she realized, but she did tuck a short kitchen knife in her apron pocket. The man knocked, and she opened the door. He was an olive-skinned, lithe man, not exceptionally tall but in cowboy boots he towered over her five-foot frame. "Mrs. Cabrera?" he asked.

"Yes."

"I'm sorry to bother you. My name is Albert Doriano. I'm with an international agency, UNINTEL." He showed her a badge and laminated identifying card. The card featured a globe imbedded in an eye, enfolded in a U-shaped wreath.

"Yes."

"Your son, Rafael, is being considered for a promotion at the UN to a very sensitive position, so we have to do a background investigation. That's my job to do. I just have a few questions."

Matilde looked carefully at the card and breathed easier. She was thrilled that Rafael might be promoted again but she hid her excitement. "Would you like to come in?" she asked politely. "Water?"

"Yes, and no thank you. I won't be long." He seated himself on a dark leather couch in the small living room. His eyes darted over the striped Navajo rug on the floor to the carved wooden crucifix on the opposite wall. "In a way I feel at home here in New Mexico, the Church is so present. It's hard to find it living in New York."

Matilde settled into a nearby, straight-backed chair. "The church has helped me in many ways," she replied, feeling more at ease.

"Mrs. Cabrera, you've always lived near here?"

"Yes."

"I mean as a child too."

"Yes." Matilde felt her stomach tighten. What she had said was only half true.

"Then maybe you could help us. You see, we couldn't find a birth certificate for a Matilde Romero. All there was, was a baptismal record at the Chimayo church. But to be honest, we've wondered about that too. It's dated August 3, 1962, but the signature on it doesn't really look like the signature on the other records from that time. In fact, it looks a lot more like the handwriting of a priest who came here around 1970, a Father Tomas."

Matilde felt an urge to get up. She suppressed it but couldn't keep herself from squirming in the chair. "I wouldn't know about that. Los niñitos and niñitas aren't the ones who keep the records. If my parents were still alive, they might have been able to help you...Mr. Doriano." She looked down at the rug and her feet, swollen from too much sitting and standing. "But you know," she added, "paperwork is paperwork, it is never quite right."

"Of course. It seems like it's always a problem we have to work through. Electronic records are so much better."

"Maybe Father Tomas could help you," Matilde offered, hoping to change the subject harmlessly. "I remember him, I think. Yes, he was a good-looking priest. We—all the girls in the church—liked him."

"We checked, Mrs. Cabrera. Sadly, he's no longer with us. He got a little too active when he was assigned to a church in El Salvador during the troubles there." Doriano shook his head in seeming regret and then turned to her sharply. "Was he active here? Was he part of the asylum movement?"

"Why...I don't know. Maybe, for sure he had ideas. But what does any of this have to do with me...or Rafael?"

Doriano smirked. "Well, we know that he was active because he left a lot of notes in the church, a journal of sorts. It seems that sometime in 1977 a friend in Albuquerque contacted him and asked if please, please could he help with a little girl who had gotten into some kind of trouble in Mexico and was likely to be killed or raped."

Doriano leaned closer to Matilde. She could smell a faint

odor of mint-masking onion on his breath. "But of course you wouldn't know anything about that, would you?"

Matilde felt her throat constrict. She dug a fingernail into her leg and shook her head.

"We tracked the story down as best we could. It seems like there was some incident in a small town in Jalisco Province. It was in the news then. There was an attempted murder charge against a young girl, Matilde Sanchez. Her mother, Flor, went to jail a year later as an accessory for hiding her. The girl was never found."

Matilde was trembling. "Cuentos y mentiras. Stories and lies. Are you accusing me?" Her shoulders hunched protectively. Abruptly, she glared at Doriano, stood up and went to the door. She unballed a fist to turn the knob. "You need to leave now, Mr. Doriano. You must be looking for someone else."

Doriano didn't budge. "Father Tomas also wrote about how generous the Romero family was with the repairs to the north wall of the church. He wrote that he had done a small favor for a middle-aged childless couple, and it was repaid may times over."

Tears came to Matilde's eyes. "My parents loved the church. The sand it sits on is sacred. It heals the sick. It shelters the Santo Niño, the Holy Child of Atocha. Only a fool who lived here wouldn't support it." Matilde heard her voice thicken and grow in volume.

"Do you have any brothers or sisters?" Doriano persisted.

Matilde pulled the door open. "Leave. Leave now." She was nearly shrieking; her vision blurred.

Doriano got up and walked to the door. "As you wish," he said, leaning over her barely a foot away. "Understand, though, our position. If we conclude that you are that girl, we don't have much choice. We have to tell the national authorities. Sad to say, the Americans still haven't repealed their terror-fed immigration laws. Illegals that are criminal suspects are rendered home. Fast."

As Doriano drove away in the SUV, Matilde felt bile rise to her throat. She gagged. She collapsed in a chair and wept. So many years ago, she thought, how could it still be? She was just a child. Her mother had been out one hot, dusty afternoon when the patrón had called her in to the main house. He had ordered a

Coca Cola with ice for her and given her a brand new doll with long blond hair to play with. He told her how pretty she was. After she drank the Coke, he asked her to sit beside him with the doll. She did. Then he began stroking her hair and arms. It didn't feel right, and when his hand went to her leg near the place her mother said she should never let anyone touch, she tried to get up. The patrón grabbed her by the arm and kept touching her. She cried out. No one was near. Panicked, she looked around. There was a knitting basket in a bowl on the credenza behind the couch. She grabbed a knitting needle and when his grip tightened, she brought it down on his thigh. Except it wasn't his thigh. He had moved. The needle pierced his right testicle and impaled him to the sofa cushion. Blood sprayed from the man's trousers; the patrón screamed.

Matilde ran out the door just as her mother was arriving. When her mother saw what happened, she dragged Matilde to their house. She removed a figurine of the Virgin Mary from a recess in the adobe wall and reached into a cavity underneath. She drew out a wad of dollars and pesos. Mother and daughter ran through the corn fields, crawled under a barbed wire fence and climbed through brush and boulders into the hills. The two hid in a rocky crevasse for hours. When it was dark, they walked to a friend's house three miles away, avoiding the road. The friend ran a sundries store below so she had a phone.

"Beti," her mother called her cousin in Albuquerque, "un desastre." A calamity. She told Beti what happened. "You have to help us," she said. "Matilde is as good as dead here."

"Santa Maria, Madre de Dios. You need a miracle," Beti responded. "Get yourself here and we'll see what we can do."

The friend who owned the store arranged for a pre-dawn ride for Matilde and her mother in the back of a pick-up truck to Guadalajara. From there a bus took them to Nogales, and somehow Matilde's mother arranged a trip across the border to Tucson and then Albuquerque. Beti, Matilde remembered, was an attractive, busty woman in her thirties. She always wore a partially open blouse that let her display the most beautiful silver cross Matilde had ever seen. Beti met them at the bus station and announced that a miracle had occurred. She had spoken to a priest in a town two hours north. It was all arranged, thanks be to the Niño Santo de Atocha, protector of convicts and children. They would go to his shrine, Beti said, and all would be well. Late one night, Beti drove them to the church in Chimayo. Father Tomas greeted them at the side door. He took her to the home of a kindly middle-aged couple whom she was soon calling *Mami y Papi*. Matilde never saw her real mother again.

Matilde made her way outside. She checked on the chickens in their roost. She patted the mule, put out some hay, and pushed the goats around to fill a trough with water. She walked the length of the sangrias that irrigated her land. Sangrias—water, the blood of the land; only the New Mexican Spanish would be so literal and call a water ditch that. And the mountains were called the Blood of Christ. And the sect that had founded the Chimayo church—the Penitentes—whipped themselves until they bled. And the pilgrims who came to the church crawled on their knees until they too bled. What did she expect? That the blood of others which she had drawn would not find here? She laughed bitterly to herself and braced herself for God's vengeance.

A sleepy-eyed dog who had been nowhere to be seen when Doriano arrived, trotted up to her and followed her back to the house. She swept the porch and living room and prepared the ingredients for her husband's dinner, in case his work ended early and he made it home that night. He didn't. Late that evening, Matilde keyed in her son's home number. When he answered, she could see on the screen that he was just finishing his own dinner. "Rafael, *mi hijo*," she said, "I have a long story to tell you. But for now, you must promise me, absolutely, no matter what, you will do whatever those UN people ask of you. We're agreed?"

CHAPTER 27

Over the whine of the turboprop an intense dark-haired, mustachioed young man was speaking animatedly to Laura. The seats on the Mexicana flight were narrow, the leg room short so that from the beginning Laura's arm had been in off-and-on contact with his shoulder, her leg resting now and then against his. The contact had been pleasant for Laura, not arousing but reassuring. She had learned to rely on her intuitive responses to human energy fields, particularly where the impressions came from touch. She had heard it said that all spiritual experiences were sensations in the body, hierarchically arranged. She had no reason to doubt it.

If she had a fear of flying, it was the fear of unavoidable proximity to a human whose energy interacted badly with her own. Laura wished she were less vulnerable but found it required a major and tiring effort of will to protect herself. So she had felt a surge of relief when this particular young man sat down beside her. He would be a good companion. She could sink into her seat and quiet her being and let the trip be a transition. Laura felt comfortable and free, free even to let her attention wander, only half listening to her companion.

Laura gathered that the young man was an agronomist. He was of Italian extraction but his parents had moved to Brazil where he hoped to return after completing his training. He was talking about the Lacondon, a Mayan group that settled in what was now the remnants of the Chiapas rainforest, refugees from the Spanish conquest. Their identity was nearly extinguished in the twentieth century by a rash of misguided policies aimed at easing the population and economic pressures that afflicted Mexico as a whole.

"They are an extraordinary people," the agronomist said, "They turned the forest into a friend and cohabited with it for centuries. Their agricultural output is amazing and when you first see the land they work, you might not even know that you are on farmland. We're not talking about acres of wheat or rows of corn or rows of anything else like that. You will think that you're still in the forest."

"Each family," he said as he gave a little twirl to the left end of his mustache, "only takes two or three acres from the forest— milpas they call these little plots. They clear it and then the first thing they do is plant trees, fast-growing fruit trees like papaya and banana that help hold the soil and shade it, and then they plant root crops like taro to anchor it, and then they put in their maize and dozens of other crops of all kinds."

His excitement was rising and he placed his hand on Laura's arm, "Everything gets mixed together, they purposely won't put the same plants together. This cuts down the pests. Every bit of space gets used; there's not an inch that isn't. And somehow they know how to put the best combinations together and which plant needs how much sun and shade and water depending on what kind of soil they're growing in. So there's this matted mess of vegetation, crawling along the ground, knee-high, chest-high, over your head and even bulging underneath your feet."

"It sounds sensuous," Laura said, squirming a bit and unbuckling her seat belt. "Does it last?"

"It does, it does, usually about five years until the weeds get bad. They don't use pesticides or herbicides, hardly even a machete. Then they move on to a new plot but they replant the old one with trees, rubber, cacao, things like that."

The turboprop stumbled briefly in an air pocket. The young man caught his breath, "I tell you, it is remarkable and here is an amazing thing. It seems that many forest animals, deer and pacas and peccaries, actually like the new growth more than the old forest."

"I've read somewhere," Laura offered, "that it's true in our Southwest too, a little bit of human activity, the right kind, actually attracts more birds and animals than you would have otherwise." Laura wished that she could remember the details. David would know, she thought, David would love to talk to this man. She considered giving the young man David's name but then decided that she was not ready to talk about David.

"Yes, yes," the agronomist continued, "I think those were native peoples too? Perhaps not; it is the love affair with nature that matters. It is her lovers that nature loves; it is those who enter with patience and fascination, those who enter into the minute intricacies of her being, who see the nourishment buried in the rot and dirt, it is those whom she rewards. This is why I came to study here."

"It's a passion for you, isn't it?"

"Yes, you are right," he said. His hands came up as if to frame the thought. He turned in his seat to face her, "A passion for the Earth. It is good that so many have it now. I think she will not abandon us."

Abandonment. Laura felt a twinge of discomfort at the word and rearranged herself in her seat again. The young man appeared not to have noticed. He had settled back in his chair and his eyes were fixed on the cabin ceiling. A steward walked by and smiled at them both.

The young man redirected his gaze toward Laura and continued, "The Earth, she has so many ways to speak to her lovers. With the Lacondon, when they grow tobacco, they don't plant by the calendar. They plant when the forest tells them to, when the wild tamarind tree flowers. We have done studies and it took us far too long to see the obvious, the variations in when the tree flowers are the product of changes in sunshine, rainfall and temperature—the very factors that determine when tobacco grows best. The tamarind measures the variations far more accurately than we ever could.

"Have I offended you—speaking of tobacco?" The agronomist leaned toward her slightly. "You are an American, yes? I know it is forbidden there."

"Not everywhere," Laura replied, "just in public places. It's okay. I know it had other uses for other peoples. We've had worse vices."

"Ah yes, the drugs." He went on to tell the story—Laura had heard it before—of how the Lacandon were saved from cultural extinction. How the remnants of the Chiapas rain forest were preserved through an infusion of foreign funds sufficiently large to persuade the Mexican Government to establish what became an extended research facility, less to study this particular remnant of forest than an approach that might be used in other threatened areas.

The Lacondon themselves broke out of their isolation, some say because of their dwindling numbers; others attributed it to their mystical contact with the earth and their ancestors who were alleged to have whispered from the other side that now as the end of the world, the end of a great cycle approached, it was time to disclose the secrets. Most of the few hundred that remained became teachers, well-paid ones, to thousands like the agronomist. Some even traveled to other settings where they served as a Peace Corps of sorts. Others continued the old planting, listening to the forest's changes.

"It is said," the agronomist added, his monologue apparently drawing to a close, "that what these people know is only a fragment of what their ancestors possessed. Can you imagine what we have lost?"

To Laura's distress the agronomist was now leading her into the world of Carlos and Don Silvestre and the lure of the hidden Mayan truth. Carlos and Don Silvestre, she felt, had made a fool of her; she wanted to talk about them even less than she did about David. The thought of them angered her, and some of that was directed at the goddess who had arranged her travel seating to ensure that she wouldn't be able to forget about them. Soon the anger passed and she felt sad. Something's wrong, she concluded, and she had to deal with it but was helpless because she didn't know what or how.

The agronomist was staring at her, waiting for her to respond. He is a nice man, she thought, and in little ways I am hurting him, too. "I'm sorry," she said, "My own thoughts... there are things that are painful... I'm sorry, I'm just lost."

She felt tears come to her eyes. She struggled to hold them back. The agronomist appeared confused, uncertain what to say.

"I have been thoughtless," he finally said. "You wish to be alone and I have intruded."

"You're right, a part of me wanted that," she managed a small smile in his direction, "but I know how to be alone. You did the right thing to talk to me."

Laura looked out the oval window. They were flying over a blanket of rolling clouds. Near the horizon a large one rose up. As Laura stared at it, it gradually took the form of a squat-bodied, small-headed reptile. The heavens always took unusual shapes for her. It was the secret of her photographic work. She had no technical skill to speak of but remarkable sky beings always walked into her frames. She thought about reaching into her bag for her camera. The window was too scratchy, the cloud too distant.

"Sir," she tapped his forearm, "look out, what do you see?"

He leaned over and peered out, squinting a little bit. "*Un lagarto*. A lizard. How remarkable. To the Maya, the lizard... " He stopped himself. "There I go again, lecturing you about the Maya when you have other cares."

"No, it's okay. You are a kind man. What's your name?"

"David, David Pileiro."

Laura let a little laugh slip out. "There is no escape," she said, recovering, knowing that only a little bit of truth would let him understand. "I was with a man, David. I left. Everything you have said today reminded me of him or of what's happened since."

"I'm sure you had good reasons for leaving," David Pileiro offered.

"No," she said with some finality, "no good reason. It was just a cruelty. I shouldn't have been there in the first place."

That was, Laura realized, the truth of it. She had been drawn by the adventure, by the lure of tropical flowers and forest canopies concealing the imagined, luminous secrets to which she always gravitated. She had liked David; she had enjoyed the intensity of his sexual attraction to her but she had not loved him, not enough to have sensed the deeper calls of his being which were, as he approached midlife, crying for the usual ordinary things: a home, a companion, children.

In a word, she had used him. She had kept him from his

fulfillment while she spun in ever more distancing orbits from her own. And she had made it far worse by sleeping with Carlos before she had left David. She had degraded the one thing that had joined them powerfully and which David could have always valued after they drew apart. The tears she felt earlier were for the most part self-pity, when what she really needed to do was cry in shame.

At least David had had the good sense to be angry. There had been a hardness in his voice when she last spoke to him, more than the time before.

"What is it now, Laura?"

"Are you coming?"

"No, I'm not." She could see on the screen that David was glancing at a document of some sort. He was wearing a guayabera with a pattern that she hadn't seen before.

"Do you want me to come back?"

"It's over, Laura." He looked squarely into the screen.

"David, I'm frightened." Maybe it was just at the ease with which she had been deceived. In the bookstall at the bus station, waiting for Carlos that Sunday, she had found it, a dust-covered, paper-bound edition of Meetings With A Mayan Magus, ©1997, 2003.

"An account," the squib on the back cover announced, *"of the author's encounter with Don Silvestre, a craggy, Mayan villager who proved to be far more than he seemed. His mysterious appearances and disappearances take us on an exploration of the Yucatan and into the secrets of its past, to a time when a temple priesthood ruled a far-flung society through telepathic command."* Even down to the details it was much the same. The author's first name was Carlos.

"I'm scared, David, there's something menacing about this."

"Why are you still there?" he asked. She knew it was a reasonable question but chose to ignore it.

"Why would they go to so much trouble to fool me?"

"To get in your pants. Isn't that what we all want from you? It'll be a great story at the cantina, good for at least two rounds."

Laura flinched but recovered, *"I'm easier than that."*

"So I noticed, but what's his name—Carlos? —he may not

have known that."

"They didn't have to drag me to Mexico."

"You were going to stay here? Crawl in for breakfast every day?"

There is more to it, Laura thought, even though nothing happened during the days and nights that she stayed at the hotel, waiting, as Carlos' note had instructed. Finally she had received a call from Don Silvestre…telling her Carlos could not come and get her…it was a little dangerous, didn't she have a friend, David, was that his name?…who could come with her into the Chiapas back country?

"Silvestre wants you to come with me," she persisted with David over the v-phone.

"No, you have to be kidding."

"No."

"Why?"

"I don't know. He said 'protection.'"

"No way. Laura, show some sense, go to Washington, look into Peter's job offer."

She remained convinced there were other motivations. Maybe she could get David to talk about it after her trip to Washington. He had given her the opening when he had mentioned the call from Peter Flanigan. "Let me know how it goes," he had said, "and give my best to Katie."

***

Peter Flanigan's office was small. It was made smaller by the stacks of bills and committee reports and yellowing piles of Congressional Records and newspapers which covered most of the furniture's horizontal surfaces and dusty corners of the floor. A large bookcase rose to the ceiling and bulged into the room. Half of it was filled with a multivolume series, *Treaties and International Agreements of the United States.* Another section was filled with twenty-five years of the *State of the World* and twenty-one years of the UN's *Human Development Report.* Various shelves were devoted to international affairs and others to treatises on Congressional and Presidential power. Boring, terminally boring, Laura thought. Why am I here! Nonetheless, she felt her mouth form words of inquiry and admiration about the book collection.

"These are the confessionals," Peter replied from behind an old wooden desk that was also covered with papers. He was pointing to the corner of the bookcase that was nearest to him, "or at least that's what I call them. For years there's been a whole industry. Top people leave government and the first thing they do is hire a ghostwriter to savage everybody else or pave the way for their next job. But the ghostwriters exact some subtle kind of revenge, a bit like the underpaid portrait painters of European courts who had to make a buck off the nouveau merchants as well. Ghostwriters show us the worst traits of the savage."

Laura smiled. It was an interesting comparison. David had said that Peter was smart. A little pompous but smart.

"It gets worse," Peter continued, "there are so many of these that no one has been able to bring themselves to read them anymore, so now they pay the publishers to print them and send complimentary ones to everyone they think is important."

Laura widened her eyes in mock admiration; she might as well have fun with this. "So that many people think you're important!"

"Absolutely, and maybe thousands more. The truth," he said with a smile, "is that they almost never send them to me, but the Senator refuses to keep them in his own office."

He has nice teeth and hair, she mused, and almost misty eyes. A little frail, maybe. She wondered why Katie had given him mixed reviews. Laura had avoided asking her too much about her relationship with Peter because she didn't want to feel obligated to talk about David. Katie had known David for years before he met Laura. She had just started at the Sustainable Development Institute and had been assigned to help David who was gathering materials before his tour in Tibet, just after the Dalai Lama's return.

It seemed like not so long ago. Beijing's centralized dominance had been challenged, first by demands for local power from Shanghai, then by similar assertions in other regions. Pro-democracy demonstrations swept the country for the second time in thirty years. To the Communist Party leadership's surprise, it was the Dalai Lama who most vocally called for patience and moderation. He sponsored a series of mediations and a new constitution was established. In gratitude, Tibet's people were given substantial autonomy. Laura remembered the broadcast of the ascension ceremonies—the prayer flags in a thousand patterns, the trumpets, bells, and harmonic chants rich in overtones. The Dalai Lama had spoken of the marriage of heaven and earth, bound in compassion for all creatures, and the land was symbolically healed with the planting of more than one million trees on the denuded mountainsides of a ravaged country. David had played a small role in that effort. He had helped introduce new varietals whose increased photosynthetic capacities had extended the altitude ranges in which trees could thrive.

Two billion people had watched. More than probably knew the place existed a decade or two before. It seemed odd to Laura that in exile a people could do so much to enrich the cultures of others. In the case of Tibet, the exile had been mercifully short, a little over half a century, for the Jews twenty centuries. *But,* Laura thought to herself, *I am still floating around unrooted, listening to disembodied voices whisper into untethered ears. When will my own pointless exile end?*

"I'm sorry," Laura said, coming back to Peter and the paper-filled room, "I spaced out for a minute there."

"Exactly, Laura," Peter replied, still smiling, "Exactly why I wanted to talk to you."

"You're making fun of me," she said after listening to Peter's explanation of what he wanted, "You can't be serious. Worse, you're mocking the very people that vote you into a job. I can't believe that you're so cynical." She paused and swiveled her upper body in the overstuffed chair to face him squarely, "What's wrong with you?"

"I'm not making fun of anyone, Laura. We have a problem and we have to solve it. I can't speak in a language these people will understand." His jaw had visibly tightened. She saw pain in his eyes.

"What's wrong?'"

"Katie said you would like the idea, that you'd be good at it."

"Did she? Peter," Laura decided to work her way back to her question more slowly, "maybe Katie didn't have a chance to explain to you or maybe she doesn't really understand.

Extraterrestrials are not my thing. I haven't seen one, I haven't heard one, I haven't even dreamed about one.

"What I do think," she continued, "is that we've lost touch with the spiritual dimensions of life. Life here on this Earth, life like it used to be when it was okay to sense an unseen force— actually a lot of unseen forces, and it was okay to say here it is, moving in our lives, so let's give each one a god name or a goddess name and maybe a story so we can understand and talk about them a little better, pull them up out of the bottomless dark of our unconscious, give them some form, and even have a real relationship with these forces...not to speak of a better one with one another and all the plants and animals that live around us.

"What I do think is that there are still special places and special people that carry fragments of the old story, maybe more than fragments. And if you're like me and you've opened yourself to these forces a bit so they start talking to you in a comprehensible way, and you get a taste, you'll be confused and elated and frightened and overwhelmed and you have to keep looking for the person or the place or the book or the culture that will help you understand, that will give you more, that will keep you alive because there's no question if you stop, you might as well be dead.

"I haven't figured this out yet. I'm not in my place yet. I'm almost as lost as you, but I do know that I'm not going to find anything out there in the asteroid belt, or on the mountains of the moon. Nothing at least that's going to get me any closer to what I have to find."

Laura stopped, as if waiting for what she had just said to catch up with her. Peter too, she noticed, had been moved to a different place. Where did these words come from? Even to herself she had never been as clear. Twice now in less than one day, barriers inside her had dissolved and truths had come out. Hope might not be too far behind.

Peter appeared thoughtful but not in an intense way; the lines of his face had softened. He intertwined his fingers together and rested them on his desk. "Maybe," he said, "what you see in the past, others see in the future, what you see in the pristine -cloud forest where native peoples once lived, others see in the underground rivers of Io.

"Maybe," he continued, his eyes now focused intensely on her, "it is just their way of describing those very same forces you feel, here, even in this room."

Laura sensed that once again she had misjudged, but wasn't sure how to respond. "In this room with books piled up like dirty clothes no one wants to wear again? I don't think so. I think it's just the two of us."

"Maybe. Maybe so," he said. He got up from his desk, "Will you have dinner with me tonight? We can talk about this some more."

To her surprise, she said yes.

CHAPTER 28

A few flakes of soft snow brushed against Almira's cheek as she stepped out of the airport walkway. She felt her sinuses contract on impact with the sudden cold. Close to a meter of snow was packed like soiled, soggy rice on the sides of the road; a centimeter or two of white powder covered the road itself. The snow began to fall more heavily, muffling the sounds of voices and machinery but, somehow, not the crackle of tires grinding it into the road.

I deserve this, she thought as she waited for the taxi to pull up. Here it is, mid-Gaia, and the snow is still coming down. Ali would say it was a sign that I should turn right around, Elizabeth would hug me and make me hot tea, and the boys would throw snowballs gently at me, and hard at each other. She already missed them all.

A sign? As if Tom Autry had not been enough. She and Tom had laughed over dinner about the bovine countenance of the English. She had enjoyed the touch of his hand on hers, his arm around her shoulder and a brief brushing of lips as he said good night to her in front of the Loaves and the Fishes. When he called a few days later to say he was in Glastonbury again, she begged off dinner—Jamal was still not well—but warmed at his offer to take her to Heathrow, her initial misgivings forgotten. Then an hour from Heathrow it had started.

"Did you hear about that Fatimah woman they found shot in

bed with a spymaster?"

Almira's pulse pounded. She said she had known Fatimah but tried to be noncommittal.

Tom asked a few more questions about her. "What that lady wanted is the next thing to anarchy. Far too much wrong for us to try that, don't you think? We could be toast—or ice cubes in a few years."

Almira didn't respond. "Hey," Tom added, placing his well-muscled hand over hers, "why don't you see if you can get an early morning flight and we can have dinner tonight." Almira withdrew her hand and demurred, her voice notably tense, certain now that Tom's encounter with her was prearranged. When she spoke to Ali a few hours later, it came as no surprise that Elizabeth's ex-husband, the solicitor, had been unable to find any record of an American lawyer named Tom Autry practicing in England, and he hadn't heard of any slow water current energy deals that could keep a lawyer busy.

A taxi pulled up in front of her and a dark-haired man of medium height put her bag in the trunk next to the banks of fuel cells. Almira climbed in and asked the driver to take her to the Hotel Kalastajatorppa. She was not sure if she had pronounced it comprehensibly so she showed the driver her reservation slip. He looked at it briefly and nodded. As they drove along, Almira saw an expanse of white, punctuated by low-slung homes, almost always surrounded by trees. She saw people walking and a few skiing in graceful strides along the side of the road. Virtually all wore bright colors, as if trying to deny the long hours to the night.

From time to time through the flurries she could see a bundled figure sitting, holding a line that disappeared into the snow. With a shock she realized that it must be a frozen lake or perhaps the finger of the bay. A good sign, she thought, the sea must be rich with fish as it once was. The Baltic Commission had done its job.

The Mediterranean, she knew, had not been so lucky. Its people were too quarrelsome to cooperate readily. Perhaps they had just been there too long to believe that anything catastrophic could happen to the sea, so the wastes kept flowing in uncontrolled well beyond the end of the twentieth century. Now she had recently read it would be at least a generation, probably two, before the Mediterranean could be called a living sea again.

As a child, she had seen a television program set in a future where beachgoers wandered around covered from head to foot by thin material to protect them from the sun and never ventured into the water. A fundamentalist neighbor watching it with her family had been ebullient and with a finger pointing toward heaven, proclaimed that it was the will of Allah that it should be so. Will of God or not, in some places it had actually come to pass.

"Is it always like this, this time of year?" she asked the taxi driver.

"Please?"

"The cold—is it always like this?"

"No, not always. Warmer usually, though before global climate change began, often like this."

The man's English was heavily accented. It was not his strength. Even though Helsinki had become a major international center, many of its inhabitants had resisted learning English even more doggedly than the French had.

"Are you with conference?" the taxi driver asked.

"No." At least not exactly. Jean Marc was there for the conference. She was beginning to feel a little bit like a camp follower, a senior civil-servant groupie. But there hadn't been any choice. After contacting Jean Marc's office, Ali had reported that her former lover was traveling, and it just wasn't going to be possible for them to meet, at least not any time soon. Almira, suspecting that this was more Ali's intention than the reality, had persisted, and eventually extracted from an officious clerk, a telephone number in Moscow where Jean Marc could be reached between the hours of eight and twelve the next day. Of course, the clerk had snidely added, in his experience, it was virtually impossible to get through at those hours. Perhaps she should wait until he was in Ouagadougou where it would be far easier.

The next day she had uttered a brief prayer each time before dialing the Moscow number from the Loaves and Fishes kitchen and on the fifth try she succeeded. As she waited for Jean Marc to come onto the screen, she felt her hands sweating and her heart racing. Their first contact in close to fifteen years could have been awful, but, as it turned out, it wasn't. He looked almost exactly the same as she remembered him, only richer, his clothes probably tailor-made. He was clearly happy to see her and yes, of course, if she were free to travel, he could find time to meet with her. Helsinki, he suggested, a Council of Europe-sponsored conference on industrial policy and environmental and consumer needs would take place there. There would be suggested consumption guidelines for European nations to follow and that would take time to work out so the pace would be slow at times, leaving him leisure. Of course, he would have a companion with him. That would not be a problem? Good, he added. He thought Almira would like her.

As the taxi drove through a suburban, almost rural neighborhood to the hotel entrance, Almira worried that his companion might be a problem after all. If she got no time alone with Jean Marc, she would resent it; she would not be able to speak freely. Then, at night she would be left on her own while she imagined Jean Marc and his friend making love. She would sense undertones, humiliating undertones. Her feelings for Jean Marc were not resolved and she knew that she has been too long without a lover. Even Tom Autry—the thought made her nauseous—had sensed her sexual longing. The air would become charged. She would become angry. Or worse, pathetic. She looked out the window again. Another mistake. She should be with Jamal and Youssef. She was angry at herself and felt her fingers clench inside the fur-lined gloves. But the sight of the snow falling, blanketing the roads and the houses and trees slowly calmed her. Inshallah, you'll be okay, she said to herself, and pressed her face against the windowpane.

The hotel was pleasant enough. It was modest in size but its rooms were large, thick-walled, tightly sealed against the cold and the boisterousness of neighbors. A maze of underground passageways led to conference rooms, restaurants, swimming pools, saunas, and shops. Almira settled in, unpacked, explored a bit and then called Jean Marc on the hotel telephone. He was not in, a vaguely accented woman's voice told her. Was she Almira, yes? The voice identified itself as Lucinda. Jean Marc would be back in two hours if all goes well. Maybe some coffee or tea before then? Almira was curious but she politely declined.

Jean Marc returned earlier than expected. "Good news," it seemed that he virtually shouted it through the receiver, "You haven't eaten, have you? We have time for a great little excursion."

Almira had been sitting in the lobby a minute or two when Jean Marc emerged from the elevator. He had remained slim and still moved gracefully, almost elegantly. The crest ring Almira remembered so well still graced his finger. He was accompanied by a boyish, light-skinned woman with short dark hair and compelling brown eyes. She moved with a light-stepped sensuality that Almira found both captivating and playful. I can see why he likes her, she said almost aloud to herself. I already do.

Almira felt Jean Marc embrace her and a confused welter of feelings that she could not separate passed through her. She was introduced to Lucinda who clasped her hand, bottom and top. Her eyes lingered on Almira's. Almira's confusion deepened, she felt like she had known this woman for years but she had hardly said a word to her.

"You haven't changed," Jean Marc said as his eyes surveyed her. "No, you have. You're much more present, almost intimidating. You're not the shy Arab girl still finding out who she is."

Almira was finding coherent sequences of words hard to come by. Lucinda interjected, "Well, I will leave you two now. I'll see both of you at dinner, yes?" She looked at Almira.

"Why yes. That will be nice."

"Where we're going," Jean Marc said to Almira, "is a museum and a restaurant, a little way outside the city.

"Three architects lived there," he said as the taxi took them into the country. The snow was falling more lightly now. "They were very young but obviously brilliant. It was their submission which won a contest and became the Helsinki rail terminus in 1904. They took the prize money and each built himself a house and studio, but the buildings were all designed to fit together and are all connected. Today, one's a restaurant, one's a museum and, I think, people still live in the third one.

"But these architects," Jean Marc continued with a gleeful smile, "were really connected. Apparently it didn't take long for one to fall desperately in love with the wife of another and for her to feel the same way. So the first gave her up but they all kept on living in this same little compound and then the first fell in love with the sister of the second and they were married too, and they all stayed in this same little compound and went on producing some of the period's finest architectural work."

Jean Marc paused to catch his breath. He reached across the back seat and squeezed her hand. She didn't withdraw it. "Actually, the story doesn't even end there," he continued, "the son of one of the architects went on to become one of America's best, the Dulles Airport, the St. Louis Arch. What do you think?"

This is so like him, she thought, enthusiastic, innocent, knowledgeable and ultimately, subtly controlling. It was not enough for him to introduce her to the experience, to let the story unfold as they toured the rooms of the house; she had to experience it as he did.

"I think that you are intrigued," Almira replied. Still, she was enjoying being drawn into his world again. "It reminds me in a way of the story of Rumi and Shams. Rumi was a lawyer and a scholar of some distinction. But it was only when Shams, a wandering dervish, appeared that the poetry started flowing. The story of the bond between the two became almost as important as the stories in Rumi's poetry."

"What I would like to know," Jean Marc said, "is whether the swaps were all as clean as the official story says. Do you think they really stayed out of each other's beds?"

"You have a one track mind. You didn't hear a word I said."

"I did, I did, but Rumi's sex life doesn't sound interesting and anyway we're not going to his house."

She whisked her hand away from his and pretended to squirm into the furthest corner of the seat. "You are a degenerate."

"Perhaps, but if I remember right, we fell quite a ways together."

Almira allowed herself a slight smile. Memories of some of Jean Marc's experimentations floated by her accompanied by a twinge of arousal. She turned her head to the window, drawn by a sudden brightness outside. The sun was slicing between two cloud masses and was reflecting off the snow and ice. The flurries had stopped.

The taxi left them at the entrance to the building complex. Jean Marc paid the attendant and they joined a tour. The three houses formed a corner. Each building was a multistoried labyrinth of small but interestingly shaped rooms. The window lighting created unusual geometric shapes and every nook and cranny seemed to have a story to tell, but the tour was short. Worse, they were joined by a class of chattering Japanese architectural students who had made a private talk impossible. The guide retold Jean Marc's story but by then the class had become serious and no one even giggled. Jean Marc and Almira left the tour and went into the restaurant, which was spread over three floors with a number of half-enclosed rooms. For the first time Almira felt as if she were alone with Jean Marc. She allowed him to order her a glass of wine. It warmed her.

"If I hadn't been so concerned, maybe afraid is the right word, I could never have brought myself to call you. I thought it was going to be hard, really hard for me to see you again."

Jean Marc's forehead briefly furrowed. "Why?"

The question, she suspected, was sincere. She fidgeted with her napkin, "I was in love, I was young and I was hurt," she said hurriedly. "We weren't equipped at that age for these things like you are in the West. But that's not what I came to talk about."

He recoiled slightly. Almira sensed a slight hurt in his eyes. "I'm sorry. I certainly didn't come here to make you feel bad," she said, "or to intrude in your life."

She reached across the table and stroked two tapered, pale fingers that were extended slightly towards her. "I need advice, Jean Marc, or maybe just information, something to help me piece a puzzle together."

She recounted the bizarre killings of Fatimah Karajan and Ariel, the lengthy police interrogations to which she was subjected, and then her encounter in Glastonbury with the American who clearly had been following her.

"You should have kept seeing him," Jean Marc observed. "You could have learned as much about him as he about you, maybe more."

"You're right, of course, but Jamal was sick, I had a ready-made excuse. And then when he started talking about Fatimah...I felt frightened and angry." And humiliated, she thought to herself.

"Jamal?"

"I have two boys, Jean Marc. Jamal's the youngest. They are a joy." She extracted a small holographic picture from the wallet in her carrying bag and handed it over to Jean Marc.

"I'm happy for you. They look like you."

"You just think all Arabs look alike," she said with a smile. "Jamal is the image of his father."

Jean Marc was smiling too. "And where is his father?"

"Dead. He was killed before the Settlement."

"I'm sorry," Jean Marc blinked and looked down at his wine glass, "I keep saying the wrong things and asking the wrong questions. I'm not being much of a help."

"You're doing fine," she said in a tone so reassuring that it surprised her. She continued, "It's the motivation for what's happened that puzzles me and why I am being drawn into it."

Jean Marc remained thoughtful for a moment and allowed a bowl of leek and potato soup to be set down in front of him. He waited for the waitress to serve Almira and step away.

"It may be quite simple. You are a suspect in a crime of passion." He broke a minibaguette in two and handed half of it to Almira. "You discover," he continued between sips of soup, "that Fatimah has betrayed the cause to which you have dedicated yourself. Worse, she is consorting with a man you believe may have been responsible for your husband's death. You run around, find a gun—and I'm sure there are plenty of them still around, Settlement or no Settlement—come back and do the natural thing, shoot them both."

"But even if it were true, I would never react that way. All our work was to put vengeance and violence behind us."

"It's hard for a policeman to believe that. It doesn't fit his experience."

"You're probably right, but why didn't they arrest me then or at least keep me from leaving Palestine?"

"Because they have no real case yet. A good lawyer would make them look like fools. You'd be out in two days and the press would be all over them."

Again Jean Marc was right, Almira realized. It would not even be clear in what court or under what set of rules she would be tried. If she were accused of killing Fatimah, it would be a Palestinian court, or at her option, the municipal court of the locality. If she were accused of killing Arbel, it would be in a special Confederation tribunal responsible for internationality felonies. Convictions were difficult, and it was even possible that protections against double jeopardy, borrowed from the British, would keep the authorities from accusing her in more than one forum, making their choice even harder.

"You are so logical, Jean Marc," she said, "We are well protected there. When the system was set up, we used to joke that it was so complicated that we would all have to marry American lawyers to explain it to us."

"Or Talmudic scholars?"

"That was the hope." The irony was not lost on her. "But bear with me," she continued, "Since they can't stop me, they do want to keep track of me so they send this American to follow me."

"Yes."

"But that doesn't really make sense. They can figure out where I am without actually having somebody try to meet me. And why an American? It's not exactly a Palestinian's favorite nationality."

"Maybe because they always seem so naive and innocent. Maybe he's so irresistible that you would confess on his pillow."

"Be serious, Jean Marc," Almira said, though she felt her face flush with the memory of her attraction to him. "And why," Almira continued, staying with the events surrounding Fatimah's death, "would they think I would call in a television camera?"

"I don't know, Almira. It's hard to guess, who knows what they're thinking."

For a few minutes Almira devoted her attention to the fillet of sole in front of her. It was browned in herbs and had a moist and flaky texture. The white Burgundy Jean Marc had chosen complemented it well. He too finished his meal. She was the first to speak again. "Maybe the big question is why. Why would somebody want to kill Fatimah and Ariel, and particularly in the way that they did?"

"Maybe," Jean Marc offered, "there is somebody out there who is very sick, who feels just the way the police suspect you feel and wanted the whole world to know about their little act of revenge."

"If I had to guess, and I knew her pretty well, she wasn't sleeping with him. I think it was a set up."

"You're losing perspective," he said. "Doesn't it always happen this way? Nonviolent, peace-making leader succeeds and then is killed.... Gandhi, Martin Luther King, Anwar Sadat, Chico Mendes, you name it. It's Newton's law. Action/reaction." Jean Marc paused and summoned the waitress to order coffee.

"This is my theory," he continued. "There's something so powerful about people like that, something so alien to the ordinary course of human experience, that there's always a reaction in their societies' common psyche and it lodges, it crystallizes in some deranged, failed person who violently acts it out."

"The Christians," Almira offered, "wouldn't agree that it's always as random as that." Almira knew she wasn't a paranoid person, but she felt certain that a concerted effort of some sort was afoot. She could see that Jean Marc had been a bureaucrat too long; he couldn't imagine a governmental institution doing intentional harm. She decided to steer the conversation in another direction, but he spoke first.

"You remind me," he said, "of a woman I met in New York. Matteo Michelson, you know of him?"

"Yes, of course."

"He died while Lucinda and I were there. The night he died we had dinner with friends and this woman who knew him slightly started carrying on about how from a dream she knew not only that he was going to die but that he was going to be killed. It was almost embarrassing. We were just friends having dinner. The woman seemed way too serious."

"And?"

"Maybe nothing, but I did read later that the police hadn't ruled out some kind of herbal poison. I haven't heard anything since."

Almira's pulse quickened. Her intuition told her to pursue this. "Who was the lady?"

"Laura, I forget her last name. A photographer, an occultist, herbalist, old New-Age type. She was with my friend David, David Grossman. He's a woodland ecologist. Professional, of the very best kind."

"Will you let me talk to him? Or would you be too jealous?"

Jean Marc smiled and pulled out an electronic device about the size of a playing card. He unfolded it open, entered the name and passed it across the table to Laura. "He's American and Jewish, you know. He could be dangerous."

Almira laughed. She gestured in the direction his ribs, "I'm used to keeping bad company." She started to write the information down. "Costa Rica? I thought he was a New Yorker?"

"An American, not a New Yorker. He works in Costa Rica. We and some other friends, we got together in New York. Let's take a walk."

Jean Marc paid the bill and led Almira outside the compound. The sun was shining, almost warmly. Water dripped from the icicles that hung from the tree limbs and from time to time a clump of snow shifted and whistled from the branches to the ground. The trail through the woods was slick, especially where it crested and dropped abruptly to a frozen lakeshore. Almira locked her arm in Jean Marc's to steady herself as they walked toward the shore.

"I'm not used to this," she said. "Walking on ice, I mean. Tell me about Lucinda. That was good of her to let us be together a while."

Jean Marc gave an abbreviated version of her life. Her father the Kosovo apparatchik, exile in Lisbon, the drug-park life and her rehabilitation at the hands of the Danish Jungians. "She will be a certified analyst soon, I'm proud of her."

"I was drawn to her. I think I would trust her…at least with my dreams. You like the wounded ones," she added, "I've seen that. Projects from underdeveloped cultures. You help bring them into the great European light."

"That's not fair." He held her closer to him as they stutter-stepped down the slope.

"But you do a good job; we're happy." While it lasts, she thought. How long does Lucinda have now that she is doing so well?

They walked to the edge of the lake. The snow was above the ankles of her boots. As she stepped forward to find a harder purchase, she was startled by a loud cracking sound and felt her heel sink into icy water. Reflexively, Jean Marc pulled her back and they both fell onto the snow-covered bank. Jean Marc turned to her as they lay in the snow and concern knitted his eyebrows. "Maybe you are in trouble," he said. "Maybe we all are." A moment passed. "Look at us," he added and then he laughed. He stood up and pulled her to her feet. Soon he was talking about his work. He described his colleagues and superiors, their brilliance and insight, his travels and promotions and a personally promising future.

"As for the planet," he said as they drove back to the hotel, "many of us are very concerned. We know there have been enormous changes—the end of consumerism, at least its excesses, environmental activity by thousands of groups around the world, global cooperation on ozone depletion and climate change, sensitivity to the poor, the dramatic reduction of armaments production. But we are afraid that this may not be enough."

Almira followed Jean Marc's eyes to a scene of a few children skating, forming a pickup hockey game. They lost sight of them as the taxi drove ahead. "Virtually all of this activity has been voluntary. If people or a group of people decided to go a different direction, there would be no real enforcement mechanism, no effective way to stop them and we know that sooner rather than later, a significant number of people are going to push in another direction. It's generational... "

"Youthful rebellion," she said. "As the danger seems to recede, sons think it's safe to play out their anger against the fathers."

"Exactly," he continued, "and it's not just that. It's that the way we are going about solving the Earth's problems is for the most part messy and disorganized. It's grossly inefficient and of course there are plenty of laggards."

"Did you hear," Almira added, "about the publisher who lit fifteen thousand gas lamps on his farm for his birthday to impress his guests!"

"I heard. Just the attitude we must fear," Jean Marc said, picking up one of his favorite themes. "Worse, we're finding that the Earth is not responding as quickly as we first thought. The rate of ozone depletion has not slowed sufficiently, the change in climate may be accelerating, biological diversity is still being diminished at an appalling rate, and a significant number of people still live in unacceptable poverty."

"But didn't a lot of people warn that it was going to take more time?"

"Yes, yes, perhaps. But the point is, how can you justify doing anything less than the utmost? We have powerful technologies available to us that with a bit of central control can dramatically reduce our environmental problems and provide for all of our needs. But we need to be able to make everyone apply them.

"We know how to organize societies so that no one is left out, so that no one's life falls below a minimum standard of well-being. But we don't have the authority to do this, except in the most egregious cases when virtually the entire world agrees.

"Almira, we're talking about an effect over time that will deeply harm millions of lives, an enormous economic cost, incalculable suffering, perhaps irreparable harm. It's unconscionable."

Almira squeezed his hand, "You feel strongly about this, don't you?" An understatement, she thought. She remembered the passions of Palestine.

"I do," he continued, "and we all think that the Convocation next year may be our last chance. We need to have a central mechanism legitimized, one that can implement its work through the central authorities of the nation states. No more of these voluntary half-measures. There will be calamities."

If Jean Marc—gentle, rational, bureaucratic Jean Marc—had become this passionate on the subject, Almira concluded, he was probably reflecting even stronger impulses in the world's larger institutions, especially among the individuals close to the pinnacle whose power would be enormously enhanced if a structure of the kind that he was describing were put into place. Strong enough that some apologists could justify taking a life or two to help make sure it would happen? People like Fatimah certainly would be impediments. Her murder, under the circumstances, would also have discredited the Palestinian Confederation as a model. But Fatimah alone was not that powerful, nor was the Palestinian example that important. If extreme means like murder were used in Fatimah's case to advance the cause of the Planetary Securitists, as they had come to be known, then there should be evidence of similarly motivated actions elsewhere in the world. Matteo Michelson's death might be just that. Almira's resolve to try to reach Jean Marc's friend and the woman, Laura, strengthened.

"I think you've answered my questions, Jean Marc," she said quietly.

"What do you mean?"

"Being with you, I'm much clearer about my own feelings. I think I'll know the difference between fantasy and reality when it comes." Not altogether inaccurate, she thought. "Your friends, David, Laura. Promise to tell them I'll call them soon."

***

In the evening Almira joined Jean Marc and Lucinda in their suite. Jean Marc had suggested it. The hotel restaurant, he said, would be filled with his colleagues of whom he had seen too much already. They could do room service or go into town. It was a ways and there wasn't that much too see, but there were some Russian restaurants. This last prospect caused Almira to vote for room service in the suite.

The accommodation was spacious, a large room with a large king-sized bed, a writing desk and bureaus, an alcove with a couch, table and chairs, and off the alcove another small room with a tiled floor and less formal furnishings. It led through one door into a sauna and through another door into the bathroom and shower area. Jean Marc had ordered champagne, which was chilling on the table. Both he and Lucinda were dressed in white terrycloth robes.

He handed Almira a glass. He led her to the tiled room and pointed to another robe, hanging from the door. "When you're ready. You can't come to Finland and not have a sauna."

She turned to Lucinda, "He's made you do this too?"

She smiled, "It's relaxing. It's a slightly altered state. We all need that from time to time. When I was in Sweden they made us jump from the sauna into the snow."

"That sounds delightful," Almira said shivering.

"I screamed that I was a child of warmer climes and would

surely be sick, but it wasn't so. It actually wasn't bad." With some urging from Jean Marc, Lucinda recounted a seemingly inexhaustible supply of misadventures with various malcontents, hedonists, and criminals during her days of wandering. The stories were entertaining, almost too much so, Almira thought. She wondered if Jean Marc didn't relish Lucinda's memories considerably more than Lucinda did herself. But the thought vanished in the second glass of champagne and her own enjoyment.

Almira had steeled herself for the sauna. When the time came, she stepped into the bathroom with the terrycloth robe, closed the door, undressed, wrapped a towel around herself and put on the robe over it.

"I'm ready," she said when she emerged. Jean Marc and Lucinda each took a towel, dropped their robes and stepped into the heated, wooden enclosure. Almira followed with the towel still wrapped around her. They were both so thin. He was still that sinewy, elegant, pale-limbed dancer whose body she had known so well, and Lucinda had just enough flesh to give a soft roundness to her well-defined bottom and belly and to keep her dark and hardened nipples from seeming harsh or out of place. Almira couldn't help herself; she kept looking at both of them and remembering the worlds where touch had taken her many years before. She knew in the growing heat that the others were aware of her attention. The towel, now beginning to fill with perspiration, was still around her. She thought of the heaviness of her hips and protruding belly, products of two births, and couldn't bring herself to take it off. She closed her eyes.

After the sauna and cold showers, after dinner and more champagne and two twelve-year-old Bordeaux, when they were all safely back in their robes, Lucinda touched Almira on the shoulder and said, "You have let the world affect you too deeply, lie down. I can feel the tension."

Almira felt somewhat confused. "I don't... "

"Right here," Lucinda said. She turned to Jean Marc, "You need to find something else to do."

Lucinda pulled at the tie around Almira's robe and guided her to the carpet, "Let me work with your back, you'll feel much better."

Lucinda ran her hands over Almira's bare back, softly at first and then with more pressure. Almira felt Lucinda's warmth as she straddled her buttocks and pressed two fingers into her neck at the base of her skull. In a few seconds pain gave way to mild discomfort, and then to an almost trance-like state. Almira felt as if her consciousness had been launched into a disconnected space, except that it was not disconnected. It was drawn helplessly, heliotropically, to each node of subtle pressure and pleasure that Lucinda's fingers and palms were creating over and over again, up and down her spine, along her sides, under her arms, around her collar bone and then last, in her tangled, spread-out hair.

Almira felt Lucinda brush her lips against her neck and then slowly roll away. It's over, she thought. How can this be? Almira wanted more but was too dazed, too limp to move. She closed her eyes. It could have been minutes or an age when she heard Jean Marc's voice echo in the room.

"Come and join us."

Gradually she opened an eye. Jean Marc was reclining on the bed, naked, on his side, his head supported by his arm and elbow. Lucinda had sunk into the mattress. All Almira could see were the soles and arches of two graceful feet dangling over the edge of the bed. The toes of one of them curled and a swath of shapely white skin rose briefly into her view.

"Please, you are wonderful to touch," Lucinda said.

Almira felt the long-neglected cells of her body, just awakened with a taste of life, clamoring for her to roll over to the bed, to be pulled up, to be embraced, to be carried away into an ocean of warmth on waves of rising sensations. You are in a far country; it's just for the night, what is the harm? She heard the words form, much as they had fifteen years before in Paris.

Suddenly the face of a striking bushy-eyed man she had never seen before appeared in her mind's eye. The face was wordless but somehow it soothed and calmed the chorus. Almira abruptly got up, naked, leaving the robe piled on the floor and calmly walked across the room and into the bathroom. She put on the skirt and blouse which she had worn and stuffed the rest of her clothes in a bag. She brushed her hair.

When she emerged, Jean Marc and Lucinda were still lying

on the bed. Almira sat beside them. She leaned over and touched her lips to Jean Marc's forehead.

"No, thank you, Jean Marc. You have been a teacher and a friend," she said, rising. "And please be careful. The world is not yours to save." Almira took Lucinda by the hand, pulled her up and embraced her. "Thank you," she said.

Almira tore the sheet off the pad where Jean Marc had written David and Laura's number and gently closed the door behind her as she left.

The message light was flashing red when Almira returned to her room.

CHAPTER 29

In the fifth year of his stay on Maui, Rashid made one of his periodic visits to New York to maintain the links of his consultancy and visit with old friends. He invited Erika to dinner. They walked from the UN building to a small Afghan restaurant on 38th Street. One wall was covered with tribal jewelry and brocaded woman's wear; the opposite wall was layered with knives, sabers, and nineteenth-century firearms. The proprietor—a Sufi sheik of some renown—was very deferential to Rashid. "There will be a dhikr later, after we close," he said. "We would be honored if you and your friend would join us." Rashid looked at Erika, "Thank you," he said, "we can't tonight."

The royal tryst, Rashid learned from Erika, never occurred. Alfred had contracted some unmentionable disease from an unfortunate dalliance during the engagement. For her part, Erika continued her rise in the United Nations and was now engaged to a British Earl twenty years her senior. "My Richard," as Erika called him, had done invaluable work in preserving endangered species in the former colonies. In his youth he had bred racehorses. "This month he's at his black rhinoceros ranch in Zimbabwe," she said. Rashid smiled at her; the candle flame gleaned in his eyes.

"Rashid," she said, "I understand now why you behaved so abominably that night with my mother."

"I knew you would, sooner or later."

Erika was silent for a minute or two. "It's not that I don't love Richard," she finally said, "but I keep thinking that a life with you would have been so much…an unending adventure."

His eyes grew misty, "We have different paths, Erika. Different paths." His voice broke. He turned away and called out to the waiter for the check.

***

The influence of the Undersecretary for whom Erika worked had increased with time. Over the years, the Planetary Defense Program, the PDP, had become more and more comprehensive in its analysis, more and more specific in its measures. The Global Convocation was less than two years away and everyone at the UN assumed that if the Planetary Securitists triumphed— and most thought that they would because the signs of planetary deterioration continued unabated—the PDP would be quickly implemented. No one spoke negatively of the Undersecretary. Key appointments would be made and certainly no one wanted to be identified as a recalcitrant resister who could wind up on a target list.

Rashid had visited the Undersecretary briefly. The Undersecretary was cordial. He remembered Rashid well and respected his abilities even though he suspected Rashid did not fully share his worldview. Rashid was also able to spend a few minutes with Senzo Sato who had by then been elected Secretary General.

Rafael, Rashid's best friend from his years at the UN, had become the Undersecretary's Chief Administrative Assistant. Rafael too had dinner with Rashid. They ate at a small Spanish restaurant on the West Side. Rafael, Rashid observed, had maintained the modesty of his New Mexican origins. He wore a loose-fitting brown suit that matched the tone of his skin. After the main course, as they waited for desert, Rafael became thoughtful and stared blankly at the undistinguished landscape on the wall.

"Rashid, this is not what I came to do," he said. "The PDP looks more like a battle plan than an environmental program. So easily it could turn into another round of conquest and oppression."

"And the Undersecretary?"

"I think he's honorable. He's treated me well but it's like he's from another era, everything's seen through a lens of conflict and struggle. And the man likes the game. He likes power. Rashid, I want to do something else."

Rashid swirled the remnants of a glass of wine and stared at the moving, burgundy liquid. "I know this is hard for you. I know that, but I also know that there is no place where you could perform a greater service than where you are right now. At least for the moment. Rafael, please stay, just a little longer, I can't explain; you'll see." Rafael stared at the landscape again, "A little longer...for you, a little longer."

Rashid saw other friends and submitted his commentaries on various structures that were being considered for involving national governments in the PDP. Jane LaForce, rickshot and mime, took him around the city during the days and they spent one night together. The morning after she mentioned that just a few days earlier, she had driven a Senator's aide whose name was Peter to the Senator's New York office and to her surprise had wound up liking him.

"Small world," Rashid said, his eyes as big as the holes in the bagels she served him, "I know him. A nice young man."

The following day Rashid returned to Maui. He was home by evening. He had barely settled into a large rattan chair on the porch looking out over the sea when he felt a whale presence stirring within him. He became quiet and for the fifth time listened to Spotted Fluke.

We feared for you Rashid. You are back. We are relieved.

You sit here again. The evening breeze rises up from the sea; it curls up the hill and passes current by gentle current around you. You do not seek to grasp it or to bend it. What is yours to breathe in you breathe in and then you breathe it out. The breeze carries the scents of nightflowers opening in the dark; they bring color to your inner eye and pleasure to your throat. You do not seek out the flowers in their hidden coppices of bloom to break them off or rearrange them in a vase.

The birdcalls are few for the birds rest, nestled in the night, clinging to branches in the brush, huddled in the eaves of your homes or flocked under the arching curve of a bridge. You do not demand that they come out to sing for you now; it is enough for you to hear the distant bark of a dog and the tree frogs raspy song.

A cloud comes now, painting the sky. It covers the stars with its brush and darkens the face of the moon. You have not launched some fearful weapon to vaporize this cloud. You sit content, knowing that Life is and that You are Life.

You are, as we have always known you, Rashid, you have not changed. We feared it might not be so. We traveled with you to where you met so many of your kind. We heard their words, fine words many that spoke of saving us all. But there was something else there, Rashid, something fearful in their voices, like an amnesiac killer, speaking love for the children of his victims and vowing to avenge the children's pain when the evil ones are found. Not knowing themselves to be the killers, havoc will be wreaked. It is killing that will be served; death that will feast at the table under the banner of the good.

We heard about these plans, about these maps where all would be set aright, the people that would be moved, the mirrors in space that would reflect back the sun, the water courses that would be changed, how each place would be rearranged, the animals and plants rebred and the people who resisted put away.

Rashid, listen to me. What would make anyone—anyone— ever do such a thing? Who would ever think to give to just one being, even to a few beings, even to a thousand beings, such power, controlling power? Power over the vastness of the sea, over the land's expanse, over the ascents to the jagged mountain peaks and the darkness of the forest. Power over the infinite variety that even you the humans are. Power over the carpenters, the farmers, the pilots, the seamen, the storekeepers, the toy makers, the scientists, the engineers, the painters and writers, the mothers, the children, the lovers, the monks, the sick, the healthy, the strong, the bookish, the quiet, the loud, the blond, the black, all speaking hundreds of diverse languages, rooted in a thousand different cultures, each with a separate history, each with a separate family going back to the beginning of your kind. And this is not to speak of taking power over the countless other beings that you share our planet with—the hawk that circles the sky, the beetle that digs in the earth, the doves, the pigeons, the swallows, the snipes and sparrows, the caterpillars forming moths, the butterflies that spin out of their cocoons, the worm in the mouth of the robin, the rabbit seized by the wolf, the mouse that escaped the owl and all the other moments of life and death and renewal.

And among your own kind, who knows when a businessman's failure is tomorrow's triumph, or what accident will lead an artist to paint the essence of a coral reef. By what absurd conceit can anyone imagine that he knows on behalf of all of these beings what is best! Who imagines to have a consciousness so vast? Who can say he always sees the effervescent traces of souls conjoined when what appears outside is pain? Who knows when a calloused hand shows a lifetime of defeat or when its lines are the sweet labors of our Mother?

If any do know such things, they will not seek power for as surely they would know that the weight of so much life and death, so much sorrow and conflict and triumph and joy, would pulverize the one who sought to bear it.

And even if some of the best of you took on vast power to perform these tasks, how long before they would measure themselves by the fruits of their work? And then how long before the power-seekers surround them holding up curved mirrors that make a wizened raisin seem round, succulent, and heavy with juice? How long before only the mirrors are seen?

It is the voices of vultures that will be heard, filtered through the ears of the dead. It is a jackal's laugh that will command.

In the Whale Nation none of us speaks for more than a few. None of us seeks to feed beyond our needs. None of us roils the water beyond the reach of our flukes. We are guided by what we know. It is only what we know that we can love—all else is whitecap's froth. And who dares act to affect another out of any place but love?

When something greater comes which we must face as it did with the great whale slaughter, we turn to the power of Humpback Whale—the One. She takes not one form but many. We each listen inwardly, knowing that our sisters do the same, then in the world we each separately know, we act as we imagine Humpback Whale would have us each do. We trust all, Rashid.

In truth we have no choice. To imagine that all of Humpback Whale could be contained in Crushing Fin or Breaching Belly or Mothered Twenty or myself, Spotted Fluke, is to swim in folly. And so it is with you. You must trust in all. No human can contain Humankind. No human can guide all humans; you must each hear the voice of Humankind.

Our Mother suckles you each a little differently, so each tastes a different-flavored milk. She speaks through different tones that echo in a secret place that is for each of you, yours and yours alone. But make no mistake, varied as the words may be, it is our Mother's voice. Each heart sounds the voice of Humankind.

You rose up from the Earth and from high above, through a few courageous eyes you saw our Earth as one, fragile, a jewel in the night, land without border, sea swirling into sea, breathing one cloud. It saved you—it saved us all—for you to see that, to know our common fate. But humans must come down again, Rashid, and see not just the One but the All, the forms without end, small and large, simple, infinitely complex, that make up the One. Each leaf performs astounding magic, powering itself with the sun. The spider makes silk stronger than your steel.

We fear, Rashid, what some of you may do. We fear the coming time. We dread it as we would a lurid yellow sky or oceans that coagulate, or green that turns to brown and broken rocks that bleed. We fear those who in aiming to make us all well again will paint us all in red.

CHAPTER 30

Peter was staring out his bedroom window, his eyes vaguely focused in the vicinity of the little cupola on the top of the Capitol. The light inside it was lit indicating that once again the House of Representatives was caught in a late-night budget struggle.

Peter dropped a small cube of ice into his brandy and stirred it a bit. It had been a day of disturbances. First Laura Feil, then the call from the Senator, and then Laura again. He was not sure which was the more important but he sensed that his life was about to change.

"Peter, what the hell is going on?" the Senator had practically jumped though the v-phone.

"What?"

"A goddamned policeman and some creep who never really said what he was have been crawling around here all day."

"What did they want?" Peter interjected.

"They were obsequious as hell, made my stomach turn, but they wanted to know if we'd seen a little boy who drowned prowling around on the day you were up here—and by the way, they wanted to know who was here and what were we talking about that day."

"Tell them it's not their business."

"Goddamn it, Peter what the hell do I pay you for! To get that kind of shitty advice? 'Senator Blocks Probe of Child's Death,'

—it would take two seconds to write that story!"

"Sorry," Peter offered, "it was a dumb reaction. What did you say?"

"I said I was sorry as hell that the kid had drowned but that we hadn't even seen the boat much less the kid, and why did they think the kid was here.

"Sources, they said, nothing firm, and back we went to who was here and where we were sitting and what we said. I said you were here and we were talking about the future and the Convocation."

"And?"

"The local cop drew a blank and the other one wanted to know if it was the kind of thing that other people might want to know about and where we were sitting could we have been overheard. And I lost it then. I said they were fucking crazy if they thought we were going to harm some kid because he was snooping around the house."

"'Oh no, no, no, not you,' this asshole says, 'and certainly not intentionally, but some questions have come up about Mr. Flanigan,' he says. An important man was killed in Peru and you were the last to see him and were you there on my behalf, he wanted to know. I said it was my policy to let anyone on the staff look into anything they thought was interesting around the world and that you thought this guy's work was pretty extraordinary and that they were as crazy to think that you would do anybody any harm as to think that I would."

"Did that end it?" Peter asked.

"Pretty much, they said they couldn't agree more but they just had to ask these questions and 'thanks'. So I called the police chief and reamed him out and he said he was really sorry but they'd gotten this anonymous call saying that the kid was seen at my house and that you were involved in a murder in Peru, and it would look awful if the Chief didn't follow up, but of course I was free not to talk to anyone and he would completely understand if I decided not to."

Peter told the Senator about the UNINTEL interview in the New York office and, more hesitantly, distaste rising up his throat, about the so-called background check that Katie had reported. "Sit tight, Peter," the Senator said, "take a break while

I get to the bottom of this, just let me know where you are."

The Senator was right, Peter mused, I'm in no position to figure out what's going on but maybe he can. He knows as much as I do now, the UNINTEL investigator, the questions to Katie. I should keep a low profile, find something to busy myself with, maybe take a trip out of town... or was he out of time? That, Peter thought, was the kind of question that Jeffery would ask. Peter realized that he hadn't seen his brother, the professor, in a while. It would be short trip to Charlottesville, perhaps Laura could join him to finish her work there. She, he felt sure, would like Jeffery too. They were equally weird.

Laura. He thought back to his dinner with her. She had surprised him. First, with what in his family they would have called a confession of faith. He would have expected murkiness; her statement was extraordinarily clear. He would have expected delusion and self-aggrandizement; she knew what she experienced and was very clear about what she didn't know or wasn't. If anything, she was self-deprecating. What was especially appealing to Peter about what she had to say was that it freed him from having to think that millions of human beings just like him were wandering around for centuries, completely off their rockers, making up fantasy figures of all kinds from goddesses to UFOs. A way of speaking about unseen forces in our lives, she had said. These people were struggling with something, they were on to something, even if they clearly didn't know what it was. Maybe it was the people who didn't have any sense of these forces at all that came up with the most bizarre and fantastic distortions of reality.

If Laura were right, then there was a good chance the Senator was right too. If there were unseen forces, intelligent forces acting in the here and now, then human history might, just might, have a purpose and you could really screw things up if you tried to ride it too tightly, if you tried to control events too closely. Especially if you were acting from the point of view of ordinary human consciousness and out of a narrow ego-based rationality. And this would probably be true even if the "unseen forces" were no more than the unconscious creations of the collective human mind.

Interesting. Peter knew that he had had no real experience

comparable to Laura's but disconnected threads in his life did seem to be pushing him in one common direction, like one of these unseen forces. What Laura had said was like the old story of the elephant and the blind men, each feeling a part of the same reality but each describing it in wildly divergent terms; gods, angels, extraterrestrials, nature sprites or power animals, the same trans sensory reality experienced through a different—atrophied, Laura might say of her contemporaries—inner lens.

Then there were people like Velasquez and O'Shea that always left him with the feeling that something bigger was going on in their presence. Maybe it was true. Maybe something bigger was going on around them—or maybe it was always going on but was just more visible to most people in their presence.

He certainly didn't expect Laura to be his enlightener, something else maybe. She was—he knew he had harbored the thought—almost too attractive to be taken seriously, yet all of this had happened and the attraction had by no means ceased. Even without the tastes of a lamb and pumpkin dinner at a nearby Afghan restaurant or the backdrop of the woven saddlebags, jeweled swords, and copper urns that created an enchantment of their own, he would have been perfectly content to watch her for two hours while she shared a few stories from her life. He had of course wondered what might be underneath the pale, full skirt and Guatemalan-patterned blouse that she had worn, but it had been quite enough to see the hints of movement—rhythmic breathing, an arm uplifted, a leg crossing—that rippled through the cloth. He had felt something akin to joy when at the end of the evening she had agreed to take the job.

Peter turned to the v-phone and dialed Laura's hotel. The call was relayed to her room and she appeared wearing a camisole on the screen.

"Hi, Laura."

"Hi," she said.

"I'm going to have to go to Charlottesville tomorrow. I thought you might start work on the space mail and then meet me down there in a few days so I can sign off on it."

"Sure," she said, "that would be nice. I've never been there."

"Great. Dinner was great," Peter took a big sip from his

brandy, "See you then."

"Good night," she said and faded out of the screen.

***

Peter's brother Jeffery did not exactly live in Charlottesville. He taught at the university there but spent the rest of the time in a small community, a replica of a late-1960s commune that was nestled in the hills of Nelson County, twenty-five miles south. Jeffery, Peter thought as he paced up and down the rail station platform waiting to be picked up, was never exactly anything that you would expect. Maybe his mother knew that from the very beginning so she gave him an English name to live with in an Irish-American family and then spelled it obscurely, Jeffery used to say, just for spite.

Jeffery was a physicist, though not exactly. Jeffery had been precocious and had completed his doctorate in the field by the time he was twenty-two. His dissertation was a mathematical model of the life of bottom-flavored quarks on the event horizon of a black hole. At the graduation ceremony, he thanked his mother for giving him the experiences that made his work possible. Peter was the only one who laughed which caused Jeffery to conclude that he had underestimated his younger brother and thereafter treated him, by Jeffery's standards, quite well.

Jeffery was in everyone's view only twenty to thirty years' work away from a Nobel Prize, so it came as a shock when he accepted a position as an instructor at a university that was not exactly known for its prowess in the field of particle physics. He said that he was attracted by the strength of its faculty in the fields of comparative religion, and on the day of his arrival he did join the Jefferson Tibet Society in order to become, he said, a part of a neo-Palladian column of Bodhisattvas.

For those to whom this answer was not clear and foolishly persisted in questioning him, he would add that it made him feel sheepish to say so, but he was drawn by the dancing of his wooly masters. Any who failed to appreciate the word play, or the hidden allusions to whirling dervishes, or the reference to a popular twentieth-century effort to bridge physics and metaphysics, were unlikely to receive in the future even a condescending glance from Jeffery.

In the following years Jeffery's mind wandered through the fields of anthropology, political economy and film criticism, interests which the university indulged by allowing him to lead a seminar here and there for young men and women in search of gentlemanly C's. In the last year or two Jeffery had returned with more seriousness—perhaps an inappropriate word—to his original chosen field. It was, he had said to Peter, time for him to take a long bath in the heavy waters of cold fusion.

Peter was not required to pace on the platform for long. Within fifteen minutes Jeffery arrived, dressed in faded blue jeans and a tee shirt imprinted with a Hubble telescope perspective on the Andromeda galaxy. Jeffery's blond hair had receded slightly and he was driving a battered, blue Model-E, the first electric car to be mass produced. It was underpowered and sold poorly when first marketed but was a prized collector's item fifteen years later. Peter's scant luggage was put in the back seat and quickly they were out of the town. As they sped on winding roads through the blooming dogwoods and cow pastures of the Piedmont, Peter realized that Jeffery had performed a form of electronic wizardry with the power plant. The Model-E moved with the speed of the gas guzzlers Peter recalled from his childhood. Yes, Jeffery acknowledged, it was not an ordinary battery. Peter was left breathless now and then but was able to finish the story of Velasquez and the Senator and all the investigators. By the time they reached the gravel driveway that led to Jeffery's house, he had told him about Laura as well.

"What about Katie?" Jeffery asked as they came to a stop.

"I need to stay away from her," Peter replied.

"Yes, but what's new?" Jeffery grabbed Peter's canvas suitcase and started walking towards the house. Peter remained silent so Jeffery continued, "I mean why did they question her? How do you know they questioned her?"

Peter described the dates and places of his recent encounters with her and Katie's apparently growing involvement with Bernie. "It got tense between us, I think I'm not going to see her anymore." Peter decided not to discuss the bedroom scenes. Jeffery, he suspected, had never had trouble sleeping with anyone.

"Can she say anything damaging?" Jeffery persisted.

"I didn't do anything. How can she say anything damaging?"

"And this Laura is coming down here?"

"Yeah, if it's okay with you."

"I'd get her here soon," Jeffery's face formed a look of concern.

Zenobia was standing on the porch, the door open behind her. Her brown hair was frizzy and long. She was tall and large-breasted, dressed like Jeffery in faded blue jeans. She tucked a plaid shirt of thin cotton into her jeans.

"I hear you're on the lam," she said and gave him a quick hug. "Welcome."

"Not exactly," Peter replied. "It's a long story. I told Jeffery."

"And you can't go through it again."

"Yeah."

"I understand. He can tell me. I hear you're having a friend come down too."

"Sort of, it's mainly work but I think she'll be a friend."

"Jeffery says you may be dropping the Katie bitch," Zenobia said, becoming more herself as she closed the door to the wood frame house behind them. "His words," she added.

"Jeffery's not very subtle, is he?"

"He likes you, that's all."

The primitive beat of a 1960s bass guitar was vibrating through the house which didn't surprise Peter at all. He knew this was Zenobia's current life. She was writing a book on existentialism, hermeneutics, and twentieth-century rock and roll. The heavy beat faded and a gentler rhythm replaced it. Someone with a honeyed voice was singing something about a garden party. There was a hint of sadness in the music but it was filled with innocence,

> ...*I learned my lesson well*
> *See you can't please everyone*
> *So you've got to please yourself...*

The refrain stayed with Peter and lifted his mood. *La-de-da-da...* And out stepped Johnny-B-Good. As he listened he grew more certain that he had done the right thing to come there.

Later in the afternoon Jeffery asked Peter to join him for a walk. The dell where Jeffery's cabin house was placed was filled with the sounds and sights of spring. For the length of the dell close to the road, a stream was running hard, almost to the edge of its banks. Robins pecked the lawns of the dozen or so nearby houses and grosbeaks, yellow and purple finches, and drabber nondescript birds flocked around their feeders. Azaleas, ubiquitous in the region, had been banned from the community as a social statement, but there was a profusion of rhododendron, daffodils, and forsythia. A bluebird pair was busy with a nest, growing it straw by straw in the split of a fence post, while a third one sat befuddled, watching from a nearby limb. Crows cackled overhead and Jeffery pointed to a red-tailed hawk, circling, maybe a quarter of a mile away.

As they headed up the hill, Jeffery gestured towards the last house on the road. A high wooden fence was attached to it. Whatever it enclosed was invisible to the passerby.

"The lady in there," Jeffery said, "has a hobby. She reintroduces captive flesh-eating animals to nature. Mountain lions, peregrine falcons, timber wolves, that kind of thing."

"I'm glad she has a fence."

"She says she saw a mountain lion around here thirty years ago when they were all supposed to be extinct. She says that she's known ever since then, that if a place isn't safe for predators, it isn't safe for us either. She tries to keep track of as many of the animals as she can. She says releasing and tracking predators is like sticking a thermometer up nature's ass."

"And nature's okay here?"

"Apparently, she was real happy the other day. She heard that some farmers were beginning to worry about livestock losses. It gives her hope, it makes her think that all the little things we've been doing for the past forty years actually did make a difference."

"The predators and the farmers. It sounds like a politician's nightmare."

"Ah…Peter the politician. I'm sure it is," Jeffery said, "but we all know that we can pay for 1.1 chickens each time that we buy one. It's not hard to make this fair. If you want to, that is."

Peter and Jeffery kept climbing up the road. It turned into a dirt trail that paralleled the stream for another half mile. The stream diminished and then veered off. Just when the sound of its waters became imperceptible, Jeffery led Peter off the trail and into the woods. They came to a large rock that overlooked the dell and some of the adjoining hills. As they sat down on its hard, sun-heated surface, Peter asked Jeffery about his work.

"It seems odd," Peter said, "with solar and wind and tidal and geothermal sources which will hold us for a while, and conductivity and long-distance transmission technologies and all the energy conservation measures that have worked so well, that you would pick this."

Jeffery remained thoughtful for a minute and pointed to the red-tailed hawk, still circling. "You're right in a way. But how many times have we had an energy crisis? We've fought wars over it, poisoned half the planet and begrudged it to other people so that they had to go out and make a desert out of the other half. I think people still don't think they'll get enough. Deep down, it's still the politics of scarcity and as long as you're in that mode, it's too easy to push the fear buttons that bring out competitiveness and greed and no cooperation."

"So if you could come up with a safe, limitless supply of energy, people might actually relax and feel provided for even at a deep level," Peter said.

"That's a big part of it. But think how crazy the whole premise is. How can you have an energy crisis in a universe that doesn't have anything in it except energy? I mean look at the sunshine all around you and the grass growing and the wind blowing and the water flowing, so even when we first woke up into the caveman dream and stepped outside, what would ever make us think that there wasn't enough.

"And then we learn that all this hard stuff we thought was matter, was really energy packed together and that if you squeeze it the right way, you can make a handful of matter or even space itself into a hot little sun, and we still don't believe that we'll figure out a way to get enough. There's something very sick happening here."

Jeffery hummed a bit and then let the lyrics out in a mellow voice,

There's a man with a gun over there

Telling me I got to beware
Hey stop what's that sound
Everybody look what's going down...

"Buffalo Springfield. It's one of Zenobia's favorites," he said. "There's another part to this," Jeffery continued. "Back in the twentieth century, when the biologists were trying to figure out how it was that an acorn knew to be an oak tree, or a sperm how to swim up the uterus or a salamander how to grow back its tail, a few came up with an idea they called morphic fields. These were preexisting, nonmaterial forms of sorts that set the patterns that the material world, the organisms, arranged themselves into.

"Then some of them took the idea further and said, you know this is sounding an awful lot like memory. There's a giant collective acorn memory that tells all the little acorns what to grow into, and for the most part that's just what they do.

"But if we're talking memory, these guys went on to say, we're talking about the past, about how the way things were done before pretty much governing how they're done now, and the word we use to describe that is habit and habit is a whole lot different from eternal, immutable law.

"Maybe, they said, what we thought were the laws of nature are just the habits of nature evolving through memory and experience. They went out and found some support for this here and there, like the fact that a lot of synthetic substances were hard to crystallize at first but once it was done a few times, labs everywhere found it a lot easier to do, or rats halfway around the world could solve a maze much faster after their colleagues in the other hemisphere had done it a number of times."

"So you thought," Peter said matching his brother's train of thought, "why not see if this might be true at the atomic and subatomic level as well. Create some new conditions that don't occur in nature, so you're not dealing with an old habitual rut and there may be a lot more room in which to play."

"See," said Jeffery with a grin, "the theory's proof, look how easily the idea came to you. That's because I'd already thought it through." He paused briefly, "Maybe something like this happened to the cold fusion folks out at Utah who were working with palladium in an electrolytic cell and getting occasional energy surges which most of the others who tried couldn't reproduce. They got a bad name but maybe they were just unlucky. They created new conditions so there were no old habits and nature was experimenting, but by the time others got around to testing it, nature had settled in on a pattern that didn't produce cold fusion.

"There were other hints as well. Andre Sakharov first talked about a muon-based fusion at a relatively cold temperature and another Nobel laureate, a man by the name of Alvarez, worked a little bit with it and later, saw it, "accidentally" doing something else with a particle accelerator, but no one ever did much to follow up. Of course the habits at the atomic and subatomic levels may be in too deep a rut.... We'll see.

"Actually," Jeffery went on as he rose from the boulder, "what really intrigues me is another question. If it's a kind of memory that shapes what we think is the physical reality, what does imagination do to that memory? We know that an internally visualized event can affect an individual's unconscious just as much as an out-there event. What happens when you turn a well-developed imaginative faculty on something outside of yourself? Can you create local anomalies? Is that what some so-called miracles are all about?"

"Or," Peter added, "what happens when a large number of us visualize a new order or a new process?"

"Like cold fusion. Or an abundant world from which we are not alienated," Jeffery concluded.

***

Time with Jeffery, Peter thought as he finished the cheese enchiladas which Zenobia had prepared, always stimulated. Even as fattened and satisfied as Zenobia's food was making him feel, his mind was still moving at a considerable pace, connecting thoughts that seemed to have nothing to do with each other before.

"Behold the fowls of the air," a dreaded, white-collared, robe-draped voice from his childhood was speaking into his brain, "therefore take no thought saying, what shall we eat."

"Jeffery," Peter said, "money. Going back to what we were saying at the boulder. We might call money a measure of human energy."

"An agreed-upon measurement of it and a few other things we put value on," Jeffery replied, "but what we value can get pretty strange. Remember—when we were kids—we had the most destructive oil spill in history? Well, the national wealth bean-counters told us that it actually made us $2 billion richer because of all the money we paid for equipment and people to clean it up!"

"So it's a measure," Peter resumed, "that gets reinforced through habit and our habits are born of scarcity. So what would it be like if we changed things around a bit and didn't focus on scarcity? Maybe the problem is to keep reinventing money to be sure that it's in a form that doesn't stand in the way of everybody's access to the wealth that we really have. There was a guy at Harvard who argued that the American West grew because the banks had no qualms about lending money that they didn't have. Everything worked fine as long as people believed the money was there or the make-believe money that the banks printed up was thought to have worth itself. Then from time to time there would be a schism in the belief system. A big panic would settle in and banks would go under by the hundreds. But in the longer term, this fellow argued, it didn't really matter because in the meantime all kinds of truly productive activities had gotten underway.

"Or in the '80s, not that long ago, people thought that they actually had savings in a bunch of institutions. They didn't; between crooks and incompetents, all their money had been lent out and spent several times over. But as long as they thought they had their money there, it made no difference at all.

"What we should have done," Peter added, gliding on his fourth beer, sensing brilliance and conviction in his growing incoherence, "is have a secret session of Congress where we authorized the Feds to fill everybody's kitty back up and never tell a soul."

Peter hammered the dull edge of a knife against his fifth bottle of beer. "A toast," he said over Jeffery's conversation with Zenobia and the chatter of three neighbors who had wandered in, "a toast to the well-filled kitties and to the fowls in the air and the lilies in the field and Zenobia's enchiladas!"

Except for Jeffery, no one paid much attention to Peter's

toast. The neighbors were passing a hash pipe among them and Zenobia had moved over to the laser disc player to put on the Rolling Stones. Brown Sugar filled the room, and Peter went to bed dreaming of Laura.

WILLIAM H. ESPINOSA

CHAPTER 31

It was the earthquake two nights before that had saved him. The tremor had come roaring up on the house like a freight train, set the hanging lamp swinging, painting the room with gyrating strokes of shadow and light as glasses tinkled and loosely shelved books crashed to the floor.

David had fallen asleep on the couch reading. He had thought he was dreaming until he tasted the plaster in his mouth, then he had bolted upright and raced to the safety of the out-of-doors. Of course it was over by then, all except the fear, the intensity of which surprised him. It was a deep-seated, primal, animal fear. He had felt it inside of him and in the silence of the forest around him. No home, no den, no lair, no burrow, no nest, not the safest of places was safe when the Earth moved, when it bared its raw, archaic, impersonal power as it briefly had.

The experience left him shaken, on edge. He had stayed awake that night, cleaning up the mess, jumpy, ready to rush out again. He went to sleep when morning came and didn't awaken until early in the afternoon. The next night he hadn't slept well either; the darkness and loneliness heightened his fear. He listened to the cadences of insect chants for clues. Every rise of the tree frogs' chirping sounded like a warning, the hum of a distant truck on the highway would come and go like the harbinger of a roaming aftershock.

Before dawn in the hollowed-out space that fear had made, he let loneliness suddenly overwhelm him. He felt shriveled and small. He wanted a warm body next to him. He yearned for the sounds of children yelling at the playground in excitement, for the regularity of books opening and closing with the schoolroom's buzzer, for his mother and father, both dead now, at dinner, listening to his stories. The three of them were often silent but they always seemed...together.... He longed for the large noisy gatherings of family and friends who were convened wherever they were on Rosh Ha-Shanah, Passover, Thanksgiving, or random weekend nights.

In his life, David had been to many wonderful places, he had tasted a dozen different cultures. He knew his work was worthwhile; he had helped bring humans and the Earth of which they were a part together, at a time when they were both at risk. But personally he had blown it. There was no other word. An ugly, implacable truth. Thirty-eight years of life, no wife, no children, no community, no one who truly loved him, a few fragile friendships at best. All of his time and energy wasted in a chase after chimerical, ungiving women whom he had wrapped in illusions of his own making. He cried in that predawn cold longer than he remembered ever crying before. When he woke up the following evening, he knew that he had slept in despair and depression, not in exhaustion.

Now he was wide awake a third night. It wasn't what he would have chosen but it wasn't inappropriate either. The tropical forest was a world that came alive at night. He had chosen to make his life's work the forest, perhaps it was time that he join it in its rhythms. So he went behind the house and set up a big-backed wooden chair with slanted-down slats for a seat. He parked the chair between the rows of flowers that Laura had planted and tended and were, he noted, still blossoming. He sat back and looked into the forest that started no more than twenty yards behind the house. Stars were visible through intermittent clouds but fortunately, he later realized, there was no moon. His eyes adjusted to the darkness, and he saw the inky outlines of trees and shrubs and ferns. It was too dark to discern much else so life came to him in the sounds of insects and reptiles, an occasional bird call, the rustling of leaves, the crack of a branch and the smells—the dank smell of too much wet vegetation and rotting trunks, the sweet smell of night blooming flowers. That was all; it mesmerized him. He lost himself in thoughts of a future life.

Until he saw a bit of color on the trees to his right, briefly, as if they had been lapped by the penumbra of a passing car's headlights. And then to his left there had been a muffled sound, like a car door closing gently, so as not to be heard. The chirp of the tree frogs dropped a few decibels then rose to a near shriek again. David got up from his chair and started to go around to the front of the house—until fear stopped him with an image in his mind's eye of a tinted-window van.

He retreated to the back, crouched low and ran uphill to the edge of the forest. He skirted it to his right, in case whoever it was—if it was anyone—chose to come through the trees and not by the road. David flattened his back against the wide-girthed trunk of a fifty-foot tree. From where he was he could see most of the approaches to the house. He could see the front and back entrances but he did not have a view of the far end of the porch. Nor of his electric car.

The car. If someone were looking for him, they would see the car and surmise that he was home. When they didn't find him in, they would look in the clearing and maybe the woods. He would be spotted where he was, even if they didn't have night-vision equipment. He was too close.

Then he saw the two shadowy figures. Two men he felt sure. His stomach knotted, his heart pounded. One was coming up the road. The figure kept walking until it was squarely in front of the house and then turned up the path toward the front door. David thought he saw a brief flash of light where the man's right hand was dangling. The other figure was twenty yards behind. When he came to the clearing, he climbed up along its edge and then trotted towards the spot where David's car was parked. David lost sight of him.

These people do not mean me well, David thought to himself. He took a few deep breaths to calm the rising panic and then took a calculated risk and headed deeper into the forest. As he climbed up, the sound of brushed and broken branches and rocks and earth knocked loose seemed deafening to him. He expected to hear crashing sounds and shouting, maybe even gunshots behind him.

So far nothing. The frogs, their croaking and chirping, must have covered for him. He could hear a clamor of loud, powerful tinks from the martillitos, the "little hammer frogs", one-inch creatures that sounded like something out of a dive steel band. He owed them one—and the earthquake that had kept him awake three nights. He came to an almost vertical incline of five or six feet and reached up to the base of a small tree for support. He put his hand around it: something slithered underneath it. He withdrew the hand in terror, lost his purchase and slipped ten yards down the embankment. Had he screamed?

Apparently not, still nothing to be heard behind him. He took a few breaths to calm himself. He reminded himself that poisonous snakes were a rarity in the Costa Rican forest and that even if you encountered one, they had no desire to mess with humans. The greater risk was probably accidental contact with the toxic skin of a poison dart toad, but even that was remote and so far the frogs had been his friends. It was odd, he thought, the intensity of fear a tropical forest can bring out in humans at night: there are far more menacing environments.

Half convinced again that he was in a benign environment, he detoured away from the tree and the snake or whatever it was and resumed his climb. Fifty yards further up he came to a ledge and stopped for breath. He turned and looked down. He could see the outline of his house. He had stumbled onto a perfect vantage point. If he lay flat on the ledge, it would be virtually impossible to be seen from below and there were a few ferns there as well, dense enough to provide some cover but with fronds set far enough apart to see through.

He had been on the ledge over an hour and there had been no discernible movement below and no sound. It occurred to him that in his mad scramble up the hill, the men could have left and he would not have known it. But it seemed unlikely. The climb could not have lasted more than four or five minutes. It would have taken them at least that long to enter the house, discover his absence and search the rooms and grounds for some indication of his whereabouts. If they were looking for him, that is. He could have panicked, the explanation could be completely innocent, a broken-down car, a need to make a phone call. When there was no answer at the door, they could have gone on. Three minutes, maybe.

As he waited he could feel more and more of his body itching as growing colonies of insects began tasting his presence. They were making him impatient; he knew he could be losing track of time, speeding it up in his mind out of discomfort.

The edge of a rock was digging into his right elbow. He moved it cautiously and as he did so, his hand brushed against a small, soft cylindrical object. He held it between his fingers and brought it close to his face. It was a cigarette filter, he couldn't tell its age in the dark.

Horror wrenched his stomach. He controlled it with difficulty. They know this place, they use this place, this is where they sit and watch me. They may know some other way here, they could be coming down on me from above. I am as visible as a pumping heart through the transparent skin of the glass frog. I wouldn't have a chance.

David regained his composure with difficulty and considered moving to another spot, or going over the mountain. The Quintanas, their iguana farm was on the other side. Long thought of as a delicacy with a taste like chicken, iguanas had become a staple for meat eaters around the world. Unlike the cattle which they replaced, iguanas could be raised in the rainforest without destroying it. Iguana ranching had become a popular and lucrative business in Costa Rica. The Quintana ranch was one of the largest, and David felt sure that he would be able to find it. He knew the Quintanas slightly, they would probably help. Bandits he could say. There were still a few around. The Nicaraguan Contras in their exile had left a whole infrastructure of banditry behind them that almost a generation later the government had never fully broken. It had spread throughout the country.

Why did he feel like he had to make up stories? What had he done?

Government authorities. Somewhere in this encircling nightmare there were government authorities, whose or how many he couldn't tell. Odd how they could still make him feel bad, guilty, out of step, antisocial. The very word said a lot—expertise, the righteousness of the first source, the enforcer of truth. But government authority, like military intelligence, was an oxymoron, it was contrary to human experience, yet at some level, unconsciously everybody still believed it. We were still cowed, even if we expressed it in revolt. David drew back; he reminded himself that this was not the time to be philosophical.

As his feelings cleared, he decided to stay on the ledge. He would probably have some warning if the men did come up and some core part of him didn't want to give in. His work, his home, his car, his links with the outside, he needed to hold on to them as best he could. Once lies and secretiveness began, he suspected, once he entered the untethered life of a fugitive, everything could unravel. He waited, keeping his body as still as possible, enduring the insect bites. Finally as a gray tinge started to fill the eastern sky, he caught a glimpse, he was almost sure, of two ghostly shapes barely materializing like deer grazing in twilight, making their way down the road. Soon afterwards he saw headlight beams head off to San Jose.

He got up to head down the hillside which was damp with morning dew, but then thought better of it and sat down cross-legged at his spot. Five minutes later, the sky much brighter, the headlights returned. They stopped in front of his house for a moment and backed into his little driveway. He heard a door close, a minute or two passed. A door closed again and the vehicle sped off towards San Jose.

David descended the hill circumspectly and when he came to the edge of the clearing, stayed in the forest for a few minutes watching the house in the early morning light. Nothing. He heard his own breathing, his heart beating, and the diminishing sounds of the forest quieting with the advent of day. No other sound. His eyes moved to a shovel near the rear door. He didn't remember it's being there but realized it would make a good weapon—if he should need one.

In a low crouch he ran across the clearing and pressed himself against the back wall of the house. He tried to contain his breathing and crawled over to the shovel. Once he had it in hand he crawled back, first to peer through the bedroom window, then to the window that looked into the kitchen and living area. Still nothing. He felt safer, though he knew parts of the living room were obscured from the rear-window view. He walked to the corner of the house and looked towards his car. It looked empty. He decided to chance a trip around to the front window, looked through, and was finally satisfied that his house was empty. The men had apparently left, perhaps not wishing to be seen in daylight.

He entered the house through the front door, gripping the shovel by its stem, his arm cocked upwards slightly. The door was unlocked as he had left it. He looked around the living room; there was no sign of disturbance. As he headed towards the bedroom he suddenly froze. The bathroom, he had not checked the bathroom. Now, there was no way to check it except to go in it. He circled the bedroom to the bathroom door and threw the door open. Nothing. Behind the curtain—the tub, Laura's favorite. Empty. His muscles slackened in relief.

It was when he went out the back to replace the shovel that he saw the first tangible evidence of the men's recent presence. The flowers on the row next to where he had been sitting had been dug up. Perhaps fifteen or twenty plants were gone, together with some of the soil, though it was possible that the soil had been scattered around. Laura, he thought, if she ever comes back, will think I did it out of spite. "Let her," he said aloud and allowed himself a smile.

When he reentered the house, the computer was in its wake-up mode. David could see the low red glow of the coffee maker announcing that it was in preparation.

[*Good morning, David. Coffee still brewing. New York Times?*]

"No. Replay Wednesday's Lifenet disk."

[*Lifenet coming up.*]

The words faded from the screen as the computer searched for the Lifenet materials. Lifenet was a disaster relief tool first tested in Costa Rica in the late 1980s. But it took a few decades of natural and manmade disasters of increasing frequency and severity for the concept to be accepted and put into place worldwide. The idea was simple. In disaster-prone areas local television crews, who would be at a disaster site anyway, were trained to shoot images which would be useful to relief experts in assessing the extent of a disaster, the damage to infrastructure, and the likely relief requirements. The images were made available to national disaster administrators and were transmitted by satellite to disaster relief agencies around the world as well. The result was a much faster, coordinated, effective, and appropriate relief effort.

David had programmed his computer to operate his dish antenna and receiver in a scan mode and to record the Lifenet transmissions. When the periodic volcanic eruptions, earthquakes, and floods did occur, he was able to tell if access to any of the project sites for which he was responsible had been blocked, or if there were reason to worry about harm to the people that lived and worked there. Now, he also wanted to make sure that there was no damage to the roads which headed north towards Miguel's family's farm. Miguel, he knew, was probably the best person to talk to about the night's events and David did not want to spend another night at the house alone, at least for a while.

David watched a little over half an hour of recorded material. There was no appreciable damage to the north. The earthquake's epicenter was further south in a much less inhabited area, not far from the Panamanian border. Even in San Jose itself there seemed to be very few disruptions. A few earth-slides, no apparent structural harm. David resolved to call the various project centers rather than visit any and then get some rest before heading for Miguel's. He exited from the video library and was ready to turn to the v-phone when the computer emitted a buzzing sound.

You have messages from last night, David, the screen announced before it faded out.

CHAPTER 32

In the Third Year of the Modern Era, Senzo Sato was chosen as the eighth Secretary General of the United Nations, the first from a major power. Sato had performed well at the UN Fund for Population Activities in various assignments all over the world, particularly in South Asia, and in encouraging the use of popular entertainment like radio and TV soap operas (an idea developed in Mexico) to deliver family planning messages. He had quickly risen to be UNFPA's Director.

He was highly regarded by the international voluntary nongovernmental agencies that were instrumental in implementing family planning programs. In the years when U.S. support of international population programs was choked off in the grip of the religious right, a number of the more prominent of these organizations, together with several environmental groups, approached Sato with the proposal that there be established an organization dedicated to consciousness raising about the importance of family planning to planetary survival, targeted particularly at governmental and religious elites. The proposal was that this be done through a series of high-level conferences that would double with international media exposure. It was the hope of the organizations that approached him that in addition to the contribution of his personal skills, he would be able to find support for these activities from Japanese philanthropists.

Sato was in fact quite successful in these efforts and through them he became known to a large and influential cross-section of governmental and spiritual leaders. Eventually, panic at ecological catastrophe had taken sufficient hold of the industrialized world's consciousness that family planning programs for the developing world would never again be underfunded. The only remaining barriers to population limitation were cultural and these were eroding, albeit slowly in some regions where governmental censorship had blocked effective educational campaigns or prevented the women's rights movement from flourishing.

Sato became a highly placed advisor in the Office of the Secretary General. In 2022, the last year of the old calendar, Sato was selected to help mediate the most recent breakout of the simmering conflict between Pakistan and India over Kashmir. He succeeded where so many had failed before and his demonstrated mediation skills, coupled with his expertise in population, ecology and development, vaulted his name into consideration when the incumbent Secretary General died in the Second Year of the Modern Era.

The greatest barrier to his selection to the post was thought to be the tradition of selecting candidates from small nations whose interests were not likely to be involved significantly in most international disputes. However, in Sato's case, it was probably his Japanese nationality which assured him of the post. For decades before, there had been an ongoing debate as to whether the permanent membership of the UN Security Council should be altered to reflect current realities, particularly Japan's economic importance. Resistance to change had been stubborn largely because of lingering anti-Japanese sentiment, but the stated rationales, such as arguments that the Japanese were bureaucratically incapable of taking a position in a fast-breaking crisis, were wearing thin and Japanese economic and political support was crucial for the United Nations to operate effectively. Electing Sato Secretary General tidily solved the problem. The Japanese could no longer claim that they were not being given a role commensurate with their importance, so the issue of altering the composition of the Security Council to give the government of Japan greater power could be postponed for a decade, maybe more, given Sato's relatively young age.

***

Secretary General Sato was finding the meeting with UNINTEL's Covert Director, Casey Hamilton, and his deputy Nikolai Ligachev discomforting. He distrusted conspiracy theories and the memo the two UNINTEL leaders had sent him in advance of the meeting seemed just that. What was more, the underlying premise of the meeting—that strong, centralized power was the answer to the world's problems— was one with which he was only sometimes in agreement. His work with family planning and environmental NGOs in the 1990s had taught him that at times the opposite might be true. It was the crescendo of activity by a large number of local voluntary associations that had forced governments to revise their priorities and address ecological problems.

As DeGaulle had put it, history precedes politics. Sato was convinced that more often than not this was right. But it was a point on which almost all of his official advisors and the Permanent Members disagreed with him. Moreover, the state of the world was certainly no worse than that anticipated by many private groups. In fact in many respects it was much better. It was only worse than the ludicrously optimistic government projections made when governments, particularly the American one, were seeking to preserve the status quo or seeking to escape culpability for their commission of a massive crime against nature. Nonetheless, dogged as he had been since his early years with accusations of self-aggrandizement, he felt extremely uncomfortable acting against the clear consensus of his advisors, and in order to preserve his ability to act as a counterweight, he knew must be cautious not to appear an obstructionist or unreasonable in dealing with related issues.

"We would not have bothered you on such short notice," Hamilton had begun, "if we were not convinced of the gravity of the threat and did not believe that we have a unique but fleeting opportunity to put it to rest."

Hamilton, a lanky, handsome Texan with an Ivy League veneer that suited his cover as a global investor, had risen through the U.S. Civil Service and the anti-terror campaigns to the position of Deputy Director of the CIA before coming to UNINTEL. He was adept at high-level bureaucratic in-fighting.

279

He is saying to me, Sato surmised, if you go around checking this one out with everybody like you usually do, the opportunity will disappear and what everyone is saying about Japan's inability to react quickly will be proven true, not to speak of the demonstration it will make of your own obstructionist attitudes.

After summarizing the material in the memorandum—the dire conditions and threats to planetary security, the opportunities to address them more effectively in a centralized context and the importance of the upcoming Convocation in that respect—the Director turned to the meat of the matter. "Nikolai, perhaps you could lay out what we have found so far."

Ligachev hesitated, as if to find the right form of address with which to begin. "Secretary General, there have been a number of events, more precisely deaths, involving certain prominent personages which may have come to your attention, though almost certainly not in a connected manner."

Ligachev was a squat, muscular man with a large, round head. He was wearing his habitual dress, a brown rumpled suit with the collar of his white shirt buttoned as tight as any tie might be. He crossed one leg over the other to dangle a foot clad in a designer loafer with a golden snaffle bit embedded across its top. The Secretary General was embarrassed by the sight of the foot, so clearly out of place. Why didn't the Russians just give this man a dascha, he mused, my life would be easier.

Ligachev continued, his eyes and voice unwavering, "The events seemed unconnected to us as well and the deaths themselves at first appeared unremarkable. There was the Brazilian, Matteo Michelson, an older man, an apparent heart attack here in New York."

"He was a friend," the Secretary General interjected, "all of us are in his debt."

"Absolutely," Hamilton added, "it's a shame he had such funny ideas about governments. He could have been a great leader."

Another warning, Senzo Sato thought, it was foolish on my part to speak so well of him.

"There was the Peruvian, José María Velasquez, an apparent roadside accident. There was Fatimah Karajan," Ligachev resumed, "Palestinian Women's Peace. You recall, Secretary

General?"

The Secretary General nodded.

"The bullet in her head was clearly no accident but the circumstances of her death, with the Israeli security man—by the way, specimens of his sperm were found inside of her—made us all think, revenge, a local problem. Even with the Settlement, there are too many embittered people in that pathological corner of the world for things like this not too happen! In the Service, the FCS, we always thought it a calamity to be assigned to that area. You couldn't trust anybody."

Ligachev rose from his seat and wandered over to the glass wall that looked out to the East River and the new buildings of variegated color and shape that glistened in the late morning sun on the river's far bank. As he stared out through stony brown eyes, he continued, "There are others, well-known, who have died recently too, but we do not know enough about the details yet, so let us stay with the three, Michelson, Velasquez, Karajan. I think you will see that they tell us enough.

"First, it comes out that Michelson may well have been poisoned, by a flower essence no less. How do you say, 'hoisted by his own petal?'" A guttural laugh emerged from Ligachev's throat but was immediately silenced by a withering look from Hamilton.

"Then we learn, thanks to the enterprise of a rural police sergeant, that Velasquez was hit on the head by the same object several times on his presumed accidental fall to the bottom of a gorge. Clearly he was murdered."

"Then," Hamilton interrupted, "the sources I recruited at EROE—the Electronic Record of Everything—came up with the real eye opener. People connected with the victims and who could be closely tied to the place and time of the deaths were in frequent communication with each other!"

"With this," Ligachev said, "we launched our own investigation—in proper coordination with local authorities of course—and have developed a most interesting picture.

"Here in New York six people meet on the day of Michelson's death. One, probably two of them, we will show, are prime suspects in Michelson's death. A third is a lifelong friend and sometime lover of the last person to be seen alive with

Velasquez. A fourth is a former and, along with a fifth, future lover of the last person to have met with Fatimah. Extraordinary is it not, sir?"

"And the sixth person?" the Secretary General asked.

"An American with the Mother Earth Investment Bank. We have not been able to clarify his role yet," Ligachev replied. "He has been helpful to us in some respects but there are strong indications of deception on his polygraph charts."

"You have already interrogated one of these people?" Sato asked with an inflection of rising concern in his voice.

"Not interrogated in any negative sense, sir." Hamilton offered, "I first approached him about a low water-current energy project, his cooperation was entirely voluntary so there was not even any need to bring local authorities along."

"May I continue, Secretary General?" Ligachev asked.

"Yes, of course."

"Michelson. Suspect Number One is a woman, herself expert in the healing and toxic effects of flowers. She and suspect Number Two live or at least lived in Costa Rica. She was seen at Michelson's lectures the day of his death and the day before, and was seen milling around the speaker's podium and then briefly talking to Michelson during an intermission. Her presence at the podium was significant, sir, because we know that Michelson had at his side, next to the podium, a case of medicinal vials that he always carried with him. We have obtained the case from his family and sure enough, on analyzing, we find that one is mislabeled and contains a powerful toxin."

"And you think this woman made the substitution?"

"She had the opportunity, sir, and we know from the sixth person, the American we interro... spoke with, that on the day of his death this woman was telling the others that Michelson had been killed, not that he died but that he had been killed. Something that neither the police nor the public suspected until weeks afterward!

"We engaged some of our best Latin American operatives to attempt to gain this woman's confidence and obtain some more information from her."

"How could you do that?" the Secretary General asked.

"Suffice it to say sir," Hamilton responded, his hands linked behind his head, his long legs stretched out in front of him, "that the lady likes dark handsome men who can give a good rap on native voodoo. We suckered her right in, got her out of her house and into Mexico where we can operate much better. We even got her on tape."

"Admitting to killing Michelson?"

"Not exactly, but admitting to knowing that Michelson would be killed before he actually was."

"Your people must be very skilled."

"Yes, Secretary General, they are," Ligachev resumed. "There is more. Our investigators in Costa Rica seized from the garden of the suspects specimens of the very flower species from which the toxic extract implicated in his death is obtained. They have even delivered to us substantial soil samples to prove their origin."

"I assume the couple has been arrested?"

"No sir," Hamilton said, "not yet, for reasons that we'll get to in a minute."

"Fatimah Karajan," Ligachev continued. "The last known, living person to see her alive is a Palestinian woman who worked for her and whose husband was killed, probably by the Shin Bet, the old Israeli internal security people."

"Revenge?" the Secretary General asked.

"You would think so but it is not so clear. After she is questioned—and acknowledges seeing Fatimah on the night that she was killed—she packs up her two children and goes to England to stay with her brother.

"We tried to get close to her there, but it backfired. The operative, an American," Ligachev said with a scornful look at Hamilton, "was clumsy and scared her out of England."

"Clumsy or not," Hamilton said dropping his hands and pulling himself up in his seat, "he flushed her good. Where does she go? Helsinki—to be with two of the people who were at that little New York get-together."

"One of them," Ligachev added, "has penetrated to the highest levels of the Council of Europe, an organization that you know, Secretary General, has given us critical support in our efforts to achieve planetary security. The other we believe to be his lover, with a long record of association with questionable elements. Actually, though, the camera angle wasn't good," Ligachev arched his eyebrows in amusement, "it may be that all three are lovers."

The Secretary General winced at the mention of the camera. UNINTEL had obviously gone a long ways beyond what most thought it to be. It had too many assets lying around from the old Cold War and anti-terror days. This conversation was confirming what he had suspected for some time, that Hamilton and Ligachev and their UNINTEL colleagues were a real danger. At the same time, they were obviously onto something here; this was not the time to attack them.

"Just to sew it up," Hamilton said, "what does she do next? She tries to contact the couple that did it to Michelson and even as we speak, she's on her way to meet one of them."

"The third case, you will also find most interesting," Ligachev continued. "The last person to be seen with Velasquez was a U.S. Senator's aide, Senator Carmichael's no less."

A look of shock passed across the Secretary General's face. Now these people are playing with fire. He turned attention to his breath to control his reactions and elected to listen a little longer.

"This aide it turns out is the lover of the third person who was at the New York meeting and he is now, as we speak, with the woman who we think poisoned Michelson! Moreover, neither the suspect nor the Senator can give a very good reason for the suspect's trip to Peru, nor can the suspect explain why he did not give this man Velasquez a ride home from a remote area the two of them were visiting on the day that he was killed."

"You have questioned the Senator?" Sato inquired icily.

"Not us, sir," Hamilton answered, "local people. Our men have just been along for the ride. It's all been completely by the book. You see something else happened. A boy drowned and he was seen snooping around Carmichael's place not long before so the police had to talk to the Senator."

"And you helpfully provided them with some background on Velasquez," the Secretary General interjected.

"Sir, that's UNINTEL's mandate, to help when suspect activities go across borders."

"Senator Carmichael is a principled man, Mr. Hamilton.

Violence is not his way."

"Secretary General, you are undoubtedly right," Ligachev replied, "but he is also an ambitious man. It would not be correct to rule him out completely."

The Secretary General decided to address the subject in a more round-about way, "You were going to tell me Mr. Ligachev, why the couple in Costa Rica had not yet been arrested."

Hamilton gave his deputy no chance to answer. "Sources, sir. Couldn't compromise them. We couldn't tell the locals about our boys at EROE and the flower snatching, well, it was done by the U.S. Embassy security team, it stretched their mandate a little bit, and the President's PSA, his Planetary Security Advisor, won't let us disclose it."

"I see," Sato said.

"The Costa Ricans are sticky about things like that," Hamilton continued. "When I was there thirty years ago, they gave us a terrible time and shit—no disrespect, Nikolai—-they had an army of Commies on their border. They just don't have good sense."

"I see," Sato said again, "but what I don't understand in all of this is what motivates these people."

"We're not sure ourselves. There are hints, we can surmise. With Karajan dead, it looks like all four of them could be at the Convocation in one capacity or another. Maybe it is maneuvering. We surmise their aim is at disruption, at power. They see strong central authorities as standing in their way. Maybe they want the catastrophes to come to pass. Revolutionaries first breed confusion and fear to manipulate passions. Then they seize the moment. We may be looking at only a cell of something much bigger. As we said, there have been other deaths that we have not looked at yet."

"And there are personal factors," Ligachev, who had returned to his chair, added. "The Palestinian woman's vengeance for Fatimah's perceived betrayal. Velasquez served in the Mideast and learned much at a monastery, perhaps the very same one that had something to do with crippling the Palestinian woman's brother. And of course there is Carmichael's ambition to be some kind of global Thomas Jefferson and fight central power."

Ligachev's upper lip curled in contempt. "He strikes me as another preachy American, maybe like Wilson and perhaps just as dangerous." Ligachev pulled a nail clipper out of his jacket pocket and ran the tip of the file under his thumbnail. "Or we may just be dealing with a degenerate Western sex cult like the many we saw forty years ago."

"The point is," Hamilton picked up, "whatever is going on is dangerous and we need to know much more about it. And that's what we need your authorization for, sir. We've searched and surveilled a lot, but the evidence we can go public with is still thin.

"We need to talk to these people, to get someone to confess. We had a shot at luring a couple of them into the Mexican jungle, but we could only get one part way and we didn't think that was enough. We thought we could get another one into bed with one of our guys, but that didn't quite work out.

"But now we've developed an asset that has a real good line to some of the suspects. He's agreed to try to get them to a Mexican resort next week for a conference where some Convocation issues are going to be talked about. From there, we think we can get them out into international waters. There, as you know, we can detain and question people ourselves. We can do it right and get one of them to break and then nail them all. Hell, in the al Qaeda days, we did our best work on ships. And nobody got upset like they did about 'Gitmo and Romania.

"One of them," Hamilton continued, "is Carmichael's man. We know that's a little sensitive so we felt that we needed to check it out with you and get your okay. That's what we're here for."

Secretary General Sato remained still in his chair, his features masking frenetic mental activity. The risk of saying yes was high, the risk of saying no or substantially delaying was probably higher. He needed to formulate an approach that would minimize his own exposure.

"Thank you gentlemen," he said getting up from his chair, "I will give you my decision this afternoon."

***

Hamilton and Ligachev picked a Northern Italian restaurant on 45th Street for lunch. Its tables were spread out enough to allow a semblance of private conversation, even at the height of the lunch hour. Ligachev, who was particularly fond of the restaurant, had, as an added precaution, arranged—unbeknownst to the restaurant's owner—for periodic 3 A.M. electronic sweeps of the premises.

The maître d' greeted the two men warmly and showed them to a table in the rear of the room. Bread and sparkling mineral water were brought and Ligachev ordered a bottle of Frascati. Hamilton pulled out a pair of bifocals, aranged them on his aquiline nose and studied the restaurant's offerings.

Ligachev dispensed with the menu. He acquired his taste in food at the same time as he acquired his taste in shoes, while he was stationed with the Russian FSB in Rome.

"The risotto, Casey," he said, "you can always tell the quality of an Italian restaurant by its risotto, especially now when we eat so little meat. And the risotto here—ah, the best there is!" When the waiter came, Hamilton settled for agnollotti instead.

"Did we do it, what do you think?" Ligachev asked.

"I think so, I don't think he has any choice. He may ask for something to cover himself but we can give him that."

"I must say I was skeptical, Hamilton, but your plan did work."

"You just don't trust computers, Nikolai, and the way you built them in Russia," the corners of Hamilton's mouth widened into a smile, "can't say I blame you."

Hamilton had spent a lifetime watching people and it had come to him a few years ago that virtually everybody he knew had a repertoire of "small world" stories, of unexpected encounters with forgotten friends, of working with friends of friends in faraway places, even of objects, books, furnishings, doing the rounds and then coming back years later into their first owner's view. It happened far more often that he would have ever expected.

This observation was certainly not original to Hamilton but what he did see that others didn't and had confirmed for himself during the American anti-terror hysteria, was that this tendency of human experience could with a couple of clever brushstrokes easily be painted into evidence of the existence of wide-ranging conspiracies, perhaps even on a global scale. Why the Bush people had taken the presence of two people in the same city at the same time and twisted it into a reason to go to war!

Access to EROE gave him a wonderful paint box. All that was needed was to identify a central person, get a high-speed computer to run through the EROE data tracking that person's contacts, do a second-generation run of the contacts' contacts (likely to total in the tens of thousands), and then a sort on all of it for political or other leaders who were likely to attend the Convocation and resist the creation of a central planetary governance.

Peter Flanigan had been the fourth person selected as the hub of a computer run. When Hamilton saw the initial printout of names, he knew he had struck gold. Not only did it present an opportunity to eliminate a couple of minor but potentially vexatious figures, Matteo Michelson and Fatimah Karajan in particular, but by blaming their elimination on Peter and his net of co-conspirators, he would be able to discredit one of the three or four most powerful advocates of decentralization, Senator Patrick Carmichael. Moreover, the fact that such conspiracies flourished would itself be an argument for centralization in order to protect the planet from another round of terrorism.

Hamilton had enlisted Ligachev's aid. Hamilton's deputy had been somewhat skeptical at first but had proved brilliant in engineering the murders. They were clever, ambiguous, replete with symbolism and suggestion. Ligachev understood human psychology well. By making two of the deaths seem accidental or natural at first, their ability to arouse fear once their nature was disclosed increased, and on a canvas of fear, malevolent conspiracies would seem far more credible. Hamilton had come to admire Ligachev.

"You know, Nikolai," Hamilton said as he raised a wineglass to his lips, "you did a hell of a job. The hits were great, but one thing I don't understand. How did you get that kid Bernie to show deception on the polygraph? I mean, as far as I could tell, he was being straight."

Nikolai blushed in appreciation; Hamilton was sparing with his praise. "An easy trick," Ligachev responded. "Before the examination, we made him watch films of his girlfriend making love to Peter Flanigan over and over again. He thought we were trying to give him reason to denounce Katie but that was not really it. What we did was replay the sound of the projector we had used while he was listening to the polygrapher.

"It was a subliminal association," he continued his mouth half full of risotto, "the sound brings up his memory of anger, an awareness of betrayal. The physiological reactions of a person who discovers that he has been deceived are not that different from those of a deceiver who has been discovered."

Hamilton was impressed. He hadn't heard of that trick. "And Nikolai, one other question. Are you sure we can trust this Rafael fellow?"

"We can trust that he doesn't want to see his mother tortured, raped, and murdered by a half-castrated vengeance-seeker from long ago." Hamilton raised the starched linen napkin and wiped his lips. He took a final sip of the no-longer-bubbling mineral water. "Nikolai, we should have worked together in the old days. The world would have been a better place."

***

The work day was drawing to a close when Hamilton's secretary buzzed him to announce that Sato was on the line. "Yes sir," Hamilton said as the Secretary General appeared on the screen.

"You may proceed," Senzo Sato slowly said, "but we must be clear on what basis you are acting and what you are proposing to do. Before doing anything you will give me a memorandum summarizing our conversation today, yes?"

"But sir," Hamilton started to reply, "security."

"The Secretary General of the United Nations is not a security risk, Mr. Hamilton. If you think your secretary is one, then type the document, or better yet, handwrite it yourself."

"Yes, sir. Thank you, sir," Hamilton replied, giving the appearance of mild dejection as he switched the v-phone off. He could do a memo; in fact, he'd already written one. Its subtle theme was that if the information that Ligachev had said he had developed was true, it was imperative that UNINTEL respond. If it were a matter of Ligachev's word against Hamilton's, Ligachev didn't stand a chance.

***

As he sat alone in his office, the Secretary General mused

about how he had played baseball as a boy, thinking it would help him learn to speak and think like an American. It didn't do much of that for him, but he did learn that small as he was, his home runs could only come against very hard throwers. It was like a martial art, using your opponent's momentum as your own. Hamilton, Sato thought as he stared out the window at the river, is about to throw heat, and I, Senzo Sato, must unleash a corker.

CHAPTER 33

"I can see the problem, "Miguel said as he took a swallow from the Coke that he had brought with him out onto the lawn of his country home, "flower-napping may not be taken very seriously by the police."

"The villainous Pistil Pete? They'll have his face on every station wall," David said, beginning to enjoy himself again.

A pack of four children ran by, squealing in front of the two men.

"There's nothing else you can say. Their car, what the men looked like, anything else they touched or took?"

"Miguel, I can't even say that they were men or even prove they went inside the house. The flowers are the only thing."

"The police, though, they could look more carefully, they could dust for fingerprints, things like that."

"True, but what would make them think it was important enough to go to the trouble?"

"At least you'd be on record, if anything else happened."

"That's comforting…it would help them find my murderers?"

"David, you're overdoing this, you don't even know what these people want. Look, I have a friend, a lawyer, he does some criminal work, perhaps he would know the right person to talk to. Will you see him?"

David put his arm around Miguel's shoulder, as he had done so many times when they were children, "Thank you, I will,

Miguel. As always you have been a friend." They leaned against the railing of a small enclosure where two ponies grazed contentedly after a day of prods and pulls from the visiting children.

"I've wondered whether this is right, to keep the ponies," Miguel said, "but the more I think about it, the more I think yes. For thousands of years they have been one of our closest ties to the animal world. Our children need to have the memories awakened."

A silence descended on them as the light slipped out of the day. Miguel broke in again, "Some of your friends, David, some of the environmentalists, they are so horrified by what we've done with nature, that they want to remove us from it all together. But in one way or another we're still here, we will always affect nature and nature will affect us. How can we love if we are removed, how can we love if we have no memories, if we cannot accept where we have been?"

"Umm...." Miguel's words stirred a nameless sensation in David but his mind was still preoccupied with the events of the day and night before. "I'll visit your lawyer friend, Miguel, but I don't think that I'm going to find much here. ...My friend Rashid, Rashid O'Shea. It's a little strange...he's asked me to meet him in Baja."

"And you're going? Who is he? Why?"

"I trust him. He's a powerful person. I mean his presence. It feels right to do it. And what's more, from there maybe I can track Laura down. This has to involve her somehow."

"Laura again?" Miguel asked gently.

"No, it's not the way that you think. I'm pretty sure I'm over that and it's not just Laura either." David patted the white blaze of a bay pony that had come over to them and then playfully flipped the pony's upper lip.

"A woman called this morning," David continued, now leaning down and rubbing his nose against the pony's. "She asked for Laura but she knew who I was too. From a friend of a friend of mine, she said, Jean-Marc Aubuisson. Did I know where Laura was. I said no, not exactly, somewhere near Washington, rural Virginia, I last heard, but maybe she was back in Mexico. I would pass on any messages, I was sure I would see her or hear from her soon."

"It turned out this woman was from Palestine and she didn't know where rural Virginia was, much less how to get there, would I help her, she asked, and go with her to look for Laura. I explained that Virginia is not exactly next door."

"It's getting a little cool, David," Miguel interjected, "and Isabel and the guests will think we are being antisocial. We need to start back." He smiled at David, "One of the guests is Maria Clara, Maria Clara Uribe. Isabel will make sure she sits next to you. She's picked her out as your future wife."

"Just what I need," David said as they turned away from the nuzzling pony and its enclosure. "But this Palestinian is a determined woman. She wouldn't take no for an answer. She is concerned, maybe even afraid, but is determined and very much in control. She says she'll just come here then, if I didn't mind, and wait for word from Laura."

"David, this woman sounds unbalanced, she's another Laura. Was the screen on? Good looking woman, I'll bet."

"Yes, her face was handsome, not pretty, handsome, that's all I saw."

"I'm going to make you marry Maria Clara, anybody before this woman comes. You didn't say yes did you?"

"Not exactly, I told her I might be going to Baja and maybe we could meet somewhere afterwards.

"But one other thing. Rashid told me to bring a friend if I wanted. I thought he meant Laura but now I wonder. He knows about these things sometimes."

"And then?"

"She said if it weren't personal or embarrassing, could I meet her somewhere along the way and maybe even go there with her. Then she would have time to explain. She said that she knew that Laura was connected with someone famous who was killed and the same kind of thing was happening to her. It was urgent, she said, and she didn't have much time."

"So with that," Miguel suggested, "the hook is baited and guppy that you are, you took one huge swallow." Miguel rolled his eyeballs, "You don't know anything about this woman. What do you really know about Rashid? They're going to put the surveillance really close to you!"

David laughed. "No, I'm not that bad," he said, "I got Jean-Marc's number and checked with him and he spoke highly of her. She was prominent in the peace movement.

"And there are other things," David added after a brief pause as Miguel opened the door to the house for him, "Remember I'm Jewish, Miguel, a Palestinian is not the first person that I would naturally trust, so if it was a setup, it wouldn't make any sense to put that kind of barrier in the way."

"True enough," Miguel said as the door closed behind them, "but maybe they don't know you're Jewish. You're not exactly a devout practitioner. If somebody put a gun to your head you might know where to find a deli in New York but certainly not a temple in San Jose."

"They would know if they knew anything about me. She knew it, she teased me about it, she said that I was probably surprised that she was so trusting of a Jew, but she said she had met a lot of American-born ones in her work and that she knew she would be safe because our mothers trained us well."

"To be used and manipulated," Miguel added sardonically.

"That's uncalled for."

"You're right, I'm sorry," Miguel replied in a muted tone. "You're my best friend and you may be in trouble, and I worry about you." They were now approaching the others. "So how did you leave it?"

David was poised at the bathroom door. "I told her I would call her back," he said as he stepped inside.

***

There were two couples in the living room and Isabel and Maria Clara. The children were still outside, playing hide and seek in the growing darkness. The living room was rectangularly shaped, a large stone wall ran along one length with a fireplace, probably never used, in the middle. Windows at the two ends were covered with lush tropical growth and blooming flowers. The windows along the other length were shaded by tall oak varietals, native to the region. A grassy yard sloped away under their limbs. Three overhead fans rotated slowly, moving the air about the room. The room was furnished lightly, a low sofa and two matching chairs, a square mahogany coffee table and a mass of pillows with Indian designs propped up along the stone ledge, which led to the fireplace.

David was quickly introduced to Maria Clara. He was pleasantly surprised; he had underestimated Isabel's matchmaking talents. Maria Clara was a stunning woman, probably in her late twenties. Black hair fell halfway down her slender back. Brown eyes looked out from behind high, lightly freckled cheekbones and a thinly sculpted nose. Her lips were full and they often opened into a smile that was surprisingly free of vanity. David liked her at once. He knew that when the effects of the previous evening's stress passed, he would find himself attracted to her.

Maria Clara, he learned, had been a kindergarten teacher and had also worked at a television station where she would do things like carry out prizes to the successful game contestants or occasionally join in singing a background song. She left her kindergarteners behind, but moved on to a television production and software-design house that specialized in creating programs for the burgeoning number of neighborhood-run daycare centers that allowed poor, urban women in Latin America's cities to bring home a cash income while helping their children succeed in school. Maria Clara's other passion was politics and as they moved into the dining room, she was describing the heritage of the 1970s and 1980s with considerable mastery of events that had preceded her birth.

"My father was a Senator from around Liberia in the northwest, he always talked to us about what was going on," she said in response to David's expression of amazement.

"You do well with memory here," David said, "Miguel and I were just talking about it. I remember from when I was first here as a little kid, a government minister talking about the country's need for conservation programs—and compared to nearly everywhere else, you were way ahead. The man openly admitted that for fifty years his country—even his political party—had followed environmentally destructive policies and that it would take fifty years to repair, even if everything went right.

"And what really struck me was that there wasn't the slightest shrinking from the truth. At the same time there was no rancor or blame of any kind. Maybe that's why you were able to deal with environmental issues sooner than nearly anybody else."

"You're a romantic, David," Maria Clara interjected, briefly touching his hand with hers, "you were impressionable when you first came here and you think too highly of us. There is a lot that we regularly forget."

She put her napkin in her lap. "I had a nanny, very old, who was black, from the outskirts of Limon, and she remembers when she and every other black had to get a special permit to leave the coastal area and come up to San Jose. You won't hear that from a lot of us who are so proud of our little socially-just democracy, or that there were systematic European-oriented immigration policies that kept our literacy rate up, or that we avoided a lot of the problems our neighbors had by simply not having an Indian population and making sure it stayed that way."

"But see, you do remember, enough of you do, and when it's held up to the light enough, the rancor will go away and the problems of the present will be addressed."

"Just like I said, you are a romantic." She touched his hand again. He knew with some relief that his libido was returning and he was beginning to weave warm fantasies around her. He could have beautiful children with Maria Clara, he thought, and live in this beautiful country. A sense of contentment accompanied his thoughts and steeped his senses.

A man on Maria Clara's left spoke to her and David's mind wandered into his childhood again. He remembered his father who he now realized had been right about so many things, sitting at a picnic table with a rum and Coke in his hand and talking about Elie Wiesel to some Costa Rican friends. The Peace Prize was not about putting Nazis in jail, his father was saying, it was about remembering, the only antidote to the poison of a new horror of a new kind against a new victim.

Implicit in this was another thought. If what was important was that the injustice be brought into public view, then it was not that important to punish the malefactors, and the malefactors might even feel a little safer letting go of their power. This had proven true in Chile and South Africa. A few people had even proposed that it become a norm of international law that every society ritualize a periodic, public examination of conscience. Failure to do so, it was argued, was a threat to the international order. It was like allowing someone to drive a twenty-year-old automobile down a windy, downhill road without ever bothering to get it inspected. No one was able to figure out how to incorporate the idea into a legal regime but by the beginning of the Modern Era, nations that didn't take at least some steps in the area of self-examination were viewed somewhat distrustfully, if not as outright pariahs. It had certainly helped Americans overcome their eight years of shame.

Pariah. Palmyra? Alma? No, Almira. A long unremembered history. No, worse. Half-remembered, each side remembering the part the other forgot. Each side self-absorbed in its ancient wounds. The flying stones, the bulldozed homes, cluster bombs, suicide bombs, plastique on a school bus, Sabra and Shatila, Munich, the Achille Lauro, the Six-Day War, the Suez Crisis, the Yom Kippur War, land stolen, land reclaimed, Mohammed and Moses, Sarah and Hagar. And what of the century after century in between? And the cultures that kicked both Jews and Arabs in the teeth? Now this Palestinian woman would be coming. It would be a journey for him but David looked forward to it. He felt sure that he was going to like this woman.

WILLIAM H. ESPINOSA

CHAPTER 34

Laura was in the shower, the hotel room bright with morning sunshine and the water-reflected light outside. The room was modestly but tastefully furnished with a bed, dresser, couch, bench, and table and chairs of blond wood, all covered with blankets and fabrics of Native American weaves. A three-foot television screen was built into one wall, a large mirror hung on a second over the dresser, a sliding door led to a tiny balcony on a third. A landscape of a painted desert stretched above the head of the king-sized bed. The two edges of the bed were rumpled; the middle was undisturbed.

With his back to the mirror and the dresser, Peter was sitting erect on the bench, his hands palms down on his thighs, his bare feet flat on the ground. His eyes were open but unfocused. The sitting posture of the Egyptian pharaohs. He was attempting to follow Laura's instructions.

Feel the sensations in your left foot, keep your attention there. Good, now the left calf, the knee, the energy coursing through your thigh. Good.

Now feel the sensations in your right foot, the toes, the arch, the heel, the tickle of the rug on your sole, good. The calf, the knee, the thigh. Good.

Now both of them together, all together, toes, feet, calves, knees, thighs, great. Now up into the belly, the chest, your spine, your seat. Feel each, add it to the rest. The right arm, the elbow,

*the hand. Now the left. Feel the tensions in your face, tighten,
release. Now the tingling of the scalp, the rhythmic breathing,
maybe even the pulse of your heart beating...*

Peter was stuck at the left thigh, his attention clinging there to
the sensation of pressure and warmth from his hand like a
barnacle to a newfound pier post as ocean swells washed over it.
He knew that a leap to his right toes was fraught with risk. His
attention, what little he still had control over, would almost
certainly get swept out into a sea of jumbled thoughts and
overpowering feelings.

Peter was amazed at the difficulty of the exercise. He had
ridiculed Laura when she had said we had practically no control
over who we are, that we couldn't even direct that little blank
space of ours that we call consciousness, much less anything
else. How could we ever think that we could do anything to help
anybody else, she had said, when he had given a speech about
how he wanted to make the world a better place.

An old pleasure center pushes up one thought, an old fear
flips it out of sight, a movement catches your eye, the taste of ice
cream on the tip of your tongue pulls you away. Where are you
then, she said, when your mouth fills with melting vanilla, and
the cold spoon brushes your lips? There is no you, there are a
thousand you's, a thousand separate sensations bouncing helter-
skelter across a screen, hundreds of imbedded mechanisms
shaped as we grow up, tugging you here and there, jumping into
action when some careening, bouncing billiard ball of a human
being, traffic jam or rainy day trips a switch.

Ridiculous, Peter had said, though he knew that he should
have known better when neither Jeffery nor Zenobia took his
side. You sound like a Skinner behaviorist, he had said, you who
talk of gods and goddesses and hidden guiding forces in our
lives.

Precisely, Laura had replied, without inner work you are
precisely what Skinner described. There are hidden guiding
forces and you must learn to choose among them, you must
choose which ones to serve. And the place where you do the
choosing is in that little island of images that we call
consciousness and that deep well underneath it that we call the
heart. You cannot control your consciousness, much less your

heart.

Start with little things, Peter, Laura said, three times a day, five minutes each, beginning with your toes...

Even the memory of the directions on how to hold his attention pulled his attention away, Peter thought, a corner of him still clinging to the pressure on his thigh. Not to speak of the habitual racing of his well-trained mind as it tried to deal with what seemed like a mountain of recent experience—Velasquez, the inquiry about him, UNINTEL, Senator Carmichael, Jeffery, Zenobia, Rashid's message, travel with Laura...Laura. He had an almost uncontainable need to touch her, to see her in front of him, to see her step out of the shower, her tanned skin wrapped in what, wearing what, anything... nothing. Each change in the sound of the water, each tinkle of an object on glass, any hint of a click, drew his eyes towards the bathroom door.

Laura. She hadn't allowed it. He was sure that they would be lovers by now. *We are lovers, she said, but not the way that you—or I a few weeks ago—would have expected. I'm finally beginning to see, Peter, gradually it's becoming clear. Be patient Peter, you don't know how far, you don't know how much this might be.*

Think of light, Peter, she had said. Close your eyes to see, see the rosette at Chartres, the yellows, the reds and greens, the hues of deep deep blue, see a crimson dawn, a golden river, a baby's face, a foamy flick of ocean spray, feel them flow together, dance and spin, forming many forms, then funneling into one light, a blinding white light, yet still you see a thousand separate hues, each separate, each its very pigment self and also all the rest.

You and I, she said to Peter the first night together at his brother's Nelson County house, we are just the tip. There are spirits on our shoulders and angels on theirs, archangels above them, a whole pantheon on top. And over all of it, for you the Father, for me the Mother, waiting, waiting to come together if only we can figure out how. Be patient, she said, and kissed his ear and left him charged up like a towering cumulus cloud.

At first, the first night at Jeffery's, he didn't mind. There would be no tension, no Katie scenes, no uncertain groping, no risk of misfire, at least nothing could go wrong. The second night was harder, she had let him sleep on the couch in the corner of the room. He had gotten up once to come closer, perhaps to touch her, to feel her warmth during a dark and lonely hour.

She had awakened before he did touch her, his face was three feet from hers. *Turn on the lamp, Peter, she said to him gently.* Smiling, even in the dark, the most beautiful woman he had ever seen. *Breathe with me. Watch me breathe.* She rolled the covers down below her waist, a light blue night shirt covered her body. *You'll be able to see it, the rising, the falling, the length of the spine, then you'll feel it. Match your breath to mine. That's it, now when I breathe out, follow it with a little sound, maybe a sigh... aaaahHHah. Again and again, keep doing it. That's it.*

Peter did. Twenty, thirty, forty breaths, probably more. Suddenly he felt himself within her, he felt a contact, a joining, an intimacy more complete than any he remembered experiencing before. It frightened him. He wanted back on more familiar ground. He wanted desperately to make love to her in the most basic of physical ways.

"I can't stand this anymore, Laura," he had said, "I've got to make love to you now."

"You wouldn't know how to build on what you just experienced," she had said.

She sat upright in the bed and crossed her legs beneath her. "We've all forgotten these simple things," she continued. "Please, Peter, trust me. I know we're onto something here, sit back, start with the sensations in your toes. Let what you're feeling fill all of your body... "

Peter had walked out in anger and frustration. He went back to his own room and crawled between cold sheets. His hand moved underneath the coverings until the sheets dampened beside him. Fuck her, he said, and then he fell asleep.

The next day he felt embarrassed. Later, on their way to the airport for the flight west, the first leg to Baja, Peter told her he was sorry; he didn't know what he was doing, he would try. Peter's embarrassment was mixed with gratitude that Laura had agreed to come with him. Laura's agreement had been nearly instantaneous when she heard his reasons why. "David knew that man Rashid," she said, "We may figure Velasquez and Michelson and all the rest of this out yet."

As he sat in the hotel room, his attention still clinging tenuously to the sensations in his thigh, it crossed his mind that he was doing this exercise because he wanted to make love to Laura. In a sense that proved her point, he had no real control even of his own consciousness but was simply pushed and pulled by mechanical desires. In another sense the awareness of this— or was this too just illusion? he wondered—seems to have relaxed the grip that his desire had on him. Not that it had diminished in any way, just that it gripped a little less tightly.

The bathroom door suddenly cracked open and Peter's eyes and head were pulled to the wet-haired, towel-wrapped figure standing beside it. His consciousness fled from his thigh.

"Your five minutes must be up," she said to him with mock reproof. "I've been thinking, Peter," she added as she crossed the room to her bag, "could we not take the bus, could we bicycle down the coast?"

Laura's question drew Peter's eyes to her legs. They were tanned and evidently strong, particularly the calves, perhaps stronger than his.

"Why? It'll take an extra day."

"Seeing the dock works yesterday. I like slow travel, feeling what's on the wayside, not just at the end."

The San Diego shipyards, once bristling with Navy superstructures and conning towers, were now devoted to converting surplus oil tankers into passenger boats, much as they had done a few years earlier with naval vessels. With the decline in petroleum consumption, so many hulls and power plants had come on the market that their price plummeted to salvage value, making it possible to produce a completed passenger liner at very low cost. So low, that even some of the world's poorer countries were able to acquire them and make passage affordable for at least their middle class.

As values changed, passenger demand for liner traffic had also grown. Most countries encouraged six-week "summer" vacations, putting less of a premium on the speed at which you arrived at your destination. Moreover, as extended sun exposure at the beach had become hazardous for much of the world's population and was likely to remain so for at least a generation, a shipboard cruise offered an alternative way in which to escape the heat and experience the sea. Even business travel increased. With satellite videoconferencing and data and document transmission, an executive could function just as well in the mid-Atlantic as in Dusseldorf or Atlanta.

The idea of the bicycle trip was beginning to appeal to Peter more and more. It would give him a chance to spend an additional day and night alone with Laura. Spread out over two days, the hundred-mile trek would probably not overwhelm even his own spindly legs. Equipping for it was one thing, and what to do about their luggage was another that would require attention. It would take a good part of the day.

"Maybe, Laura, we might be able to," Peter said curling his toes into the rug as Laura headed back to the bathroom in her towel, a thin orange blouse and loose-fitting white cotton pants in hand. "If we do, do I get a reward?"

"Virtue is its own," her voice said from behind the bathroom door.

"BS."

"Anything you want, anything at all," she said as she emerged again from the bathroom. Peter could detect the gentle bounce of her breasts under the blouse, the silhouette of her legs in motion against the fabric of her pants. "The first thing that I'm going to do tonight," she said laughing, "is take off all of my clothes in front of you so that I won't feel like you're undressing me every time you see me."

"You mind-read too?"

"It's not your mind I'm reading, love." Laura walked over to him and embraced him, running one hand through the hair on the back of his head, putting the other at the small of his back. Peter felt a dancing vitality penetrate through his clothes. A shock of uncertain impressions shot up his spine from her hand. "Thanks," she said, "I appreciate it, I know it's not what you would normally do."

Peter knew that she was right. The picture of the rickshot mimicking his motions the day of the UNINTEL interview came to him. While he laughed at times at others' addiction to work, he knew he was a victim of it himself. A week ago he would have seen the trip as a wasted day.

"And the work, Laura," Peter said a little hoarsely as she

released him, "the work, you've got to finish it, so that I can look at it and send it back today."

Her eyes were looking into his, drawing him to their true point of focus, a point receding into infinity inside of her. "I promise. Your brother made me rethink it all. I had to write the letters all over." Laura dropped her eyes for a moment, "He's a remarkable person, your brother," she said, and then looking back at Peter, added, "and so are you."

***

Peter left Laura to her work while he arranged for the logistics of the bicycle expedition. She found herself an open-air cafe and sat in the shade of a striped canopy, sipping an iced cappuccino. A stack of form-letter responses for the Senator's constituents was on the table in front of her but her attention was not on the mail nor on the passing sidewalk parade of faces and shapes that would normally have drawn her eye.

Nothing could have been more unlikely, she thought. Peter, a city dweller, a politician's aide. Seemingly as removed from metaphysics as a mountain goat from the sea. Pleasant-looking but a little flimsy, certainly not strikingly handsome like Carlos or possessed of David's rugged strength. But from the beginning—even before she saw him, while she was on the way to seeing him—she had felt the internal shifts. Understanding, transformation, the little settlings and rearrangements of feelings, memories, and beliefs into a more proportional internal space—a prefigured space that seems always to have been there, awaiting only for her to discover it—that signaled new levels, new possibilities of being within.

Laura had felt the stain of debasement from her time with Carlos, and humiliation at the ease with which Carlos and Silvestre had seduced her into believing she was an oracle for the ancient Maya. There had been the agronomist on the plane, talking of his own obsessions but leading her to understand David and herself. Then, when she first sat with Peter, she had found herself suddenly expressing—to herself as much as anyone—the more subtle and universal truth that lay behind her dreams of goddesses and her search for the ancient ways. That night at the Afghan restaurant, and when he had called her later to say good night, she had felt at peace in her heart.

When she woke up the next morning, another set of memories had fit into place. Her mother—the daughter of an American-educated Bolivian oligarch and a French diplomat—had been swept around the world in her father's career. When she was twenty, her father was assigned to the French UN delegation in New York. There she met and quickly married Robert Feil III, an international investment banker whose career also proved peripatetic. They did settle for six years in Toronto at a time when Laura, their only daughter, was entering her teens. In Toronto, her mother would search far and wide for meditation centers, theosophists, occultists, and gurus. Toronto attracted its share and when the prominent ones came to speak, she would invariably drag Laura along. Laura had resisted the experiences. She usually found them depressing so she insulated herself from them even as they happened. Nearly everybody who came to the lectures seemed so serious—often silent and always intense, seeming to travel in isolated islands of weirdness. The few who were less serious walked around with angelic smiles that covered…nothing.

In her own way, she now saw, she had put together a parallel world. Her goddesses were a little more cheerful, a little lighter to be with even when they expressed their sadness at being driven from the world, and they were much more inclined to take her to green and watery places. But what was missing from the old guru-seekers and spiritualists was also missing from her goddess world. It was her own sense of worth, of the power and value of the feelings of the life force, of the being within her. Laura had had no trust in her own intuition, in her own ability to be attuned to a greater wisdom. This too had become clear during her time with Peter and it was probably why she was putting Peter through what must seem to him a bizarre ritual. If just once she could achieve a sexual union that really did transcend the physical, if she could suffuse the energy throughout her being into every molecule and subtle center and then raise blissfully in an upward flowing, golden river as her dream goddesses described, she would feel as if she had left a tangible mark on the world around her, and, in doing so, she hoped, lose herself in a brief taste of heaven as well.

Laura also wanted a relationship with Peter that wouldn't

self-destruct. She knew that she was being drawn to him more powerfully every day. It occurred to her that perhaps our deepest attractions were to those who wittingly or unwittingly immersed us in the most powerful transformative experiences. Her father had had his own way of putting that. "We marry our worst problems and our highest dreams," he said during one of those rare moments when he communicated meaningfully with his daughter, on a day her mother commanded that he take her to the zoo.

Laura's eyes returned to the unanswered stack of mail in front of her and felt the dread of work that wasn't getting done. Jeffery and the Deep Space Pulse. On her first evening with Peter outside of Charlottesville, not long after she had arrived and been given her room and a taste of one of Zenobia's herbal teas, neighbors, first one or two, then more, finally seven or eight, filled the house, gathering for no apparent purpose, talking loudly, asking for a beer or tea or some little snack to eat.

When the room filled, Jeffery set out to separate her from the rest, like a wolf thinning a sick one from a caribou herd. "Let's go outside," he said, "I want to show you my stars."

Laura, uncertain of what to say, had glanced around the room, hoping to catch Peter's eye to tell him where she would be. Peter was nowhere to be seen. "Shouldn't we tell Peter," Laura said, "he may wonder where we'll be."

"Zenobia's teaching him how to bake cookies," Jeffery took her arm and led her toward the front door. "She thinks he needs more nourishment, he'll have his hands pretty full."

"We all want to mother him, don't we?" Laura said.

"He needs it," Jeffery replied, guiding her outside into a warm evening breeze, "but the trick is to give it to him in a way that frees him of the need."

"And you know how?"

"No, but something tells me you do. That's why I wanted to show you my stars," Jeffery said leading her away from the star-obscuring light that poured from the windows and the porch.

"Your stars?"

"My own little joke," he said. "Take that bright one there, Vega, I think it is. It's sending its light to me and when it gets here it's going 186,000 miles per second which is okay, except that we're also moving away from it at a good clip. This is where it gets strange. Even if I were standing still with respect to it, in fact even if I were speeding towards it at 100,000 miles per second, the light would still reach me at 186,000 miles per second. It's like saying that there's no difference between a head-on collision and nicking someone who's moving in the same flow of traffic as you are. So if that's true, Vega and all the other stars must be doing some very special dances for me to make it happen that way. And if that's true, why not call them my stars?

"Of course they do the same for you or for anyone else that watches them, no matter where you are or which way you're going." Jeffery paused briefly. The murmur of the gushing stream grew louder as they neared it.

"And here is something else we've learned," he continued, "it turns out that wherever you are, when you measure the background radiation, it appears that you are at the center of the universe. Einstein didn't pick his words well. Relativity sounds like there is no truth, no absolute. Maybe what he was really saying was that there were five billion truths or however many sentient beings there were then. I would have called it the theory of the Eyes of God." Jeffery draped his arm around her shoulders and squeezed affectionately. "It's like a peacock's tale. Just a little joke. Actually two."

The breeze rustled the branches, a frog started up a throaty rivet song from somewhere near the steam, and a bird, oblivious to the dark, trilled with a night-time exuberance that only comes in the spring. If she had been alone, Laura would have taken off her clothes, sat on the bank and dangled her feet in the stream.

"Let's sit by the stream," she said, looking up again at the stars. They walked to the edge and found adjoining rocks on which to rest. Laura took off her shoes and dipped her feet into the water. It was shockingly cold, so cold that she almost withdrew them. She felt the cold penetrate the bones of her arches and toes.

Jeffery kept his feet on the bank, "Peter says that you're doing the Senator's space mail," he said.

"For a while anyway," Laura replied, "it amazes me how many people care. Pretty weird stuff sometimes."

"The Deep Space Pulse?"

"That's a lot of it, people waiting to know why we're exploring Ganymede instead of arming near-space to the teeth."

"Laura, do you know what the Fibonacci series is?"

"The what?"

"Fibonacci, it was the nickname of maybe the greatest Leonardo of them all, Leonardo Pisano. He introduced Arabic numerals and decimals into the West, twelfth century, and his famous series.

"You start out 1, 2... and then from there on you get each succeeding number by adding the preceding one 3, 5, 8, 13, 21 and so on, but what's remarkable is that any number divided by the following one approximates .618 and any number divided by the previous number approximates 1.618. Those numbers are what the Greeks called the golden mean—what you get when you divide a line so that the ratio of the smaller part to the larger is the same as the larger to the whole."

Laura pulled her feet out of the water and massaged them gently. "I remember, I took a course in ancient architecture."

"That's right. It's in their art, the Greeks and nearly everyone else's, as far as we can tell," Jeffery continued. "It's in the spirals of a sunflower's seeds and in the curvature of a nautilus shell. And in us. If you take the other Leonardo's famous drawing of the ideal man, it's everywhere. It's a symbol of our own beauty.

"Well, about twenty years ago, an obscure graduate student whose name was Leo Rabinowitz got permission to send radio pulses out into space to see if anybody would answer."

"And he sent out the numbers in the series," Laura guessed.

"Exactly. Now think of a movie and a projector. This Deep Space Pulse is exactly what you would get if you run young Leo's movie backwards through a projector, speeding it up a little as you go along. Or think of it another way. Imagine that you are inside, in the middle of a hollow sphere and the inside surface is a mirror. Now imagine the sphere getting smaller and smaller like a deflating balloon. When that happens, we'll see our own reflections, larger and larger, closer and closer."

"So we send out this symbol of our own—and the universe's—beauty," Laura said as she returned one foot to the water, "and now it's coming back."

"And," Jeffery added as he slipped off his shoes, readying his own feet for immersion, "what happens? People freak out. They want to arm to the teeth to shoot the image or at least scare it away, they want to project all sorts of monstrosities on it." He winced as his feet touched the cold of the rushing water.

"So I should explain all this to the Senator's constituents," Laura said with a smile, "in two easily understood sentences."

"You can if you want but the reason I'm saying all of this to you is Peter." Jeffery's tone changed.

"Love is like the pulse," he said. "It's a projection of our own beauty and when it gets reflected back at us, when it gets close and intimate, we freak out, we start seeing monsters and even want to shoot them sometimes, or if that's distasteful, we just move away. Peter needs to love and be loved but it could be a real fragile thing with him."

Laura was about to protest that she was not Peter's lover, that she liked him, yes, but she was just working with him for a little while. She swallowed the words and listened instead to the sounds of rushing water and the rhythmic trill of the songbird oblivious to the night. A few minutes later they had walked back in silence to the house.

As she sat alone at the café in San Diego, tears formed in her eyes. She reached for her sunglasses to hide her face. Peter, I want you here, she said to herself, this mail isn't doing it for me. I've had enough of aliens and goddesses and Mayans and trying to be some kind of priestess. I need to be loved too.

**

Two days later, when they rounded the last bend, where the loading cranes, fishing piers and cruising ships of Ensenada all loomed into view, it was Peter who was pedaling faster, two hundred yards ahead of his companion, his mind filled with impressions of the trip: the bare slopes, rock-filled and scruffy, punctuated with oases of green; the shimmering blue of the Pacific; the ground growing cactus with the eight-foot spikes, century plants as they were called, waiting to flower into semaphores of yellow, red and green; the fruit orchards newly planted with low-water-consumption varietals developed in Africa and the Middle East and vegetables planted in their shade;

the cries of children returning from school; an athletic, graceful girl, hitting fungos to a mixed-sex softball team; the power-generating windmills scattered in the open sites; the plate-sized satellite antenna perched on nearly every structure, modest as it might be, pointing towards the sky.

The images seemed to come pounding through his veins, pumped up by the action of his legs. He was filled and exhilarated, he could drive the spinning wheels beneath him forever; through the fish smells and the dust; through the taste of sweet water; through the memories of Laura's shrieks of ecstasy on the no-hands, free falls down the hills, of Laura naked diving into the breaker's foam with a grace he thought no human could possess, of Laura holding him the night before, each of them shaking, shuddering with relief.

"It's like coming home," she had said, "except it's better, it's the home you never had. But everything's so familiar, like you knew it all, long, long, long ago, maybe an eon or two before."

Peter's legs kept driving, the water-cooled wind pushing and refreshing him the more he sped along. He let out a loud yell into the air and then glided back in a circle through the traffic to bring Laura to his side. They pedaled together to the Ballena Loca, the Crazy Whale, the hotel Rashid had named. As they drew nearer they started to laugh, there was a circus tent pitched beside it.

CHAPTER 35

David's dark skin allowed him to enjoy the sun. On the afternoon that Peter and Laura arrived, his muscular legs were stretched out on a deck chair, a margarita was in his hand and he was considering whether to do a few laps in the oversized pool before Almira joined him. At the far end of the pool, set in a canted white slab was an eight-pointed, multicolored star, with wheels within wheels each containing Aztec glyphs—a reproduction of the Calendar of the Sun. There were a few other people in the pool area. No one seemed remarkable to David and it was by no means crowded. Piped mariachi music was responsible for most of the noise.

The sun could have been unbearably hot but the current-cooled ocean air softened it. The music and margarita proved too alluring. David gave up on the laps, sank into the deck chair, closed his eyes and replayed the events of the past few days. First, there had been the lawyer, Miguel's friend, a slender man who exuded good humored cynicism through an aristocratic veneer. He had called the morning before David's departure, several days after they had met.

The lawyer appeared relaxed on the v-phone, but there was an edge of concern to his voice. "David, I've talked to my friends, particularly one. He's in charge of dealing with other agencies. Do you understand me?"

"I think so."

"There is encouraging news."

"Oh?"

"They took what you said quite seriously. To be honest I thought they might laugh—as I know you did too. But there is also disturbing news."

"And what's that?"

"The reason they took it seriously is that they knew about you, or at least about your friend Laura. You know a man named Michelson?"

"I've admired him, I don't know him."

"They seemed to think Laura knew him rather well. Someone, I was told, thinks she was connected with his last speech. Do you understand me?"

"Yes."

"That someone wanted to know more about her. That's how my friend knew."

"But it's ridiculous."

"Maybe. My friend says it sounds to him like they're trying to get more evidence, that they don't have enough to do anything formal yet."

"They're going to have to make it up," David said.

"They may. My advice, David, is that you stay here. You can be protected, you have civil rights here."

"I can't, people are on their way to meet me. The first in L.A. tomorrow."

"The U.S. is okay too," the lawyer said with a smile. "Now that the terror obsession has passed, most people have civil rights there too."

"After that I'm going to Mexico."

The lawyer muttered an obscenity involving as best as David could tell intermarriages between several animal species. "Be careful, David."

David had been nervous when he met Almira. It wasn't just what had happened and what the lawyer said. His fear had awakened a little boy within him who still believed that every Palestinian was a terrorist, waiting for a chance to turn a blade in a Jewish back. It was ludicrous he knew. He had been in Israel, he had talked with and liked a number of Palestinians when he was there, and the Settlement had now been in place more than five years.

When he met Almira at the ticket counter where he had had her paged, the words had come to him with difficulty, not because of his fears, but because he had not expected to meet someone with whom he felt at once so familiar. Neither had he expected to meet anyone who at roughly his age, and with a handsome though not striking appearance, radiated so much dignity and a modest playfulness at once.

On the bus to Ensenada she had gone over the whole story of Fatimah Karajan's death, the interrogation, her trip to England, the man who followed her while she was there, her rendezvous with Jean-Marc and Lucinda in Helsinki, a brief stop in England again to see her boys—how much she missed them—and the trip to meet David.

He told his story—Michelson and the New York dinner, Laura, surveillance, the raid on his house. They had talked about her boys, Youssef and Jamal, about the death of her husband and about her brother Ali. David had said he was sorry and it quieted them both for a while.

"No, David," she said finally, "that's a guilt without reason and wherever there's guilt, there's fear. We have to be done with fear." She had taken his hand and squeezed it and when the sensation of her hand had left, the thought arose that the two of them would lead lives intertwined in ways he could not guess.

He told her about his travels and his trip to Israel. "I was even going to write a tour guide then. A journalist, a Palestinian, was going to help me. We were to meet again but he never came."

The color faded from Almira's face. There was a brief shadow in her eyes. "When was that?" she asked and when David told her, she said "It could have been my husband you were waiting for. He told me once that he was helping with a travel guide. Who knows?" Her shoulders sagged as if weighed down by memories of another time. "It was a common cover if you were a Palestinian and needed to travel or write."

The mariachi music was drawing to a close with a flourish of trumpets; a high tenor voice held a note and then let it softly expire. In the silence that followed, David heard the rhythmic splashing of a swimmer and through eyes half open to the reflected glare saw a woman's long arms executing graceful strokes. He was tempted to go into the pool and take a closer look but was arrested by a new song—or actually a very old one. His mother had sometimes played it. At the beginning it wasn't even a song but just a man shouting over an occasional background strum.

Jeremiah was a bullfrog
And he was a friend of mine
Couldn't understand a word he said...

A loud splash of a body diving into the pool covered the words and sharp squeals and laughter followed. There were more splashes, and then he heard the music again upbeat.

...Joy to the fishes in the deep blue sea,
Joy to you and me.

"Peter, not here." A woman's voice, loud and excited, rose up. David was stirred by a growing sense of familiarity. He sat up and his eyes gradually adjusted to the light and focused on the woman swimmer, now standing in the shallow end. A knot formed in his throat when he recognized who it was. The tension passed as he realized that there was no anger, no jealousy, no infatuation, no out-of-control desire burning in his veins. There was only a protective fondness for Laura—fondness and amazement at the workings of a universe that had brought them together in an obscure Mexican coastal town.

"Laura," he shouted over the music which had switched to a different tune.

She heard him the third time he called her and looked in his direction. She put her hand on the shoulder of her young, somewhat slender companion and then climbed over the edge of the pool. There was a time, David thought, observing her exit, that he would have lived on that sight for a day. She walked over to him and sat on the end of the chair next to him.

"Rashid?" she asked.

"How did you know?"

"Peter, the Senator's aide you talked to about work for me, he knows Rashid too."

"He what?"

"He knows Rashid too. That's Peter who's with me."

David absorbed what she said and turned to face her, "Laura some things have happened, we need to talk. I think we're all in danger."

Laura put her arms around his shoulders and pressed her cheek next to his. "David, before that, there are things I need to say. I've done really hurtful things to you," her voice was constricted, slightly louder than a whisper. "I'm sorry...what can I do?"

"Nothing, Laura," he responded, conscious of the warmth of her body, the shudder that passed through it and a hint of moisture dammed up where their cheeks met. "We're all children still. These things pass."

He drew away from her and put his hand to her face gently, to the place where he had felt the tears, wiping one away with his thumb. "We're all children and we're having a real adventure," his face formed into a smile. "Nobody gets to have these anymore. The Earth's gotten too tame. Let's all enjoy it. We need to find Rashid and why he wants us here and then get to the bottom of all of this."

"In surreal Mexico," Laura added, now smiling slightly herself, "always generating new mysteries. David, I was such a fool. I let them convince me that I was a key to unraveling all the old mysteries! But they used me, Carlos for sex and an old man for I don't know what else." She gave David's hand a little squeeze. The tension around her jaw relaxed as she spoke and a light went on in her eyes. "But I feel different now. On the road here, there was a great big outrageous football-field-long sign of bleached white rocks on a mountain slope—you could see it for miles coming down. VIVA LA TIERRA MADRE, hooray for Mother Earth!"

"I missed it," David said.

"We—Peter and I—we bicycled down," Laura added. "You see so much more that way—and feel it and smell it too. Do you know Peter? I think you'll like him. He's kind, he has a brilliant crazy older brother. He's still an innocent, and if he lets Her do it, the Goddess will write his destiny."

"Katie speaks pretty well of him. I've known Katie a long

time and so has he. She said—"

Laura put a fingers to her lips. A pale-skinned, thin young man joined them. "Peter," Laura said, "this is David."

***

Almira came out to the pool not long afterwards dressed in a blue cotton shift that covered a modest one-piece bathing suit. David introduced her to the others as they gathered around a table near the pool. David talked about being followed and the night the two men had raided his house and garden. He told Laura that apparently someone thought she was involved in Matteo Michelson's death. As Peter and Almira told their own stories the patterns became clearer. Almira and Peter had each been questioned about the deaths of prominent people; in Peter's case, there had also been a break-in at his apartment, and a search for something, much as David had experienced in Costa Rica. Almira had been befriended in England by an American but she had then discovered that the American wasn't who he said he was. Laura related her similar experience with Carlos and Silvestre. But no one had any ideas on how these events could all be linked or, if they were linked, what might motivate someone to try to blame them for Michelson's, Velasquez's and Fatima's deaths. Nor did they understand much about Rashid's request that they come to Ensenada. Peter and David both knew Rashid and admired and trusted him, but the more the group talked, the more obvious it became that no one really knew Rashid well and no one had any explanation for how he knew that Almira would be contacting David.

"It's like Carlos and Silvestre," Laura said. Her eyes shifted from David to Peter and back again. "An enticing trip with virtual strangers…. And God knows what else."

"And what do you mean, he knew I would be coming…." Almira added, looking nervous as well.

"He didn't name you, Almira. He just said I would have a friend and she could come and then you insisted on meeting me on the way."

"Almira's not accusing you of anything, David," Laura interjected, regaining her optimism. "You don't need to be defensive. I trust you, I trust Peter. Something interesting is going to happen and it's going to be alright. We're all together.

That's a gift—and a strength." Laura put her slender hand on David's shoulder and smiled. David couldn't help himself. He felt the tension run out through her fingertips and his anger dissolve in her smile.

Peter fidgeted with his drink as he watched Laura's hand as it settled and lingered on David's shoulder with a discomfiting familiarity. But his unease turned to bravado, "Laura's right. We are together. It was being alone and separated that made me— each of us—vulnerable. We're going to get to the bottom of this. It's going to be okay."

***

There was no sign of Rashid. David, Laura, Peter and Almira decided to go to the early-evening circus show, something none of them had done since childhood. The circus had the usual complement of clowns, acrobats and jugglers, and gravity-defying moments of suspended animation as a young woman with streaming blond hair flipped from trapeze to trapeze, seemingly held up by the oohs and aahs of a thousand transfixed mouths. Lions and tigers responded to the crack of their trainer's whip while the self-proclaimed world's shortest midgets watched accompanied by a crew of Hideous Hooded Alamos Gilas, the mutant, nuclear-testing-ground successors to the teenage turtles of an earlier age. Chimpanzees somersaulted around; well-disciplined pachyderms and poodles walked erect on their hind legs modeling various historical, human fashions.

When they walked back to the hotel the temperature had fallen rapidly in the clear, dry night air and Almira leaned close to David for warmth. "The poodle with the parasol and the ankle-length red taffeta dress," she said to all of them, "I couldn't help myself, I was drawn in, I was walking down the muddy streets of Paris on a Sunday afternoon a couple of centuries ago."

"*Chien* on you," said Laura who had been inspired by her time with Jeffery and childhood memories to venture forth with a cross-lingual pun, "it was bad enough to force those dresses on women."

Everyone laughed. Laura became thoughtful. "It is sad for the animals, especially the wild ones, there is only so much solace they can get from the love of humans."

"It's true," David said, "but did you see the kids' faces? And they'll grow up to be the animals' protectors. Maybe what we have are lion martyrs being thrown to the humans for Nature's sake."

"I think," said Almira, "that we've had enough of martyrs. I think we cage animals because we feel that our spirits are trapped in a cage of flesh and pain and it's one of our little ways of getting back at God."

"I think," said Peter, still ebullient from his recent experiences, the bicycle ride and his growing attachment to Laura, "that what we should do is learn to live like the woman on the flying trapeze."

When the group reentered the hotel, the reception clerk waved at them. Both Peter and David had messages and the man who had left them was waiting at the back of the lounge. "He says," the hotel clerk informed them, "to tell you that he was sent here to get you by your friend Don Rashid O'Shea."

The clerk gave a brief description of the visitor and the four headed to the back of the lounge. To get there they had to step around a space that was sometimes used as a dance floor but was now filled with moving three-dimensional images of six-inch men with shorts and colored shirts chasing a black and white sphere over a carpet of green grass. A roar went up from the loungers when the man nearest the sphere was tripped up from behind. The Mexico-Quebec World Cup preliminary was not expected to be close but any national match still excited the passions once spent on warfare. The holographic devices that were generating the images from a compressed stream of digital transmissions had not yet become affordable for individuals, but a good number of bars around the world had profitably invested in them. Peter kicked at the tiny ball as it rolled near him and as his foot passed through the ball's image, he impaled a Mexican striker as well. A chorus of good-natured boos erupted.

The man seated in the back of the lounge seemed pleasant enough. He appeared to be in his thirties. He was of medium, slightly rotund build that was accentuated by ill-fitting but nondescript, trousers and shirt. He had unmistakable mestizo features. When the four arrived, he was nursing a soft drink and rose to introduce himself. His name, he said, was Rafael, Rafael

Cabrera. Mr. O'Shea, he explained, was staying in a home outside of town, and wanted them all to join him for a late dinner. If they would care to come, he had a van waiting for them. He would bring it to the hotel door.

The four looked at each other and then David said yes, they would be delighted to come, but Almira said she would require a few minutes to get ready. Peter asked if perhaps they should call Rashid to tell him they would be late. Rafael insisted that it was not necessary but after some prodding from Peter and David, he gave them a telephone number.

While Almira was in her room, David dialed the number several times from the lobby v-phone and each time got a flashing OCUPADO, OCUPADO, FAVOR MARCAR DE NUEVO. Almira exited from the elevator into the lobby and David turned to Peter and Laura. "Am I being paranoid or should we wait until we get through to make sure this is all okay?"

"How would anyone know that we are here to see Rashid?" Almira answered.

"And if they—whoever they are—do, are we any less likely to be safe by refusing to go tonight?" Peter asked rhetorically. The truth of the matter, he knew, was that he was growing tired of his fugitive status and wanted some finality so that he could return to his Senator's work and, he hoped, to a deepening relationship with Laura. He felt a strong urge to touch her but was inhibited by David's presence. Laura had told him that David bore no animosity but Peter couldn't help himself; he felt like an immature dolphin in the presence of a dominant bull. Peter had heard that dolphins put up their fins to be bitten as a sign of submission and he regretted that there was no socially acceptable human equivalent that came to mind so that he could get on with his life.

Through the glass entrance of the lobby, David saw Rafael standing by a dusty white van. He squinted at the license plate and then wrote a scribbled note. He tried the v-phone again and at the first flash of OCUPADO, switched it off and went to the desk where he left the note.

"There is a chance," he said to the clerk, "that we may miss Mr. O'Shea. If he should come by here, please give him this." And then to the others, "I guess it's time to meet Rashid."

After Laura and Peter climbed into the back of the van, David and Almira took the middle bench. From where he was sitting, David could see that there was a box and two magazines resting on the front passenger seat next to Rafael.

"How do you know Rashid?" David asked.

"We used to work together."

"At the supermarket?"

"No, not in Hawaii, in New York."

David felt reassured. The man obviously did know Rashid. "With the UN? What agency?"

"I just did office work but I got tired of it." After a few moments silence, Rafael added, "I missed Mexico."

David sensed that Rafael's reticence hid a less than happy experience. They rode on in silence. Rafael drove them south on the peninsular highway and after fifteen minutes turned off the main road onto a rougher and narrower surface that veered west towards the Pacific. From the occasional lights scattered on its slope, David concluded that they were paralleling a tall ridge that fell steeply towards the bay. Traffic was sparse. The road was becoming more windy as it began to creep up the slope of the ridge.

David opened his window slightly. He could hear the roar and hiss of the sea pounding against rock in the darkness below. As they rounded a particularly sharp curve, they came up on two small and unilluminated roadside structures. David heard a voice cry out over the ambient sounds. Rafael quickly brought the van to a halt and a uniformed man carrying a small automatic weapon emerged from the darkness into the outer edge of the headlight beams. Nestled against the far wall of one of the unlit structures, David noticed, was a vehicle which had been concealed from their view. He could distinguish the outline of two circular objects on the vehicle's roof which he surmised were police emergency flashers.

"What's going on?" Laura asked from the back, her view apparently obstructed.

"Police," Almira said, "they've stopped us for some reason."

"Maybe it's just a checkpoint," Peter offered. Rafael nodded his head, as if to show agreement.

David was less sure that this was a routine matter. The

uniformed man shone a light first through the front windows and then, as he walked around the van, through the side and rear windows as well. Apparently satisfied, the uniformed man pulled at the front passenger door latch and opened it. It was when Rafael moved the box off the seat without being asked, that David knew that they were in trouble. By the time he was ready to react, however, the small barrel of the automatic weapon was leveled at him and the man was sliding into the seat.

"Quietos todos," keep quiet, the uniformed man said in a tense voice through a mustache-covered lip to the passengers, and he then spoke to Rafael, *"Bien hecho! Andemos."*

Directing himself again to the passengers as the van picked up speed, he continued, in lightly accented English, "Señores y señoritas, you are under official detention. I am with the Northern Baja District Police. You are wanted for questioning by international authorities, and it is our duty to comply with their instructions."

"Please cooperate," he said with the cultivated impersonality acquired in years at his job, "none of us have any desire to hurt you. You will, all of you, please keep your hands on your lap. I am sure that you all understand that any sudden movement could have tragic consequences in these close quarters, a situation I'm sure you all wish to avoid. I'm sure that you have nothing to hide, so I am sure that the international authorities will be releasing you quickly after you have answered their questions. You will probably be released back into our custody and I want you to know," he said casting a meaningful look at Almira, "that Rafael and I will be at your service to return you to your hotel or otherwise meet your pleasure."

David could feel his heart pounding. He was sure that more was going on than the official indicated. He wanted to be sure that the others were aware of this too. "If what you say is true," David asked as an unexpected clarity settled into him, "why this ruse? Why not simply detain us at the hotel?"

The thin lips under the moustache betrayed a hint of cruelty as the man pondered his response. "My cousin is the hotel manager. It's bad for business to have the guests arrested." The officer looked at Rafael, obviously amused at the cleverness of his response.

"That's right, Jorge," Rafael supported him, "very bad for business!"

The van was laboring with its load, the climb had become much steeper. David's sense of clarity and command started to crumble in the darkened cab. This he hadn't expected. He no longer knew the value of his ace in the hole, the message he had left for Rashid with the van's license plate. He had figured that he could use the existence of the message to forestall violence, if any was threatened, even before Rashid or others came to their rescue. But now he wasn't so sure. The story about why they weren't detained at the hotel was obviously an invention, but David knew that more often than not lies have at least some truth imbedded in them. There was a good chance that Rafael's cousin or someone else close to him or Jorge really did work at the hotel and if that was the case, their captors could easily get access to the message and have it destroyed before Rashid or someone else read it.

For that matter, the more he thought about it, could he really trust Rashid? It was Rashid who had asked them all to come for unknown reasons and now he was nowhere to be found. Rafael, or whoever he was, almost certainly knew Rashid.

A clawing fear like the one he had experienced on the night his house was raided spread through him. The lawyer was right. This was a stupid country to come to. Its "authorities" were too easily manipulated. Worse, David surmised, whoever was behind this probably had no compulsion about killing. David was convinced now that it was Michelson's and Fatimah's—and maybe even Velasquez's killers—who were circling around them. It was just as bad that he had dragged Almira here to expose her to unknown risks and the sexual innuendos and leers of the armed man in the front seat. Given time and opportunity, the man's behavior towards her was likely to get much worse.

He should have followed his first instinct, not to budge from the hotel. That would have been so simple. How many warnings did he need? Surveillance, raids on his house, the realization of his stupidity seeped through his veins like acid.

"It's not your fault, David. I pushed you into bringing me," Almira said in a whisper. She rearranged herself in her seat as the van leaned around a sharp curve so that her leg and body were pressed against his. "I've seen far worse than this," she added.

David absorbed the warmth of her touch. It calmed him a bit and he was both taken aback and grateful for the skill and sensitivity with which she had sensed his state. He knew that her most important message was in the last sentence. I've seen far worse than this. *We can survive. But you have to get your faculties back; don't drown in guilt and remorse.*

The van was descending now, its tires squealing occasionally around the rough-edged curves. Rafael slammed on the brakes suddenly and veered to the left down a dusty rutted lane. After bumping along for two hundred yards, he stopped. The van came to rest by the sea. In the scant light David could make out what appeared to be a boat ramp and a skiff pulled up onto its surface. A man stood next to it, holding a line.

The susurration of water flowing in and out of the rocky shore and the slapping sound of the larger swells crashing against the nearby cliffs were all that David heard. There seemed to be no one else present. If there are only three of them, he conjectured, and only one of them is armed with a gun, there might be a chance to overpower them.

But why even take a chance on someone's getting hurt? These international "authorities", whoever they were, might actually exist and want something from the four of them. It was unlikely to be their lives. But then why had he hidden in the forest when the two men had come to his house? David realized that he couldn't reason his way through this dilemma. He would have to act on intuition, and do his best to make sure it wasn't distorted by fear.

"Two of us," Peter announced loudly from the back, breaking David's train of thought, "work for one of the most powerful senators in America. If there is anything in the least improper about this, even if you don't know about it, I promise you the Senator won't rest until your asses are in the nastiest jail we can find. If I were in your position," he continued, "I would check very high in your government and with our embassy too before turning us over to anybody."

It was Jorge who answered. "We know exactly who you are, Mr. Flanigan." He turned around in his seat to face his captives.

He gave Peter a malevolent look and then took on an ingratiating expression as his eyes shifted to Laura.

"What we didn't know," he said, "was that your companion would be so beautiful. Had we known it, we might have planned a little detour. A picnic perhaps. There is a place near here, *La Bufadora,* a blowhole I think you call it, where when the sea caresses the earth just right, a spout of spray flies through a crevice in the rocks fifty feet high into the air. We could have a little contest, yes... "

A look of revulsion crossed Laura's face. David could feel Almira's body next to him tense as well. Peter lost control. "It's a good thing you guys have guns," he said looking squarely at them, "because without them, you couldn't get a mangy street mongrel to screw you, even if you fed it steaks."

Jorge did not smile. He got out of the van and went around to the side door. When he opened it, he stepped outside and with the gun trained at the van's occupants, handed it to Rafael. He signaled for him to step back until he was twenty feet away. Jorge stayed next to the door and instructed the occupants to get out one at a time, and to stand next to the van on the opposite side of the door. David and Almira exited and did as they were told. Peter was next. As he stepped down onto the ground, his head was still bowed from his effort to duck under the sill of the van. Seemingly from nowhere, a fist flew up into his face knocking his head against the van. Another plunged into his stomach and when he doubled over, a kick swept his legs from under him and he fell to the ground.

Jorge stepped back with a satisfied smile. *"Gringo de la madre."* Son of a bitch.

Laura, Almira and David clustered around Peter to help him up. Peter's nose was bleeding and his breath was raspy but he did not appear seriously harmed. David took advantage of the jumble of concerned voices. He had noticed that Rafael flinched when the fist went into Peter's face. Rafael might not be trained. They might have a chance.

"Be ready," David said to his three companions, "we have to try something." To his disappointment though, when they boarded the skiff, Rafael did not come with them. Instead, the man who had been holding the line boarded with them. He was barefoot and wore tan trousers that ended just below the knee. There was a deep scar on a muscular left arm and a smaller one down his left cheek. He looked competent and cruel. Jorge called him Javier.

"Hasta luego, Rafael," Javier called out as Rafael walked back to the van. *"Bien hecho. Se lo diré a Nikolai y Silvestre."* Well done. I'll tell Nikolai and Silvestre.

WILLIAM H. ESPINOSA

CHAPTER 36

When the puttering sound of the skiff's outboard reached Don Silvestre, he pushed one starter button and then another. The Egg Harbor's engines roared to life and then settled down into a rhythmic, muffled rumble. After glancing briefly at his instruments, Don Silvestre spoke to his companion.

"Carlos, the anchor, go up on the foredeck and make sure she comes in cleanly." Carlos moved gracefully to the bow. Don Silvestre pressed the radio hand-held microphone and spoke into it, "Guardian One, this is Guardian Two. Cargo now arriving, should be at your position in about an hour."

Static and then the radio crackled with an American voice, "We copy, Guardian Two. Be gentle with the cargo. Out."

The puttering of the outboard was growing louder and the shadowy form of the skiff, low in the water and filled with passengers, emerged from the black. The plan was working even better than expected, they would be gone before moonrise so the chances of the boat's being identified from shore were virtually nil. There were hundreds of deep-sea charter fishing boats still operating up and down the Baja coast. The activities the boats supported had been grandfathered in as a hardship exception to the global climate carbon emission rules. A poor area would have been made much poorer robbed of even a portion of its tourist trade.

The skiff was within a few yards now, its engine cut back.

Jorge deftly guided it alongside the fishing boat and took advantage of a rolling swell to grasp the gunwale of the bigger vessel. He motioned for the four captives to get out and then Jorge, his automatic weapon still trained on his guests, followed. Javier let go of his grip on the gunwale and steered the skiff away.

Jorge gestured for the four to enter the cabin where Don Silvestre was operating the boat. Laura was the last of them to enter, instinctively placing herself between Peter and their captor to make another outbreak of brutality more difficult. She stopped, stunned with the recognition. She hardly felt the cold prodding of the gun barrel on her back.

"Peter, David. It's the old Mayan, Silvestre," Laura said. All turned to look at him.

Silvestre seemed to bask in their surprise and smiled at Laura, "You had no faith, Laura, I told you that we would meet again. I thought that your friend David would follow you to Merida, but he didn't, so we had to rearrange the schedule a bit to get you all together and now it seems we have even more." He pushed the engine throttles forward and the boat angled back as it gradually gained speed. "Please, introduce me to your friends."

Laura's shock turned to revulsion when she saw Carlos walking back from the bow. He briefly disappeared from view and then ambled into the cabin. He was wearing tight-fitting blue jeans and a blue and white striped shirt open to his solar plexus. There was a gold chain around his neck.

"Laura, querida!" he shouted out in mock surprise as he headed towards her.

Disgust, shame and rage were still clouding Laura's responses. She saw David's fists clench and Peter's hand drop from his injured face. Images of blood and violence swept through her mind. She knew that she needed to say something to head it off but the words refused to come.

"Stay away from her," Almira said in a level but determined voice. She too must have sensed impending violence at a time when they were not prepared for it.

Carlos turned towards her. "We haven't met, have we?" He smiled sardonically, "You must be the Palestinian, the asses-for-peace person."

"Cut it out, Carlos," Don Silvestre interrupted, "you're acting like an animal."

"Animals don't act like this," David said coldly.

"Quite right," Don Silvestre responded, "just an expression we've inherited. A European one, one of its many deceptions."

The fishing boat was reaching its cruising speed as they came to the mouth of the small inlet. The looming cliffs that fell to the ocean like black curtains could no longer be seen. The pitch and yaw of the boat were increasing as they entered open water and left the protective shore behind.

"You have the nerve to talk about deceptions?" Laura said, having recovered her composure and steeled herself with anger, "or are we to believe that this too is one of the Mayan mysteries? Or is this just how you treat all of your people's friends?

"Or maybe, Don Silvestre," she added a bit ruefully, "you've just been kicked so much that the only thing you know to do is kick everyone else."

"What I said to you in Merida," Don Silvestre replied, "is truer than you will probably ever know. This is a new age, Laura. The old world has come to an end, and a new world needs new governance."

***

Don Silvestre paused to peer through the cabin windshield. Spray splattered against it as the bow plunged into a wave. "Carlos," he said, "the depth finder and the radar, watch the screens. There are some rock formations out here."

Peter spoke to his captors for the first time since Jorge had hit him, "What does any of this have to do with governance?"

Don Silvestre considered the question for a few seconds, "Eleven hundred years ago the center of my people, the Maya, fell apart. Every shaman wanted to do his own brujeria, his own sorcery. Every petty prince wanted to be great king and every town saw itself as the center of the world. The great projects of the past that brought all my ancestors together were no more. The astronomy, the building skills, the agronomy and most of all the deep knowledge of both the other worlds and our connection to this earth became moribund. And the degree of suffering and humiliation that we experienced after that was indescribable, especially when the Spanish came, when those rage-filled pigs

331

and their stupid little superstitious priests came to make us their slaves.

"The people you are about to meet have no intention of playing planetary Mayas to extraterrestrial Spaniards. They have no intention of letting irresponsible elements desecrate the Earth or letting petty people ruin the planet for all of us."

He paused and looked over at Carlos and the glowing instrument screens. Apparently satisfied, he continued. His voice was calmer. "I'm not sure about the extraterrestrials, but there are a lot of other ways that harm can come when the center isn't holding. My friends seem to think that you four are standing in the way of a strong center and maybe involved in worse, and they want to have a talk with you. That's all. We have no ill will but we had to do what we did."

Almira had been listening with interest and she exchanged looks with David. She whispered, "I told you David, there are already powerful, power-seeking men who think they have to control it all. They're making examples of us or setting us up or something like that. This is not good."

David didn't answer. He surmised that they were heading towards international waters, twelve miles from shore, where they would be handed over to Silvestre's "friends" and where the Mexican authorities couldn't be held accountable for whatever happened. He had no good idea of how far they had come but he guessed two to three miles. They had forty minutes at best in which to do something.

David considered the possibilities. The key of course was disarming Jorge, the policeman. If they could do that, then they had a chance. But the man was not going to put his gun down and hand it over. The approach had to be to mentally disarm him, to make him hesitate before using it just long enough for one of them to tackle him. After that the gun would probably be useless.

A distraction? Hard to visualize. A shield? More promising...place himself so that Silvestre or Carlos was in the line of fire? Better yet, have two of them, he and Peter, come at the armed man from two different directions, one with Carlos behind him, the other from Silvestre's direction. It could buy an added fraction of a second. Still, it would be extremely risky. If the man got off a round or two, someone in the cabin was likely to get shot. But an insistent inner voice kept telling him that the risks of doing nothing were even greater.

***

David surveyed the cabin. The four of them were clustered on the left-hand side, Carlos was at the front maybe five feet away, seemingly absorbed in his instruments. Don Silvestre was at the wheel on the right-hand side and Jorge was standing in the rear at the cabin entrance. He had lit a cigarette which dangled from his lips. He was holding the weapon with one hand aiming it generally in their direction but somewhat downwards towards the floor. Don Silvestre was intent on his steering and a radio conversation with a voice that had a Russian accent.

David needed to communicate with Peter, Laura and Almira. If he couldn't do that, at a minimum he needed to make sure they spread around the cabin more and hope that they reacted instinctively once he started a charge. He noted the four steps going down to the head and sleeping berths next to where Silvestre was standing. At least one of the women should be able to claim incontinence. Or Peter might get away with going next if he said he wanted to clean up the blood...

The arc the boat was tracing over the swells was becoming steeper, the spray on the cabin windshield denser. A quarter moon had crept over the shore behind them but visibility was, if anything, worse. A mist seemed to be forming in front of them.

David feigned loss of balance on a downward arc and stuttered a step or two towards Almira. He resteadied himself with his back towards the man with the gun. "Don't worry," he said to her to get her attention, "we'll be okay." He gazed out the cabin window but as he did so, he traced his finger along the ledge to show the movements he would like everyone to make. It was like diagramming football plays in the park as a kid.

Almira, he knew, had never seen a football play, much less seen one diagrammed. Please God, he said to himself, let her understand. Apparently she did. "Is the bathroom down below?" she asked Don Silvestre a minute later.

Don Silvestre nodded noncommittally. "Quickly, eh," he said.

David could feel his heart pounding as the adrenalin rushed in. Now they were launched on an irreversible course. He might be killed, he might have to kill. He had no idea whether he could do it. He breathed deeply to settle down and was thinking of how to get Peter's attention focused when Carlos looked up from his monitors and spoke, "Don Silvestre, I'm getting blips on the radar, maybe half a kilometer in front of us."

"How many?"

"It changes, sometimes three, sometimes one, sometimes none. And there was nothing there before."

Don Silvestre pulled the throttle controls back to slow the boat down. The boat leveled out as it dropped from its plane. "What's the depth?"

"Nineteen, twenty feet, it was a hundred a minute ago," Carlos added.

"Shit," Don Silvestre squinted into the night, "They told me there were a few rocks cropping up, not a fucking underwater island."

"Four of them now. I think they're moving, Don Silvestre." Carlos' voice had risen a few decibels.

"Idiot, we're the ones that are moving." For the first time Don Silvestre appeared to have lost control.

"No, no, no. The spacing between them is changing."

Don Silvestre slowed the boat down further, switched on a spotlight and started sweeping the area in front of them. The beam got lost in the murk. "Get up on the bow, Carlos. I can't see shit through the windshield. As soon as you actually see something hold your right hand up."

Carlos left his station at the instrument panel and holding onto the rail for balance, slowly moved to the prow. When he got there, Carlos forgot to raise his right hand but everyone heard his words, "*Cabrones, ballenas!* Whales jumping out of the fucking sea!"

A few seconds later the cabin occupants saw a breaching humpback leap from the water into the spotlight. As they heard it fall back with a thunderous crash, the depth finder alarm let out its piercing, warning scream. A moment later there was a thump and a groaning. The aft part of the boat was tilted into the air as if lifted up on the shoulders of a waking giant who had been slumbering in the sea. In the cabin, the man with the gun was the only one who had a long ways to travel after he lost his feet. His mouth opened wide but the cry never left his throat. He flew with a crunch of bone into the wooden bulkhead and the Uzi in his hand went clattering down the stairs.

The boat was only tilted for a few seconds. Its descent was gentler. The boat's stern sank into the water, the high speed whine of propellers racing died back to the monotonous, gurgling throbbing to which they had all become accustomed, the deck returned to level. Fifteen yards to port what appeared to be a thirty-foot log of massive girth surfaced and let out a towering blast of oily mist which would have put La Bufadora, the shore-bound blowhole, to shame.

***

On the boat, underneath the umbrella of the whale's effluent condensation, David checked to make sure that Jorge was unconscious and then helped Peter subdue Don Silvestre. For his age the man was unusually spry but he was no match for David, much less the two of them together. Almira emerged from the lower area, Uzi confidently in hand. Laura was looking through the windshield for any sign of Carlos but saw nothing. In all likelihood, she thought, he was thrown off the boat.

Almira kept the Uzi trained on an unconscious Jorge while she searched for a few lengths of rope. She found some in a wall cabinet and handed them to David who with Peter's help lashed Don Silvestre to one of the fishing chairs on the rear deck. Then they dragged Jorge's slumped body and lifted him into the other chair and tied him in as well. Jorge was recovering consciousness and began to moan in pain.

"I don't think I can listen to him," Laura said, "is he okay?"

"Probably," Peter replied. "We'll see. Where's Carlos?"

"I think he went over. I didn't see anything move up there."

"We better look," David said and headed towards the bow. He returned a minute later, "No sign of him," he said.

To everyone's surprise, it was Laura who expressed concern, "He'll drown, we have to look for him." As soon as she had spoken, there was a swishing of water on the port side. They all turned in time to see two enormous flukes rise above the water. The flukes seemed to wave at the boat's occupants and then sank back into the sea.

Peter had taken over the guidance of the boat and had cut back its engines to keep it stationary. "Laura, we don't even know where we are, much less how to look for a place we passed five minutes ago."

Jorge's moaning stopped; quiet descended on all of them, except for the lapping of water against the hull and the persistent murmuring of the engines. "We could ask Don Silvestre," Laura suggested, "He would want to help his friend."

"We can't trust him, and I'm not sure he would help anyone, much less Carlos," David said. "He seemed almost contemptuous of him."

Almira had become visibly angry, "Laura is right, we have to try, we're becoming as dangerous as they are." She slammed the Uzi into David's hand and walked up to Peter. "Just head east for five minutes and then we can spiral out in a circle."

No one argued with her and Peter started to turn the boat around. As he was doing so, they all picked up the approaching buzz of a motor boat moving at high speed. David felt his muscles tense again and his senses heighten with a shiver of fear. He looked at the Uzi's mechanics and prayed that all he had to do was pull the trigger. He crouched down so that his head was only slightly above the gunwale and the weapon was resting on it, pointed out toward the sound.

The approaching engine was suddenly cut back and a smaller boat of some twenty-five or thirty feet bobbed into view fifty yards away. A bullhorn-magnified voice carried across the water, "David, Peter, it's me, Rashid. Where have you all been!"

Rashid approached the larger boat more slowly and finally drew alongside. He threw a line to Laura and asked her to tie it to a cleat. Rashid was wearing white pants, a red and blue-striped polo shirt and a captain's hat with golden leaves embossed on its brim.

"I've been looking for you everywhere," he said, "But all I could find was a fellow swimming in circles ranting about whales. He just wasn't much help at all."

Rashid displayed a set of long and shining teeth in a broad inviting smile, "I left him a life jacket with a light and a radio beacon. His friends will be here to pick him up soon. We really shouldn't be here then, so it's probably best if you all climb in with me."

Peter, Laura, David and Almira followed his suggestion.

They made sure Jorge and Don Silvestre were still securely tied to the chairs and then cut off the fishing boat's engines, leaving two running lights on. The four climbed into Rashid's boat. Rashid steered the craft north and an hour later, still answering questions about the role of whales in the Modern Era, turned east towards shore. When they arrived at the small-boat docking cluster in the Ensenada harbor, Rafael was waiting for them at the end of a pier. "*Gracias a Dios*. Thank God, Rashid. You got them all back." He threw over a line.

CHAPTER 37

"A great job, Peter," Senator Carmichael's satisfaction showed through the v-phone, his booming voice testing the limits of its speakers.

"Thank you," Peter replied. He was still logy from the experiences of the night before; his face and midriff ached. He had pulled the curtains in his room at the Ballena Loca and slept in late. "But the truth of the matter, Senator, is that I'm not sure what happened."

"Not to worry Peter, when you get back, your confederate here will tell all." The Senator was visibly savoring the moment. "For a start though, should you ever meet him, you will want to thank Senzo Sato profusely, him and his friend Rashid.

"Rashid's here, Senator."

"Sato and I," the Senator continued, "we don't see eye to eye on a lot of issues, but the man has integrity, solid right to the core. If somebody's going to play king of the world, he's the kind of man it should be. He knew something was foul in the way they were going after you and he had the decency to let me know."

"They?"

"We got them red-handed or I should say red- and red-white-and-blue-handed this time. Ligachev and Hamilton...they're quite a pair. You know who they are?"

"They're at the top of UNINTEL, aren't they?"

339

"Yep. It seems that they nearly had you and your friends framed for murder, even for your friend Velazquez's. And of course that would have been a sweet way to discredit me too. Hamilton's had it in for me for years—ever since I broke up an old CIA black ops that targeted American citizens." The Senator paused briefly. "Who knows? We're still trying to figure out if there are other people behind it all. Maybe some of the Planetary Defense people, it could be tough to get an answer.

"Ligachev and Hamilton aren't going to talk, though, unless we can link them to the actual murders. And you know they're so used to operating with a wink and a nod and never anything explicit from their superiors. Everybody leaves room for plausible denial. It's like an honor code with these covert action types. About all we really have on them for sure is that they threatened to send some UN employee's mom back to a nightmare that she came from but that's so close to what they're supposed to do, we can't really do very much with it."

Peter was still half asleep. His head pounded and his entire mid-body region pained with every move. He had no real idea what the Senator was talking about. It probably showed because the Senator paused again and an expression of concern crossed his face, "I hear you got roughed up a bit, Peter. No harm done?"

"I'll be fine." Peter looked around the room hoping that Laura might be within earshot but saw that she was gone. He looked at his watch; it was almost noon. No wonder.

"That New Mexican guy—the guy whose mother they went after. Have you met him?" The Senator didn't wait for an answer. "He showed some real character. Instead of crumbling, he went to Rashid and Rashid went to the very top. We let Ligachev and Hamilton think they had him and we used it to break up what they were doing."

"You still with me, Peter?" the Senator asked. Peter nodded. "The best part of this, Peter, is what this will do for us at the Convocation. We may have it, Peter, a real, pluralistic, planetary, cooperative confederation, not another armed-to-the-teeth-top-down monstrosity of the kind that's made a mess of human history for the past five thousand years.

"Can you imagine, Peter," the Senator continued, as excited as a little boy on Christmas morning, "for the first time in I don't know how long, it won't just be governments as we know them that will have a recognized governing role but human groupings of all kinds—environmental coalitions, children's advocates, religious affiliations, ethnic groups, multinational businesses, even, God help us, universities and ex-professors."

Peter finally smiled a bit at the Senator's self-denigration. "We have work to do," the Senator added. An understatement, Peter mused to himself. He was beginning to share the Senator's vision. The key was to create a cross-current of allegiances in many dimensions so that no single stream had a grip on an individual's identity and most of all so that no one got tied down to seeing themselves as a map of one territorial boundary that needed armies and police to defend. The mechanics of governing in a new kind of world like the Senator saw would not be simple but perhaps they were already evolving. Perhaps they had already evolved and just needed to be given a name to be recognized. He thought of Almira and her explanation of the Palestinian settlement.

"Senator," Peter said, "there is a woman from Palestine with us here, I think she can help a lot. You need to meet her soon. I think she may already know how it can be done."

"Good. And Peter, the other woman with you, the space lady. Great letters she wrote. We need to keep her on."

"Laura, Senator. Her name is Laura, Laura Feil." Peter paused for an instant and his voice thickened, "I think I am in love with her."

The Senator was visibly taken aback at Peter's evident and unexpected emotion. He didn't speak for a few moments. "Great, Peter," the Senator finally said. "Well, we'll see you both soon." His image faded from the screen.

Peter had surprised himself as well with his unguarded comment to Senator Carmichael. He knew as he descended the stairs to the lobby that his first concern should be food to help his body repair, but all he really wanted to do was find Laura and be near her. He walked into the restaurant hoping to find her but without success. Peter wandered out to the poolside terrace and saw her sitting at a table with Rashid. Laura was wearing a turquoise two-piece bathing suit, Rashid was in indescribably garish flowered trunks. Peter pulled up a chair to join them in the sun. When he had seated himself, Laura pressed his hand and told him that he looked more rugged with a battered nose.

The sun's warmth soothed Peter and Rashid summoned a waiter and ordered huevos rancheros and a large glass of orange juice for Peter to eat. "From what I hear," Rashid said smilingly to Peter, "you gave the lie to Edmund Burke. The age of chivalry isn't gone after all."

Peter laughed. Peter knew Burke well. In college he had studied the Political Philosophy of the English-Speaking World. Hobbes to Hobbits, as his classmates called it, with discordant notes from the not-so-pliant colonized like Jefferson and Gandhi. "No, to the contrary, just showing my loyalty to the little platoon, just as he would say."

Peter grew pensive. "Rashid, I still don't understand. Why did you bring us here? We could have been killed."

"The Senator didn't tell you?"

"No."

"But he told you about Ligachev and Hamilton?"

"Yes."

"And about my good friend Rafael whom you met twice last night?"

"Not really. He talked about a New Mexican and his mother who was helping you. I guessed it was Rafael."

"Yes. Well, we weren't really putting you at risk. Some very powerful people were already casting around, trying to land you with pretty barbed hooks. They had some plot. As best as we can tell, it was to make you a model conspiracy for why we need an all-powerful state as well as killing or discrediting some people that might stand in their way. They nearly pulled it off, too, but even with raids and seductions, they didn't think they had quite enough evidence. So then they used their electronic net to figure out who might be able to attract some of you together again. My name came up and they thought they could get to me through Rafael. They threatened his mother. They thought they had him cornered and pliable but he wasn't really. He told me what was going on. I worked with him and then with Sato and some other friends to stop their efforts. But to do that we had to let them try to kidnap you."

After the juice and eggs arrived Peter ordered coffee and

pastries and devoured them too. Laura excused herself and dove almost noiselessly into the pool. She lapped its length with a few fluid strokes and kick-turned, apparently set on making the swim a full exercise session.

Rashid seized on her absence to speak to Peter. He spoke in a resonant but gentle voice that left Peter feeling as if he were hearing with more than his ears. "You have important work to do, Peter. All of you—you, David, Almira—are no less important than the Senator or what he will do.

"And Laura. Laura is less political than the rest of you, but Laura's role is special." Rashid paused, the features of his face shifted almost imperceptibly but did so in a way that enhanced its compelling power, "She is one who could speak for the angels. She can know the faeries and rock spirits and understand the language of trees. The plants and animals can find a voice in her," Rashid's face broke into a smile, verging on outright laughter, as his eyes shifted briefly to capture Laura's graceful strokes, "and even the water sprites and the merpeople. Or God knows, the bullfrogs and the whales! The whales without whom I might never have found you last night—they are all your companions in the human journey, Peter." The insistent tone of his words remained unchanged, "They should all be at the table when a new course is set.

"I have spoken to Laura already," Rashid continued. "We will spend some weeks together in Maui. She and I and a few of my friends from the sea, we will work with her to help her find her center and perhaps to learn how to hold onto it when the vastness comes into view.

"Then she will come back to join you and the two of you must take care of each other." Rashid looked out at her swimming figure again, "Laura loves you. It may be hard for her at times. It is a difficult life that she has picked, belonging to neither matter nor spirit, yet trying to give expression to both. Sometimes she's tossed around by the slightest eddy, prey to the faintest current. At her best though, she's a solid force, anchored beneath the waves."

Peter was listening intently.

"It will be hard for you too," Rashid added, his eye drawn to a distant place, "but every once in a while she will take you by the hand in an ascent into heaven that, however brief, will by its depth weigh more in your balance than years of ordinary experience, and you will know that you did the right thing in joining your life to hers."

Rashid became silent. His silence was a penetrating one that repressed not only Peter's tongue but his thinking processes as well. Peter's mind lunged to grasp the echo of Rashid's words, to store them in his memory, but the words were elusive and one after another, like bubbles of blown soap, they vanished. Peter's futile grasping slowly stopped and with it, his inner silence deepened. His connection to the table and the terrace and the people milling around it seemed severed as if by a barrier of dense particulate energy. Time seemed to have no passage and fell away.

***

Finally, Peter did not know how much later, Almira's clear and ringing voice broke through the trance.

"Dr. O'Shea," she was saying with a gleam of mischief in her eye, glancing down at his bathing trunks, "I had no idea that you could dress so tastefully."

"Almira," Rashid said, putting on a set of sunglasses so as to admire her better without embarrassing her. She was wearing a sleeveless white cotton frock with needlepoint-flowered patterns spiraling around the neckline, a purchase at a local craft shop, "Mother and bride to us all, you look splendid!"

"And Peter," she said, rumpling up his hair with her hand, "how is our warrior-statesman today?"

Peter smiled appreciatively. "Improving with every touch," he said.

Almira massaged the top of his shoulders and his neck went limp. "You reminded me," she said, "of my husband, Farid. What you did in the van, it is just the kind of foolish thing that he would have done."

And last night on the boat David would have done worse, Almira thought, and she would have helped him. She had held a gun, an Israeli-made gun in her hand, and would have used it without a moment's hesitation. Ali would have done the same, as would Youssef and little Jamal. Even Elizabeth. Ai, if those who are so close to me would bathe the ground in blood so easily, what hope is there? Where will we ever rest? When will it ever end? She felt a darkness rise within her and her shoulders slumped. The only refuge was in small things.

God, bring me back to Youssef, bring me back to Jamal, she prayed silently, let me hold Jamal and comfort Youssef again, straighten out the one's clothes and comb the hair of the other as they run out the door to school. A few more times, let me do it, before the next knife comes slashing into our lives—or worse, embeds itself in one of their little backs.

At least, God, show me your face again in the way I've come to know it. In the sandy air filled with the cries of men, in the morning light and the call to prayer, in the animal smells of the market and the jostling of two impossible peoples and three impossible faiths all crammed together, living impossibly, somehow together on a little corner of arid dusty land.

Almira realized that her hands had come to a full stop on Peter's shoulders. Laura had set herself down beside them to dry in the sun and David was now only a few steps away from the table. "I'm sorry, Peter," she said, straightening herself and letting her fingers now knead Peter's neck. "I got lost there for a moment. It must have been thinking of Farid."

"It felt good, Almira," Peter placed one hand over hers, "comforting."

Almira became aware of the piped-in music. It was an American song. Her command of English had always been excellent but one thing that had given her trouble was making out the words to English and American popular music. With French it had been the opposite, the songs were more understandable than day-to-day speech. This song, though, seemed an easy one, whenever she listened, she could catch the fragments clearly, "... bullfrog... singing joy to the fishes... joy to you and me... "

Rashid broke in, speaking over the song, "This song reminds me of my friends the whales, they have something like this bullfrog joy. Only they call it glee. Actually they spell it differently than we do, G-L-I, Great Loving Intelligence, an acronym, a pictosonograph of sorts.

"Actually," he continued, his face displaying utter seriousness, "at first they called it G-I-L, the Great Intelligence that Loved, but this was rejected. GIL reminded too many of the whales of the animist fish cults of the early cetacean period." He turned his gaze to Almira, "We all have our histories to overcome."

"I don't see how you can joke about this, Rashid," Almira said. She took her hand away from Peter and her voice rose with anger, "Here we see it all again, violence, secrecy, plots for power. We are caught in our histories and we always seem doomed to repeat them somehow."

"Jeremiah," Rashid replied, "the man that song was about, when you read him, for pages and pages all you see is the blindness and stupidity of those around him, the horror and grief that is likely to come to them, he sees it all, and then you turn a page and quite suddenly, unexpectedly, is a vision of a new day, of the unimagined possibilities that lie on the other side of the horror.

"Jeremiah was in a pit," Rashid continued, "where nothing had visibly moved except down, and he still saw beyond it. But Almira, you—we—are in a very different place.

"When the twentieth century began, young men saw war as glory, and rulers were measured by their empires. When the century ended, almost everyone saw war as a barbarity and rulers were condemned for the empires they sought to create. When the twentieth century began our caring by and large stopped at the nearest border; not long after the century ended most of us had made all the world's children ours.

"When the century began we had an atomistic, billiard-ball view of the world and cause-and-effect concepts that left little room for the inner human experience; when it ended we had a far more integrated cosmology where the line between matter, energy, mind and spirit was no longer clear at all, but where, in a certain sense, we were much more at home. At the outset of the century, we measured ourselves by our prowess in conquering nature; at its end, we prized those who were attuned to it.

"When the century began, we were still crawling on the face of the Earth, barely aware of what was happening in the next town. When it ended, we had traveled far into space. More importantly, nearly every sentient human saw the image of our planet seen from out there, a blue and white jewel, fragile and glistening in the vastness. Ever since then, even if it's unconsciously, we've had to think in terms of the underlying unity of our fates," Rashid's eyes were still riveted on Almira, "and the underlying unity of our faiths.

"You have seen it in your own life, Almira, in the Palestinian settlement, in the speed with which billions have responded to the crisis of ecology, in the disappearance of large-scale warfare—especially after the Americans transcended their fears. For all that was accomplished, a terrible cost was paid in the past hundred years." It was Rashid's voice which was now taking on an overtone of anger, "In blood and anguish and spiritual confusion and emotional numbness, in your husband's death and your brother's pain.

"It is for us now to gather in the harvest of what was sown then. Almira. When you are gloomy and depressed, you devalue what has gone on before. You are digging yourself into a hole of projected negativity. You can't cling to some alienated identity of yourself as helpless victim of the world's cruelties. You have far more important work to do."

Rashid stood up and took Almira's hand in his. He brought her fingertips to his lips and kissed them softly. "You are magnificent, Almira." He set his sunglasses down on the table and plunged into the pool. As he swam away in a graceful free-style, the seat of his multihued trunks bobbed to the surface, seemingly transformed into an eddy of flowing jewels.

CHAPTER 38

[MICHELSON FLOWER DEATH CONFIRMED | Toxic Flower Essence Ingested]

New York, New York. Monday 15, 5/6. UNINTEL confirmed yesterday that a battery of tests conducted after Matteo Michelson's body was disinterred have revealed trace amounts of the toxic substance found in the rare South American flower, *lycaste mycemosa*. The investigators also found one unlabeled vial in Mr. Michelson's traveling case which contained lycaste essence. UNINTEL concluded that ingestion of the unlabeled essence was the likely cause of death of the renowned Brazilian herbalist. Mr. Michelson died unexpectedly just before receiving this year's Planetary Citizen Award here in New York.

UNINTEL stated that it presently had no reliable leads as to how Mr. Michelson came to ingest the plant. The UNINTEL spokesperson concurred that it was unlikely that Mr. Michelson would have knowingly ingested the poisonous essence. The UNINTEL spokesperson added, however, that it would be extremely difficult to detect how the vial had come to be in Mr. Michelson's belongings. UNINTEL had identified certain persons of interest in the case but further investigation had failed to establish sufficient grounds for further suspicion...

[HUNDREDS MISSING IN WAKE OF PERUVIAN QUAKE | Mudslide Dooms Dozens in Bus]

Lima, Peru. Friday 26, 5/6. On Wednesday at 3:35 AM local time, an earthquake registering 5.7 on the Richter scale was recorded here. Its epicenter is believed to have been approximately one hundred and fifty miles southeast of Lima at the base of the Andean range. While not of unusual strength, it triggered mudslides that buried two villages near the provincial city of Ayachuelo. Reports from the buried villages suggest that most of the residents, who were likely sleeping when the slides occurred, are missing and the majority of these are presumed dead. Search and rescue efforts are now underway.

Yesterday, a medical relief team recruited by a local constable, Sergeant Arsenio Sucre, set out from Cuzco. Tragically at approximately 4 o'clock in the afternoon the bus carrying the team was knocked off the narrow highway into a chasm by another landslide near Ayachuelo. It is believed that the slide was caused by one of dozens of aftershocks that the region has experienced. However, there were reports of one or more explosions several thousand feet above the road just before the slide. The local authorities noted that mountainous terrain could play tricks with sound but indicated that the reports would be investigated after the more urgent search and rescue tasks are completed. Ironically, Sergeant Sucre had been spearheading the inquiry into the death of José María Velasquez, a well-known local activist who was killed in what was described as a road accident on the same highway only twelve miles from the site of the mudslide. Sergeant Sucre leaves behind his wife, Imelda Perez de Sucre, and two sons, Diego and Roberto.

[FORMER TERROR FIGURE FOUND DEAD | Adib Yarkis Stabbed in London Flat]

London. Monday 1, 6/6. Adib Yarkis was found dead last night in his Chelsea flat. He died of multiple stab wounds. Mr Yarkis, also known as "The Cobra", was a shadowy figure in the terror underground. Little is known of his origins but it is believed that he was of Turkish-Syrian background. Mr. Yarkis was associated with several Middle Eastern organizations, the most prominent of which was Hezbollah, the Party of God. Mr. Yarkis was reputed to specialize in the planning of dramatic assassinations, particularly of Lebanese political figures. Using different identities he is said to have operated in many countries including Israel and the former Occupied Territories.

The Cobra's presumptively true, Yarkis identity was revealed as part of the Levant Truth Commission report following the Israeli-Palestinian settlement. It was also rumored that the Cobra was trained by the

KGB, the former Soviet foreign intelligence service, and that following the KGB's successor agency, the FCS's, dissolution, he had been retained as a consultant by UNINTEL for his counter-terrorism expertise. As is its practice, UNINTEL refused to confirm or deny any link to Mr. Yarkis, although it did say that it had been asked to assist with the investigation of his death.

Mr. Yarkis was one of several figures mentioned in speculative reports concerning the widely reported bedroom deaths of Fatimah Karajan, the Palestinian peace activist, and Ariel Arbel, a former Shin Bet operative. Palestinian and Israeli authorities connected with the Karajan-Arbel investigation made no official comment on the Cobra's death. However, one source with knowledge of the police's deliberative processes indicated that it now seemed unlikely that the twin murders would be definitively solved and that the resources assigned to the case were likely to diminish significantly.]

EPILOGUE

[YOUR GATESWAY DAY | Monday 15, 8/6 | August 2, 2028]

[*Good morning, David. Coffee warm, New York Times?*]

"Yes."

[*Headlines or Index?*]

"Headlines."

[CLIMATE CHANGE SEEN SLOWING | Cloud Formation Is Key | Gaia's "Negative Feedback Loops" Aiding Human Efforts]

[*Story?*]

"Later."

[HUMAN SUFFERING DECLINING | U.N. Report Released | Data Correction Shows More Basic Human Needs Being Satisfied]

[*Story?*]

"Later."

[UNINTEL LEADERSHIP REPLACED | Hamilton, Ligachev Ousted | Directors Removed in Wake of Kidnapping Scandal]

[*Story?*]

"Yes."

David waited for the story to come up on the screen, then he turned to his companion, "Well at least a small bit of justice has been done—even if we still haven't unraveled the killings."

Almira smiled as she stood behind him reading the headlines on the screen. "The story of my life. A lot of death, unavenged thank God, or there would be even more death—but you're right, baby step by baby step, maybe we—the world—are getting a little better."

It was so easy to communicate with David, Almira thought to herself as she looked at the story over his brown shoulders and unkempt hair. She shared with him a common view of the world, at least as it might be, and both of them had given over their working lives to help a better world come about. He was thoughtful and considerate. He liked children. Sometimes she wondered if she had been right in discouraging a deeper involvement. But she knew her place was in Palestine, his elsewhere. David needed to make a family that was all his own in order to be whole, and she just couldn't see herself having children again. Still, on solitary nights she wondered. David was kind and strong. Who else with so many good qualities would enter her life to break the loneliness? She turned away and walked to the stove to make herself a cup of tea. She wasn't entirely sure that it had just been working on the Convocation and a chance to let her boys experience a rain forest that had brought her to David's. She was lonely but the more she considered, the more she felt confident that it was a desire to seek something new in her life, not David, that had made the trip so appealing.

A few minutes later the v-phone rang and she saw David's attention shift away from the story to the caller on the screen. It was Rashid. Almira's heart skipped a beat and she moved a little closer to David and the v-phone. Rashid, she could see, was bundled in a white hooded parka; ice crystals dangled from his eyebrows. "David," he said, "it's nice to see you. I thought I'd check in to see how you're doing."

"What are you doing?"

"A little change of pace. The Bering Straits, visiting some of my friends," Rashid offered good-naturedly.

"Almira is here. So are Youssef and Jamal."

Rashid arched his icy eyebrows. "Oh?"

"Almira and I, we've both been selected by our organizations to be their delegates to the Convocation."

"Oh?"

"The boys have vacation. Almira asked if she could bring them to see a tropical rain forest so they're all here." David rearranged himself in his chair to look at the v-phone screen more directly. "We're working on a strategy. Groups from all over the world are contacting Almira. Peter and Laura and the Senator and his allies, they're always talking to her too." David became reflective, "She could have a big role, possibly?"

"Yes."

"You were harsh on her that last day at the pool."

"Not really...she heard me, she understood." Rashid's eyes were briefly drawn away from the camera by some unknown disturbance in his environment. A cloud of snowflakes swirled onto the picture. When the screen cleared and his gaze returned, he spoke again, "How's your love life, David?"

"There's a woman I met a couple of months ago, just before Baja. Costa Rican, Maria Clara's her name."

"Tell me." Rashid said, his presence somehow filling more than the screen.

"She's beautiful and smart. She works with children and wants to have her own. I think she's ready to settle down—and I am too."

"You're in your home, you're where you belong."

"You think so?"

"Absolutely. I don't have too much time, David. I should speak to Almira. I truly miss her." David turned to look for her but was called back by Rashid's voice. Rashid was smiling into the screen; the ice crystals in his eyebrows were beginning to melt, "David, before you call her, there's a story I heard, it's about a farmer, and his horse that runs away, and all the things that happen after that. I'd like to tell it to you... Have you heard the story before?"

Visions of new earthquakes, whales, losses, and loves poured into David's mind. He felt the walls of his future turn wavy and its floor and ceiling buckle. He resisted the temptation to cut off the screen. He swiveled in his seat away from Rashid's smiling face and called out, "Almira, the phone, it's for you..."

Almira came a few steps nearer, brushed her hair into place with her hands and then took David's seat. The close-up image on the screen chased away her nervousness and made her laugh, "That hood looks silly, Dr. O'Shea. With an outfit like that, am I really supposed to take you or your stories about whales and horses seriously?"

Rashid paused thoughtfully. His eyes seemed to moisten (or could it have been the blur of a snowflake dissolving on the camera lens?) and when he responded, it was in a slow and soft voice, "You need only do so, my dear Almira, if they are pleasing to your heart."

ABOUT THE AUTHOR

William H. Espinosa is an international lawyer and NGO
director. He is a Harvard and Georgetown graduate. His
background includes environmental game design, international
development, global broadcasting, diplomacy and intelligence.
He lives in Charlottesville.